For
David

Enjoy The Story

D1713406

QUANTUM

Before you embark on a journey of revenge, dig two graves.
Confucius (504 BC)

QUANTUM

a novel

T. Milton Mayer

Simon Publishing LLC

T. Milton Mayer

Text copyright © 2020 T. Milton Mayer
All rights reserved.

Published by Simon Publishing LLC, Naples, FL ®
Simon Publishing LLC logo is a registered trademark

ISBN: 978-0-578-23592-9 Trade Paperback
ISBN: 978-1-73618812-5 Hard Cover/Jacket
ISBN: 978-1-7361881-1-8 ebook

Library of Congress Control Number: 2020923529

Cover Design by Robin Ludwig, Robin Ludwig Designs
Printed by Ingram Spark in the United States of America

First Edition
1 3 5 7 9 10 8 6 4 2

For my son, Christopher
An excellent author in his own right.
Your edits and recommendations
have been invaluable.

PROLOGUE

Liuang Computer Technologies Corporation
Chengdu, China
Three Years Before YAOGUAI!

Bodies were stacked everywhere. The official count was one hundred thirteen dead, a third of whom were children. Dozens more were alive but in critical condition. Dr. Chow's head pounded as the guilt bore down to the inner depths of his soul, creating a psychological sore that could never be soothed. It was worse than any physical pain he had ever endured, worse even than the childhood burns on his legs sustained during a bombing. Those wounds healed. He feared this never would. Like a recurring nightmare, ominous visions of the bodies plagued his every thought. Chow raked his fingers through his disheveled hair, trying to convince himself that it was not his fault. He worked ferverishly for months to make sure the device was safe before its preliminary trial. More work was needed but the Ministry insisted that a wide-spread test be performed immediately in a small village to the north—and the Ministry always got what it wanted. It resulted in a tragic disaster due to an unexpected lack of specificity in the design of his creation. The mistake unmasked the catastrophic potential of YAOGUAI, something Chow never anticipated. In the wrong hands it could be perverted into a weapon of unparalleled destruction on a global scale. He could only hope that nobody else but he appreciated the significance of the mishap.

QUANTUM

What had he done? Because of him, the world was about to experience something horrific, even more catastrophic than Wuhan's Covid-19 pandemic. One hundred thirteen innocent people were already dead. There would be more—many more. Billions might die.

He needed a containment plan and wracked his brain, searching for some solution, but he was having difficulty remaining focused. His thoughts kept drifting back to the creation. He walked over to close the blinds to his office, as if he could shield the outside world from the device. Impossible. It was already too late.

He removed the tiny box from his office safe and held it up for inspection, cradling the object in his hands as though it were his baby. In many ways it was, being the result of over two decades of devotion to his research. Glare from the overhead fluorescent lights reflected off the sides of the clear glass cube as he rotated it, examining its contents from all angles with the pride of a parent. Inside sat the device, so small it appeared trivial— tiny, but exceedingly dangerous. It represented the first step on a dark path which could only lead to disaster. There would be no turning back from this Armageddon. He should never have allowed it to progress this far, but there were no other choices.

Chow sat at his desk. Every available surface was covered with reports, books, and articles dealing with his areas of expertise. He glanced around his office and his eyes lingered on the plaque hanging on the wall. "Dr. Chow Chi Wong, Director of Sub-atomic and Photonic Research, Liuang Computer Technologies Corporation." He took great pride in his laboratory, a place where he cast aside the chains of reality and opened his mind to the impossible. He squared his shoulders. *That's what I have accomplished – the impossible. Yet I remain an unknown.*

Only a select few individuals outside his laboratory were aware of his groundbreaking discoveries. Any praise from the world's scientific community would, of necessity, elude him. He was forbidden from sharing his work with anyone outside the inner circles of the Ministry of Intelligence. His life was destined to be one of forced obscurity. After the deaths at his disastrous trial run, he was thankful for the anonymity.

Chow pushed his black frame glasses up the bridge of his nose as he continued to study the device. Did American scientists have the same misgivings when they detonated the first nuclear explosion at Trinity, New Mexico? Did they ask themselves, "What have we unleashed upon humanity?"

Chow had asked himself that same question almost every day since the deaths, losing countless hours of sleep pondering the potential consequences of his discoveries. Science was intended to be pure and untainted by outside influences, a search for truth for the sake of knowledge that might benefit mankind. He pushed the boundary of scientific possibilities to better understand the universe, but his discoveries led him into a swamp of scientific irresponsibility. He had considered the possibility of sabotaging the entire project but knew that any such attempt would be futile. Things had progressed too far, and the Ministry had its expectations. Refusal to produce the final design on schedule would have had serious consequences: arrest and probable execution for treason.

"Maybe that would have been better," he muttered to himself as he protected the small box in his hand. "Maybe it would be best if I simply disappeared." It was possible. He could do it. He shook his head. "I must think of Liu-Fawn." She was the only thing in his life more important than his research. Without her love, nothing else mattered. "I couldn't do that to her. She's would pay a heavy price for my treason if I ran."

His thoughts were disrupted by his secretary's voice over the intercom. "Dr. Chow, Colonel Meang is here."

The mere mention of the Colonel's name struck fear. Chow's heart raced and his hands trembled. Beads of perspiration formed on his upper lip. He pulled a stick of spearmint gum from his desk to sooth his nerves. He started chewing — too rapidly.

The Colonel approached the research complex door until his image filled the monitor screen on Chow's desk. He was tall, athletic-looking, and crisply dressed in his military uniform with a cascade of medals displayed across the left side of his wide chest.

"You can fool the others with all those medals, but not me," Chow said to the screen. "I know better, Meang. China hasn't been in a significant war in over fifty years. You're a fraud, just a bully hiding behind a military uniform decorated with useless trinkets to boost your own ego." Chow studied the screen. Yes, Meang was a fraud, but an extremely dangerous one. A man who wielded a great deal of power.

The Colonel stopped at the mandatory retinal scanner to confirm his identity before being cleared for final entry into the top-secret laboratory.

Chow checked the time. He was obsessed with the relativity of it, something only a quantum physicist could appreciate. Exactly 10:13 a.m. It had taken him a year to make the necessary modifications to the watch. There were two sets of small buttons on either side capable of unlocking the power of the device. Those on the left were yet to be activated. That would have to wait until all was ready. He pressed the upper button on the right side, replacing the time display with a photo of Liu-Fawn. Her picture always served to soften the worries that plagued him. He caressed the image with the tip of his finger. "I miss you, my love."

When Meang entered the room, Chow closed the image and stood, almost at military attention. He pushed his thick glasses further up the bridge of his nose. No greetings were exchanged. Meang never bothered with social niceties. He held out his right hand. "Where is it?" He approached until his face was only inches from Chow's. The man smelled of death. Chow's hands shook as he relinquished the clear box.

"This is it?" Meang tossed the box over in his hand studying its contents. "This is the result of thirty-seven billion dollars and ten years of research? This is what killed those villagers?"

Chow's pulse again quickened, and the stab of guilt shook him. He wanted to remind the Colonel that he had warned against the testing, but he had nothing to gain and a lot to lose by arguing.

Chow bowed his head and searched the floor for an

acceptable response. He had to be careful with his words. The Colonel did not tolerate any disrespect. "That was due to a glitch in the system, Colonel."

"Your glitch, Chow."

Chow had no response. The Colonel was correct. It was his mistake, one he should have foreseen.

"It doesn't look like much!"

Chow raised his head and looked Meang square in the eye. "Yes, but size can be deceiving, Colonel. In time you will find that my device far exceeds your expectations. This is only the first working model and it's almost ready for mass production. I expect further improvements in its power and efficacy over the next several years." He chewed his gum more rapidly and bit his lip. His head jolted back, and he wiped away a small droplet of blood with the back of his hand.

Meang smirked. "I expect you to have it ready for production within the month."

"I'll call Mr. Liuang and let him know as soon as all the final tests are complete."

"That won't be necessary, Chow." Meang puffed out his chest and glared into Chow's eyes. "The Ministry and Mr. Liuang put me in charge of the final stages of the project from here. They are making it a top priority, so I will be taking over." He tossed the box back to Chow. "How quickly do you estimate it will become widespread enough to be effective?"

"It will begin working immediately. My computer models predict minimum world-wide penetration of seventy percent within the next year. As we continue to refine the device, those numbers will improve exponentially."

"Make it six months." Meang grinned, evil and intimidating. "Don't disappoint me, Chow."

"Yes sir," replied Chow, relieved that the meeting seemed to be over.

His hand on the doorknob, Meang turned. "By the way, how is your good friend, the newspaper reporter? I think Liu-Fawn is her name."

The question sucked the air out of the room. Chow struggled to breath and his knees buckled. He again bit his lip. More blood to wipe away. "Uhm, she's not actually a friend, Colonel. She's more of an acquaintance."

Meang nodded his approval. "That's good for you, doctor. Liu-Fawn's editorials have attracted a great deal of attention from members of the Politburo in Beijing. She's walking a fine line and could be arrested soon. I'd hate for you to be tainted by your association with her. I'm sure you're familiar with the punishment for treason." The Colonel again grinned and left the office.

Chow collapsed back into his chair and exhaled. Meang was up to something. Why had he taken charge? Did Meang know about the dark potential of his device? He needed to develop a countermeasure as soon as possible. The future of the world could be at stake.

Three months later, Chow received the report. What he had feared happened. A sales representative from Liuang Technologies Corporation had waited in the Delta VIP room at LAX Airport in Los Angeles, on his way to the International Consumer Electronics show in Las Vegas. He selected a chair in the middle of the crowded room, opened his briefcase, and pushed a single button. The result only took a millisecond, so brief as to be completely unnoticeable. Over the next four hours, the other travelers around him left the lounge to board their respective flights for destinations in the United States and around the world. YAOGUAI had begun — possibly the beginning of the end of civilization.

ONE

Home of Jacob Savich
Parkview Hills, Kentucky, United States
Present Day: Six Months Before YAOGUAI

Jacob Savich rested against the back of his chair and allowed the warmth of the mid-day sun to relieve the aching in his shoulders. He stretched his tight muscles, leaned forward, and ran his fingers over the flowing lines of his newest creation. A few rough areas still needed sanding, but already the maniacal image of the man's face was there, preserved in the swirling grain of the wood. Jacob had plunged a knife into the man's neck seconds before he had a chance to assassinate the president. All it needed was some stain and a few layers of varnish to give it depth. *That'll have to wait until after Los Angeles.*

He massaged the arthritic cramping from his fingers. Sculpting wasn't the best hobby for a surgeon, but it was necessary for him to maintain his tenuous grip on sanity. He sighed and gazed up at the cerulean blue skies as if they might contain the answers to his problem. He had witnessed things no young boy should ever see, events that gave rise to a deep-seated rage within his soul, an unquenchable thirst for revenge. It was the birth of the Entity, a force that had wormed its way into his soul, demanding to be fed by the spilling of blood. Killing became an essential part of Jacob's life, as normal as eating and breathing.

Jacob spent over a decade trying to purge the thing. Three

years of seeing a psychiatrist had been a waste of time. Self-treatment for PTSD had also failed. The Entity was too enmeshed within him. His only option was to refocus its demands for killing in a more acceptable direction. He turned to neutralizing terrorists to save the lives of innocent civilians.

He carried the unfinished sculpture inside the house, his footsteps echoing across the marble floor and down the hallways. The home was modern, exquisitely decorated, and overlooked the river valley. It was much too large for only one man but the Entity would never allow anyone else into his life. Except for the team, he was destined to be alone. The lives of too many innocent civilians were at stake. He placed the new piece on a shelf inside a large glass display cabinet where it joined thirteen of its brethren. *Getting crowded. Going to need another case soon.* Something big was happening. More lives would be lost in the coming battles. The enemy was relentless. For each one he killed, two replacements seemed to pop up. The responsibility for protecting the country was all-consuming.

I need a drink.

He filled a glass with Bombay Sapphire and added a little tonic, then turned on the outdoor sound system. Returning to the openness of his deck, he stood at the railing and pushed his dark hair back from his forehead. It was a full and thick, just like his father's was the day he was murdered. Streaks of grey invaded the temples, a change that began the year he was recruited by Winston Hamilton to lead the team. He took in a deep breath and stared into the valley. The waters of the Ohio River rolled by a hundred feet below as the haunting sounds of Beethoven's Moonlight Sonata drifted across the treetops. A mouthful of the gin burned as it washed down his throat, promising it's numbing effect. The alcohol disappointed. It did little to dispel the sense of foreboding that had been plaguing his thoughts ever since he thwarted the assassination attempt on President Wagner. He had failed to kill Scorpion, the mastermind behind the plan. That meant there would be more attacks to come. Something ominous was brewing out there, just over the horizon, worse than anything he had ever encountered before. He could sense it but had no specifics as to what it might be. There had been subtle clues, a suspicious email here, an enigmatic text there, but no concrete leads to pursue. *Elusive.* Like trying to wrap his arms around a cloud of smoke.

It would pose the greatest challenge for the team, a five-person group selected by Winston Hamilton III three years ago to combat terror threats to the country. His mind drifted back to their meetings at the Solitude compound where the team gathered to plan their missions. Dan Foster, the oldest and most combat savvy member of the group was a special forces veteran who had served three tours in the Middle East. He had been a close friend of Jacob's ever since their childhood days in Whitesburg, Kentucky. Tank Chmeilewski was a mountain of a man, selected because of his enormous size, but he was more than just muscle. He was bright, having earned a PhD in English Literature, an unusual career selection for a black man who had been drafted as a defensive lineman in the NFL. The newest member, Norman Deets was a quintessential nerd who rarely saw the front lines. He remained in his computer lab, hacking into enemy information systems and harvesting critical information for each mission.

Enough reminiscing. Jacob took another sip. "First things first," he said aloud. He pulled out his iPhone and placed the call to his team leader and trusted friend Dan Foster. When the man answered, Jacob's only words were, "Status report."

"I've secured a position directly across from the target. It's a dump, but I've been in worse, and the room provides good visibility of the subjects. Looks like they're waiting around for the van, so I don't expect anything to happen until tomorrow morning at the earliest." Dan paused for a few seconds. "We have one problem."

"Terrific." said Jacob. He swirled his drink and emptied the rest of the glass. "There's always a problem when it comes to terrorists. What is it?"

"We can't take the van at the house. There's a school only a couple blocks away. Stray gunfire might hit one of the kids."

"No problem. We can intercept it in a safe location. Have Tank scout out the best options and I'll check them when I arrive."

He paced back and forth across the deck, watching a hawk gliding on currents of warm air, searching the ground for a meal. "How about Lisa?" His sister was the final member of the team and its best shooter. Using her talents for these missions was always a risk, but she was a fierce warrior and an irreplaceable asset. She was one of the few individuals who understood his inner problems. She would willingly protect him with her life. However, being able to protect her life was another matter.

"She found a good spot a few hundred yards away from the intersection," said Dan. "It should be an easy shot for her. She'll be in place and ready if needed."

"Good. I'm flying out early this evening. I'll be in L.A. by nine."

The voice of the Entity, deep and throaty, rumbled up from the dark recesses of his soul.

Finally gonna see some action again, eh Buddy Boy?
I'm getting tired of all this sculpting bullshit.

Jacob shook his head to dismiss the intrusion. Stay focused on the mission. Must stop them in L.A. Too many lives at risk there.

TWO

Corporate Headquarters
Parisian Telecommunications Corporation
Paris, France

Philippe Mitterand looked about the conference room where representatives from all European Union countries were assembled. He had been chairing these meetings for the past three years. Standing at over six-foot-four with a strong chiseled face and a full head of black hair, he was an imposing figure. The others naturally deferred to him as their leader during the negotiations. The group was concluding a year of final talks in Paris. All major roadblocks to the major communications mergers were resolved. After the final vote of approval, each signed the preliminary agreements. "Is that the last of the documents?" he asked.

"Yes, Mr. Mitterand," said one of the attorneys. "Everything has been executed per your instructions. My legal team is prepared to file the necessary papers with the individual member governments. Ratification should be automatic, and the program will be ready for full implementation with integration of all systems in three months. I'd like to congratulate you and all members of the commission on their diligence in the negotiations."

The individual representatives stood, shook hands, and discussed the far-reaching implications of the plan. After they were gone, Philippe gazed out his sixth-floor office window and looked down upon the Paris skyline. "The world is rapidly changing," he whispered to himself. "I hope to God it's for the better."

His secretary called out from her desk outside the room. "I'm sorry, Mr. Mitterand. I didn't hear you. Were you speaking to me?"

"What's my schedule look like for the rest of the afternoon?"

She scanned through the appointment calendar on her computer screen. "You have a meeting with a Mr. Faizel Sassani at three."

"My niece's friend?"

"Yes sir. He said the two of you will be discussing some merger opportunities."

Philippe checked his watch. "I have over an hour. I think I'll head down to the bunker and recheck our new security systems. I'll be back in time for Mr. Sassani."

He took the elevator down to the basement level and walked through a connecting tunnel to one of the company's adjacent buildings. After a hundred feet, Philippe opened a door with his keycard and entered a small concrete antechamber. He patted his hand against a second door on the far wall. *Solid steel. Completely impervious to attack.* Philippe placed his right hand on a black glass plate, the top of a stainless-steel box mounted into the wall next to the door. The box glowed as his palm print was scanned by a red laser. A computerized voice said, "Identity confirmed, Mr. Mitterand. Please enter your passcode."

The rectangular facing opened and a small keyboard projected outward. Philippe typed his personal password. He heard the hum of the door's electronic locking system disengage. It opened inward with a hiss. Three faulty passwords and a tactical unit of the French National Gendarmerie would have been notified and the entire area placed in lockdown mode for twenty-four hours. He smiled. Impregnable.

Once inside, he scanned the room. It looked like a science fiction movie set. A bank of large monitors lined the entire back wall as a multitude of technicians sat at individual computer terminals, scrutinizing different aspects of the system. It reminded him of what a military command center might look like.

"All is ready," he said to himself.

THREE

Los Angeles, California
United States of America

Lisa Savich positioned herself atop the flat rooftop of a three-story office building in Los Angeles. The two-foot concrete parapet around the periphery of the roof offered excellent cover. She set the bipod of her rifle on the top ledge and peeked over the side. The city was coming alive. Already the rising sun at her back was partially obscured by a hazy veil of Los Angeles smog. Drivers honked their horns while switching into and out of lanes. Pedestrians on the sidewalk below scurried about apparently in a hurry to get somewhere important. All were looking down, studying their cell phones and oblivious to anything happening above them. *Perfect.*

Looking through her rifle's telescope, she checked the distance to the intersection. *Target site is one hundred eighty-seven yards. Like shooting fish in a barrel.*

"We're too late! They're already gone!" Jacob Savich voice said into her earpiece.

"Are you sure?"

"Yes," said Jacob. "We were hoping to intercept them shortly after they left the house. They must have moved up their schedule. Dan reports that a white van arrived a couple hours before sunrise. We believe it's packed with hundreds of pounds of ammonium nitrate and ball bearing shrapnel. It left a few minutes later with two men inside."

"Description?" she asked.

8

"It's a 2011 Ford Econoline with a 'Pacific Carpet Company' logo painted on the side. We tapped into LAPD's information systems and found that it was stolen several days ago. We had them issue a BOLO alert, but nothing's turned up so far. Looks like it's all going to be up to you."

"They're probably being extra cautious," she said. "They might have caught wind that we were on to them."

"That's possible. Do you think they could have already passed your position?"

"I doubt it. I got here before sunrise and haven't seen anything. The stores won't open for another few hours, so I suspect they're holed up somewhere. Probably don't want to get too close to Rodeo Drive until the time is right."

"Let's hope so," said Jacob. "Stay alert and watch out for a trap. That last cell fell into our lap a little too easily for my taste. It seemed prepackaged. I'm getting the feeling that we're being played and missing the big picture. Something else is going on here besides another urban terror attack."

Lisa kept her eyes focused on the intersection. "Should we abort?"

"Not yet. Too many lives at stake this morning. Keep your eyes open. If it looks like a trap, stand down."

"Copy that." *Stand down. No way I can do that, no matter what Jacob says. Like he said, too many lives at stake.* Thousands of unsuspecting shoppers would be massacred. Trap or not, this had to be a go.

Jacob's voice crackled with tension in her ear. "I'll head along the secondary route in case they change their plans."

"I'm ready for them, locked and loaded." She attached the rifle's sound suppresser and reconfirmed the exact distance to the intersection. It would be an easy shot. The sun was still at her back so there would be no worries about light casting a telltale reflection off the rifle's scope.

She waited an hour before she spoke into her throat mike. "Commuter traffic's picking up and there are more pedestrians on the sidewalk. They'd better get here soon, or this is going to get ugly."

"Be patient. Keep us posted."

"Copy that." Her knees were aching, and her back was stiff. Didn't expect to be here this long. Should've brought a cushion.

She rested her back against the wall, stretched her legs and rubbed her thighs to get the circulation going.

"Remember them," Jacob's voice said.

"Always," she responded. That was the problem. She could never forget what had happened. "Nor should I," she admonished herself, but the memories were poisoning her soul. She didn't like what she had become. She was about to kill today. Again. As a warrior, it was a responsibility she and the others had accepted after being recruited for the team. She had always slept well knowing that what she did was for the sake of her country. In the beginning it had all been crystal clear, black and white. Kill terrorists to save innocent American citizens. Recently, the job had become a more complicated matter.

The diamond on Lisa's left hand reflected the sunlight into her eyes, disrupting her concentration. She never expected to be engaged, but her fiancé had proposed just over three months ago. He had only one condition. Lisa had to retire from the team. "Just one more mission," she had told him. The following month there was another, then another, then she lied.

What was she going to do? She promised him she'd stop, but here she was, ready to kill again. If he found out, it would fuckin' destroy him. There would be no arguing or yelling. He'd just walk away and take with him any chance for a normal life. That would be it. No wedding. No family. Nothing.

She shook her head. Concentrate, Lisa, she scolded herself. Deal with this later. You have a mission this morning.

She peeked over the ledge and redirected her attention to the intersection in time to see the vehicle exiting Santa Monica Boulevard and approaching the stop sign. "I have target acquisition. A white Ford van, but it doesn't say 'Pacific Carpet' on the side. It says 'Premier HVAC.'"

"Wrong one?" asked Jacob.

"Wait a minute." She centered the scope's crosshairs on the van's logo and noticed a fine line of demarcation along the edges. "No, it's the right one. Looks like they used a magnetic decal to cover up the original logo. That's why there were no hits on the BOLO alert."

"Roger that."

"Reconfirm. How many targets in the vehicle?" she asked.

"Two: a driver and Qaiser, the cell's top honcho in the front passenger seat."

"Confirmed, two occupants. They're pulling down the ramp now."

The van sat third in line before the intersection. She set the selector switch on her rifle to three-shot bursts and steadied her breathing, willing her heart rate to slow below fifty as she entered "the zone." The van moved up to second in line, and she again checked the targets. The driver was sweating, his head darting from side to side, tapping on the steering wheel with both hands. *First timer. It's also going to be your last.*

Sitting in the passenger seat, Qaiser appeared calm and calculating as he scanned his surroundings apparently looking for potential threats to his mission.

"Qaiser, you son-of-a-bitch," she whispered. "I bet your finger's twitching away on top of that detonator switch right now, ready to push it in case anything looks wrong."

"What's that?" Jacob asked into her earpiece.

"Nothing. Hold tight," she answered.

By now there were at least a hundred pedestrians within the impact range of the van. The shot had to be perfect. A miss and Qaiser would detonate the bomb. Dozens of innocents on the street below would die. Failure to make the shot meant thousands would die within the hour when the van reached Rodeo Drive. Lisa caressed the cold steel trigger of the rifle and slowly squeezed until death was delivered. Pfft, pfft, pfft. The first burst struck the van's windshield, exploding it inward and showering the two occupants with hundreds of shards of glass. The debris slashed through the driver's neck, ripping out his throat.

Qaiser grabbed his eyes, blood oozing between his fingers. Lisa squeezed the trigger again. Before he could press the detonator, the second burst of shots found his head, shearing off the top half of his skull. The van collided with a utility pole. There was no movement inside. Dozens of bystanders scattered in all directions. None of them looked up. *Mission accomplished.*

Staying low, behind the wall, she collected the six shell casings and dropped them down a heating vent in corner of the roof. She removed her black knit commando hat and shook out her long blond hair. She peeled away her outer black jump suit, exposing a taupe, fit-and-flare dress underneath. After slipping on a pair of cream espadrilles, she collapsed the rifle and stuffed everything into an oversized portfolio bag. A layer of light pink lipstick and a pair of dark sunglasses completed her disguise as she calmly headed toward the roof's access door. *No rush. Cops won't respond for another fifteen minutes.* She left the building, and sashayed down the sidewalk, her hair blowing gently in the breeze, her head up straight and shoulders back, looking like any other beautiful Hollywood model on her way to a photo shoot. "Both targets are neutralized," she said into her throat mike as she made her escape.

"Copy that. Good job," replied Jacob. He turned the wheel of the car and headed back toward the house.

FOUR

South Watts District
Los Angeles, California
United States of America

As soon as they arrived at the neighborhood, Jacob parked the Suburban a block from the house. The South Watts district had never fully recovered from the LA riots several decades ago. It was still dotted with crack houses and abandoned buildings. Jacob spoke into his throat mike, "Sitrep?"

Dan Foster, one of the team's snipers, sat in a second-floor apartment across the street from the target house, "No change. I don't think they've heard about what happened to their buddies in the van yet, but they're moving around a lot and carrying gear out to a car parked in the rear. I suspect they planned to use it to pick up Qaiser and his driver as soon as they abandoned the van. Looks like they're getting ready to run."

"How many?" asked Jacob.

"At least three, maybe four."

"Copy that. Let's finish this one." He and Tank exited their vehicle and approached the front of the old house. Jacob wore a hoodie sweatshirt to conceal his face. Tank's Harley Davidson t-shirt stretched tightly across his impossibly wide chest. His bald head looked like a giant black bowling ball perched upon a scaffolding of broad shoulders, without the benefit of an intervening neck. He towered over the other team members. Jacob considered him to be the perfect wingman. He remained unfazed when under heavy fire. If unprovoked, he was about as mean as a marshmallow, but if threatened, he was explosively lethal.

Jacob stopped behind a cluster of bushes and whispered, "Cover us."

"Copy that. You're clear to proceed," replied Dan. "Watch your lines of fire. There's that school."

Jacob and Tank attached silencers and racked the slides of their semi-automatic handguns. Staying low, they walked up the front porch steps. Jacob peered through one of the front windows. Two men were inside, scurrying about, packing up their gear. One had a Glock tucked into the back of his waistband. The other had an assault rifle leaning against a coffee table next to him. A third man tossed a paper bag onto the table, turned, and ran down a hallway. A rear exterior door opened, then slammed shut.

Using hand signals, Jacob told Tank that he could see two armed men. Tank was to go right, and Jacob would cover the left. He held up three fingers and began the countdown. On one, Tank drove his foot into the door right next to the lock where it was most vulnerable. It splintered open, catching the two men inside by surprise. The one with the Glock pulled his weapon and fired too quickly. He missed high. Jacob dropped him with double-tap shots to the head. The second man stood and stared at his rifle, sitting only a few feet away to his right.

Tank shook his head. "Don't try it."

The man ignored him and went for the gun. Big mistake. Tank rewarded him with a shot to the middle of his chest.

Jacob said into his mike, "Two down. Can you see the other one?"

Before Dan could respond, Jacob heard the back door burst open. He and Tank immediately started receiving automatic rifle fire from the kitchen area. They took cover by diving behind an old couch. Puffs of fabric and stuffing flew in all directions. They returned fire but were shooting blindly. They couldn't see their target or even be sure how many there were. During a brief pause, Tank got a quick look down the hallway.

"Looks like just one guy," said Tank. "He's reloading." A

second later, the man resumed fire, laying down a hailstorm of bullets, shredding the couch.

Jacob fired the rest of his clip to keep the shooter at bay while Tank inserted a fresh one into his gun and started shooting.

The return fire stopped. They heard the shooter rummaging through drawers. "He's out and looking for another magazine. This couch isn't going to protect us much longer," whispered Jacob. He hurdled over it and charged down the hall, firing his gun as he ran. Ten feet away from the kitchen he heard the unmistakable sound of a pin being pulled.

"Grenade!" He was trapped in the hallway with only one door for escape. When he saw the grenade flying toward him, he jerked the door wide open deflecting it back into the kitchen. The explosion blew all the windows and most of the shooter out into the backyard. It was over for now.

> *Now that's what I call fun, Buddy Boy. Let's see if we can find some more of these bad boys,* said the Entity.
> *I'm just getting started.*

Jacob approached the body of the man he had shot. He was face down on the floor, a pool of dark red expanding from around the two holes in his head. He turned him over with his foot and stepped back. He was only a boy, no more than sixteen. Why?

> *It's his own damn fault, Buddy Boy. He's like all the other terrorists we've stopped. They're all consumed by hatred for us and our way of life. This is the result.*

The Entity was right. Bitterness led to the boy's death. For a brief second Jacob saw himself lying dead on the floor. Hate and the pursuit of revenge had plagued his own life; ever since he was a boy and witnessed the massacre of his brother and father. He tried to shake off the guilt.

> *No time for that guilt shit, Buddy Boy. You're the good guy, remember? You're killing terrorists and saving innocent Americans. It's all for the greater good, right? You're the hero! Nothing wrong with having a little fun in the process. Right?*

Jacob pushed the voice aside. There could never be

enough blood to quench the Entity's demand for revenge. If he didn't keep it contained, it would eventually consume his life. He turned his eyes away from the dead young man. "Gotta clear the rest of the house, Tank." The two men looked for more threats.

A minute later Jacob yelled, "All clear."

"Second floor clear," responded Tank.

"Roger that. Your six is secure. I'm coming in." Dan's voice echoed through Jacob's earpiece. A minute later, Jacob saw Dan pull up to the front of the house in the team's black Suburban. He was wearing his usual frayed old army jacket and a stained hat with a bullet hole through the top. Called it his good luck charm. He ran inside the target house to join his teammates. "What's with all the fireworks?"

Tank shrugged and said, "Grenade. A minor diversion."

"A diversion loud enough to be heard a mile away," said Dan.

"You're right," said Jacob. "We need to hurry and get out of here. That explosion's bound to attract a lot of attention." He turned to Dan. "Check that car in back and see what you can find. Tank and I'll look around in here, hurry, we don't have much time."

Jacob searched the room and his eyes fell upon the paper bag sitting on the coffee table. He emptied it and found a half dozen flash drives. *Strange. I'd think they'd put these in the car first thing. Yet, they left them sitting right out in the open.*

Tank directed his attention to the two bodies on the floor. He patted them down. There were no wallets or any other forms of identification, but each had a cell phone. Tank placed them in his pocket. "Probably untraceable burner phones."

"Probably," replied Jacob, "but maybe Deets can get some usable information from them."

When Dan returned, Jacob asked, "Anything in the car?"

"A stash of automatic weapons, several thousand rounds of ammo, and a dozen grenades in the trunk." He smiled and held up a laptop. "You might like this. Found it in the front passenger seat."

"A computer? That's the big prize of the day." He paused to study the laptop for a second and shook his head. "Why didn't they take the bag of flash drives out to the car with it? Why leave them behind on the table?"

"Maybe we surprised them before they had a chance."

"I don't think so, Tank. Something's not right about this." He turned to Dan. "Pull their vehicle around to the front of the house. You can follow us to the airport. We don't want to leave all those weapons behind, and we don't have time to transfer everything to our car."

As Dan pulled the terrorists' car around, Jacob completed one final search of the house. Nothing else of significance. He exited through the same front door he had entered eleven minutes earlier. Before walking down the steps toward the car he lingered on the front porch for a few seconds. Dan looked at him and raised his eyebrows. "What is it?"

"We're being watched. I think this entire thing might have been a setup, but it backfired on them."

"Watched? By whom?" Dan searched up and down the street. "All the bad guys are dead."

"Not sure yet, but there's no doubt. Someone's out there. We'd better get moving."

Tank said to Dan, "What was that about? Being watched."

"It's instinct," replied Dan, "honed to the precision of a sixth sense. Jacob's had a knack for as long as I've known him. When he says something is wrong, we'd better pay attention."

"If you two are finished with all the chit-chat about me, we need to head out."

They left in the two cars and set out to pick up Lisa at the pre-arranged rendezvous point. Jacob kept his eyes on the rearview mirror, looking for tails. There were none.

FIVE

Pelican Bay Resort
Naples, Florida
United States of America

From across a canal, Rozhin studied the back of Tom Foley's vacation home through a pair of binoculars. She knew he would be there. She knew everything about him. He brought his family to Naples every year after the "snowbirds" left so they could relax and he could write in peace. He was working on the third installment of his five-article series, *The Terror in Our Midst*. Roshin glanced down at the newspaper sitting on the table next to her chair. She had read through the first two artictles several times. Foley was a good investigative journalist—too good in fact, and he was getting dangerously close to the truth. He would ruin everything if allowed to finish.

A light came on in the kitchen, but the moring fog was still too heavy for her to see details inside. As the haze lifted, the predawn sun cast a blood-red glow as its rays penetrated the dissipating shroud of mist still hovering over the water. She could barely see the faint outlines of a flock of egrets working the opposite bank, foraging for breakfast. An eight-foot alligator slowly glided by, apparently hoping to snatch one of the birds for its own meal. "It's the way of the world," she said quietly to herself. "Eat, then be eaten."

She watched as Foley entered the kitchen carrying his laptop. *He's still wearing the same clothes he had on yesterday. Looks tired. Probably worked all night. Must be a deadline.*

Tom's first article in the series attracted a great deal of international attention— far too much attention for Rozhin and her organization. It was explosive and well received by both sides of the political aisle in America. The initial report was vague and sparse on details, but future installments promised to include names and specifics about her group and its leaders. Rumors circulated around Washington about a possible Congressional inquiry. Rozhin's job was to prevent that from happening. "Foley's exposé is a threat to our organization's plans. He must be eliminated immediately," demanded her boss, a man who she only knew as the Scorpion.

"Scorpion," she whispered. Saying his name caused her heart to race. She allowed herself a few seconds to dwell on the warm passion of his touch and the image of his intense eyes staring into hers as they made love. Her hand drifted down toward her lap, but she pulled back from the fantasy. *No time for that, Rozhin. You have a job to do.*

She focused the laser microphone on the kitchen's sliding glass door and checked the alignment. It had to be perpendicular to the surface to insure good reflection back to the converter. Once satisfied, she studied the reception monitor. It was perfect. Any speech set up minor vibratory patterns in the glass pane. The laser read the variations and transmitted them to the converter. Using a USB cable, she connected it to her laptop where the laser transmissions were translated to real time conversations into her earpiece.

Foley brewed a pot of coffee and poured a cup. Amazing! The system worked better than she had expected. The liquid splashing in the bottom of the coffee cup sounded as though she were in the room standing next to him. Foley sat at the kitchen table and opened his laptop. He took a sip of the coffee and began working. His fingers typed furiously on the keypad.

He looks excited. Bad sign. He's probably almost done with the next article.

A few minutes later a little boy walked in, carrying his teddy bear. Tom stood. "Good morning C.J."

"G'morning, Pawpaw."

"What would you like for breakfast?"

"Fruit Loops," the boy replied with a wide smile on his face. "I want Fruit Loops."

"Then Fruit Loops it'll be, kiddo," said Tom. He filled a bowl with the cereal and milk.

Across the canal, Rozhin felt a pang of regret as she watched and listened. She hadn't seen her own children in over three years. Personal sacrifice was expected. The Scorpion demanded that the mission always be the top priority. All else, including family was secondary. She pushed the emotions aside and continued her surveillance.

"What's all the commotion out here?" a female voice called out. She was tying a robe around her waist as she entered.

"We're having Fruit Loops for breakfast, Grandma. You want some?"

She winked at her husband. "Thank you, C.J. That sounds delicious, but I think I'll just have my coffee and toast this morning." She walked over and kissed Tom on the cheek. They both looked at their grandson and laughed. He was wearing cowboy boots and his bathing suit. "He was so excited about going to the beach today he slept in them," she said. "Last night he arranged all his toys on the living room floor. He didn't want to forget anything."

The boy looked up from his cereal. "Will you come with us, Pawpaw? You can help me catch some fish with my new net. Maybe we can take some home for pets!"

Tom looked toward his wife. "I don't know, C.J. I still have some things I must wrap up this morning."

"He really wants you to join us, Tom. It's all he's talked about since we got here."

Tom closed his laptop. "I guess my work can wait a few hours. I only need to make a few changes. I want it to be perfect though. My editor said that the entire five-part series was Pulitzer Prize material."

"It's a good report," said his wife. "It's about time someone exposed the Jamaat-e-Islami for what they're doing in those military camps. We're both very proud of you. If you can't make it today, we'll understand."

Tom tousled his grandson's hair. "Sure, I'll go with you, kiddo. I can finish my piece and send it back later this afternoon. That'll still give my editor enough time to have it ready for the Monday morning edition."

This afternoon! Rozhin replayed the conversation to be sure. *There's no time to plan an accident.* It had to be done today. Things were going to get messy.

Tom's wife made toast and set it on the table for him. "Do you think you'd better lock up your computer before we leave? You don't want to lose everything you've been working on."

"No worry. I have everything backed up on a flash drive." He pulled the drive out of the USB port and dropped it in his shirt pocket. He patted it and stretched. "I've been working most of the night trying to get everything finished, and I'm a little stiff. Need to go to the gym and loosen up a bit. We'll leave for the beach as soon as I return."

"We'll be ready when you get back. She stood, kissed him on the head, and grimaced. "You're not going anywhere until you shower first," she said.

"Nobody showers before going to the gym."

"Tom."

He held up his hand. "OK, but it makes no sense to shower when I'm going to be walking over two miles to the gym. In this heat, I'll just get sweaty again. Then I'll need another shower when I get back."

He emerged from the bedroom fifteen minutes later, dressed in an NYPD t-shirt and gym shorts. "I'll see you in a couple hours."

"Hurry, Pawpaw! I can't wait to see the ocean! Maybe we'll see some sharks."

"Maybe, kiddo." Tom patted the boy on the head and kissed his wife on the cheek. Then, he headed out the door.

Rozhin had been watching Foley for over a week and had

his routine down pat: early-morning writing, breakfast with the family, then a workout at the Players Club. Next, it was back to the computer for more writing. The beach trip was a new wrinkle, but it provided a window of opportunity. It would be tight, but doable. She had to hurry. It would take him at least thirty minutes to get to the gym. Should be just enough time to pack up the equipment and scout out the club before he arrived.

SIX

Player's Club
Naples, Florida
United States of America

Thirty minutes after packing up her gear, Rozhin entered the resort's gym and took a towel from the shelf. Being petite had s advantages. People didn't perceive her as a threat, a fatal mistake n their part. Being plain was even better. She was unremarkable nd warranted no interest from others. She kept her head down, voiding any eye contact with the other gym patrons.

Rozhin set her gym bag in the corner and searched for a ituation where she could stage an accident. She tried disabling the afety measures on the weight bench and several other machines but vas unsuccessful.

Tom entered the main room. *He's here!* She needed to mprovise. He grabbed a mat and headed into the free-weight room. provided a perfect opportunity, but she needed to act fast. Timing vas critical. Rozhin allowed him a few minutes to get comfortable oing stretches on a floor mat. She put on a pair of weight gloves nd analyzed the crowd in the adjacent room. Most were wearing eadphones and involved in their own workouts, oblivious to nything else happening around them. Her pulse quickened as she vaited for the right moment. If things went sideways on this, she vould be caught before she could complete her assignment. She had be careful. Like a cat stalking its prey, Rozhin circled around her rget, searching for his most vulnerable spot. She selected a five-ound weight from the barbell rack and tested its balance in her

23

right hand. Too light. She picked up a ten pounder. Perfect. Rozhi
casually walked over to Tom's mat and smiled. He sat up and smile
in return. "Do I know you?"

Her eyes scanned the room, then without warning, smashe
the weight into the left side of his head. The crunch was sickening a
Tom's skull split open casting blood and bone fragments against th
wall behind him.

Rozhin yelled out. "Oh my God. Some guy just killed thi
man. Call 911! Someone call the police before he gets away." Sh
knelt at Foley's side, pretending to provide comfort. Her hand wa
on his carotid artery checking for a pulse. There was none. Sh
exhaled a sigh of relief. Tom Foley was dead. The sudden brutalit
of the attack appeared to stun the other gym patrons, their mind
apparently unable to process the violent event that had taken plac
They looked to the exit, searching for the non-existent male attacke

Rozhin retrieved her gym bag, pulled out what she wante
and melted into the background as others swarmed to help Foley
She screamed, "Bomb. He has a bomb," and tossed a grenade into th
room. Nothing like a catastrophic attack to give witnesses amnesi
She rushed out the door and ran in to a security guard. She pointe
"He's still in there! Hurry."

There was still a lot of work to be done and little time in whic
to do it. She jumped into her car and drove directly to Tom Foley
home, pulled her Glock out of the gym bag, and tried the front doo
Unlocked! Towels and a beach bag sat just inside the door. The bo
was playing on the floor with a toy starfish and looked up as soon a
she entered.

"Grandma!"

Tom's wife rushed into the room. "Who are you?" sh
screamed. "Get out."

Rozhin lifted her gun. "Both of you, on the couch." The ol
woman hesitated. "Now!"

The woman scooped up her grandson into her arms and sa
with C.J. on her lap. The boy buried his face against her. Mrs. Fole
looked up at Rozhin, terror in her eyes. "Just take what you wan
Please don't hurt my grandson."

"Where's the office?" asked Rozhin.

"I don't understand," said Tom's wife. She pulled little C.J. closer. He clutched his teddy bear.

"The office. Where's your husband's office?"

"It's . . .it's down the hall on the right."

"Take me. Bring the kid with you."

Rozhin followed the woman until they entered the small room. Foley's laptop was sitting on top of the desk. The flash drive wasn't plugged in. She searched the desk drawers and threw everything on the floor. *Found it.* She inserted a drive into the computer but couldn't open it.

"Password," she screamed.

"I don't know."

Rozhin pointed the gun at the little boy's head. "Password now."

The grandmother sobbed. "He never told me."

Most people were the same when it came to passwords, simple and easy to remember. "What's the kid's name?"

She replied, "C.J."

"Too short. What's his full name?"

"Christopher James."

She tried it but the computer didn't respond. "When was he born?"

The woman told her and Rozhin entered the letters CJ followed by the numbers of his birth date. The computer came to life. When she searched the flash drive, it was blank. Wrong one.

"Where's the flash drive, the one he was using this morning?"

The old woman was shaking. "I don't know. He had it in his hand." Her eyes widened. "He put it in his shirt pocket."

Rozhin pointed her gun to the corner of the room. Both of you, over there and sit, facing the wall. If you move so much as an inch, I'll shoot. The old woman grabbed C. J. into her arms and carried him.

Tom's shirt had been tossed over an easy chair. She searched the pockets and found the flash drive. Inserting it into the computer, she opened the files. It was what she needed. No time left. The boy and his grandmother were cowering in the corner. Witnesses. She fired twice. Casualties of war.

After a quick search of the house to be sure she left nothing behind, Rozhin went to the kitchen stove and turned on the gas burners. Then she started a fire in Foley's office. She needed to destroy the possibility of any trace evidence that could implicate her. *Should blow in about ten minutes.*

By the time the SWAT team arrived, Rozhin was already thirty miles away on I-75 North. She stopped in a Cracker Barrell restaurant parking lot to switch cars, then continued north toward West Virginia. She had accomplished everything she had been assigned. The Scorpion would be pleased.

SEVEN

Solitude Compound
Owen County, Kentucky
United States of America

After completing their mission in Los Angeles, Jacob and his team boarded their boss's private Citation CJ-4 jet. Three hours later, they landed at the Solitude training compound. The facility couldn't be found on any official CIA organizational charts. The property had been a drug cartel manufacturing and distribution center located in a remote corner of rural Owen County, Kentucky. It was confiscated by the FBI after a drug raid and sold at auction to Doctors Jacob and Lisa Marie Savich.

The Savich farm retreat provided a total of thirty-five hundred acres of secluded rolling hills that were protected by a ten-foot chain-link security fence. It provided the perfect training facility for a non-sanctioned group. The drug cartel had excavated a subterranean vault under the main house. It had been created as a state-of-the-art meth lab and drug storage facility. Jacob repurposed the room as an interrogation center. In addition, the property possessed a runway large enough to accommodate medium sized planes including Winston Hamilton's personal jet.

The team members unloaded their gear and the items seized during the raid. After quick showers, they convened in the dining room to eat and discuss the events of the day. They congratulated each other on another successful mission, all except Jacob. He paced the floor in deep thought before finally speaking, "I think we walked into a trap."

Tank stepped forward, towering over the others. "I don't see how that's possible, Jacob. If it had been a trap, we would have been surrounded and killed. Other than the guy with the grenade, no one even attempted an attack."

Jacob continued pacing the room. "They were expecting us, but we got lucky and stopped them before they could clear out. Someone was watching."

"What would simply watching us give a terror organization?" asked Tank. "If they were there, why didn't they attack us and save their cell members and their weapons cache? Makes no sense."

"I'm convinced someone was there."

"Could it have been the FBI you sensed?" asked Lisa. She fidgeted with her dress and seemed worried.

Jacob noticed. "What's wrong?" he whispered.

She gave an almost indistinguishable head shake. "Later."

"I doubt it was the FBI, Lisa. They would have stormed in as soon as the shooting started."

"How's it even possible that the cell members would be expecting us?" asked Dan. "Nobody except President Wagner and his security chief even knows of the team's existence much less our operational plans." He turned to Jacob. "Do you think we could have a mole somewhere in the organization?"

"I don't think so," said Jacob, "but it's always a consideration, especially if someone's willing to spend millions of dollars to turn one of our people. I don't doubt the loyalties of anyone in this room, but maybe someone else discovered who we are and leaked the story. We need to be very careful until we can get more information about what happened today."

"Hopefully, Norman can come up with something when he goes over their equipment," said Dan. "What do you think, Deets? You're the computer genius. Can you open their flash drives?"

Deets was the team's IT expert. "If there's something on the drives, I can find it. They're probably encrypted and might have a self-destruct feature if the files aren't opened properly, but I've been able to circumvent their measures before. I'm sure I can do it again."

After Lisa and Dan left Solitude to head home, Norman Deets hobbled into his computer lab and laid his metal crutches against the wooden table. Ever since he was crippled by childhood muscular dystrophy, the internet had been his life. He had been arrested years earlier for breaching the firewall of a major credit card company and deleting the balances of several thousand customers. Mr. Hamilton pulled a few strings and arranged to have the boy released into his custody. He told Jacob that the boy's mind was too brilliant to be wasting away in a prison cell.

Jacob and Tank carried in the seized computer, flash drives, and cell phones, and set them on the table in front of Deets.

"Need anything else buddy?" asked Tank.

"No, this should do it. Thanks."

Jacob watched as the kid sat at his desk, multiple large monitors surrounding him. It was as though the boy was sitting at an alter preparing a religious ceremony. He arranged the confiscated items in a precise sequence, placing the flash drives in a straight line. He adjusted them until their edges were perfectly parallel to each other. Behind them, he placed the cell's laptop, and to the right of it, the three burner phones. When all appeared to be arranged to his satisfaction, Deets said, "We're ready." He turned on his bank of computers and the screens flickered for a second. Jacob watched as the boy set about the process of extracting information from the flash drives. He inserted the first one into the USB port on a quarantine computer. He explained that he used it to protect his main network from contamination by outside systems. He turned to Jacob. "Occasionally, drives contain suicide programs that erase not only its own content but also crash any interfaced computer that attempts unauthorized access. Before trying to open anything, I need to be certain all destruct programs have been disabled. I can afford to sacrifice the quarantine device, but not my primary information systems. They're tied directly into the NSA and Homeland Security databases."

Jacob remained quiet as Deets opened the first drive. "Empty," Deets said and tossed it onto a trashcan. The next two were also blank and were discarded. He inserted the fourth and studied the screen. "Finally, here are some security measures. They must be trying to protect some important stuff inside." He bypassed the password without difficulty, but soon Jacob noticed a frown on the boy's face.

"What is it?"

"Amateurs," Deets said. "This is too easy. Where's the challenge? A high school freshman could easily hack into this thing." He scrolled through a multitude of files. "Holy shit! I can't believe this!"

"What?" asked Jacob as he looked over the boy's shoulder.

"Looks like these guys were actually planning to poison the water supply for L.A. They have aerial photographs of the major aqueducts and various pumping stations. Things were still in the planning stages, but the file indicates they were definitely going to do it sometime soon. They've been stockpiling arsenic."

Jacob stood straight and ran his fingers through his hair. "Holy shit is right. These guys are crazy. We need to let Mr. Hamilton know about this so he can warn Homeland Security ASAP."

Deets inserted another flash drive and again bypassed the security measures without difficulty. He sat on the edge of his chair. "Here we go. This might be interesting. There's a large file here titled 'West Virginia.'" He clicked it open. "It contains correspondence regarding some kind of a camp."

"Like a military installation?"

"It sure looks like it. There are lists of training schedules, budgets, and provisions. There's another list that includes armaments, AK-47 rifles, RPGs, and C-4 explosives. It's enough to arm a small army."

Tank took off his hat and rubbed his head. "Sounds like someone is planning to start a small war."

"It looks like a place where they might train for another attack, a big one like their assassination attempt. We need to find this camp now. Let Mr. Hamilton know."

Deets copied and encrypted the file, marked it urgent, and sent it to Mr. Hamilton along with the information about the L.A. water systems. He checked the last two flash drives. They offered no new information, so he picked up the laptop Dan found. He ran a USB cable from it to his quarantine computer and turned it on. "This one's going to be fun. It's password protected and it's a good one, at least fourteen random characters and numbers. I need to run a 'Cyber Buster' program to circumvent the password prompt."

Deets activated the program. The screen flickered for a second and Deets moved to the edge of his chair, almost knocking over his crutches. "Now this is what I'm talking about. There's a complex self-destruct program. I almost triggered it because it was hidden behind a second password. You two might want to step out for some coffee. This is going to take me a while."

When Jacob and Tank returned an hour later, they brought a cup for Deets. He had been working on the files for over two hours and Jacob figured he might need a little caffeine. Jacob was wrong. Deets appeared so preoccupied, he didn't even acknowledge their return. He looked to be running on adrenaline, his face buried in the computer screen. "Did it! I'm in!" He scanned the files and leaned back in his chair shaking his head. "What the hell is this? Nothing here but video games and pornography. Why all the sophisticated security measures if there's nothing in here except this shit?"

"Doesn't make sense," said Jacob. "Why would a terror cell make sure they took their laptop in their car, when all it had was useless garbage? I'd expect at least some Google searches regarding those potential targets you found or communications with other cells regarding West Virginia."

"I know," said Deets. "I found a lot more information on the flash drives and they were barely protected."

Jacob took a sip of his coffee. "Maybe the laptop files were erased. The guys at the house looked like they were scrambling to destroy evidence."

"Of course! That would explain things. I should have thought of that myself." Deets pulled out a disc from his file drawer and uploaded it into the quarantine computer. He interfaced it with the laptop.

"What's that?" asked Tank.

"Data Recovery Wizard. It's a program that can allow me to open any erased files and emails."

"You can do that even after they've been removed?"

"Sure. Most people don't realize it, but deleted information remains on the hard drive until it's been recorded over. If it hasn't been too long, I should be able to retrieve almost everything that was there. It's an old computer and it's slow, so this is going to take a little while."

It was a half hour and another cup of coffee before Deets finally said, "Here we are!" He leaned closer to the computer screen. "There are dozens of emails from some guy called, 'RQ3/12.' I'll start with the most recent one." He read the message aloud for Jacob and Tank:

May the hand of Allah guide and protect you on your holy quest tomorrow. By your actions, the word of Muhammad, praise his name, will be heard throughout the world.

Jacob studied the monitor screen. "What was the date of that message?"

"The day before the Rodeo Drive bombing attempt. The rest of his emails deal with similar subjects, praising the holy jihad and encouraging future attacks."

"It sounds to me like the sender could be one of their leaders rallying his minions into battle." Jacob leaned closer and pointed to the email. "Who do you think this RQ3/12 guy is? Sounds like he might be an important player."

"I have no idea," said Deets. He studied the username. "Wait a minute. I think I might have something." He turned to Jacob. "What was the name of that cell leader in L.A., the one Lisa shot?"

"Qaiser, but we never knew his full name."

Deets turned to face Jacob. "The Q in this guy's screen name might stand for Qaiser. Do you think he might be related to our guy from L.A.?"

"Might be," said Jacob. "It would be one hell of a coincidence for one terrorist to go by the name Qaiser and someone else in the same organization to use the initial Q in their screen name."

"I don't believe in coincidences," said Tank. "Most are statistically improbable."

"I agree, Tank. One thing's for sure, whoever he is, he's one of the group's leaders, maybe even the top man himself, the mastermind behind all the terrorist activities in this country. The only way we'll know for sure is to find him."

"If he's still transmitting emails, I might be able to run a reverse trace to the source. Might even be able to identify where he lives. It's going to take me some time, but by using the IP address I can probably backtrack to the original server. If we're lucky, I might even be able to come up with a specific address. If you want, I can start to bleed out his organization's bank accounts and bankrupt them."

"Let's not get carried away, Deets. I don't want any of their people to know we're onto them yet."

A sheepish grin crept across his face. "Just thought it might be fun to mess with their heads." He turned his attention back to the laptop, again combing through the files until he turned to Jacob. Near the bottom of the list was a file labeled YAOGUAI. He said the name aloud.

"Yaoguai?" questioned Jacob. "What the hell does that mean?"

"I can't say for sure," said Deets. "There's no reference to it in any of the other files. Could be a person or even a code name for a mission."

"Like a large-scale attack?" asked Jacob.

"Who knows? Let's see what I can find out." Deets turned to another computer and did a Google search. "It says here that Yauguai is an evil demon from Chinese mythology. It seeks to attain mystical powers by destroying the innocent."

"What could a Chinese demon have to do with radical Islam?"

"No idea. Let me open this thing. Maybe I can find out." Deets double clicked on the file. The computer immediately flashed, and a series of nonsense symbols waterfalled down the screen.

"Shit! Double shit!" Deets yelled as his fingers danced across the keyboard. His glasses slipped to the end of his nose and he knocked his coffee cup onto the floor.

"What?" asked Jacob.

"I triggered a hidden self-destruct sequence! Damn computer's erasing everything!" He frantically downloaded the file to his quarantine computer before it was completely gone. "Not so sloppy after all. I got a little too cocky because things were easy — up until now. They really didn't want anyone to see this file. Clever bastards!"

"Can you save it?"

"Working on it. The laptop is a dinosaur so it's a little slow. That's good for us." He saved what he could and printed what was left of the file. By now, the text was severely corrupted. There were only a few handfuls of isolated words, most of them arranged in short phrases or nonsense jumbles of letters. The only usable bit of information was a fragmented sentence which read, "Raphael p/q&x Paris ... %xj#0--key."

Deets studied the printout. "I wonder what this Paris stuff is all about. What's the key for? A hotel room? A locker?"

Jacob rubbed the back of his neck. "I don't know. Maybe the jihadists are planning to ramp up their activities in France. They've been rioting in the streets and burning churches over there, but that's not our concern. Right now, we need to focus on that damn training facility and the guy sending the emails."

Deets was unable to salvage anything else from the corrupted computer. He set it on the table and examined the three burner phones the team had seized. He copied all the incoming and outgoing phone numbers and forwarded the list to Mr. Hamilton.

Jacob studied the list. "Looks like most of the calls on the logs were made to and from various areas around Paris. Maybe this French connection is something we must consider after all. We need to notify Mr. Hamilton about this."

Jacob watched as Deets typed an email.

Jihadist training camp in West Virginia?
Must locate ASAP. Impending military assault!

Raphael--Paris: connection? Key to what?

YAOGUAI: have you heard of it before?

EIGHT

CIA Headquarters
Langley, Virginia
United States of America

A bespectacled Winston entered his Langley office at precisely 7:00 a.m. The plaque on the door read: *Supplemental Section of the Office of Research and Reports: Winston Hamilton III, Director.* He appreciated the irony, knowing the department appeared to be just another insignificant cog in the CIA bureaucracy. It was anything but that, a fact few people outside the White House realized, including his superiors in the Agency. His track record and family connections resulted in multiple opportunities for advancement, but he declined. As the sole heir of the Hamilton Family Trust, he didn't need the money. He already wielded more power than most politicians in D.C. His present position afforded him all that he required and provided the level of anonymity he needed to accomplish what was necessary. Winston Hamilton used his position to amass the most valuable commodity in the nation's capital. Information was king in Washington and Winston had accumulated a library of incriminating facts on almost every influential politician and power broker in D.C. He knew the details of their many indiscretions. It was a powerful weapon and Winston had become a master of how and when to use it.

He hung his suit jacket and black fedora on a wall hook and inhaled. The aroma of fresh brewed coffee filled the air. Several cups were part of his morning ritual, helping him to kick-start the day.

"Good morning, Jeanine," he said to his secretary of twenty-three years.

"Good morning, sir." She poured a cup, prepared to his specifications: black, no sugar, and strong.

He took a sip and relished the hot liquid as it ran down the back of his throat, stimulating his neurons to life. He sat behind his antique desk and placed the cup on a coaster. Behind him, an original oil by his favorite American painter, Andrew Wyeth, hung on the wall. Its somber portrayal of isolation loomed over Winston's shoulders. Appropriate. On the corner of his desk, an obligatory family photograph stared at him. It had been sitting in that exact spot ever since he took over the office fifteen years ago. Winston picked it up and traced the outline of the images of his wife and two boys with his finger. It was a reminder of better days—before his wife packed up the kids and moved to Glendale, a quiet community just north of Cincinnati. She had demanded that he choose between her and his mistress. His choice destroyed their marriage. It wasn't another woman who had captured his heart. It was the Agency and its attendant intrigue that he couldn't give up. All that was left of those earlier times were fading memories and the knowledge that everything he did was to protect his family and the future of their country.

One of his two computers, the personal one on the left, pinged. It was a personal message giving instructions to move his opponent's bishop to take Winston's queen. He chuckled at the thought of his opponent's glee at capturing the most powerful piece on the board. A bad decision, Mr. President, but predictable. He walked over to a small table in the corner. Atop it sat a chessboard, its well-worn pieces in mid-game arrangement. He made the move as instructed by President Wagner, and in response, he advanced one of his rooks. Three more moves and his unsuspecting opponent would be in checkmate. He emailed his instructions back to POTUS and returned to his desk.

Winston turned his attention to the secure agency computer on the right and started plowing his way through a slew of interdepartmental messages. Boring stuff. *That's the problem. Too many meetings and reports, but no action.* The bureaucrats were too busy covering their collective asses, afraid of political repercussions and endless subpoenas to testify in front of congressional committees.

In the beginning, the CIA had been a powerful international force. Now it was an ineffective shell of its former self, something used mostly as a political weapon. The country was under attack and no one had the courage to address the problem head on. Agencies like Homeland Security and the NSA had become feckless behemoths, bogged down in a quagmire of bureaucratic protocol. They were great at accumulating data but that was all. It was useless information if no one was willing to use it to formulate effective responses. President Wagner had been trying to turn the situation around, but it was a painfully slow process. Knowing that the President's efforts were continuously thwarted by deeply entrenched holdovers from previous administrations made Winston furious. *Spineless bureaucrats.* They were more interested in protecting their jobs than protecting the citizens of the United States. Some drastic changes were needed.

Winston's solution was the creation a small nimble team with the moral flexibility to do whatever was necessary to safeguard the citizenry. He empowered his clandestine group with the mission of protecting the country at all cost. They were charged with the task of extracting information from the enemy by any means necessary and then acting upon that information with extreme prejudice. Winston didn't care that they functioned outside the accepted tenets of the Constitution. Old procedures had failed to protect Americans and he wouldn't allow his team to be hamstrung by the same bureaucratic limitations that hampered the nation's traditional law enforcement agencies. It was essential that his team establish its own set of rules. It took a special breed of individuals to do whatever had to be done.

He needed people who could think independently. After years of searching, he discovered a most unlikely leader around whom he could build his team. The man was intelligent and possessed an uncanny ability to almost read the thoughts of his opponents. He could rapidly analyze changing situations, anticipate the response of his adversaries, and formulate effective countermoves. If Winston had to come up with a phrase to define Dr. Jacob Savich, it would be "ferociously clever."

The man was a paladin of sorts with a compelling need to protect those who couldn't protect themselves, to rain down punishment upon those who deserve it: murderers, rapists, and pedophiles, anyone who had eluded accountability for their crimes through slick manipulations of the courts. Winston simply redirected that quest and refocused it on the protection of U.S. citizens and the preservation of western culture. The man had an instinct for what he did. It's not something that could be taught. You either had it or you didn't, and Jacob Savich definitely had it.

Savich more than lived up to Winston's expectations. Two years ago, the new leader and his nascent team thwarted an assassination attempt on President Richard Wagner during his inauguration ceremony in Washington. They prevented the detonation of a dirty bomb that would have wiped out most of the federal government and shut down the nation's capital for decades. Since then, the team had neutralized over a dozen sleeper cells and prevented a multitude of terror attacks around the country.

Winston sipped on a second cup of coffee as he awaited a status report from his team leader. Jeanine's voice came through the intercom. "Mr. Hamilton, sir, Dr. Savich is on line three." Winston picked up his most secure phone line, the one that provided direct access to Solitude, the team's base of operations.

"Hello, Dr. Savich. What have you found?"

"Sir, we have several major problems."

"Major problems? You mean beyond what we already know?"

"Affirmative, Mr. Hamilton. We've uncovered the existence of at least one jihadist training facility hidden here deep within our borders. There's a direct connection between it and the attempted bombing at Rodeo Drive."

"A training camp! That's all we need. A military-style training facility in our own damn back yard." Winston stood, switched the call to speaker phone, and paced the room, his hands locked behind his back. "There have been some rumors about such camps circulating around Washington for years. Even I had my doubts about their existence."

"It looks as though those rumors were true, sir."

"Where is it? We need to know."

"We can't say exactly, but Norman Deets has been working on it. He uncovered some emails between Qaisar, the leader of the L.A. sleeper cell and what might be his brother. The emails mostly refer to the attack on Rodeo Drive, but there was also a file that referenced the existence of the training camp. That corresponds with other information we already uncovered. Using some reverse tracking and triangulation techniques, Deets was able to isolate the general vicinity of the brother's computer to a ten-square-mile region along the eastern portion of West Virginia."

"And it's your belief that Qaiser's brother heads that training compound?" asked Winston.

"It certainly looks that way, Mr. Hamilton. At the very least he's a major player in their organization. He might even be the mastermind behind what's happening in this country. If so, taking him out would cut the legs out from under their terror network."

"You need to make that happen ASAP." Winston withdrew a Padron Reserve cigar from his desktop humidor and lit it. He enjoyed a few puffs and set in down in the ashtray. Something needed to be done, and soon. "What do you suggest, Dr. Savich?"

"That's why I'm calling. I need to find the camp's exact location. As I said, I can give you the general vicinity, but I need your boys at Homeland Security to pinpoint it. Once that's done, I'll need access to one of the country's surveillance satellites. I want detailed overhead maps of the area including the location of all structures, an estimate of numbers of personnel present, and the types of vehicles they might have. When we have all the necessary information, the team will infiltrate the place and confirm that it's an actual training facility. If we find evidence of a military compound with sophisticated weaponry, we plan to take them out."

Winston picked up his cigar and tried to take a puff. It was out. He relit it and took a long drag, allowing the smoke to fill his mouth, then leaned back in his chair and exhaled toward the ceiling. "It'll take some behind-the-scenes work and I'll have to twist a few arms, but we should be able to locate the site. I'll speak to the White House and ask the president to have one of our satellites redirected so it's just about parked on top of the location. That should give you all the reconnaissance information you need to plan a raid. In addition, I'll arrange for a live feed so you and your team can have real-time updates when you need them. Give me a week to get everything set up." *So much for chess games. This is the real thing!*

Winston scribbled a few notes. "I assume if you raid this training compound in West Virginia you'll want to retrieve more than just another set of hard drives. You'll want to get your hands on someone you can interrogate."

"Yes sir, I need to get the kind of details that only one of their leaders can provide. I strongly believe that Qaiser's brother is that person, and I'm certain he's there in that camp. Something big is in the works, and I need to squeeze as much information as I can out of him."

"Do whatever you must do to destroy that camp and neutralize its leaders." Winston knew his meaning was fully understood. "Is there anything else?"

"Yes sir. Three names have surfaced. The first is Masterson."

Winston leaned forward in his chair. Savich had his full attention. "As I recall, the name was Masterson Properties Corporation and it surfaced several years ago in conjunction with the assassination attempt on President Wagner. The company owned the three hotels where the assassins were hiding. It was owned by a Martin Darpoli." He returned the cigar to the ashtray.

"The Scorpion," said Jacob.

"I've been expecting his return," said Winston. "It was inevitable. Does the file give any indication as to what he might be up to?"

"No sir. I can't say with any degree of certainty that he's actively involved in anything specific right now. It's possible that the name was used in a historical context or it might be a code name for a future attack. Bottom line, we don't know for sure."

"He's a dangerous character, but there's nothing for us to do right now. We don't even know where he is. All we can do is to keep in mind the possibility that he's planning something. Hopefully more information will surface later." Winston reached into the top drawer of his desk and retrieved a soft cloth. After cleaning his wire rimmed glasses, he replaced them on the bridge of his nose. "What else do you have?"

"More names sir, but I don't know if they're significant. Have you heard anything about a terrorist called Raphael?"

"No, only that Raphael was one of the more famous Italian Renaissance painters, known for his portraits of the Madonna. Magnificent artist."

"Yes sir, but have you heard that name in the context of any terrorist organization?"

"No, I haven't come across the name, but I can check with my contacts at the National Security Agency to see if they have anything." Winston made another note. "I'll have to get back to you on it. What was the second name?"

"Yaoguai." Jacob spelled it for him. "I think it could be the code name for their next attack. I'm getting the feeling it might be something big, but I have nothing more than the name."

Winston made another note and replied, "I've never heard of it and I definitely would have remembered the word, Yaoguai. I'll do some research on it."

"And sir?"

"Yes."

"I'm going to need your private jet again."

NINE

Chengdu, China

Chow was standing in the dark on the sidewalk in front of the apartment building when Liu-Fawn saw him. She approached him from behind and tapped him on the shoulder. He flinched and turned to hug her. "I was afraid something happened to you."

She watched him scan his surroundings in all directions. Beads of perspiration along his upper lip glistened in the moonlight. "Are you sure you weren't followed?" asked Chow.

"That's what took me so long. I was tailed for a while and had to backtrack down several side streets. I finally lost him when I switched cabs." She held up two fingers. "Twice. If he picked up my trail again, I would have seen him." She checked the streets in all directions. "How about you?"

"I don't think so, but I'm not as good at this as you." He looked over his shoulder. "You never can be sure. Are you certain this place is still safe?"

"Yes. We can trust her, Chow," said Liu-Fawn. "She's been a good friend of mine since we were children. She's a simple teacher and is not being monitored."

"I hope so. If they catch us together, we could be arrested. Maybe even shot."

For Liu-Fawn the initial intrigue was part of the excitement of getting the story. She tried to meet with Chow at least once a month, and her friend's home was the only safe place where the two could rendezvous privately. Surveillance systems had been installed in their own apartments: him because of his sensitive research, hers because of her political activities. Each of them was frequently shadowed by members of the Ministry of Intelligence and losing a tail was a dangerous challenge.

"We should go inside." She looked over her shoulder one more time before using her key to open the front door. It was a tiny apartment with only a combination living room/kitchen and one small bedroom. The air smelled of jasmine, her friend's perfume. Liu-Fawn turned to face Chow. There was a child-like naïveté about him. He appeared to have no political or personal agenda. He seemed to be motivated only by the purity of his science.

I never expected the relationship to evolve into something intimate.

Her original intent was to gather information from him for a news story about his research. He wouldn't ever discuss the details of his work, but the more time she spent with him trying to coax the story out of him, the more impressed she became with Chow as a person. Never before had she met a man with a mind as brilliant as his. *How could I fall in love with the subject of my own investigative report? Love? Is that what this is?*

In the privacy of the apartment, the two kissed briefly, something they could never do in public. Liu-Fawn suspected she was Chow's first and only love. He had spent most of his life in his lab, sequestered from anything normal like female companionship. She had changed this by exposing him to many of the more important aspects of life besides his scientific research. She allowed him to discover the exquisite joys that only the tenderness of a woman's touch could provide. She also unveiled the ugly treachery of their government and those in power, how the average person in China suffered the same degree of oppression that they suffered prior to Mao's revolution. "The only difference is the face and names of the oppressors," she told him.

Liu-Fawn went into the tiny kitchen and made tea. She took a sip and offered to pour some for Chow. He was shaking so hard he could barely hold the cup. She filled it for him.

He looked into her eyes. "I hate that we must meet under

these circumstances." His eyes dropped to the floor. "We can never hope to have a normal relationship."

"We wouldn't have to hide if we didn't live in this oppressive country."

"What else can we do? This is our home, and our country isn't going to change."

"But that's what I've been trying to do, Chow," she said, "force a change. There are serious problems in China. The original ideals of communism have been perverted. The average citizens no longer benefit. They are little more than workhorse automatons used by the elite to amass greater wealth and power for themselves. Then the government used the coronavirus to sacrifice hundreds of thousands of our people to stop their protests for reform. Our entire system is a charade. The Ministry engineered that virus and unleashed it upon our cities. Exposing their part in the Covid-19 pandemic is the topic of my next internet blog."

Chow interrupted her. "Maybe it's not such a good idea to openly criticize the government. Those doctors who initially spoke up have disappeared. You already spent a year in prison for joining in the Tiananmen Square anniversary demonstrations. If you keep antagonizing them like this, you might wind up being jailed again." He held up his hand. "Or worse. Maybe you should stop for a while."

"If I don't do it then who will? Who will speak up for the people? Someone has to take a stand."

"Let someone else do it for a while. I think it's getting to be too dangerous." He caressed her cheek. "I can't bear the thought of losing you."

"Then we should leave," she said.

"You mean defect?"

"Yes, I know you don't like to talk about it, but I can tell that you have developed something extraordinary in your lab, and I believe it has something to do with all those deaths in the village of Nam Pen. You must have developed some type of weapon. Most nations in the world would be more than willing to give asylum to a scientist of your caliber. I'm sure any country would provide whatever you need to continue your research. If we left, I would be free to write what I want about the failings of communism and the corruption in the Politboro."

"But we can't defect! The Ministry would have us shot for certain. What good is trying to defect if we die in the process?"

She took Chow's hand in hers. "If we die, then we die pursuing freedom. At least we will perish together."

She looked into his eyes and gently kissed him on the lips. "You'll never lose me, Chow. We will be together forever." When the kiss became deeper, Chow reached under her blouse and tried to caress her left breast. He lacked finesse. She lowered her hand toward his lap and began exploring through the fabric of his jeans until she felt a shiver of anticipation surge through Chow. He was still new at this, his response clumsy and premature.

He turned away. "I love you Liu-Fawn. I'm sorry, but I'm afraid I'm still not very good at this. I'm sure there are other men who . . ."

She turned his head to face her, put her finger over his lips, and slowly shook her head. "I don't want any other man. It's you I love, Chow. Stop analyzing everything with your mind and let your body take over."

That's what he did. Their love making was still awkward, but at the same time, blissful. They became lost in each other for the next hour. By the time they left the apartment, Liu-Fawn noticed several lights across the street were out. Those still working cast eerie shadows along the buildings. Liu-Fawn squinted her eyes, peering into the darkness. Her heart raced. She thought she saw movement of two men in a small alley across the street. She pulled Chow closer but when she looked back, they were gone. *Probably just being paranoid.*

TEN

Liuang Technology Corporation
Chengdu, China

Chow preferred to ride his bike to and from the lab, but that was no longer an option. Meang had arranged for him to be driven every day for the past week, ever since his last rendezvous with Liu-Fawn in the apartment. As the car pulled to the front, the huge Liuang Computer Technologies complex loomed over him. The corporation was the largest company of its kind in China, exporting electronics, computers, and micro circuitry parts to almost every country in the world. Three six-story research buildings were arranged in a semi-circular fashion around the central Administration Building. He had never set foot in it before but was aware that it housed Meang's office and sections of the Ministry of Intelligence.

His driver watched him and would continue to do so until he entered the first building on the right. Unlike the Administration Building, it was a rectangular-shaped, utilitarian structure lacking any attempt at architectural nuance. An armed security guard stood just inside the door of the small lobby. It contained only a single table and a set of elevator doors. Chow allowed the security camera to scan his face and a second later the door opened. He pressed the button for level C, three stories below ground, away from the probing surveillance technologies of China's enemies.

Each of the research buildings was constructed the same. The six floors above ground housed a multitude of laboratories devoted to various legitimate research activities including, nanotechnology, artificial intelligence, superconductivity, and controlled nuclear fusion. Three subterranean stories beneath the complex housed the clandestine People's Liberation Army Unit 61398. It was formed to spearhead strategies of business espionage and electronic warfare against the West. It also housed Chow's special lab.

After being cleared by the retinal scanner, Chow entered and headed for his office where he sat at his desk and studied the newest prototype for his device. It was twenty-seven times more powerful than the one he originally designed three years earlier. It's capacity never failed to amaze him. He pushed a button on the right side of his watch. The picture of Liu-Fawn appeared on the small screen, her tender almond eyes gazing back at his. "Good morning, my love. Where have you been?" he asked. He hadn't heard from her since the last time they met. Several seconds later, he depressed the set of buttons on the left side of the watch in a precise sequence, activating the system. *Careful.* Failure to execute the procedure properly would result in the watch and its programs going into a self-destruct mode. He completed the maneuver and the side of the watch opened, exposing a micro-USB port. Using a mini cable, he connected the watch to his laptop, and pressed the 'enter' key. The computer screen flickered for a second, after which the word "**YAOGUAI**" appeared, followed by the message:

> **Good morning Dr. Chow. How may I assist you?**

Chow typed: **Status report**.

> **The system is fully functional and is presently coordinating all input data. The identification and activation codes are already organized according to geographic vectors. All is arranged in decreasing order of strategic importance.**

Chow entered: **Extent?**

> **Estimated 94.739% world-wide penetration, plus or minus .002%. Detection possibility 0%.**

He typed: **YAOGUAI-II?**

Fully functional and ready for activation upon your approval.

Chow asked: **Antidote status?**

Also, fully functional, but still must be subjected to a rigorous set of test formats to ensure efficacy. I have already designed the appropriate models and will begin evaluation protocols on your command.

Up until last year, the world had been unaware of Chow's accomplishments. The Chinese Ministry had allowed him to publish a small amount of his earliest research work. Though the paper was admittedly groundbreaking, it intentionally excluded his most dramatic breakthroughs. He allowed himself to smile. Finally, he was receiving the recognition he deserved from the international scientific community. Even though the paper was based upon work he had completed almost a decade ago, it was still light-years ahead of anything being accomplished elsewhere. Even those in China's Ministry of Intelligence were unaware of how far his work at LCT had progressed.

He picked up the tiny clear box from the top of his desk, the glass container only a one-half inch cube, its contents barely visible to the naked eye. He held it under a magnifying lens and examined the device inside. He pondered the ancient philosophical question, *How many angels could dance on the head of a pin?* He knew the answer because he had created the angels, but they weren't actually angels. No, they were Yaoguai and they were astonishingly powerful. They had already invaded almost every computer system in existence.

After the deaths of the villagers three years ago, Chow could never allow the power of his device to also become its downfall. He built several failsafe protective measures into the activation protocols. Just as a human body can be immunized against disease, his network now had the equivalent of an electronic injection to protect select systems from unwanted activation of specific codes. The problem was the antidote program was yet to be tested.

Chow's interaction with YAOGUAI was interrupted by

his secretary. "Dr. Chow, Colonel Meang is here to see you."

A surge of adrenaline pulsed through his body. Meang wasn't scheduled to see him. *What does he want?*

He disconnected the mini cable from his watch, closed the laptop and hid it in a drawer. He bit into a stick of spearmint gum as the Colonel stepped into his office. He didn't knock or ask permission.

"I understand congratulations are in order," Meang said.

"I'm not sure I understand Colonel." Beads of sweat formed on his upper lip. He licked them away.

"Of course you do, Chow. I heard from the Ministry of Science that you have been invited to present a paper at the International Conference on Computer Sciences in Paris. Some say it can be a steppingstone on the path toward a Nobel Prize."

"Yes, I did receive an invitation several months ago, but I didn't give it much consideration. I figured my work demands here would preclude any travel abroad, so I dismissed it." International acclaim was a fantasy that he never allowed himself to indulge. He possessed far too much knowledge regarding China's cyber-espionage program. He was sure the Colonel would never permit him to leave the country.

"The Ministry insists that you attend. In all our history, the People's Republic of China has never been able to boast a Nobel Prize recipient in science. You represent an excellent chance to be our first. We have become the world's leader in the field of quantum information technology development. It's a staggering accomplishment Chow, and you are the one responsible. The Ministry is anxious to show you off and demonstrate to the international community how much our Republic has advanced."

Meang flashed a crooked smile. "Of course, I recommended against you leaving the country. You represent a significant security risk, especially in light of your association with that radical newspaper woman. She has been warned on multiple occasions."

Chow's mind raced at the suggestion of a threat to Liu-Fawn.

Meang pressed on. "I'll protect your friend for as long as I can, but if she continues to offend our leadership, it'll be out of my hands. There's only so much that I can do if she faces charges of treason. You must be careful, or she will pull you down with her."

The Colonel walked over to the window and gazed at the lab where dozens of Chow's associates worked. "Arrangements have already been made for you to travel to Paris, but we certainly can't have you going there unescorted. Therefore, I will accompany you. In case you get any ideas that might embarrass the Republic, I'm going to make sure your friend is placed in custody the moment we land in France."

Chow trembled as the floor beneath his feet shifted. International recognition wasn't worth it if the acclaim came with a risk to Liu-Fawn. For her sake, he was going to have to be extremely careful regarding this trip. He was relieved when Meang changed the subject.

"Give me a report on the most recent upgrades of the device."

"I've been able to harness the quantum characteristics of the sub-atomic universe as the new byte storage unit. They're called qubits, and they far surpass any prior capacity. Using these principles, I've been able to condense the calculating ability of millions of super-computers into something as tiny as a small group of molecules. Over a trillion, trillion, trillion simultaneous functions can now be processed in an instant."

Meang picked up a plastic model of a hydrogen atom and studied it. "That's very good, but what's the range?"

"I developed a photonic transmission program which uses surrounding wave lengths of light and fluctuations in electro-magnetic fields to transmit signals. Using those and traditional Wi-Fi as conduits, the functional range of the device is limitless. Almost everything in the world is connected by the internet and other information systems. Just as the human body can be racked by disease, the world's nervous system can also be infected."

"Like a computer virus or one of those botnet things?"

asked Meang.

"Yes, and no. In simple terms, a virus is a malicious piece of computer code designed to corrupt the host's programs and steal data. When a botnet program is inserted into a computer it allows an outside individual to take partial control of the device. Both are fairly easy to detect and remove using standard security software.

"Yaoguai isn't a virus or any other type of malware program. It's an individual self-contained super-computer sitting undetectable inside the host device. Security programs are completely ineffective against it. It remains dormant until it senses another electronic device within its range. In less than a nano-second, it commandeers that device and sits dormant until activated by the proper code sequence. Once activated, the primary computer and its entire network of slave devices are under our control." Chow avoided discussion of the true potential of Yaoguai and its derivative, Yaoguai II.

"That's excellent Dr. Chow. I assume you're organizing all of the access codes?"

"Yes. There are over one-hundred-ninety billion of them, but I'm almost finished."

"Good. Let me know as soon as everything is complete. What about phase two of the program?" asked Meang.

Chow swallowed his gum. It was a topic he was hoping to avoid. He locked his hands behind his back trying to conceal his trembling as he lied. "I'm working on it, but it's still a year or two away, at least. It's extremely complicated."

"Well, make it a priority. The Ministry wants phase two available as soon as possible."

The Colonel looked at his watch. "You are to clear the rest of your afternoon calendar. There is a representative of the Iranian government scheduled to meet with you later today. I'm picking him up at the airport in an hour."

A meeting! I'm never allowed to meet with outsiders.

"What's it about?"

"The Iranians want to revamp all of their information

systems and need your expertise in doing so. They want every-thing consolidated under one central command. It's going to require complex reworking of their entire organization. They claim that it's all for non-military purposes, but I suspect it's more about their new nuclear weapons program. The People's Republic and the Iranians have mutual geopolitical interests so it would only make sense that we work together in some areas."

"But what about the security of my work here?"

"Not a concern. I checked the visitor out personally. He's a high-ranking member of the Iranian government with top security clearances. Of course, any discussion of your quantum research is off limits"

"But why me? Iran must have dozens of people in their own country who are more than capable of handling that type of project."

"I don't know, but they requested you specifically. The man you are meeting said he has reviewed your recent paper on the theory of quantum-based information systems and was impressed. The Iranians were willing to pay handsomely for your expertise."

"Most of which will go directly into your own pockets," Chow muttered to himself.

"What was that?"

"I said I'll help in any way I can."

"Good, and Dr. Chow?"

"Yes?"

"Remember, I'm watching you closely. That includes your good friend, Liu-Fawn."

T. Milton Mayer

ELEVEN

Liuang Technology Corporation
Chengdo, China

Several hours after Colonel Meang left the research center, Chow's intercom buzzed.

"Mr. Faizel Sassani from Iran is waiting for you in Meeting Room 217 in the administration building. He says you're scheduled for a meeting at two o'clock."

"Yes, of course. Tell him I'll be there in several minutes."

Chow checked his watch. It was only 1:53. *Impressive.* The man was seven minutes early. Chow depressed the top right button on his time piece and Liu-Fawn's picture appeared, her smile disarming and reassuring. "What could this be about?" he asked the image, then left.

Room 217 was plush by Chinese military standards and used only for meetings with VIP outsiders. Three leather chairs sat on either side of a large mahogany table over an ornate Aubusson rug. A window afforded a view of the courtyard below. On two of the walls hung the obligatory framed portraits of Mao Zedong, Deng Xiaoping, Zhou En-Lai, and other heroes of the Communist revolution. In the rear, a large mirror reflected the room. Chow suspected that hidden behind it sat probably a half-dozen of Meang's men, filming and recording every word of the meeting.

The Iranian, a dark-complected man with black hair and a wide smile politely stood when Chow entered the room. Dressed

54

in a perfectly tailored grey suit, white shirt, and a silk yellow tie, he extended his hand to shake Chow's, his grip firm and authoritative. "Dr. Chow, my name is Faizel Sassani. I appreciate your taking the time out of your busy schedule to meet with me," he said in perfect English.

Chow was unaccustomed to this level of courtesy from a government official. At over six feet, the man stood at least eight inches taller than him. He was athletic looking but, unlike Colonel Meang, he gave no overt indication of trying to intimidate. The man seemed cordial enough, but his intense dark eyes were unsettling. The two men sat opposite each other. Chow suspected the meeting, might be a trap to test his loyalty before the Paris trip. The Colonel himself was probably standing there behind the mirror. *Must be careful about what I say.* His mouth went dry. He reached into his pocket for a stick of gum. There was none. He'd left the pack on his desk in the lab.

After a moment of awkward silence, Chow said, "I understand your country is interested in upgrading its information systems."

"Yes, I'm afraid that years of economic embargoes levied by the United States and the other western powers have rendered our present systems antiquated. They no longer have the capacity to serve our needs. We need to update with the most modern and sophisticated technology available."

"But certainly, you must already have a number of computer engineers in your country, ones who are more than qualified to handle the task."

"Yes, but none of them are of your caliber, Dr. Chow. Iran needs the advice of the brightest man in the field. I've done my research, and that man is you. I'm aware of your work in the cutting edge of computer design using quantum principles."

Chow looked down at the table. "I'm afraid my work is still only in the early developmental stages. A workable prototype won't be available for a least another decade. My research will have no practical applications for the improvements you seek. Using me as a consultant might be a waste of your time."

Sassani remained undaunted. "My country is committed on this matter, Dr. Chow. We are willing to pay whatever is necessary to secure your services."

The way the Colonel worked to set up this little meeting, I'm sure you already have. He pushed his glasses up the bridge of his nose. "Exactly what is it that you need from me, Mr. Sassani?"

The visitor withdrew a pamphlet from his briefcase and placed it on the table. Next to it he set a pack of gum. "Do you mind? My mouth always gets a little parched after a long flight like the one from Tehran. It's that dry cabin air in the plane, you see." He unwrapped a stick of the gum and placed it in his mouth. He held the up the pack. "Would you care for a piece, Dr. Chow?"

It was Wrigley's Spearmint, his favorite, a treat rarely available in China. *How did he know?* He accepted the stick of gum and unwrapped it. His pulse raced. There was writing on it. Printed in small block letters was a single word: DANGER. That was it. *What danger? From whom?* He needed more clarification, but he couldn't exactly ask any questions, not while the entire meeting was being monitored. He placed the gum in his mouth to destroy the message and made a conscious effort to chew slowly lest he raise Meang's suspicions.

The two talked for another hour about the type of information systems the Iranian government required. Mr. Sassani possessed a conversational knowledge of the subject of integrated computer systems. However, it wasn't to the degree he expected from a man who was supposedly arranging for the establishment of a complex technology to integrate the entire Iranian government, possibly including coordination with a nuclear weapons program.

Chow tried to focus on what Sassani was saying during the remainder of their meeting, but he was too distracted by that word. "DANGER."

At the end of their discussion, Sassani looked at his watch and stood. "I see it's getting late. I'm afraid I must return to the airport to catch my next flight." He pushed the pamphlet across the table to Chow. "Read through this carefully and if any problems seem to catch your eye, simply email me at the address on the inside cover of the booklet. It's listed directly under my photograph." Sassani pointed at the picture and tapped it several times with his index finger, "I look forward to seeing you again in the near future, Dr. Chow."

With that, the visitor left. He had mentioned nothing about scheduling a follow-up appointment. Chow sat alone in the room. *What was that meeting really about?* It certainly had nothing to do with the development of a plan to coordinate Iranian information systems.

TWELVE

Solitude Compound
Owen County, Kentucky
United States of America

Jacob gathered his team around a large dining room table in Solitude's main house. He spread the satellite photos provided by Winston Hamilton across the top. Norman Deets sat in a chair at one end, his crutches leaning against the table and his laptop in front of him. Tank sat to the left, the bright ceiling lights reflecting off his head. Dan sat next to Tank while Jacob and Lisa stood on the other side. She fixated on the ceiling as though she were gazing into an endless abyss. Absent was the normal enthusiasm in her bright blue eyes. *She's disconnected.*

Jacob turned his attention to the group and began. "I asked Deets to do some background research on the owners of the West Virginia camp property. What do you have for us, Norman?"

Deets opened his computer. "According to local tax records, it was purchased eleven years ago by The New Green Horizons Foundation. I checked their website. The foundation presents itself as an ecofriendly company. According to their mission statement, they are dedicated to global warming research."

"Sounds pretty innocent to me," said Jacob. "Maybe we're wrong about this entire training compound theory."

"Based upon their website information, one might think so," said Deets. "There is a problem, however. The foundation has no other property holdings. They manage no actual laboratories, have no staff, and are involved in no other activities other than this parcel of land in West Virginia. Their bills are paid from a post office box in New York."

Jacob ran his hand through his hair. *A shadow company.* "Keep on it. They probably claim to be a tax-exempt organization. If so, they must provide a list of donors. See if you can uncover one. We need to know whose bankrolling this group. It might give us a clue about what we'll be up against."

Jacob picked up a red sharpie. "Mr. Hamilton provided us with some great satellite images." He marked the training compound's location on one of the photos with a small star.

"This is the target. As you can see, it's surrounded on three sides by the Monongahela National Forest. That's a million acres of buffer zone to protect it. "

Tank stood and braced his arms on either side of the picture, his biceps bulging like a pair of cannons. He tapped his finger over the area. "It's a pretty isolated place. I have family in West Virginia. That part of the state is almost completely undeveloped."

Jacob nodded. "Being isolated is both good and bad for us. Access is definitely going to be challenging, but on the positive side, it's unlikely anyone will be close enough to hear if a gun battle breaks out." He turned to the team's senior member. "What do you think Dan?"

Jacob watched Dan Foster study the map.

"From the way the buildings are arranged, it certainly looks like a military installation," Dan said. He pointed to the map.

He's shaking. It was a slight tremor, maybe not even noticed by the others, but very apparent to a doctor like Jacob. *Thirty years of fighting wars have taken their toll on you, my old friend.*

Dan continued. "It looks to be pretty well fortified by the surrounding mountains and it's camouflaged under a heavy canopy of vegetation."

"No wonder it's never been noticed before," said Lisa.

Jacob turned to her. She was refocusing on the meeting. *Good.*

"Almost impossible to see if you're not specifically looking for it," said Dan. "It's well protected and a perfect site to conceal military activities." He drew a line with the red marker. "The only direct access is this long winding gravel drive in the front. I'd estimate its length to be around five hundred yards, and it's protected by a gate with at least one guard. There might be more hidden in the trees. Dan selected one of the enlarged images of the camp and drew small red circles around two buildings in the center. "These two medium sized cabins in the middle look to be the camp's living quarters. I'd guess they each house at least a dozen men, maybe more. The two vans parked in front look similar to the one Lisa took out in L.A." Dan shifted his attention to another building. "I'd bet anything this large building to the north is a weapons armory. It looks like they have two guards posted by the front door."

"That makes at least three guards and probably more we can't see," said Tank. "A global warming research facility sure as hell shouldn't need three armed guards."

"Roger that," said Dan. "They shouldn't need any guards at all unless they're up to some bad shit."

"Is that door the only access to the armory?" asked Jacob.

"Can't tell. It's the only spot where guards are posted, so probably," said Dan.

Probably?

"What about this small cabin to the left of the living quarters?" asked Lisa, pointing to the structure. She was getting more engaged in the planning.

Deets studied the image for a few seconds. "Based upon the satellite dish on the roof, I suspect it's a command and communications center. Information systems and files are probably housed there. I bet that's also where Qaiser's brother lives. He's probably the only one who would have the clearance to establish contact with the rest of their organization. I'd love to get my hands on his computers. With a setup like this, I bet they have a ton of info stored in them."

"Computers are nice, Deets, but we need to get our hands on a live prisoner so I can interrogate him. I want the guy who lives in there." Jacob tapped on the communications hut.

"We should be able to do that if he doesn't blow himself up before we can grab him," said Lisa.

Jacob studied the building. *And us along with him.*

"I don't think he'll do that," said Dan. "I've had a lot of experience with these types in Afghanistan. While the everyday jihadist is more than willing to die for the cause, the commanders are more reluctant to do so. They prefer to stay behind the scenes while sending the grunts out to sacrifice their lives in exchange for their seventy-two virgins. Their leaders aren't that anxious to meet Allah any sooner than they must. That presents an excellent opportunity for us to take him alive."

Jacob pored over the maps for a minute. "You say there are at least a dozen men in each of those two cabins, Dan?"

"That's not including the three guards we can see on the satellite images," said Dan. "There could be maybe up to a couple dozen more."

That's around forty potential hostiles to cover. Jacob stood straight. "We're dealing with a lot of unknowns here." *Maybe too many.*

Lisa picked up the sharpie. "If we use a sniper stationed either here to the south or here on the north, he should be able to provide good cover while the others check out the camp." She placed a star over each location.

"Good point, Lisa. That and working under the cover of night should help even things up a little," said Jacob, feeling a little better about the mission.

"Let your plans be dark and impenetrable as night, and when you move, fall like a thunderbolt," said Tank.

"Sounds poetic, Tank, but what the hell is it?" said Dan.

"Words by the ancient Chinese warrior, Sun Tzu. He wrote *The Art of War.* Did my dissertation on it. You should read it."

"Don't need to," said Dan. "I've spent half my life in the military and don't need some fucking dead Chinese general to explain to me the benefits of darkness." He paused and looked across the table. "Sorry for the language, Lisa."

"No fucking problem, Dan." The sparkle in her eyes returned. Everyone, even Jacob laughed.

Deets shifted in his chair. "If Mr. Hamilton can arrange to give us access to a real-time infrared satellite feed, it'll be like having a dozen extra men ourselves. I should be able to get it set up without a problem."

Jacob paced the room for several seconds and stopped. "OK then. But that'll work only if we're quiet and maintain the element of surprise." He turned his attention back to the maps. "The next problem is, how do we get there?"

Deets typed on his computer. He studied the screen display for a minute. "The Greenbrier Valley Airport in Lewisburg is about two hours away by car."

"That should work," said Jacob. "We can fly in on Mr. Hamilton's Citation and drive the rest of the way by car. I'm sure he can arrange for a vehicle to meet us when we land. Then, it's only a matter of selecting a spot from which to mount our attack. We can't exactly approach the front gate via this gravel entrance road. We'll be too exposed. As soon as the guard sees us coming, he'll pin us down with automatic fire. Then all hell will break loose before we even get started."

Dan pulled a crumpled pack of Camel cigarettes from the breast pocket of his faded army jacket, stared at them for a second and put them back, the tremor barely noticeable. "I don't see any obvious access options from the rear. That entire mountain range looks to be impassable."

Deets worked frantically on his laptop. "I've opened Google maps and I may have something here." He zoomed in, printed the map, and had Tank spread it out on the table. Deets stood on his crutches and took possession of the red Sharpie. "If you follow route 219 north, you can turn onto this secondary road. After about thirty miles, there are several trails which head east toward the compound. One of them looks like it might be an old dirt road, maybe even a deserted logging trail. It looks mostly overgrown, but with a four-wheel drive vehicle, it might be passable." He outlined the route and circled a spot on the map. "It looks like there might be a small clearing here. You could leave your vehicle and approach the compound on foot by heading east over the mountains."

"How far?" asked Tank.

"I'd guess about two or three miles," said Deets.

"What if the trail isn't passable?" asked Lisa.

"Then we have no other choice but to slug our way through that front gate," said Tank.

"So, we'd better make Norman's plan work," said Jacob.

―――――――

When all was finalized, Lisa stepped back from the table. "I need to discuss something." The room went quiet, everyone staring at her. She fidgeted, shifting from one foot to another. "This is going to be my last mission."

Jacob watched tears well up in her eyes. It was bound to happen eventually, but the harsh finality of the statement hit him like a punch in the gut. Lisa was his only remaining family, his closest advisor, and the one who understood him best. She was the buffer who helped hold the entity in check. The loss would be painful.

Dan stepped forward and placed his hand on Lisa's shoulder. "We're sorry to hear this, Lisa. I know it must have been a difficult decision for you."

"It was. All of you have been like a family to me. Leaving the team is one of the most difficult things I've ever had to do, but I have no choice. If I'm going to be married, I want a normal life, and I want to be able to raise children in a normal home. I can't do that if I continue to be a member of the team, running all over the country chasing terrorists."

Tank lowered his head. "I'm going to miss you, girl." He squeezed Lisa in a bear hug and kissed her on the cheek.

Dan embraced her next. "We can't begrudge you for wanting that, Lisa. God knows you've earned it." He laughed. "I guess that means we'll have to be extra careful tomorrow night.

Your future husband might get a little pissed off at us if we let you get shot."

Everyone but Jacob joined in the laughter. It was a frightening possibility he had always dreaded. *At least now she'll be safe.*

Lisa smiled. "He just might, Dan." She looked at Jacob. "Make sure you keep an eye on my big brother here. He's a brilliant tactician and a fearless warrior, but sometimes he thinks he's invincible. That gets him into some bad situations."

"Roger that," said Dan. He stared at Jacob. "It's gonna be a tall order, but we'll try to keep him out of trouble."

Jacob exhaled slowly and put his hands on Lisa's shoulders. "You worry about me too much. I'll be fine. He pulled her into a tight hug and whispered in her ear. "Remember them . . .remember us."

"Always."

Tears flowed down her cheeks.

THIRTEEN

Avenue des Champs Élysées
Paris, France

An acidulous knot coiled up in the pit of Faizel Sassani's stomach. It was a feeling he hadn't experienced in over two years, ever since his attempts to assassinate President Wagner were thwarted by the Americans. The plan had been perfectly designed, but he had underestimated them. They turned out to be more cunning and tenacious than he had anticipated. He would never allow that mistake to happen again. Nothing would prevent him from successfully exacting the revenge he deserved.

For over ten years, he had cultivated a close relationship with Abo Bakr al-Baghdadi, one of the founders of the ISIS organization. With extensive financial support from Sassani, al-Baghdadi was able to expand the influence of his jihadist group across the Middle East and into parts of Europe. Sassani provided billions of dollars in cash while, in exchange, al-Baghdadi provided Sassani with the manpower and logistical support he needed to complete his own agenda. Though the ISIS plan to establish a Middle East caliphate had been neutralized, the organization remained viable.

It had been a mutually beneficial relationship. Through his ISIS connections, Sassani had access to hundreds of sleeper cells scattered throughout the United States and Europe. He had planned to use them to unleash a multitude of terror attacks on the West.

And then it began. Cells in America started coming under assault. The attackers were well-organized and didn't follow the same rules as the country's traditional law enforcement agencies. His men were simply executed on sight. Whoever was doing it had to be stopped before they caused any further damage to his organization. *Can't risk them uncovering information about about my plan.* He devised a trap for those responsible, intentionally leaving subtle clues that ultimately led his enemy to the Los Angeles crack house. A photographer was there waiting for them. *Soon, I will have your identity.*

Sassani sat in front of his computer screen and studied the images sent by the photographer. The first was of the home his men had selected, a ramshackle structure in the middle of a depressed L.A. neighborhood. They had chosen well. It was clearly visible from the photographer's station. The next picture showed two men approaching with handguns drawn, a white man about his own size with jet black hair, and a gigantic black man. They kept their heads down and their faces obscured. "Professionals," he said to the screen. "So, you're the ones who have been taking out my cells. You might think you're clever, but I'm smarter. I was ready for you this time. Now, I've got you. I knew you wouldn't be able to pass up on the Rodeo Drive target. You had no other choice but to show up. But who are you?"

He scanned through the next dozen photographs carefully. In the last picture, one of the men stopped on the house's front porch, looked up, and appeared to check his surroundings. His face was fully exposed. Sassani tapped on the computer screen and yelled, "I have you now, you bastard!" He enlarged the screen and examined the photo more closely. "You must be the one in charge." He magnified the image. "I've seen that face before—but where?"

He poured a snifter of Suntory and walked out onto his balcony. Paris was like any other large city, with the same large city sounds and smells. The viral pandemic had passed, and the city had returned to normal. A cacophony of horns assaulted his ears as drivers jostled for better position along the Avenue des

Champs Élysées. It was late and to his right the Arc de Triomphe lit up the night sky. Thousands of tourists milled around the shops and restaurants below him as he pondered the image of that man. He had seen him before but couldn't quite place where it had been. By the time he poured a second glass of brandy, it came to him. He rushed back inside and did a Google search of the Inauguration Day ceremonies of President Richard Wagner from several years ago. There were dozens of videos recorded that day, feeds from a multitude of different television networks from around the world. While focusing on one video from Fox News, he finally saw it.

During the archbishop's convocation address, the film showed a momentary disruption in the ceremonies. *That was the explosion meant to kill President Wagner.* During the confusion, the television camera panned the area behind the presidential podium. There, near the corner of the capital building, stood a group of a half-dozen men speaking into radios. It was only for a few seconds but that was enough. Sassani froze the video and zoomed in on the leader of the group, the athletic one with the black hair and bright blue eyes. He was giving the orders. Sassani clenched his fists as the storm inside his gut raged.

"You!" he exclaimed and threw his brandy against the wall. "Now I know who you are and soon I'll have your name. You'll not stop me this time. You'll not live long enough. My trap has been set, and you won't escape. Once you and your team are dead, I can begin implementation of my final plan."

While he poured a third glass of brandy, his computer chimed, indicating a new email notice. "Must be Dr. Chow. That didn't take long." Everything was beginning to fall into place. The storm inside him abated.

FOURTEEN

Chow's Personal Apartment
Chungdu, China

The day after meeting with the Iranian, Dr. Chow still couldn't get the message off his mind. **DANGER**. Written in bold letters on a stick of gum. The man had to know the room was being closely monitored, which would explain the clandestine way of delivering the warning. What did it mean? How would the Iranian know he was in danger? Chow needed to find out what was going on, but he couldn't exactly contact Mr. Sassani directly.

He paced his apartment for several minutes. Sitting on the kitchen table was the brochure Mr. Sassani had given him. He picked up the booklet and paged through it looking for a solution. It was of no help and he tossed it back onto the table. He replayed the meeting in his mind and recalled some unusual phrasing Sassani had used. "If any problems seem to catch your eye, simply email me at the address listed under my picture." He had made a point of tapping on the photograph. Why? On the surface, it appeared to be an innocent statement, but the wording was awkward. Why not simply say, "If you have any questions, email me"? It might have been because they were speaking in English and Sassani wasn't comfortable with the language, but the rest of the conversation had been normal. In fact, Sassani's English was otherwise perfect. No, he was too articulate to speak that way in clumsy phrases.

Chow sat in front of his computer and entered Faizel

Sassani's web page as listed in the brochure. Immediately the man's picture appeared and there was a column of selection options along the left-hand side of the page. He clicked on each and scanned the different sections. Everything seemed innocuous, dealing only with Iranian governmental departments and the man's curriculum vitae. There was nothing to explain the warning of danger. There had to be an explanation hidden here somewhere. Sassani had made a point of mentioning his picture, so Chow studied the photograph of the Iranian carefully and focused on his piercing eyes. Something eerie about those eyes. The man kept using the word see. "It's the dry air in the plane, you see; nice to see you; looking forward to seeing you again; I see it's getting late; if any problems seem to catch your eye."

Before proceeding further, Chow switched to another computer he had hidden in his bedroom. He had installed his own encryption protocols so no one, not even the Ministry could monitor what he was doing. He again called up Sassani's photograph. He dragged his curser across the screen, suspecting the possibility of a steganographic, a hidden micro link. *See.* He clicked on Sassani's right eye. Nothing. He then clicked on the left eye, and again there was nothing. Chow studied it. *There must be something.*

He zoomed in on the photograph to enlarge the eyes and noticed a slight imperfection in the left pupil. *Maybe a light reflection, maybe not.* He centered the curser on the small irregularity and left-clicked, Nothing. He right-clicked on the same spot. His computer screen flickered briefly and went blank. After a few seconds, a message appeared.

Sassani:

> ***Hello, Dr. Chow. There is no need for you to worry. If anyone is monitoring your computer right now, they will still be seeing my photograph, the same one you must have been studying a few seconds ago. Your Colonel Meang has no idea you have contacted me. Rest assured that our conversation here is completely protected from**

intruding eyes.

Chow typed:

> I have already taken my own precautions. Your message said 'DANGER.' What kind of danger and from whom?

Sassani:

> *It's Colonel Meang. He's aware of the intensity of your relationship with the newspaper reporter. The only thing keeping you and your friend alive is your highly classified work at the LCT research center.

Chow's head snapped back:

> How do you know about that? Few people are aware of my research.

Sassani:

> *I know that and more, Dr. Chow. You are heavily involved in China's cyber-espionage programs. I've discovered how far you've progressed with your quantum computer systems. You've accomplished what no other scientist in the world has been able to do. More importantly, I know of the work on your special program, and how far it's developed.

Chow's mouth went dry and he was unable to reply for several seconds. He opened a piece of gum and began chewing. Had Sassani discovered the existence of Yaoguai and its destructive potential? His hands trembled as he typed.

> But that's highly classified information. How did you find out?

Chow waited, almost afraid to read Sassani's reply.

> *I'm a very wealthy man, Dr. Chow, one of the wealthiest in the world. Nothing is outside my grasp as long as I'm willing to pay the right price. Everyone is approachable, even the most dedicated followers of your communist regime. Colonel Meang himself is a man whose allegiance

is easily diverted for the right incentives.

Chow's response:

> Colonel Meang! Is that why he arranged our meeting?

Sassani:

> *His loyalties are guided only by what's best for him and his own agenda. His cooperation cost me a great deal of money.

Chow shook his head slowly as he tried to digest this new information.

> Are you actually affiliated with the Iranian government?

Sassani:

> *No, it was a ruse to facilitate our meeting. The point is that you and your friend are in grave danger.

Chow asked.

> How?

Sassani:

> *The amount of data associated with your program is astronomical, but I suspect you have already organized and categorized the information. I assume that access can only be obtained through a specific activation protocol. Once that has been turned over to the Colonel, he will have no further use for you. He's not interested in your future research potential.

Chow's pulse quickened.

> You believe that once I turn over the necessary codes and the activation sequences, the Colonel will have me killed?

Sassani:

> *Yes, both you and your friend, Liu-Fawn. I've been trying to reach her, but it appears Meang has silenced her computers and cell phones. My sources tell me she's under house arrest.

House arrest? A surge of fear pulsed through him. Could he believe this man? Who was he? They had just met a few days ago and already he knew more about Chow and his work than anyone else, even Liu-Fawn.

But why are you concerned? You don't know us. Why would you want to help?

Sassani:

> ***You're too brilliant a scientist for the world to lose. You must be allowed to continue your research.**

Chow fingers hovered over the keyboard. Sassani's explanation seemed plausible.

What do you suggest?

Sassani:

> ***You are scheduled to present a paper to the International Conference on Computer Sciences in Paris. That's where the Colonel plans to have you shot for selling your secrets, but you must keep that commitment. I have a plan.**

Chow typed.

What kind of plan?

Sassani:

> ***You will be given instructions when you arrive in Paris. I promise, once everything is complete, you and Liu-Fawn will be given new identities and sent to a safe location where you can live out the rest of your lives in peace. I can even arrange for you to continue your work at a prominent university and your friend can pursue her career as a journalist. I will contact you in Paris.**

Sassani terminated the communication and the computer screen returned to his photograph. Chow studied the man's picture. His plan was exactly what Liu-Fawn always wanted, to leave China and be together in a free country. But could he trust this Faizel Sassani? How would he keep his promise, and what were the risks? Those were the overriding questions.

FIFTEEN

Monongahela National Forest
West Virginia
United States of America

Jacob checked the GPS, brought the Hummer to a stop, and spoke into his throat mike. "This should be it. Deets, how do we look?"

"I have you on the satellite feed. That's the spot, but you're about an hour behind schedule. It's almost two in the morning."

Jacob drank the last of a cup of cold coffee. "That old logging road of yours turned out to be a dried-up creek bed. We had to push a few fallen trees out of the way."

They had driven the last several miles by moonlight, not wanting their headlights to give away their position. The four team members exited the vehicle, retrieved their equipment from the cargo area, and put on body armor. Dan and Lisa each shouldered a sound/flash suppressed sniper rifle. They put a half dozen thirty-round ammo magazines into their tactical vest pockets. Tank and Jacob selected H & K automatic MP5s, also fitted with silencers. All secured Sig Sauer 9mm semi-automatics in belt holsters. Dan and Jacob strapped combat knives to their thighs while Tank loaded his tactical vest with a handful of grenades.

Jacob pulled out several sticks of camo face paint and handed them to the team.

Tank completed the application and said to the others. "We are the terror in the darkness."

Dan shook his head. "More of your Chinese military shit, Tank?"

Tank chuckled. "No, it's Thomas Nash. He was an Elizabethan poet. Maybe you should spend more time reading."

"No time. Too busy protecting your ass."

Jacob raised his hand, palm out. "OK guys. We are the terror in the darkness. We have a lot of ground to cover so get ready."

After donning night vision goggles, they set out in the direction of the target. A few hundred yards into the woods, Jacob whispered into his throat mike, "Communications check." All responded.

Dan put on his good-luck army hat, the one with the bullet hole on top. He adjusted his earpiece. "Dan here."

"Lisa receiving."

"Wo ting dao nile," said Tank.

"What the fuck is that?" asked Dan.

"It's Chinese for 'I hear you.'"

Dan stared at him. "For Christ sake, can we just use English for this mission—like normal people, Tank?" The big guy shrugged like a kid.

Jacob shook his head and pushed on his throat mike. "Deets, are you getting this?"

"Affirmative. Loud and clear."

"How's everything look from there?" Hamilton had arranged for the overhead satellite to feed directly into Deet's Solitude lab.

"I have the infrared imaging up and running. I can see the four of you clear as day. Wait a second while I focus on the compound site."

Jacob rechecked the clip on his sidearm while he waited. Finally, Deets said, "I can see the heat signatures of a few guards sitting in front of the armory building, and there's still only one man protecting the front gate. I can't see any additional guards hiding in the woods, but that's never a guarantee, so you'll have to be careful."

"How about those two bunkhouses?" asked Jacob.

"It looks like there's about a dozen or so men in each. It's hard to say for sure exactly how many because of possible super-imposition of images. It looks like they're all asleep, though. There is one more man sleeping in that communications cabin."

"OK. That last one must be Qaiser's brother," said Jacob. "He's the one I want." Jacob scanned the darkness around him with his night vision goggles. "Keep a close eye out. I'm getting a funny feeling about this thing."

"Terrific," said Dan. "There goes Jacob again with his funny feelings. That's a bad sign."

"Enough chatter. Maintain radio silence until we reach that hill behind the compound," ordered Jacob.

The team pushed forward and after another hour they stopped just below the crest of the small mountain. Dan was lagging twenty yards behind and short of breath. Jacob took him aside. "Are you OK?"

"I'm fine."

"I don't think so, Dan. I've seen you do a five-mile run in combat boots and not break a sweat. Tonight, you can barely make it up this mountain."

"I said I'm fine."

"When this is over, you're seeing a doctor."

Jacob returned to the team and pulled the map from his vest pocket. "The camp should be just over the next rise." He marked the time on his watch. "It's zero-three-nineteen. Dawn is over four hours away, so we're still good on time. This is where we split up. Dan, you head to the north observation point and Lisa, you head south." He pointed to the two locations on the map.

"Split up?" said Lisa.

"You're the second sniper," said Jacob.

"No way, big brother. We only need one shooter and that's Dan. You need me at your side."

"Nope. Tonight, you're a shooter," said Jacob.

"This is all about my wedding, isn't it? You don't want me to get hurt." She stared into his eyes. "I can take care of myself.

I've done it over and over before and I can do it tonight."

"This has nothing to do with your wedding. I still don't know what we're facing down there. Tank and I are going to need all the support we can get. That means both you and Dan are snipers."

"Fine," said Lisa and turned her back.

Jacob looked to the team. "Make sure the flash filters on your night vision goggles are switched on. I don't want anyone being blinded by the light of a sudden explosion." Each team member complied. "Final weapons check."

All had full magazines and chambered a round.

"Don't open fire unless you absolutely must."

Jacob turned to Dan. "Your positions are about four hundred yards above the camp. Is that distance going to be a problem?"

"Like shooting fish in a barrel. The only potential difficulty could be the density of trees and underbrush. If it's too thick, we might have to relocate to find better shooting lanes."

"Adjust if you have to. When you're in position, let me know. Deets, how're we looking from overhead?"

"Good to go."

Jacob put his hand on Lisa's shoulder. "Remember them."

"Always." It was a terse reply.

Lisa and Dan made their way to the sniper positions, while Jacob and Tank slowly headed down the mountain toward the compound. Fifteen minutes later, the silence was interrupted by Lisa's voice on the radio. "In position. You're clear from the south." Still terse.

After another five minutes Dan said, "Too much underbrush. Had to find a better spot, but I have good visualization now. You're all clear to proceed. We've got your six."

"Deets?"

"No change. You're good to go."

Jacob turned to Tank. "Let's head down."

Dan said into the radio, "Hold on. You have what looks like a firing range directly in front of your position. It's wide open

QUANTUM

and there's not much cover there. If you head that way, you'll be exposed for at least a hundred yards."

"Ideas?" asked Jacob.

Lisa's voice came across soft, but focused, no longer angry. "I can see what looks like an obstacle course fifty yards to the south. That should give you good enough cover until you reach the armory."

"Roger that." Jacob and Tank crab-walked their way through the course, hiding intermittently behind the obstacles. Once through it, Jacob said, "Deets?"

"Still clear."

"Where to now?" asked Jacob.

"The armory building is another hundred yards to your left," said Dan. "I'll paint it with my laser."

Jacob checked his surroundings with the night vision goggles until he saw the red light. "Got it."

"Be careful," said Lisa. "Two tangoes standing guard at the front of the building. Both carrying automatic rifles with thirty-round magazines. Bad guy ammo."

"That guard by the front gate?" asked Jacob.

"Still there. Looks relaxed. Might even be asleep. I have a clear shot if needed," said Lisa.

"Hold on," said Deets. "I've got another one guarding the back of the armory. There must be a rear door."

Jacob whispered into his throat mike, "We didn't know about him. Where'd he come from?"

"Not sure. I could only make out the two in front a few minutes ago," said Deets.

"Dammit, keep a better eye on things! We can't afford surprises," said Dan. "You want me to take him out, Jacob?"

"Negative. No firing at anyone until we're sure about what's going on here.

Jacob worked his way through the trees. When he got closer to the building, he whispered in his throat mike, "That rear door might be a good thing for us. What's the guard up to?"

"I have eyes on him," said Dan. "He's about thirty yards

directly in front of you. Looks pretty relaxed. Not on to you yet."

"Roger that. Stay dark as long as we can. Got to keep the element of surprise on our side." Using hand signals, Jacob instructed his partner to approach the rear guard from behind while he hid in the brush. When Tank got close enough, Jacob rustled the bushes with the tip of his rifle. After the guard looked in the direction of the sound, Tank ran up from behind and hit him in the back of the head, knocking the man unconscious. He checked his face. "This son-of-a-bitch is no fucking climatology scientist." He looked over toward Jacob and gave a thumbs-up.

Jacob approached the back door of the building and checked it. *Damn.* It was locked and it was the only way in unless they stormed past the two guards in the front. That would mean some loud gunfire. He whispered into his mike, "We've got to open this door and it's going to get a little noisy. Get ready to cover us but wait for my signal."

"Roger that," said Lisa.

"Already have one of the guards in my sights," said Dan.

"Deets?"

"Clear from my viewpoint. Everybody's still asleep in the same places. I'm going to zoom out with the satellite camera to get a wider view."

> *Enough pussyfooting around, Buddy Boy! Let's get this shindig started. I'm getting hungry. We need to start killing some bad guys.*

Jacob looked at Tank. "On my mark...three, two, one!"

Tank drove his right foot next to the door's lock. It splintered open with a loud crash. Jacob ran inside and tore open some crates. They were filled with automatic weapons, mortars, and grenades.

"Take them!" he yelled into his mike.

As soon as the door broke open, the two front guards ran around the side of the building. Neither made it more than a few yards. Pfft, pfft. Both collapsed to the ground as their heads exploded into misty red clouds. Lisa scanned with her night vision scope. "That front gate guard's running up the drive toward you."

"I don't have a shot," said Dan. "You'd better take him."

Lisa squeezed the trigger on her rifle and downed the guard with a three-shot burst to the center of his chest. "Neutralized."

Jacob and Tank stood just outside the armory door, their weapons pointed toward the huts, awaiting a response to the noise. Deets yelled into Jacob's earpiece, "We have a problem! A big problem! I scanned back to get a better view. At least a dozen more hostiles are coming up on your six from over the mountain."

Dan's voice blasted into his throat mike. "Where the hell did they come from?"

"They must have been out of my view on a back road," replied Deets. "There are several vehicles parked next to your Hummer. They must have followed you in."

"Shit. This thing's about to turn in to a major cluster fuck!" said Dan.

A surge of adrenaline coursed through Jacob's body, preparing his muscles for battle. His pulse raced. "It's an ambush!" he yelled. "You two get out of there! I repeat, abort! Head for cover and protect yourselves!"

He looked at Tank. "There's at least a dozen tangoes coming at us from over the mountain, and dozens more sitting inside the dorm buildings. Lisa and Dan are trapped and won't be able to help. It's just the two of us."

Tank shrugged his shoulders and smiled. "As I see it, us against maybe forty of them are damn good odds.

Jacob willed his emotions under control. Everything shifted into slow motion allowing him to analyze every second and calculate potential responses. He yelled into his mike, "Lights!"

Lisa and Dan shot out all exterior lights.

"We need to hightail it into the bush where we have the advantage of night vision," Jacob said.

"Need a distraction," said Tank. "I want something from inside." He ran back inside the weapons armory and came out with an RPG launcher hung over his shoulder. "This should help even things up a little. Amongst chaos, there is opportunity"

The front doors of both dormitory buildings exploded open and men rushed out, spraying automatic fire in all directions. Tank threw one of his grenades at the nearest building and took out three of them. Jacob returned fire and eliminated another four. One of them fired back, barely missing Jacob's head, the bullet smashing into the side of a tree to his right. Before the guy could get off another round, he was knocked back five feet. The shot came from Dan's position.

"Thanks, Dan, but I told you and Lisa to clear out!"

"What? Can't hear you. Damn earpiece must be broken!"

More men rushed out of the two cabins. Jacob turned to Tank. "We need to split up. I'll keep the guys in the far cabin contained while you do your thing. I'll meet you back here when it's over." Would he ever see Tank or the other team members again? He took off in the direction of the two vans parked in front of the compound and dove behind the nearest one. From that position, he unloaded an entire magazine keeping most of the enemy pinned down inside the far cabin. He reloaded.

Tank unshouldered his RPG launcher and fired into the structure. It exploded in a large ball of fire. "That's over a dozen we don't have to worry about."

Two of the men from the near cabin made their way toward Jacob's position firing their weapons as they ran, peppering the side of the van with bullets. *They're trying to trap me by attacking from either side. There's no escape.* Jacob rolled under the vehicle and flexed his fingers around the Sig's grip. He took aim and shot one of the guys in the ankle. The man fell to the ground, screaming in agony. The second one was downed the same way. Each stopped yelling after Jacob quieted them with double tap rounds to the head.

Jacob rolled out from under the van when Deets yelled into his earpiece. "There's a third one coming at you from the left." Jacob swung his weapon around and unloaded the rest of his clip into the man's chest, stopping him ten feet away. He slammed a fresh magazine into his Sig and did a quick three-hundred-sixty-degree search, looking for the next attack.

Through his earpiece, Jacob heard Dan's voice yelling to Lisa. "Here they come, just over the crest of the hill."

"I see 'em," said Lisa. "A hundred yards out. About as subtle as a herd of buffaloes."

"They don't have night vision," said Dan. "I've got the right. You take the left. Start with the ones in the rear. The guys in front won't know what's happening."

Pfft, pfft, pfft. One by one, they picked off seven of the enemy. Suppressors helped to reduce the muzzle flash, but at night there was still enough light to localize their positions. They began receiving return fire.

Deet's frantic voice exploded over their earpieces. "The rest just split into two groups and are advancing toward your positions."

Sounds of heavy gunfire and the light of muzzle flashes filled the night near Dan.

"Shit, they're attacking your position, Dan" Lisa said. "Need help?" All went quiet. She whispered into her throat mike, "Dan?" There was no response.

"Dan?" No reply. "Do you read? Over." Still, no response.

"Deets, can you see Dan?"

"His position was overrun. I can see five or six bodies lying on the ground."

Calling into her throat mike, she said, "We lost Dan."

"Dammit," Jacob's voice spat into her ear. "I told you two to abort. Now clear out of there immediately! Circle around back to the Hummer. That's an order!"

"Watch out, Lisa," Deets hollered into the earpieces. "More hostiles headed toward you from the west."

"How many?" she asked.

"Hard to say. Five at least." Seconds later Deets said, "They're splitting up and it looks like they're going to try to outflank you! You'd better run!"

Lisa heard them closing in. Her lanes of escape were blocked. She was trapped. She turned on a flashlight, set it on the ground, and crawled through the underbrush to a spot about fifty yards away. When the group of attackers reached the light, she put her rifle's selector switch to full-automatic fire and sprayed their position with an entire magazine. All of them fell to the ground.

"You got 'em!" said Deets. "Wait . . .shit . . .still two others approaching from your south."

"Get around them," yelled Jacob.

She slammed a fresh magazine into her rifle and using a low military crawl, she clawed her way through the underbrush, her rifle cradled in the crook of her elbows. The branches and thorns tore away at her skin, but she continued to head further down the hill toward the camp. Suddenly, something stopped her. She was looking up at the barrel of an AK-47 rifle. She had no chance. She was prone on the ground with her rifle under her chest. The man grinned, raised his gun, and aimed at her head. She would never see her fiancé again. The wedding would never happen. No family. Closing her eyes, she waited for the shot she would never hear — but she did. The bullet whistled high into the brush inches above her head. *I'm still alive!*

When Lisa opened her eyes, her attacker was still there but his rifle was on the ground. He was standing over her with bulging eyes and a shocked look on his face. He tried to yell, but only a gurgling sound came out with a cluster of crimson bubbles from his neck. The man's trachea had been severed, and a gaping wound in his neck pulsated blood out of both carotid arteries. Behind him, Dan stood, grinning and short of breath, with one hand around the guy's forehead, and the other pulling a bloody combat knife across his victim's neck. Dan's lucky hat was covered with fresh stains. He pushed the dying man to the side and said, "Now that's what we call a close one!"

Lisa hugged him. "Your alive! I was afraid they got you."

"Nah, Just a little preoccupied for a while. Couldn't talk. Had to stop shooting and start using this." He held up the blood-stained knife and wiped it off on the dead man's pants. "It's quiet, and a lot better in these up close and personal situations, especially when you're outnumbered. I saw your little flashlight trick and thought you might need some help. Couldn't have the bride-to-be getting shot up on this damn mountainside."

Lisa quickly looked around. "Careful, there's another one out there."

"Not anymore. I took care of him on the way over here," said Dan. "Let's head down to that camp to see if the other two need help."

***

After another fifteen minutes, it was all over. The coppery smell of blood filled the air. Dozens of bodies lay scattered around the compound and along the side of the mountain. Three of the team members met outside the armory building, faces bleeding and their sweaty skin reflecting the light from the surrounding fires.

Jacob approached through a cloud of smoke, his Sig still in his hand. "Everybody OK? Any injuries?"

"A few scratches and bruises. We're all doing a lot better than those suckers who tried to ambush us. What the hell happened?" asked Dan.

"We were set up."

"How?"

"Don't know yet, but I'm going to find out," said Jacob. "Let's get a better look at what they've been collecting in here."

The team entered the armory building. "Holy shit," said Tank. "They have enough stuff in here to start their own war!"

"That was their plan," said Jacob. He went outside and paced the grounds, checking the bodies. "All dead."

"Good," said Tank. "That's a lot of bad guys who won't be doing any more of that terrorist shit anymore."

"Roger that," replied Dan.

Jacob shook his head. "I was hoping to get the top man, the one financing and organizing whatever has been happening.

Now all I have is a bunch of dead bodies."

"Maybe one of them is still alive," said Lisa. "Dan might be able to patch one up and take him with us."

"Maybe," said Jacob. "Deets, still got eyes on us?"

"Affirmative. Everything looks secure."

"Can you tell if any of these guys are still alive?"

Seconds ticked by before Deets replied. "No, I don't think so. None of them are moving and their heat signatures are fading—wait a minute! There's still some movement inside that small cabin to your far left. It's the one with the satellite dish."

"The communications cabin," said Dan. "I bet Qaisar's still in there, hiding."

"I figured he came out to join in the fight," said Jacob.

Dan shook his head. "Like I said before, the leaders don't always like to get their hands dirty. Probably thinks we're all dead."

The four approached the small cabin staying low and using trees for cover. It was little more than a shack, but it had the potential of yielding the greatest prize of the mission. The only door faced them.

Jacob circled around the hut. "No windows." He turned to Dan. "Cut that satellite feed. I don't want him contacting his superiors and calling for help.

Dan ran behind the building while the remaining three prepared to storm the front door.

"Tank, kick it in and go high right. I'll go left. Lisa, stay out here and cover our backs in case we missed someone. Remember, don't shoot to kill."

When the door crashed open, they saw the back of someone in military fatigues trying to destroy a desktop computer. A long black ponytail hung behind her head. She spun around to face them, withdrew her sidearm, snarled, and fired a round at Jacob. She missed. "A woman!" yelled Jacob, hesitating for a second. He fired a little late and his shot went wide. Dan rushed in and pushed Jacob aside as the woman fired again. Before she could get off a third round, Lisa put a bullet in the woman's left leg, just above the ankle. She fell to the floor, dropping her weapon. Lisa quickly ran over, kicked the gun away and stared at her brother. "Men—what the hell is it with you guys when it comes to women? You hesitated, Jacob. If it wasn't for Dan, you'd be dead."

She looked from her brother to Dan. "There's blood all over your shirt!"

Dan felt his left shoulder. "Just a flesh wound. Can't be too bad. I have my lucky hat on." His smile was more of a grimace.

Jacob rushed to him. "Let me take a look at that, old friend." He removed Dan's tactical vest and cut away his shirt. The bullet entered an inch to the side of his armored vest. It was through and through and more than just a flesh wound. *My fault.* Jacob hesitated and Dan took the bullet meant for him. At least no major vessels or nerves had been hit. "You're not going to die but you're definitely seeing a doctor as soon as we get back." Jacob applied a combat compression dressing and looked Dan in the eyes. "You saved my life, old friend."

"You call me old friend again and you're the one who's going to be needing a doctor." He forced another smile.

Jacob turned his attention to the woman still writhing in pain on the floor. He applied a tourniquet and tended to her bleeding leg wound. "It's clean. Bullet exited." He applied a dressing as Tank and Lisa foraged through papers in a filing cabinet.

"There's too much important stuff here. We'll never be able to carry all of this and a wounded prisoner back over the mountain," said Tank.

Lisa searched the desk where the computer had been sitting. She opened the top drawer, paused, and withdrew a stack of photographs. She leafed through them for a few seconds. "You guys gotta see these!"

She handed Jacob a half dozen close-up pictures of himself, Tank, and Dan.

Jacob clenched his fist. "Now I'm certain this was a set up!

We were lured here so they could kill us, but how did they find out who we are?"

Must have a mole in the organization. Gotta knock some heads together. Time for some payback, Buddy Boy.

Dan studied the photos. "They were taken outside that crack house in LA. You were right, Jacob. Somebody was watching us. There's none of Lisa because she wasn't there."

"So, they've known about us for a while," said Jacob.

Jacob looked at their captive and said into his mike, "Deets, can you patch me through to Washington?"

"Sure. Give me a few minutes."

Jacob turned to Tank. "Take one of those trucks parked out front and drive back to our Hummer. Bring it to the camp. You think you can find it from here?"

"Deets can guide me with the satellite."

"Good. Get started."

"I have Mr. Hamilton on the radio," said Deets.

"It's definitely a training camp," Jacob told Hamilton. "We have a pretty big mess here. There are bodies scattered everywhere and I'm not sure how you want to handle it. Also, we might have a major problem with our security. We were set up. I'm afraid we might have a mole." He looked at the woman still writhing on the floor, screaming and cursing at them. "The good news is we took a prisoner, a very pissed-off woman. Unfortunately, she's probably just a second-level pawn."

"That means her boss is still out there," said Winston. "When he finds out his ambush failed, he's going to come after you and the team with a vengeance."

By the time Jacob finished his conversation with Winston, Tank returned with their Hummer. They loaded up all the files and computers, gagged their prisoner and secured her in the back of the Hummer with flex-cuffs

Dan struggled to get himself into the front passenger seat, complaining that he didn't need any help. "This damn thing's no worse than a fucking paper cut."

They headed out on the two-hour drive back to the

Greenbrier Valley Airport in Lewisburg. Hamilton's Citation CJ-4 waited on the tarmac with the engines running. The team was airborne within five minutes and headed back to Solitude, still unsure of what had happened.

SIXTEEN

Solitude Compound
Owen County, Kentucky
United States of America

While Jacob arranged transport for Dan to see a doctor about his wound and the tremor, Tank took their prisoner to the compound's subterranean holding cell. He flex-cuffed her ankles to the legs of a galvanized metal chair. A wooden table in front of her had a U-bolt screwed through its top. Tank secured both of her wrists to it with handcuffs. Despite the gunshot wound of her ankle she struggled against the restraints. The only result was self-inflicted abrasions and more leg pain. Tank took several pictures of her, placed a black bag over her head, and left.

Jacob forwarded encrypted copies of the prisoner's photographs to Mr. Hamilton at Langley. An hour later, Jacob's cell phone buzzed and the screen glowed with an incoming call. It was larger and heavier than the iPhone he once used. It was CIA issue and made to Winston Hamilton's custom specifications, completely impenetrable by hackers, including those in the country's own intelligence agencies. The call could only be from one person.

"Yes, Mr. Hamilton." Jacob pushed several buttons on his phone. "I'm going to put you on speaker phone so the rest of the team can hear what you have to say."

"That's fine," replied Hamilton. "First of all, I've done a thorough search of our systems. We don't have a security breach. L.A. was the ninth sleeper cell your team has successfully eradicated in the past two years. Their leaders figured it out and needed to stop you. They led the team to LA knowing we couldn't allow their planned attack on Rodeo Drive to go unchecked. They must have stationed someone near the crack house and that accounts for the photographs."

"Precisely," Lisa said. "It was a classic chess strategy, the queen-sacrifice move."

"A diversionary tactic?" asked Jacob.

"Exactly," said Hamilton. "They were willing to sacrifice the LA cell in the hopes of leading you to the West Virginia compound."

"That explains why Norman was able to open their flash drives so easily." Jacob ran his fingers through his hair. "It was a risky maneuver, and it cost them over three dozen lives. If they were willing to risk that and exposing their training camp in the process, they must've been worried about us uncovering something more important."

"I agree." Hamilton paused for a second. "They probably don't know that they failed yet, but when they do, you can be certain they'll come after you again. They have to stop the team."

"We might be able to use that to our advantage," said Jacob, "but first, I need to gather more information about their leader. Who is he and what's he up to? I guarantee it's more than just another act of urban terrorism. Something big is in the works. A least we have the woman. I'll get something useful from her."

"Next point," said Hamilton. "Deets asked me to help him identify the financial backers of the owners of the land, the New Green Horizons Foundation. It's the Masterson Properties Corporation."

"I knew it." Jacob paced the room. "Now we know for certain that the Scorpion has returned and is still active."

"I have something else for you," said Winston. "We used computerized facial recognition software from Homeland Security and successfully identified the woman. Rozhin Qaiser is her name."

"So, she is the RQ on the emails," said Deets sitting in his usual chair at the end of the table.

"Yes," said Hamilton. "Incidentally, she's the primary suspect in the murder of journalist Tom Foley and his family in Florida several months ago. Burned Tom's wife and grandson to death."

Lisa scowled. "What kind of person does that to a little boy? It's plain evil."

"If Satan wanted a bride to reign as queen of hell, it would be Rozhin," said Hamilton. "As you might have already suspected, she's the wife of the L.A. sleeper cell leader."

Tank looked up from a book he was reading. "The one Lisa shot in the van near Rodeo Drive?"

"The very same." said Hamilton.

"So, the leader of their organization threw Rozhin's husband under the bus to get to us," said Jacob.

"Looks like it. I wonder if Rozhin realizes her husband was sacrificed. You might be able to use that fact to get her to talk, though she might not care. Her dossier suggests that she was having an affair."

Lisa wrinkled her nose. "With whom? Who would have an affair with a psychopath like her?"

"Probably another psychopath," said Hamilton. "The report didn't list a name, but I wouldn't be surprised if it was one of her superiors. Rozhin's husband grew up in Flint, Michigan after his parents emigrated there from Iran. They joined a fundamentalist Sunni mosque that preached a radical Wahhabi interpretation of the Quran, the same one Rozhin's family attended. When the two were old enough, their parents arranged a wedding, so there might not be any real love involved in their marriage. Might explain the affair. They have two children: a boy and a girl. Rozhin's husband became a tailor and the small family lived a typical middle-class American life for several years."

Jacob stopped pacing and leaned toward the phone. "When did Rozhin and her husband become terrorists?"

"The husband was radicalized by his family when he was a boy. His father was heavily involved with CAIR which was named as an unindicted co-conspirator in the 2007 Holy Land Foundation case. It provided support for Hamas and other known terror groups. His mother has ties to the Pakistani radical group, Jamaat-e-Islami."

"That's the same group to which the San Bernardino shooter belonged," said Jacob.

"Yes." Hamilton continued, "We believe Rozhin became radicalized shortly after the marriage to her husband. Four years ago, the two parents left their children with the grandparents and fell off the grid. Looks like they used that time to help organize a network of sleeper cells. Meanwhile, their children have been living the American dream."

"Being raised by jihadist sympathizers." Lisa scowled. "They're continuing the family tradition of molding terrorists to attack the same country that gave them a safe home."

"There's one other matter, Jacob," said Hamilton. "You and your team are going to have to stand down for a while. You've been too successful, and it's getting to be more difficult to cover up your operations. The White House is twisting as many arms as they can to keep a lid on this thing, but they can do just so much.

"That's fine. I'm tired of chasing down these sleeper cells one by one. It's taking too long. They've even infiltrated the ranks of ANTIFA, stirring up riots and unrest wherever they can. We'll never get ahead of the curve. Meanwhile, innocent people are being slaughtered. Maybe we've been approaching this problem from the wrong direction. We've been trying to identify individual cells in the hopes that we could follow a trail back to the leadership. We should leave that process up to the FBI. We can feed them information as we obtain it, but it's time for us to come up with a more aggressive approach. We need to refocus in the direction of their leaders and sever the head of the serpent."

"I agree," said Hamilton, "though I'm afraid that this organization is much like the mythological Hydra of Lerna. There are many snake heads to be severed, and once you remove one, two more grow back in its place."

"Then we'll cut out its heart," said Jacob. "That means finding the one who ordered the ambush on us in West Virginia."

"How do you plan to find him?"

"Like my father used to tell me when I was a young boy. If you want to catch the big fish, you have to go where the big fish are swimming. I need to find that place. Maybe the interrogation of our prisoner will lead me in the right direction."

"That's it then," said Hamilton. "Call me back after you've had a chance to speak to the woman."

SEVENTEEN

Solitude Interrogation Center
Owen County, Kentucky
United States of America

Rozhin Qaiser remained in the stainless-steel room where Tank stood behind her as intimidation. He removed her hood. Rozhin's eyes squinted at the bright light as Jacob pulled up a chair and sat across from her. She looked like a wild animal, her long black hair in tangled disarray and her once-mocha complexion now mottled with bruises from her recent battles. Under better circumstances, she might have been beautiful, except her eyes sparked with a hateful fury. The wooden table separated them by only four feet, close enough for her to reach over and kill Jacob, but her hands were still secured to the U-bolt. She struggled violently to get loose, but it was no use. She couldn't move.

"How is the ankle?" Jacob asked.

She scowled in reply.

"Would you care for something to drink?"

She tried to spit at him, but it was a feeble attempt. She had to be dehydrated. He set a bottle of cold water on the table, inches out of her reach. The offer was received with only a snarl.

"If you cooperate with us, you can have a drink. I know you must be thirsty. Answer a few simple questions and I can make this much easier for you. I can even give you something to take away the pain in your leg."

"You have nothing I want! Now let me go, American pig!"

she said with a slight middle eastern accent.

Jacob leaned back in his chair; his fingers locked behind his head. "We both know that's not going to happen."

On it went, questions being asked, and no answers being given. He tried to establish a flow of dialogue as he struggled to remain patient.

Come on, Buddy Boy. Smack the bitch around.
Beat the answers out of her. Make her bleed.

He hadn't heard from the Entity in a while. He had been so busy killing jihadists, it had remained quiet, but it was always there, just below the surface. He pushed it aside and continued with the unsuccessful interrogation of the woman.

"Tell me about your plans to launch an attack at The Mall of America."

No response.

"How about your plans to poison the L.A. water supply?"

Her eyes widened, apparently surprised that he knew about it, but her only answer was to again spit in his direction. He moved the water bottle a little closer, still out of her reach. Tempting droplets of condensation ran down the sides. He asked, "Who's your boss?"

For another two hours, Jacob continued to ask questions that remained unanswered. He was getting nowhere.

Lisa and Deets watched the process on video screens in the observation room. Lisa studied her brother closely on the monitor. He wasn't himself. "What the hell's he doing in there? It's been almost three hours and he has nothing. Why's he pussy-footing around with her like that. If she were a man, Jacob would have broken her an hour ago."

Lisa paced back and forth, keeping her eyes fixed to the monitor. "Enough," she said. "We don't have time for this nonsense. He's getting nowhere with that nice-guy approach. Get him out of there, Norman. Tell him to take a break."

Deets called into Jacob's earpiece, "Lisa said to stop for a while."

Jacob stood, left the interrogation room, and entered the monitor area. He took a long drink from a bottle of water and looked at his sister. She slowly shook her head.

"What?" he asked.

She stepped nose to nose with him. "Jacob, you're the toughest man I've ever known. You've done things most men wouldn't even begin to think of trying, brave things, very dangerous things, but when it comes to dealing with women, you're a patsy. I know our father told you to respect and protect women, but that was different and you know it." She jammed a finger toward the monitor. "That person in there isn't a woman and doesn't deserve to be treated gently. If she could, she'd reach over that table and rip your throat out with her bare hands. She's a murderous psychopath who's directly or indirectly responsible for the deaths of countless innocent men, women, and children! We need to get tough with her. We don't have time to wear her down like this. We don't have a month. We don't have a week! We don't even have a day! Something very bad is in the works, and we'd better get to the bottom of it today."

Lisa turned to Deets. "Turn off the video and audio." She spoke into Tank's earpiece. He was still standing behind the prisoner. "Put that hood back over her head, and don't be gentle about it. I want to shake her up a bit. If she tries to spit now, she'll get it all over her own face." She turned to Jacob. "I need to borrow your combat knife."

"Why?"

She held out her hand. It wasn't a request. "Because I need it."

Lisa raised the temperature in the interrogation room and let the prisoner stew for a while. She thought about the woman. She wasn't just a terrorist sympathizer. She was a murderer who enjoyed what she did. She had personally slaughtered the Foley family in cold blood and God only knew how many other lives she had taken. What Rozhin had done made what Lisa had to do next much easier. She took a deep breath, entered the room, and stood next to the prisoner. Under the hood, the woman turned her head from side to side as Lisa approached. Lisa stomped her foot against the woman's wounded ankle. A rosette of red expanded across her white dressing.

"Owww!" she howled. "You infidel pig, you'll—" Rozhin didn't get the chance to finish her sentence. Lisa ripped the hood away and punched her in the mouth. A stream of blood trickled down from her split upper lip and a look of shock transformed her eyes.

Lisa leaned closer, "Did that get your attention? We tried to do this the nice way, but the easy times are over, bitch. It's time to start talking. What's your name? Who are your superiors?"

Rozhin spit out a mouthful of blood and started screaming, "You whore! I want my lawyer! In a few years we'll take over this . . ." Slam! Her sentence abruptly ended with a scream of pain as Lisa plunged Jacob's combat knife through her left hand, impaling it on the table.

Lisa yelled into her ear, "You think this is some kind fucking game? Look at me!" Rozhin stared down at the table in defiance. Lisa twisted the knife deeper into her hand. "I said look at me!" The woman looked up, grimacing in pain. Lisa slowly and deliberately twisted the knife deeper into her hand. "Look into my eyes and tell me what you see there."

Nothing.

"No reply? No clever 'infidel' retorts? Well, I'll answer the question for you. What you should be seeing when you look in my eyes is contempt, hatred for all that you and your gang of psychopaths stand for, and hatred for your perversion of the Muslim religion. You people fancy yourselves as soldiers of Allah. You're not soldiers! You're not warriors! You're not even Muslims! You're no more than a gang of thugs who wrap themselves in the cloak of a phony religion. I know who you are, and I know what you did to the Foley family in Florida. You burned to death that poor grandmother and her young grandson while they were still alive, and claim you did it all in the name of Allah?

Rozhin looked down.

"I didn't give you permission to look away from me." Lisa twisted the knife deeper into the table. A fresh rivulet of blood trickled across the surface. "You see — I can be just as ruthless and brutal as you, Rozhin."

The woman's face transformed from a mask of resentment to surprise, astonishment that her captives knew who she was. She started to say something, but Lisa again hit her in the mouth, starting a fresh stream of blood flowing down her chin. "You don't get to speak until I tell you to."

Rozhin's defiance faded. Lisa continued. "That's right! We already know who you are. We also know that our attack on your training compound was a setup. We were supposed to be killed, but you and your group failed, Rozhin. That failure isn't going to sit well with your superiors. Your family's going to have to pay for that failure. We know who your husband was. I say was because he's dead. I killed him myself. Your leaders used him and his L.A. cell to get to my team, but it was all for naught. Your leaders didn't care a lick about him, and they certainly don't care about you or your family."

Terror spread across Rozhin's face. She was shaken by the information that the father of her children had been sacrificed like a pawn. Lisa pressed on. "We know your children are hiding with their grandparents in Flint, Michigan. We even have the address, so if you don't start telling us what we want to know, I'll personally make sure that they each experience the same slow painful death as the Foley boy."

"You can't do that! It's illegal!" cried Rozhin.

"Who can't?" Lisa conjured up the most maniacal laugh she could muster. "Me? I don't care about the law! I don't exist. My team? They don't exist. This place doesn't even exist. That means I can do whatever the fuck I want, and right now I'm giving your brats a long, hard look. It was illegal for me to shoot your damn husband, but I did it anyway. And you know what? I enjoyed it. I shot him right through his fucking head. His brains splattered all over the back of the van. I sent him straight to

Jahannam. You see, my friends and I don't play by the rules. Our mission is to eradicate each and every one of you animals by any means necessary. We've started with your sleeper cells. Then it was your training camp. Next in line will be your family."

Tears threatened as Rozhin's trembled, her hard shell appeared to fracture.

Lisa clenched her teeth. "When I say by any methods necessary, that's exactly what I mean. You aren't the only ones capable of killing and maiming children. We can play that game too. I'm going to personally make sure that both of your children and your parents are beheaded. I think I'll start by practicing on the grandparents. Your children will have a chance to witness what's in store for them. I must confess that I'm new at this whole decapitation stuff. I don't have as much experience as you. When I do it, I'm afraid things will be slow and painful—much more fucking painful." Lisa twisted the knife further into Rozhin's hand for emphasis.

Rozhin screamed and pulled in vain against her restraints. It was no use. She broke down and sobbed. "Please don't hurt my children. I'll tell you whatever you want to know."

The first few questions were answered reluctantly, but once the small leak of information began to trickle out, the dam ruptured. The flow of dialogue had been established and there was no turning back for Rozhin. It was time for Jacob to ask the important questions. Lisa walked across the room and whispered into her microphone, "She's ready to talk to Jacob now. Send him back in here. Make sure the video recorder is turned back on."

"Already did when she started talking," replied Deets.

Jacob and Tank re-entered the room. Jacob took a chair across the table from Rozhin. He stared at the hand, still pinned to the table, pools of blood clotting around the wound. Lisa stepped aside and Tank reassumed his position behind the prisoner. Jacob nodded and Tank pulled the knife free and handed it back to Lisa. Rozhin screamed in pain.

Jacob gave her the bottle of water and she guzzled half. He wrapped a towel around her hand. "We'll put a dressing and antibiotics on that as long as you continue to co-operate."

"OK, OK, just keep that crazy woman away from me and my children." Rozhin's eyes fixated on Lisa who was standing in the corner, still holding the bloodied knife.

"You need to look at me, Rozhin," said Jacob. "I want to see your eyes as we talk. I'm very good at this and I'll be able to tell if you try to lie to me. If you do, I'll leave the room again and place you back in her hands." He tilted his head in Lisa's direction. Forcing Rozhin to look back and forth between himself and Lisa was a way of throwing her off balance while unmasking any attempts at deceit.

"I won't lie. I promise."

Jacob resumed the questions. "How many other training facilities are there like the one in West Virginia?"

"Four others, I think."

"Where are they?"

"I don't know." She glanced at Lisa. Her voice raised a pitch. "I'm telling the truth! I don't know! They keep it a secret."

"Who keeps it a secret?"

"My superiors."

"Who are they?

"I don't know their names. It might be only one, maybe more, I don't know." She looked down.

Jacob wasn't buying her story but kept a straight face. The look in her eyes already told him what he wanted to know. There was only one man in charge, and she knew who he was. "Continue," he said.

"We were instructed to train an army of soldiers to launch attacks on each state capitol building and major tourist attractions in America several years ago. The cells were told to await a signal which was to follow the assassination of President Wagner, but the assassination didn't happen. The command never came, and most cells were told to stand down. Others were instructed to carry out intermittent attacks on soft targets."

"Why?"

"Recruiting."

"Explain," said Jacob.

"Even though ISIS had been weakened, we had to let everyone around the world know that we were still a formidable force. Even the powerful United States couldn't stop us."

"And the rest of you were told to stand down?"

"Yes, most were told to await the new signal."

"A large-scale attack, like the assassination attempt on President Wagner?"

"Yes, I believe so."

"Tell me, what, where, and when is the next attack. I know your group is building up to something big."

"I don't know." She looked nervously at the knife still in Lisa's hand. Light reflected off the blade into her eyes. "Honestly, I don't know." Her eyes filled with tears. "Just that it's called Yaoguai."

The same word Deets found on the captured computer.

Jacob leaned closer across the table, looking directly into Rozhin's eyes. "Yaoguai? What's that supposed to be?"

"I've already said, I don't know!" She cried.

"Who gave the order?" Keep her off balance.

"What order?"

"To stand down."

"I don't know. Each cell and camp leader is given an untraceable burner phone. When a message is to be delivered, a few leaders are contacted. They in turn, contact ten more cell leaders. The process is repeated until everyone's been notified. That way only a few individuals are aware of the full scope of the organization. We never know the identity of the superiors who give the orders."

Her eyes said otherwise. She was lying. "So, you're saying you only know of the cells for which you are responsible, the ones you are assigned to call? I want each of those numbers, and every cell leader you know."

"I already retrieved them from her cell phone," Deets

said into Jacob's earpiece. "It's more than just ten. Must be over a hundred."

She was a more important member in their organization than he originally thought. It was time to take a chance and shoot for the bullseye. "What about the Scorpion? When's the last time you were in direct contact with him?" Jacob asked.

Her face turned ashen and terror oozed from her pores. She tried to hide her fear and denied knowing about the Scorpion, but Jacob already had the answer to his question. They were close.

"Are you still sleeping with the Scorpion?"

"I don't know what you're talking about?" She was shaking. He didn't need to pursue it further.

Jacob paused to consider his next line of questions. "Who is Raphael?" She flinched. "Don't lie to me now, Rozhin. We're the only chance your family has. Once your superiors find out that you've been talking to us, your children are as good as dead."

Rozhin looked at Lisa. "All I know is that his name is Raphael DuBoise and he lives in Paris. He's the key to the next big attack, but like I already told you, I don't know exactly who he is."

After another thirty minutes of questioning, she had little to offer except that she admitted to her own involvement in the murder of investigative reporter Tom Foley and his family. Her organization was involved in the planning of the Boston Marathon and the Stanford University bombings.

Rozhin was finished. Her days as a terrorist were over. The only remaining option she had was to protect her children whom she would never again see. Jacob re-dressed her wounds.

———————◆———————

The team convened in the monitor room. "Wow," said Deets. "That was some pretty intense shit in there, Lisa! Did you mean what you said about her kids?"

"Of course not, Norman," said Lisa. "The important thing is that Rozhin believed me. She thinks I'm crazy and that's exactly what I wanted her to think." It had been necessary, but she still didn't like what she had done. The interaction had reignited the rage inside her soul, the same one afflicting her brother. She had to push it away if she ever hoped for a normal life.

Tank placed his arm on her shoulder and looked into her eyes. "I know it was hard, but you did the right thing in there, Lisa. To understand your enemy, you must become the enemy."

"Sun Tzu may be right, Tank, but sometimes you can become so much like them you forget who you truly are."

Don't worry" he said. "You are not them and never will be."

"I hope not." She had said that this would be her last mission, and she intended to keep that promise to herself. If only Jacob could do the same, but there was a war going on in the world. Without men like her brother and the team, that war would be lost.

She looked at Rozhin's image on the monitor screen. "What're we going to do with her?"

"I need to talk to Mr. Hamilton again," said Jacob. "We'll arrange to send her down to Guantanamo."

"It's a good thing President Wagner rescinded the prior administration's order to shut the place down. If they had, we'd have no place to keep these psychopaths."

"Roger that," said Tank. "What now?"

"I have to clear my schedule for a few weeks," said Jacob. "I'm probably going to be doing some traveling soon."

"Where?" asked Lisa.

"Paris."

"What about us?"

"This mission's going to be a one man show," said Jacob.

Lisa shook her head slowly from side to side. Not the answer she wanted. Jacob planned to go fishing and he was going to use himself as bait. It was going to be extremely dangerous but there would be no talking him out of it.

EIGHTEEN

Washington, D.C.
United States of America

The chauffeur drove the black Mercedes limousine north on Pennsylvania Avenue between Lafayette Square and the White House. The park was dedicated to French General Marquis de Lafayette, a key figure in the success of the American Revolution against King George III and the British. It had been the site of frequent political protests, but on this day it was filled with a throng of reporters and photographers awaiting the visit of the Chinese ambassador at the White House. A bespectacled Winston Hamilton slouched down in the back seat and pulled his fedora low over his forehead. "Drive on to the east side," he instructed his driver, hoping the press would ignore him. Anonymity was of prime importance.

Hamilton normally avoided the White House. Too many preying eyes, but he needed a face to face meeting with the President. Relaying information through the usual back-door channels wasn't going to work this time. The situation with a possible terror attack was evolving too rapidly. His vehicle came to a halt at the guardhouse outside the service entrance of the East Wing. A guard walked over and instructed the driver to lower his heavily tinted window. Hamilton knew enough about White House security protocol to realize that there were at least four snipers with their sights trained on the car, two on his driver and two on him. If the car tried to ram through the gate, rocket launchers were ready to be fired.

The guard studied the driver closely. Holding out his left hand and keeping his right hand on his sidearm, he demanded, "Identification." There would be no denying him. The Secret Service had been taking no chances ever since the attempt on President Wagner's life two years ago. The guard examined the ID, comparing it to his face. "Mr. Hamilton?" Winston nodded in the affirmative. The guard returned to the gate house and made a phone call.

The guard spoke into his headpiece. "Yes sir." The steel crash-gate pillars were lowered, and the car was waved through. The diminutive Winston Hamilton exited his vehicle and turned to his driver. "This might take several hours. I'll call you when I'm ready."

As the car pulled away, Hamilton was met at the ground-level side entrance by Parker Davis, the Chief of White House Security. He had worked with Davis ever since the team had uncovered the assassination plot. Davis was discreet and absolutely dedicated to the President. He was a valuable ally who could be trusted with the most sensitive of secrets.

"This way, sir." He led Hamilton through a metal detector and down several back hallways. They wound up inside the huge White House kitchen, a stainless-steel palace where meals were prepared for the most powerful individuals in the world. Several faces turned to stare. A herculean man in a white shirt and black vest stepped forward but stopped short when he saw that the visitor was accompanied by the Chief of Security. He nodded and let them pass. They walked across the room and past several cooks until Davis opened a small door in the rear. It led into a smaller kitchen, one that looked much like a staff break room. It had recently been nicknamed "Wagner's Retreat," a place where the President could get away for some much-needed privacy. It was the perfect location for a confidential off-the-books meeting; one of the few places in the building without surveillance cameras and hidden microphones.

Davis dismissed the staff except for Mary, the head chef.

"Have a seat, Mr. Hamilton. President Wagner will meet with you in here. Believe it or not, outside the First Family's living quarters and the Situation Room, this is one of the most private rooms in the White House."

Hamilton pulled up a wooden kitchen chair.

"Would you care for something to eat while you're waiting? Mary is one of the finest chefs in all of Washington. She's been here for over twenty-seven years and has prepared meals for five different presidents." Mary blushed but said nothing.

"No thank you, but a cup of coffee would be nice, black, no sugar."

After a second cup of coffee, President Wagner walked in, leaving his entourage outside. Hamilton stood to greet the Commander in Chief. At six-foot-two, Wagner was a full eight inches taller than him. The man was lean, with square shoulders and a determined jaw that one might expect from a Special Forces veteran. He possessed the aura of a natural leader, but his demeaner was unassuming and cordial.

"I'm sorry for the delay. I was tied up in a meeting with the Russian ambassador. They're up to some of their old shenanigans again."

"I understand, Mr. President. I appreciate your taking the time to see me. I've just been enjoying some of Mary's wonderful coffee." The cook blushed again.

President Wagner held up his finger. "I need to check on one important matter before we get started. Mary, what ice cream do we have on the menu today?" He looked at his friend and winked. "One of the great benefits of being president is I get the best ice cream in the country."

Mary said, "It's New Orleans Praline Pecan from Kilwin's, Mr. President."

He smiled. "One of my favorites. You want a scoop, Mr. Hamilton? You won't be disappointed."

"That would be nice, Mr. President, and another cup of Mary's delicious coffee, please."

Wagner nodded to Mary. "Ice cream for two." After the

two men were served, President Wagner said, "Thank you, Mary. That'll be all for now." When she turned to leave, he added, "And Mary?"

"Yes, Mr. President?"

It was the president's turn to blush. "I see no need to tell the First Lady about my secret trips to the kitchen. She has me on a low cholesterol diet."

"I understand, Mr. President. Mum's the word," Mary smiled warmly at him and exited the room.

Wagner turned to Hamilton with a sheepish grin on his face. "You know, I'm the leader of the free world so I'm not afraid of much. I'm not afraid of my critics or the press. I'm not even afraid of Putin. But I am afraid of the wrath of my wife when she gets angry with me. That's something everyone should fear."

"I understand completely, Mr. President. I was married at one time." They exchanged a knowing nod and shared a laugh.

The President took a bite of ice cream, a twinkle in his piercing grey eyes. "You suckered me in on our last chess game."

"Mr. President?"

"You're a clever man, Mr. Hamilton. You allowed me to take your queen and both bishops. I thought I was about to beat one of the world's finest chess players. You had me in checkmate four moves later."

"Playing chess is similar to international politics. It's a learning process, Mr. President. Each mistake makes you stronger."

"Have you ever lost a chess tournament?"

Winston answered with a smile. "I look forward to many more games with you in the future— after you win reelection."

The President finished his ice cream, gathered up both bowls and placed them in the sink. He began pacing the room. "There is one thing I actually do fear, Winston. It's something that every president has feared since the Twin Towers were brought down. I worry that some crazy group will detonate a nuclear device, crippling one of our cities. Had it not been for your team and what they were able to accomplish several years ago, it would have happened in the Nation's Capital. We could have lost Washington and most of our government."

Hamilton neatly folded his napkin and placed it on the table. He brushed a small piece of lint off his leg. "We are at war and must remain vigilant at all times, Mr. President. Unfortunately, our enemies are already imbedded amongst us. That's the reason I wanted to meet with you personally today. We have a problem, a very serious problem. I believe it might even be worse than the assassination attempt during your inauguration."

President Wagner stopped pacing and took his seat opposite Hamilton. He leaned forward, hands on his knees. "What's going on? I sure as hell hope it isn't another nuclear device."

"I don't think so, sir, but someone is definitely hatching a new plan to attack our country. It's big, and I have reason to believe that someone might be the Scorpion."

"The Scorpion! Damn! I was hoping we were rid of that guy." The President exhaled slowly. "What makes you think he's back?"

"After we failed to capture him, it was inevitable that he'd show up again, sir. We discovered the name of Masterson on a terrorist laptop computer last month. Does that name ring a bell?"

"It certainly does. Masterson Properties was the name of the Scorpion's hotel corporation. He used it as a cover for his organization."

"That's why I think he's active again, Mr. President." Hamilton relayed all the information he had obtained from his team regarding the numerous terror cells and their attempted attacks over the past two years. He discussed what they had uncovered regarding the jihadist training facility in West Virginia, but he avoided giving him details of the team's activities and how they obtained their information. Wagner was one of the very few to know about the team's existence and he needed to be able to claim a degree of plausible deniability regarding the specifics of what they did.

"So, your team has eliminated the training compound?" asked President Wagner.

"Completely, Mr. President. It no longer exists."

"Excellent work" said Wagner. "So why do you think this all implicates the Scorpion?"

"I can't say with absolute certainty that it's him, but his name turned up during a recent prisoner interrogation, and it fits his modus operandi, sir. He likes to utilize attacks on soft targets to divert our attention away from the real threat. It's a classic misdirection maneuver. It happened repeatedly in the year leading up to your assassination attempt."

"A diversion like your allowing me to take your queen."

Winston tried unsuccessfully to hide the smile on his face. "Yes, sir."

"What exactly do you think he's up to now?"

"Unfortunately, we can't say for sure yet. We only know that the attack is possibly being referred to as Yaoguai."

"Yaoguai?" The President's eyebrows almost seemed to meet. "I've never heard of that term. What the hell's a Yaoguai?"

"It's a demon from Chinese mythology. It supposedly has magical powers and is capable of inflicting hideous amounts of evil upon the innocent."

"And you believe this Yaoguai thing is being orchestrated by the Scorpion?"

Winston nodded. "It looks that way, Mr. President. A lot of evidence is leading us in that direction."

"Does that mean you think his plan will originate in China? I have enough trouble with those characters without dealing with some powerful Chinese demon. We've already had to deal with that damn virus they engineered. Their lies cost us a several hundred thousand lives and almost destroyed our economy. Now, they're ratcheting up their cyber-espionage programs again. Are you familiar with Wang Liuang?"

"Some. I know he's the founder of the Liuang Computer Technology Corporation. Forbes Magazine lists him as one of the ten wealthiest men in the world."

"He's that and more," said the President. "He has close ties to the Chinese Ministry of Intelligence. We suspect he's the coordinator of China's extensive cyber espionage programs. Through the use of wide-spread illegal political contributions, Liuang has been influential in almost every major American congressional, senate, and presidential race for decades. Hundreds of millions of illegal dollars have exchanged hands in the process. The maneuver has given him unfettered access to the United States government and our economy.

President Wagner shook his head. "It disheartening to witness how a member of a foreign nation has been allowed to influence our country to this degree. Many doors have been conveniently opened for him. Working under the umbrella of his international company, he's been able to hack into a multitude of crucial American institutions. Stealing our technology has allowed his corporation to become the largest exporter of electronic systems in the world. The DOJ has been trying for a long time to put the screws to Liuang, but he's a powerful man with a stable of influential friends."

Hamilton listened without interrupting.

President Wagner stopped to pour himself and Hamilton another cup of coffee. "What I don't understand is what could the Chinese have in common with a terrorist like the Scorpion? Maybe a cyber-attack?" The President scowled. "Do you have anything else on it other than the Yaoguai name?"

"We believe there's some kind of connection through Paris."

"France? A Chinese and French collaborative? That's a stretch. They're not exactly known to cooperate with each other. How'd you come up with that theory?"

Winston removed a cloth from his coat pocket and cleaned his glasses. After replacing them on the bridge of his nose, he said. "From our intelligence gathering efforts, sir. We've uncovered a great deal of communication back and forth between sleeper cells in our country and those in Paris. That's where the Yaoguai reference originated. Thus far we've been unable to confirm that the Scorpion is the source of the communications. We've only been able to identify one name, a Raphael DuBoise."

"A Frenchman? Who is he?"

"Unfortunately, we have the man's name and little else, but I believe it's a legitimate lead. One of our sources told us that Raphael was the key to their plan. My IT expert completed a search of the French databases and he was able to find only one individual by that name. He lives in Paris."

"Is he on any of our known-terrorists lists?" asked the President.

"There's been no mention of anyone by that name. The fellow in question has been a private museum tour guide for over ten years, and he doesn't exactly fit the profile of a member of a terrorist organization. It could be a dead-end, but we need to establish contact with him to find out if he has a connection to Yaoguai. That's why I wanted to see you today, Mr. President. We have a plan and it is predicated upon you contacting the President of France."

"You want me to ask him to allow your group to operate in his country?"

"Yes, Mr. President. I know it's a tall order. I realize the French government can be recalcitrant sometimes but considering what they've been experiencing with their own recent terrorist massacres, I think they might be willing to cooperate with us. We need them to turn a blind eye to whatever we must do.

The President's brow furrowed. "I'll do my best to persuade the French to help us. As you said, they can be a little obstinate at times, but if we're facing a crisis to the extent that you believe, we're going to have to work together to stop it."

President Wagner's aide stepped in the room. "Mr. President, the Chinese ambassador is waiting in the Oval Office."

"Damn Chinese," said Wagner, almost to himself. "They're being tough on the next stage of trade negotiations. We're at some disadvantage because they hold a huge stake in our national debt. The good thing is they can't afford to see our country fail. They have too much to lose financially. That's why I doubt that the Chinese government is directly involved in the Scorpion's Yaoguai thing."

President Wagner stood. "I'd prefer to let the Chinese

bastard wait, but I'm afraid I must end our meeting." He shook Hamilton's hand and turned to leave. He stopped and placed his hand on Hamilton's shoulder. "Do whatever you must to protect our country, Winston."

"I will, sir. That I can promise you. Before you leave, there's one other thing."

"Yes?"

"We need to have a guest transferred to Guantanamo."

Wagner's eyebrows raised. "When and whom?"

"As soon as it can be arranged, but it might be a little complicated. It's a woman."

The President's eyes squinted. "Now that is a new wrinkle. I'll personally speak to the commander of the base."

"I would recommend that she be isolated from the other prisoners. They'll probably kill her if they get a chance, and she might still be a source of useful information."

"Understood." President Wagner turned and left,

When Winston Hamilton returned to his car, he called Jacob on his secure phone. "Everything's been arranged, Dr. Savich. You'll need to clear your schedule for the next several weeks."

"It's already been taken care of, Mr. Hamilton."

NINETEEN

Avenue des Champs Élysées
Paris, France

Sassani walked out onto the balcony of his luxurious apartment and gazed down at the thousands of tourists walking along the famous Champs Élysées in Paris. They were shopping or enjoying a glass of wine at one of the many sidewalk restaurants. *Fools.* They had no idea about what was about to rain down upon their world. Modern civilization was going to end. Millions would perish like his family and friends perished when their mountain village was incinerated in Afghanistan. 'Collateral damage,' the Americans called it. Soon they would all know the true meaning of collateral damage on a world-wide scale.

He returned to the confines of his condo, loosened his tie, and unbuttoned the top button of his shirt. After pouring a snifter of Remy Martin brandy, he swirled it and studied the amber liquid in the light before enjoying a sip. The taste did little to calm him. The photograph of Jacob Savich sat on the table in front of him, staring up, almost mocking. *What happened?* Rozhin should have reported in about the ambush by now, but there had been no contact in over four days. Unusual for her, especially after such an important mission. She wasn't responding to his calls or emails. He threw the brandy against the wall, shattering the glass as the anger of realization coiled up inside his chest.

"She hasn't answered because she's dead, or worse, she's been captured!" He shouted and paced back and forth across the room like a caged animal. "If they have her in custody, it could ruin my plans. I should have never had sex with the woman. It clouded my judgment." Had he told her any details about his plans during the heat of passion? *Maybe.* Rozhin was loyal and knew how to keep her mouth shut, but even the toughest have their breaking point if you know which screws to twist. She couldn't know much, but the Americans have proven themselves to be clever. They could find out about Raphael. They might even uncover the existence of Yaoguai! That might be enough to destroy everything.

All was at risk, even his own safety. *Need to be ready to run.* He was prepared. His escape bags lay where he had placed them six months ago: two days of clothing, a collection of passport identities with corresponding credit cards, and a half-million dollars' worth of European currency. He hadn't expected to need them for at least another three months, but things weren't going well with this Jacob Savich and his partners still lurking about. He had to be prepared for the worst, in case everything fell apart.

He poured another glass of brandy and considered the potential ramifications of Rozhin's capture. Even in the worst-case scenario, the situation was salvageable. The plan was still solid. It simply needed to be adjusted and the schedule accelerated. Unfortunately, he was still at the mercy of Chow. He sneered at the photograph of Jacob Savich. "And you, I must stop you before you get any closer, before you can again keep me from fulfilling my destiny."

Sassani swallowed a mouthful of his brandy, allowing the alcohol to finally calm the storm raging inside. There was an upside to Rozhin's capture. Maybe she did mention Raphael DuBoise by name. *That could become a positive.* It meant Jacob Savich would be headed to Paris soon. He pulled out his computer.

TWENTY

Limone, Switzerland

The smell of chocolate and freshly baked pastries permeated the small shop on the outskirts of the peaceful village of Limone, nestled in the foothills of the Swiss Alps. Carla Coyne, the owner of the establishment, was rearranging a stack of coconut macaroons on the counter when she saw a black SUV pull across the stone bridge leading into the town center. The driver slowly pulled around the small central plaza fountain and parked outside her store. Two athletic looking men, each wearing tight, black t-shirts and jeans, exited the vehicle.

"Americans," she said to herself with contempt. She brushed her short brunette hair back from her face. "I've been expecting you for a long time."

The two men adjusted their matching mirrored sunglasses as they stepped onto the sidewalk and entered the shop. The bell over the door chimed as Carla reached under the counter, exposing a Death Before Dishonor tattoo on her right forearm. She wrapped her fingers around the grip of a Glock semi-automatic and racked the slide, chambering a round. The handgun had been a favorite during her years in the service. It was also the same sidearm her father carried when he died from a sniper wound in Operation Desert Storm, and the same gun her brother used when he was killed by an IED in Iraq. The weapon held special meaning to her. All Carla had ever wanted was to continue in the family tradition of honorable service to her country. Eleven years ago, she received her first sergeant stripes. Subsequently, she applied for the United States Special Forces, becoming one of the first women to complete the grueling program. Initially, her teammates resented the presence of a female in their elite group and she was constantly under pressure to resign. She refused, and after six months, her tenacity paid off. She had more than proven herself to most of the other squad members — but not all. Halfway through the program, it happened. Her dreams of a military career were destroyed in one evening.

The memory shook her as Carla followed the two Americans with her eyes. *Should have known better when the commanding officer asked me to meet him in the General Staff Office building. The fucker said he needed to clear up some discrepancies in my evaluation numbers.* It was after hours and, except for the two of them, the building was empty. He raped her. After he finished, he zipped up his pants and said, "You might want to reconsider your resignation. The Special Forces Unit is no place for a woman." He told her to clean herself up, and then summarily dismissed her as though nothing of significance had happened.

The memory still made her stomach twist in knots. When she went to his superior officer to report the incident, she was reprimanded for bypassing the military chain of command. How was she supposed to do that? Report the incident to the rapist himself? Subsequently, she approached the base commander with her accusations. The results were the same; she was again reprimanded and told to forget the matter or face disciplinary action. She sought legal assistance outside the military, only to be demoted and transferred to an army psychiatric hospital for a mandatory six-month inpatient evaluation. The discharge diagnosis read: 'Manic-depressive disorder with a tendency toward delusional thinking.' She was found to be unfit for active duty and forced to leave the army.

It took her a year to recover emotionally, and even longer to plan her response. She had learned many useful skills during her tenure in the Special Forces and decided to make the most of them. She surveilled her attacker for months until until she became intimately familiar with his routine. He didn't deserve to be killed. That would be too easy. She opted for something worse than death. She struck as he was leaving an off-base bar where he always went for his weekly poker night. A shot to the crotch with a high-powered rifle gave her the justice she wanted. It was a fate much worse than receiving a bullet in the head. The man who had brutally raped her was no longer a man. For all intents and purposes his military career was over. Within four hours of the incident she had already left the country with a new identity and plans for a new life in Europe.

Carla refocused her attention on the two Americans. *So, you've finally found me.* She was sure the two had been assigned to bring her back, but they were going to need more help. Things are about to get bloody. She tightened her fingers around the grip of the Glock as the men approached the counter. Each ordered a chocolate éclair and a cup of espresso. They sat at a window bistro table overlooking the small mountain stream which cut under the town's stone bridge. They talked and laughed, seemingly oblivious to her presence. When finished, their eyes fixated on hers. A surge of adrenaline put her finger on hair-trigger status. Just before she lifted the gun to fire, one of the men raved about the pastries. "Oh my god. They were divine. Weren't they Brad?" His partner nodded his head. "Best ever."

They ordered a bag of the coconut macaroons to go, left a generous tip, and walked back outside. They stopped for a minute to take a selfie on the bridge, then returned to their car, hand in hand.

Carla exhaled slowly in relief and released the grip on her Glock. *Tourists – just a couple of gay American tourists.* She returned the Glock to its usual hiding place under the counter.

Her computer chimed, indicating that she had a message. It read: **From a secret admirer.** Carla smiled. It was always the same. When she opened the email attachment, an assortment of a dozen fresh-cut yellow roses filled the screen. They were neatly arranged in a circular fashion with the stems bound together in the center and the buds strategically arranged in a circle like the numbers on a clock. She had a job offer. Each time it was a different species of flower, but always arranged in the same manner. It was July, the seventh month, so she focused her attention on the rose in the seven o'clock position. She zoomed in and studied the flower carefully until she found it, a slight irregularity in one of the thorns on the stem. Moving the computer's curser to the spot, she carefully right clicked. If she did this maneuver improperly, or clicked on the wrong set of pixels, the flower picture would have disappeared, and the hidden message erased.

The screen flickered for a half-second and an image appeared. It was a photograph of a man, mid-forties, with dark hair and crystal blue eyes. Windows to the soul, Mom had told her. "Always check their eyes," she whispered to the screen. It was advice she had ignored the night she had been raped. If she had paid more attention, life might have been different for her. That mistake would never happen again. She had since become an expert at reading eyes. This man's eyes were alert, scanning his surroundings and analyzing his situation. They were the eyes of a leader. At the same time, there was an inexplicable sadness there. *Why*, she wondered, but it was a question born out of curiosity more than anything else. It made no difference why, as long as he wasn't an innocent civilian. She didn't do revenge or business assassinations. Her contracts had to deserve to die. Beyond that, she wasn't paid to care. *He is remarkably handsome, and those soft blue eyes could melt any woman's heart. Another time, another place, maybe?* Pity to take him out but killing was the career life had forced her to select.

She swiped her finger across the screen from right to left and a second photograph appeared. This man was older, maybe approaching sixty, with a broken nose and chiseled facial features. There was a determined look in his eyes. He was a warrior and would be a formidable enemy. He had killed before and wouldn't hesitate to kill again to protect his leader. A third picture showed a huge black man with a scruffy beard. Again, she studied the eyes and said to the computer screen, "And you sir, are a fraud. Your appearance is a disarming façade. You're supposed to be the

muscle, the knuckle-dragger, but you're much more than that."
Intelligent eyes. Another formidable foe. The final photograph
was of a Chinese military officer. His eyes were cold and empty,
completely unreadable. He didn't seem to fit in with the rest of
the group.

She never knew the identity of the contractor but always
insisted on a target's background. She typed:

Why?

The screen read:

**International arms dealers…supply terror organi-
zations. Responsible for the deaths of thousands.**

Most paid assassins wouldn't concern themselves as to
why these four men were being targeted. However, she always
insisted on a reason. If it wasn't satisfactory, she reserved the
right to refuse any contract offer. She poised her fingers over the
keyboard and typed in the message:

Contract amount?

When she saw the numbers, she blinked several times to
be sure she was reading them accurately:

**One for the first and five hundred each for the
other three.**

"That's a two and a half million-dollar contract for four
men!" It was by far the largest one she had ever been offered. She
could retire. She typed:

Accepted. Where, when, and in what order?

After several seconds, the screen replied:

**Paris—leave immediately. Further information
upon arrival. Marriott Champs-Elysees. Client
will contact you directly.**

Her fingers curled over the keys:

**That's not how we do this. I only deal with you.
Never directly with the client.**

Carla read the response:

**I understand but the client insists. You will
need extra assistance for this job and the client
has an entire network under his command. This**

is ten times greater than any previous contract. Make it work.

The screen went blank.

TWENTY-ONE

Charles de Galle Airport
Paris, France
The week of YAOGUAI

Jacob retrieved his luggage from the baggage carousel. One important item was missing, his Sig Sauer. He couldn't exactly travel on an international flight with a gun, and he felt uncomfortably vulnerable without it. He exited the Charles de Galle Airport. Outside, dozens of taxi drivers honked their horns and jockeyed for a prime position in the pickup area. Exhaust fumes and the screeching of tires assaulted his senses. Some thrived on this level of mayhem, but not Jacob. It was a far cry from the sweet smell of laurel and the peaceful sounds of the mountains surrounding his childhood home in Whitesburg, Kentucky. They were innocent times when every day offered endless possibilities for exploration and adventure.

> *It's also the place where the local sheriff murdered your family, Buddy Boy. Remember that, always. There's evil everywhere. Trust no one.*

In front of him stood a tall man in a black suit and tie. He held a sign with "Savich" printed in large bold letters. Jacob shook his head. He had hoped for a lower profile until he was ready to face his enemies. As the bait, it was a danger he readily accepted, but he didn't want to openly broadcast his arrival at the airport. He didn't plan on exposing his identity until he could control the environment, and right now, Paris was unfamiliar territory. Jacob forced a smile as he approached the man. As was his habit, Jacob completed a visual sweep of the crowd, checking to see if anyone showed any inappropriate interest in him. All looked safe. He slowly exhaled in relief and got into the rear seat.

The driver loaded Jacob's bag into the trunk of the limousine and sat behind the wheel. He looked over his shoulder. "Destination?"

"Hotel Lancaster on Rue de Berri."

"Oui, monsieur." The driver pulled away from the curb and began the twenty-minute drive to the hotel. He said nothing during the short trip.

Quiet was appreciated, not mindless conversation about the sights. He was on a mission and had to think. He needed to lure the enemy out from whatever rock he was hiding under, and he'd have to somehow use Raphael DuBoise to do it. The trick was to stay alive in the process. He opened his secure iPad and read the message Mr. Hamilton had sent. It contained vital information about Curt McClure, his embassy contact.

McClure had been a twenty-year veteran of the CIA. Initially, he was recruited out of the Georgetown University Law Center after demonstrating excellent cunning and athletic ability. At "The Farm" training facility, his superiors quickly came to appreciate his special skills in covert field operations. That's where he began his successful career. He earned his stripes in Somalia, Afghanistan and Iraq doing black-ops work. It was in Iraq where he sustained shrapnel wounds to his left knee. The injury resulted in a total knee replacement that rendered him unqualified for the field work he loved. Therefore, he was transferred to his present position at the U.S. embassy in Paris. Jacob noticed Winston's handwritten note at the bottom of the official report: "Not cut out for a desk job. He'll wither away in that position. Could be an excellent asset!"

On the surface, it appeared as though Curt McClure was a solid man who had more than paid his dues for his country, but outside his team, Jacob trusted only a small handful of individuals. People had a tendency to change over the years and it wasn't always for the better. He would take things slowly with

McClure until he could get a more accurate assessment of exactly who he was now.

It was mid-afternoon by the time Jacob reached his hotel. The doorman removed his luggage from the car and carried it up a short flight of marble stairs to the front desk where he presented his passport and signed the necessary registration papers.

Jacob entered the penthouse suite and checked every room, searching for areas of vulnerability and potential escape. Nice place, but not really his style. Winston always did everything first class, except when he couldn't. That's usually when the mission got down and dirty. That was where Jacob felt most comfortable. Dark streets and alleyways were a safe refuge for those who didn't want to be noticed until the time was right. The problem was that he couldn't meet up with a professional museum tour guide if he didn't look the part. That meant a high-profile presence. Jacob took a quick shower, changed into khaki pants and put on a navy-blue blazer over a long-sleeved blue, button down shirt. He returned to the front desk.

"May I assist you, sir?" asked the clerk.

"How far is it to the Place de la Concorde?"

"Around two kilometers. You can easily walk there by heading East down the Champs Élysées, or I can have the doorman hail a cab for you."

Though he would normally prefer to walk, Jacob was running a little behind schedule. "Thanks, a cab would be great." By the time he exited the lobby doors, the car was already waiting for him.

"Bonjour, monsieur. What is your destination this afternoon?" asked the driver in a heavy French accent.

"Two Avenue Gabriel," Jacob replied.

"Yes, sir. The United States Embassy?"

"That's correct. Take me to the front entrance."

"I hope you have an appointment. Ever since the terror attacks in Paris, security has been very tight there."

Jacob didn't reply. Five minutes later the cab pulled up to the front of the embassy, a three-acre piece of American soil in the middle of Paris, governed solely by the laws of the United States. Surrounded by a tall wrought iron fence, the embassy building was a four-story structure designed to be in architectural harmony with the rest of the nearby French buildings. Ten feet in front of that barrier, rows of steel-reinforced concrete columns protected against any attempt to ram through the outer perimeter defenses with a car bomb. The front entrance faced the magnificent gardens around the Champs Élysées where thousands of tourists and local Parisians strolled about enjoying the sunny afternoon. Jacob walked up to the security gate and was immediately met by a U.S. Marine in formal uniform. Several others kept a close eye on him from twenty feet away, hands on their sidearms.

"May I help you sir?" asked the marine with a no-nonsense tone.

"Yes, sergeant. I have an appointment to see Mr. Curt McClure."

The guard held out his hand. "Passport?"

Jacob handed over his passport. The booklet was run through a scanner. A brief call later, he was allowed to enter the grounds, still under the watchful eyes of the marine guards. He walked across a cobblestone courtyard and past a bronze statue of Benjamin Franklin, the first U.S. ambassador to France. The front doors of the embassy building were guarded by two more marines, also in full military dress. An American flag flew proudly above them.

Inside, a wide marble staircase dominated the lobby. The seal of the Department of State of the United States decorated the wall above it while statues of George Washington and Marquis de Lafayette, heroes of the American Revolution were poised on either side of the room. Jacob was met by a receptionist who escorted him up the flight of stairs and down a hallway to a small office furnished with a white French Provincial desk and two plush leather chairs. A man about his own age with rust-colored hair entered. Jacob noticed he walked with a slight limp. He extended his hand and introduced himself. "Dr. Savich, I'm

Curt McClure."

The man scrutinized Jacob for a few seconds. "I don't know exactly who you are, Dr. Savich, but you must have some major connections in very high places. I was given specific instructions to help you with anything you need." McClure stepped closer and smiled. It was a fake, predatory grin like you would expect from a used car salesman. "What is it that you want from me?"

"For now," Jacob said, "let's simply say I'm a tourist who wants to get a better feel for the lay of the land here. I don't want to wander into some neighborhood where I don't need to be."

McClure took a seat behind the desk and motioned for Jacob to sit in one of the chairs. "A tourist? Hardly. Let's be straight with each other, Dr. Savich. You're no more a tourist here in Paris than I am. In one way or another we probably work for the same boss. I have a level five security clearance, so let's put our cards on the table and maybe we can help each other."

"Fair enough, Mr. McClure." Jacob had no intention of revealing all his cards.

"Curt."

"Jacob."

"Alright, Jacob, tell me what's going on and the real purpose behind why you're here."

"We have reason to believe that a major attack against the United States is in the planning stages. Our investigation has led us to possible terrorist cells in Europe. It's our feeling that everything is being coordinated from Paris. Have you uncovered anything that might support our theory?"

McClure retrieved a Montblanc pen from his coat pocket and twirled it around in his fingers. "It wouldn't surprise me. The European Union has created a mess for itself, and France is no exception. There's a ticking time bomb here and the governments of Europe have set the fuse themselves. In an attempt to embrace cultural diversification, the countries have left their doors wide open to a wave of immigrants from the Middle East. It's been going on for decades and without any effective vetting process. They have no idea who's actually crossing their borders. Providing refuge for the displaced was a noble concept, but it resulted in the creation of multiple, self-contained parallel societies within major European cities. Rather than becoming assimilated into the local culture, they have segregated themselves from mainstream European society. The immigrants have established their own communities governed by laws based upon Islamic doctrine."

"The No-Go zones?" asked Jacob.

"Exactly." McClure leaned forward, encroaching on Jacob's space, still twirling his damn pen. It was a power play. He obviously didn't like an outsider working his territory. Jacob countered by leaning closer. Message sent and received. McClure retreated and continued. "The official position of the European central government is that such 'No-Go' regions don't exist. That claim is a misdirected denial spawned by the politically correct movement. The fact is that multiple studies have confirmed the existence of the zones and they can readily be found in cities throughout Europe. In France alone, they've been documented in Marseille, Roubaix, and especially here, in Paris. If you talk in private to local officials, they readily admit to the presence of the zones. The police tend to give the areas a wide birth. The rule of democratic law is ignored. Even the peaceful Muslims fear for their lives if they fail to support the jihadist agenda. God protect any unwary tourists like yourself who might wander in by mistake. Odds are they won't make it out unless it's on a stretcher. If local police attempt to enforce the law in those communities, central governments restrict them from taking any aggressive measures for fear that any assertive action would disrupt the potential for social peace."

"I personally have no problem with immigration as long as it follows the dictates of the law and if a strict vetting process is in place," said Jacob.

"Same here, but too many of the politicians in Europe feel otherwise and have turned a blind eye to the present problem. Some in the news media try to claim that the rise in the number of radical Islamist attacks in France is the result of high unemployment and poor living conditions in the Muslim zones. That's hogwash. For most, their lives here are the equivalent of a middle-class life in their native countries. Relatively speaking, things are much better for them in Europe. The primary reason for the increase in jihad activity in Europe has little to do with the living conditions and everything to do with the fact that the radicals simply hate our Western culture. Most of the Muslim community would like to live in peaceful coexistence, but the radicals want to destroy our civilization. They despise our freedom of choice. Democracy is an anathema to them, and they are fighting to replace it with Sharia Law."

McClure continued, still twirling the pen. "The 'No-Go' zones have become ripe recruiting grounds for the jihadists. Radical mullahs have been free to distort the Muslim religion and brainwash young men into killing innocent civilians in the name of Allah. They have been able to plan and carry out raids against the general public with impunity. It began with the attacks at the Charlie Hebdo offices."

Christ! Does this guy ever stop talking? You keep flipping that pen around and I'm going to shove it into your right eye. Why don't you shut him up, Buddy Boy?

Not now. This guy wasn't the enemy. He may need McClure.

"They lambasted Islam, but they've also ridiculed everyone and everything else that represents the western establishment. Twelve innocent people were gunned down that day."

"I guess that opened the door to the Paris nightclub attacks and the slaughter in Nice," said Jacob.

"One hundred thirty people killed and hundreds more injured. That's only the tip of the iceberg. It hasn't received much press, but dozens of churches have been burned or vandalized recently. Christian clergy have been murdered. I'm not surprised that Paris might be the command center for the next major assault against the U.S."

Jacob leaned forward in his chair. "I think you need to speak to the ambassador and ask him to warn the French president. They should look beyond the attacks themselves. There's a bigger endgame here and it's being coordinated by a sophisticated multilayered organization."

"ISIS?" asked McClure. "I had hoped that when their plans to establish a caliphate in the Middle East failed, their organization would fragment. I guess they're still are a significant threat to the West."

"They're certainly a major part of the equation, but there are more groups involved in whatever's happening. Their financial backing is extensive and so convoluted it's been impossible to track down the sources of their funds. Something bigger than isolated terror attacks is going on here, something which might affect the entire world."

"Like what?"

None of your goddamn business. Come on Buddy boy.
Just for fun, take the damn pen, and stomp on it.

Jacob tried to concentrate as the Entity infiltrated his thinking. "I'm not sure yet." He leaned back in his chair. "Have you ever heard of the term, 'Yaoguai?'"

McClure shook his head. "No, the name hasn't come up in any of our briefings. What is it?"

"That's one of the major reasons I'm in Paris. It has to do with the impending attack, but we don't know what it is. I'm here to find out. How about a Raphael DuBoise? Have you seen his name show up on any of your terrorist watch lists?"

McClure finally set the pen down and shook his head again. "Raphael, like the Italian Renaissance painter? No, I haven't seen the name. Is he a terror cell leader?"

"I don't know that either, but I plan to find out."

The two men talked for another half-hour. McClure was a loudmouth but looked to be a person who could be trusted. Still, Jacob didn't want to discuss his plans in any more detail. Thank God, the Entity was finally quiet. He excused himself and promised McClure that he would keep him apprised of anything he might uncover.

It had been a pleasantly warm afternoon with the sun shining brightly through the occasional wispy cloud. It was getting late, but the park across from the U.S. embassy was still crowded with tourists and native Parisians enjoying the final hours of daylight. Unbeknownst to Jacob, one of them was the spotter. He wore sunglasses and a thick, black beard. The park bench had been carefully selected to provide him with a direct view of the entrance to the U.S. embassy. It was the same position he had occupied every day for the past two weeks. He pretended to feed the birds when he noticed the embassy front doors finally open. His target had been inside for over two hours. The spotter took off his sunglasses and rechecked the photograph stored on his iPhone. There was no doubt in his mind. It was him! He placed the call. "You were correct. Praise be to Allah. He is here."

"Are you certain it's him?"

"Absolutely. What would you have me do next?"

"Follow him and find out where he's headed. Be careful, he's smart and very dangerous. Stay far behind. If there's the slightest chance he might notice you, break off the surveillance. We already know where he's going to be in the morning. Be there early and keep me posted.

TWENTY-TWO

Louvre Museum
Paris, France

The following morning, Jacob dressed in his usual blue blazer over a white polo shirt, khaki slacks and comfortable walking shoes. Even at forty-three, he still had the same body and reflexes that had helped him become an All-American quarterback in college. After a light breakfast, he exited through the hotel lobby and headed east down the massive thoroughfare of the Champs Élysées. It was time for Dr. Jacob Savich to meet Mr. Raphael DuBoise. He strolled past the throngs of tourists who were already lined up to enter one of the many exclusive stores along both sides of the famous Parisian avenue. Guards stood outside, limiting entrance to only a small manageable number of patrons at a time. Jacob slowly shook his head in bewilderment. So many people waiting in line for hours simply for the privilege of spending thousands of dollars on a purse or a new pair of shoes. The Avenue was admittedly exquisite, but much too crowded and materialistic for his taste.

Fifteen minutes later, he reached his destination. As instructed by the tour company, he waited in front of the famous Arch du Carrousel at the far end of the Champs Élysées Park. Behind it, the Louvre Museum wrapped itself around an immense plaza, consumed by a multitude of gardens, triangular pools and fountains, their angles complimenting a huge glass pyramid standing in the center. It had to be over seventy-feet tall. He bought a can of Diet Coke from one of the nearby vendors and continued to scan the crowd, searching for the mysterious Raphael DuBoise. An uneasy feeling prickled at the back of his neck. He was certain he was being watched, although the feeling wasn't a complete surprise. The terrorists who had failed to kill his team in West Virginia were lurking out there somewhere, ready for another opportunity to take him out at the right moment. Drawing them into the daylight was the plan, but it was happening sooner than he had expected. He needed to identify them before they found him. Out of habit, he patted at the small of his back, under his blazer where he usually wore the holster for his 9mm Sig Sauer. He didn't have it. *Shit! I'm a sitting duck out here.*

"Dr. Savich?" a soft voice inquired from behind him. He turned around to see a petite woman, around five-four and in her mid-thirties. She wore a short black skirt, cream silk blouse and low business heels. A solitaire diamond pendant hung from her slender neck. She extended her hand. "Bonjour, I'm Raphael DuBoise. You've scheduled several private museum tours with me over the next few days." Her voice was lyrical, caressing each syllable as she spoke. Her English was perfect with a charming French accent.

He accepted her handshake. "You're Raphael? I was expecting—"

"A man?"

"Well, ah, yes after the tour company gave me your name."

Raphael stared down at the stone pavement for a second and kicked a cigarette butt into the grass. "A gift from my parents, I'm afraid. They were both artists who achieved a moderate amount of acclaim here in Paris. Like many in the creative arts they had a quirky sense of humor."

"Hence, they gave you the name of an Italian Renaissance painter—and a man at that."

She shrugged with a pouty smile. "And the fact that they were expecting a boy. They had the name pre-selected. I believe I was a bit of a disappointment."

"I seriously doubt that. Raphael is a beautiful name, and perfectly fitting for a very lovely woman." Jacob realized he was still holding her hand, her skin soft and surprisingly cool. He slowly released it, and his hand felt suddenly cold.

"Still, my burden to bear." She brushed her hair to the side concealing a small scar he noticed over her left eyebrow. She had delicate features and silky dark hair that curled around the sides of her face. She wasn't glamorous but was decidedly beautiful. There was something innately sensual about her voice and the graceful way she moved, a seductive aura that was difficult to ignore. It wasn't contrived, but as natural as her soft blue eyes that became flirtatiously playful when she smiled. She certainly didn't look like a terrorist sympathizer or the key to an attack.

"So, do your parents live here in Paris?" asked Jacob, regretting the question as soon as asked. *Pushing too hard Jacob. Slow down.*

Her smile faded and her face became more somber. "They died when I was only seven. It was a car wreck on the winding roads that overlook Monte Carlo."

"I'm so sorry."

"That's all right. The accident happened a long time ago. It was to be a second honeymoon in celebration of my mother's first solo art exhibition. I was told that an oncoming car took one of the turns too wide and hit my parent's convertible head on. They died instantly." Raphael nibbled at her lower lip and stared into the distance as though her thoughts were lost in the memory. After a few seconds, the moment seemed to pass. The brightness returned to her blue eyes and the captivating smile reappeared. A rush pulsed through his body. What was it: pity, admiration, a physical attraction?

What the fuck is that! the Entity shouted in his ear. *You gotta push that shit aside Buddy Boy. You've only known this woman for what, maybe five minutes? She's probably a terrorist. Then you're gunna have to kill her before she kills you! Don't let your dick get in the way of your head.*

She stepped back. "Enough with the talk about me, Dr. Savich. We have a busy day ahead of us and some magnificent works of art to see. Are you ready to begin the tour?"

"Yes, but first I have a question." He gazed toward the huge glass pyramid occupying the middle of the Louvre courtyard.

She grinned. "You're wondering about La Pyramide?"

"Yes, it's just that it seems . . ."

"Out of place?"

"Yes."

"You're not alone in your feelings," she said. "It's been the source of a great deal of controversy in our city for decades. Some love it while many refer to it as an obnoxious monstrosity." She leaned into him and whispered. "Personally, I hate it, but don't tell anyone I said that. I could lose my job. I think it destroys the elegance of the Louvre's classical French Baroque Architecture." She swept her hand toward the museum. "At one time, these buildings comprised one of the largest Royal Palaces in the world. It was a majestic structure." She crinkled her nose as she leaned closer and placed her hand on his arm. "But now, with the pyramid, I'm afraid it looks more like a Disney theme park."

The scent of her perfume wafted over him, disrupting his thoughts. He ran his fingers through his hair, pushing it back from his forehead trying to clear his mind. *She's distracting me. On purpose? Is she setting me up?* He eyed his surroundings, checking for a blindside attack, but saw nothing. Jacob refocused on the conversation. "How did the pyramid come about if so many disliked it?"

"There were those who believed the Louvre was getting too stale. They claimed that it had to be brought into the modern era, so Francois Mitterrand, the president of France at the time, commissioned a committee to solicit recommendations on how to enhance the museum's appearance. Unfortunately, his mistress was a curator at the Louvre, and she was appointed as chairwoman of the search committee. Of all the presentations, she preferred the pyramid design and lobbied Francois hard to back her. The rest is history."

"His mistress? How could you possibly know that?"

Raphael again nibbled on her lower lip. "Everyone knew about it. This is Paris, after all. Extramarital love affairs are a part of life here. Besides, he was my great-uncle."

"Francois Mitterrand was your uncle?"

"Yes, but again, the conversation seems to have drifted back to me and my family history. Today is about you." She checked her watch. "We should begin the tour. The Louvre is the largest and most famous art museum in the world. It would take us weeks to see everything and you have only scheduled three hours. We'd better get started and focus on the highlights. Once inside, we'll start with the Mona Lisa."

Before entering, Jacob scanned his surroundings. He couldn't shake the feeling that he was being set up. Problem number one, he had no idea what they looked like. Problem number two, he didn't have a gun.

You have a third problem, Buddy Boy. That little cutie standing next to you is probably one of them.

TWENTY-THREE

Café Du Monde
Paris, France

They were getting ready to exit the museum when Raphael asked, "Is there anything else you'd like to see Dr. Savich?"

Jacob turned to look her in the eyes. "We've known each other for over four hours now, and I think we should be on a first name basis. You can call me Jacob."

She blushed. "And you can call me Raphael."

"Which I've already been doing all morning."

"So, what did you think of the Louvre, Doctor . . . I mean, Jacob?"

"It's an amazing place, one of the most impressive museums I've ever visited. I must admit, the Mona Lisa was a little less than I had expected."

"It is disappointingly small, isn't it? That's what most people say."

"And yet, it's obviously the most popular work at the Louvre. I know it was painted by Leonardo da Vinci but what makes it so valuable? He has other excellent works like 'The Last Supper,' and 'The Virgin of the Rocks.' There must be a hundred other paintings in the museum with the same degree of artistic content and value."

"That's true. It might be the Mona Lisa's enigmatic smile or maybe her mysterious identity which has been the source of endless academic speculation in the art world. It didn't enjoy its present level of notoriety until it was stolen from the Louvre in 1911. The citizens of Paris were devastated, and it remained missing for over two years. It was found hidden under a false bottom in a handyman's trunk. The story made the Mona Lisa a media sensation and it's been the world's most famous painting ever since."

"I'm not surprised it was taken. There isn't much security in the museum. Some of the most valuable paintings in the world are hanging on the walls, out in the open with no protective glass cases, and only red velvet ropes to keep visitors away."

She smiled. He loved watching her do that. "Rest assured, there's a lot more security than you can see. There must be to protect all the priceless treasures displayed here. You may not notice them but the containment measures are extensive. I wouldn't try to run off with anything. You wouldn't make it more than a few feet before alarms were triggered and steel section gates dropped. Any perpetrator trying to remove a painting would be trapped inside until the security police arrived." She dodged a group of tourists stepping in front of her. "What else caught your attention?"

"Everything was magnificent," said Jacob. "I especially enjoyed Venus de Milo and the Winged Victory of Samothrace sculptures, things I've seen in books but never fully appreciated until I saw them in person today. I never cease to be amazed how ancient sculptors could take a block of cold marble and convert it into a lifelike figure with supple skin and flowing robes. It's almost as though they create life out of inanimate stone."

"You have a greater appreciation of the intricacies of sculpture than most of my clients. If we had more time, I'd show you more pieces, but the museum's just too big to be seen in one day."

"What I found most intriguing was the fact that the Louvre was a royal palace constructed upon the foundation of an old castle during the fourteenth century. It's hard to imagine how the engineers were able to excavate the entire subterranean area under the Louvre, without risking the structural integrity of the buildings. They've even recreated the moat."

Raphael nodded her head. "You'd be amazed at some of the ancient relics and skeletons they found in the process. Many tourists don't realize this, but much of Paris is the same way. It's built over layers of previous civilizations. Running under the city is an entire labyrinthine complex of tunnels, caves, and sewers left over from centuries of limestone mining. It's where the old catacombs are located. Those and the old sewer tunnels are two of the more popular tourist attractions in the city. Much of the system has been mapped, but it's believed that there are still miles and miles of unexplored areas. Every few years, construction workers uncover a new vein and the archeologists get excited."

"Caves always get archeologists excited; the older the caves the more excited they get. I can't blame them though. They're almost like time-travelers, bringing back information about ancient civilizations."

"Most of it is good, but I'm afraid that some is bad," she said.

What did she mean by that? Was she bitter about something? Could it be bad enough to make her a terrorist sympathizer?

The two walked together quietly for a minute. Rachael turned to face him. "You left our afternoon open, Dr—I mean Jacob." Again, there was a slight blush to her cheeks. "What would you like to do now?"

He searched the street. "Are you hungry?"

"Famished. I didn't have time to eat breakfast. There's a quaint sidewalk café a few hundred meters up the street and it's a perfect afternoon for people-watching."

"That sounds great, but let's eat inside." He glanced over his shoulder. That prickling at the back of his neck would not go away. Sitting outside in the open made him uncomfortable.

When they turned to head toward the restaurant, Jacob bumped into a heavily bearded man. The guy's sunglasses were knocked to the ground and a book fell out of his hands. "I'm so sorry. I wasn't looking where I was going." Jacob bent down to pick up the glasses and the book. It was a copy of *Les Misérables* by Victor Hugo. When he returned it to the owner, the man didn't reply. He glared at Jacob with dark eyes, ominous and angry. *The guy's pissed about something, but what? He stepped almost directly in front of me. The collision was his fault as much as mine.*

"I'm sorry," Jacob repeated. The man rebuffed him with a scowl. He replaced his sunglasses, grabbed his book, and rushed away. Curt McClure had warned him about the pickpockets who like to work the crowds in tourist areas. Jacob checked his back pocket for his wallet. It was still there. He looked at Raphael, who could only shrug one slender shoulder.

"Sorry. Some Parisians seem perpetually angry."

"How could anyone be angry while living in this beautiful city?" Within ten minutes, they reached their destination. The sign over the restaurant read Café Du Monde, as charming as Raphael described. They shared it with three other couples, apparently tourists involved in an animated discussion, about what, Jacob couldn't tell. Two lovers sat at a table to their right. They were holding hands across the table and staring into each other's eyes, unaware of any other presence in the café. They both wore wedding rings. Were they married to each other? *Probably not.*

There were no apparent threats, but Jacob requested a small bistro table in the rear that faced the front door and allowed him to monitor the entrance and sidewalk traffic. The waiter asked for a wine order and Jacob deferred to Raphael. "You probably appreciate the subtleties of French wines better than me. Why don't you select one?" There was no better way to loosen a person's tongue than several glasses of good wine. They shared a cheese and olive plate over a bottle of French chardonnay. He raised his glass to Raphael's in a toast. "To art."

"To art," she replied and took a sip.

He cut several slices of bread from a French baguette and placed one on her plate. He was still trying to get a read on her. Usually, he could size up another person without difficulty, but Raphael was different. Who was she? And who was following him? Was it because of her?

He decided to take a more direct approach. "So, tell me

about yourself. Who is Raphael DuBoise?" He poured them each another glass of wine.

She again nibbled at her lip. *Disarming.* "Like I mentioned earlier this morning," she said, "my parents died when I was a little girl. I spent most of my life here in Paris where I was raised by my Uncle Philippe."

"Philippe DuBoise?"

"Oh, no, no. Philippe Mitterand, my mother's brother. He's been my guardian ever since my parents died."

"And I assume he's also related to the former French president?"

"Yes, the Mitterand family is large and still quite influential around Paris."

"And is Philippe also involved in politics?" It might explain why Raphael could be the key.

Raphael giggled. "Goodness no! Uncle Philippe detests politicians. He thinks they're all corrupt scoundrels."

Jacob chuckled in return. "In my experience, your uncle's opinion isn't far from the truth. It's a universal problem, I'm afraid."

"Power corrupts," she said. A scowl crossed her face, but it did nothing to deter her innocent beauty.

"And absolute power corrupts absolutely," added Jacob as he completed the quote by Lord Acton. "So, what does your uncle do?"

"He works for Parisian Telecom."

"The huge telecommunications company? That sounds fascinating. What's he do there?"

"He was vice-president in charge of acquisitions and development. A few years ago, he was promoted to president of the company. It was a well-deserved promotion, but he's been extremely busy interfacing France's systems with the rest of Europe. As a result, I don't get to see him as often as I'd like."

Jacob considered this new information. That might be the reason why Raphael could be the key to whatever was going on, but what would a terrorist organization want with a telecommunications company? "Well, your family certainly is influential."

Raphael took a sip of wine and didn't comment. She pulled at a loose thread on her skirt and looked uncomfortable. He had been pushing too hard for personal information. He waited for her to take over the conversation.

"And what about you? Who is Dr. Jacob Savich?"

He gave her a history that was partially true. He had also been orphaned as a child. He and his sister had been raised by their grandmother in an impoverished small coal town in Kentucky.

Raphael's eyes lit up in recognition. "The horse racing and bourbon state?"

"Exactly. I'm kind of surprised you'd know about that."

"I've read a lot about America. Of course, I've never been there, but it seems to be a beautiful country with a rich history."

They didn't sound like the words of a terrorist who hated America. "After college I attended medical school and then went on to become a plastic surgeon in Cincinnati, Ohio."

"The Buckeye State."

"Yes." He laughed. "Again, you impress me with your knowledge of my country."

"And your surgical background explains your interest in art?"

"Possibly. That and I've been sculpting in wood since I was a little boy." *The only way I could capture the essence of the evil people I killed.* By preserving their image in wood, he controlled them.

They continued with small talk for the next hour as Jacob tried to get a better understanding of who Raphael DuBoise was. She was a little elusive and he didn't learn much more, other than the fact that she was exceptionally bright and loved what she did. After they finished the last of the wine, Jacob grabbed the check just as she was reaching for it. He scanned the sidewalk in both directions before they left to continue their tour.

TWENTY-FOUR

Basilique du Sacré-Coeur
MontmartreParis, France

"What would you like to see now, Jacob?" Raphael asked as they stood on the sidewalk.

He didn't respond. He was lost in thought, again experiencing the nagging feeling that he was being watched. He took Raphael's hand and cut across several streets. Pretending to shop, he looked in a number of display windows, checking the reflection to see if he could identify a tail on the other side of the street. Seeing none, he backtracked down several narrow side streets that also provided an excellent opportunity to check for a shadow. Still, he saw no suspicious activity.

If they're following me, they're good.

Raphael seemed confused by the apparent aimless wandering around. "Maybe I should lead the way," she said. He didn't reply. It was hard to think of her as being part of a large terror organization, but serious questions remained unanswered. She could very well have an associate following them.

When they passed a camera store, it gave him an idea. He stopped and turned to Raphael. "Let's duck in here for a minute. There's something I need."

"You go ahead. I think I'll wait out here and enjoy the afternoon."

When he exited the store five minutes later, he had a pair of binoculars hanging from his neck. They were capable of taking high resolution photographs through a sophisticated lens system. He was surprised to find Raphael talking on cell a phone. She closed it abruptly when she saw him. "Needed to check on my messages."

What's that about? Talking to a partner? Maybe the one following him? Planning a good spot for a shot to the head or a knife in the ribs?

She stared at the binoculars. "I thought you went in to buy a camera."

"I need these to get a closeup view of the sights. This is what I use for photographs." He pulled out his cell phone. "In fact, I think right now would be a good time for a selfie." He looked around and found what he wanted. He put his arm around her waist and positioned the two of them with a background containing two tall towers. They looked to be less than a quarter mile away. He took the photograph.

"Before you do anything with that picture, like posting it on Facebook, let me see it first. I have veto power." She laughed and studied the photograph. Apparently, it met with her approval. "OK."

Jacob fiddled with the phone for a minute, pretending to save the picture to his photo album. In fact, he was forwarding it to Winston Hamilton's office with the note:

Run this through our facial recognition programs. Need to find out who this woman is. On any terrorist watch lists?

He pushed the send button and turned to her. "Saved for posterity. A perfect couple." After again showing her the selfie, he pointed to the two towers behind them. "What are these?" He already knew the answer.

"Those are the bell towers of the Cathedral Notre Dame de Paris."

"The one that burned?"

"Yes, but the president promises to rebuild it."

"Is it possible to tour it? I'd like to see the artwork and climb the tower to get a better view of Paris."

"I'm afraid its closed to the public and won't be opened again for years. If you want a overall view of the city, there is the Basilique du Sacré-Coeur. I can take you to see that."

"Sacré-Coeur?"

"Sacred Heart as in Jesus. It sits atop Montmartre, the highest point in Paris. The view from the church is breathtaking and should provide the view you're looking for. It's only a ten-minute ride from here and there's a taxi stand just several streets away." She gently took his hand and led him down another group of narrow streets.

> Don't be a fool, Buddy Boy. She's probably leading
> you right into an ambush.

"I don't think so," said Jacob.

"You don't think what, Jacob?"

"Uh, nothing, just saying I don't think it's too far."

She pointed. "The taxi stand is directly ahead."

The cabbie looked to be from the Middle East. *Coincidence?* Maybe, but Jacob never believed in coincidences. Dismissing chance occurrences could be dangerous. A healthy level of paranoia was mandatory in his work. The driver grabbed the steering wheel with tight white knuckles, his head turning from side to side like a bobble-head doll, looking for potential collisions. The possibilities for a crash were endless. The car sped through a roundabout where there were no lines and fewer rules. The drivers changed lanes with complete disregard for other vehicles, passing cars and herds of motor scooters with only inches to spare. Everyone seemed to be in a deadly game of demolition derby. It was like his driver was on a suicide mission or had a death wish.

> He's in cahoots with your pretty little girlfriend,
> Buddy Boy. That's why she was on her damn phone.
> He's trying to kill us!

Raphael must have noticed the look of concern in his eyes. "Many of the cab drivers in Paris are like this. It's a Darwinian thing. Survival of the fittest. You'll get used to it."

When the cab came to a stop, Jacob paid the man and added

a generous tip, thankful he and Raphael were both still alive. They set foot on an old cobblestone street. He craned his neck to look up. The basilica dominated the entire region, towering over the surrounding buildings. It was an impressive sight. To the right stood a funicular that could carry people up the hill. Jacob walked over to buy tickets, but Raphael pulled at his arm and shook her head. "That's no way to see Paris. Getting up there is part of the fun. Come on, Jacob. Bet you can't keep up with me." She laughed and took his hand again. She seemed to do that a lot, not that he minded. He enjoyed the feel of her soft skin against his. The Entity tried to protest but Jacob pushed it aside. They dodged their way through a tapestry of multi-colored blankets covered with displays of knock-off Gucci and Louis Vuitton purses. They walked along the front of the Moulin Rouge cabaret with its giant windmill and headed uphill, passing dozens of low-end bars, kebab shops, and sex stores. It was the perfect place for a hit. Jacob longed for his Sig. He stepped up his pace.

"I know it's a little seedy down here," Raphael said. "The neighborhood can be dangerous at night, but it's perfectly safe during the day. Things will get much better as we head uphill."

Raphael was right. As they continued their climb, the neighborhood became a maze of small streets, each taking on a more Bohemian look. The porno stores below were replaced by quaint boutiques, sidewalk cafes, and art galleries. Garish neon signs yielded to antique streetlamps and tree-lined streets. Ivy and hanging flowers cascaded down from old window boxes. The scent of French pastry shops and chocolate stores wafted through the air. The poetic charm was intoxicating to the point of distraction. *Stay focused, Jacob. Someone around here might be targeting you right now.*

Throngs of tourists pushed closer together as everyone was funneled to the same spot near the top of Montmartre. Jacob didn't mind the crowd. The more people around him the less likelihood there would be of a blindside attack. He stopped to take in the surroundings. It was a delightful afternoon. The skies were blue, and a gentle breeze provided welcomed relief from the heat of the climb. The Sacré-Coeur church stood several-hundred feet above them. The white travertine stone cast a heavenly glow in the sunlight, several large arabesque domes creating the appearance of a giant wedding cake. Two patina covered bronze equestrian statues stood guard atop the church portico.

Raphael noticed him staring. "The one on the right is Saint Joan of Arc holding her sword and on the left is King Saint Louis IX, holding the crown of thorns." Between them a huge statue of Christ, the sacrificial lamb, gazed down upon the multitudes of God's children.

"Come on, Jacob. Only another two hundred steps and we'll be there."

When they reached the cathedral's forecourt, they turned to look down at the enlarging crowd of tourists in the plaza below. A turquoise-topped carousel entertained the young at heart. The soft sounds of a jazz saxophone bled out of a nearby bistro club and drifted across the plaza. Native Parisians and tourists alike sat at tables in front of sidewalk cafes enjoying a glass of wine or espresso. A few white-faced mimes performed their acts and made balloon hats for the children. Local artists stood behind their easels, working to capture the magnificence of the Basilica and its surroundings. Many displayed their works on the pair of stone steps that led up to the base of the church. The grounds in front of the Basilica were terraced with lush green grass and landscaped with flowers. Students sat in small groups, flailing their arms about, probably discussing how they would solve all the problems of Europe. Lovers lay on blankets gazing into each other's eyes, apparently oblivious to the world around them. Hundreds browsed through the many boutique shops, smiling and buying souvenirs. Others sat on park benches to read. Any of the people down below him could be an assassin— maybe none of them, but Jacob still had that feeling. He needed a better view of his surroundings.

Before he could speak, Raphael said, "We must go inside. It's not as grand as Notre Dame but it's beautiful." She released his hand as they entered through a massive bronze door decorated with scenes of Christ's life. It was cool inside, and the lights were kept low to protect the works of art inside. The footprint of the basilica was that of a Greek cross. Byzantine arches supporting the soaring ceiling drew the eyes upward as though looking up toward heaven. *Probably the architect's intent.* The distal end of the nave was dominated by a magnificent bronze altar, topped by an immense mosaic of Jesus and His Sacred Heart, the cathedral's namesake.

"It's one of the largest mosaics in the world," said Raphael. "It's a depiction of Jesus after His resurrection."

"Amazing," said Jacob, but what caught his eyes the most was the huge dome in the ceiling directly above the architectural center of the building.

"After the Eiffel Tower, it's the highest point in Paris," said Raphael. "It has a wonderful observation deck."

Exactly what Jacob was looking for. "How do we get up there?" he asked. "Maybe an elevator?"

Raphael giggled and pointed. "The entrance is on the outside. No elevator though. Three hundred narrow steps."

Jacob groaned. "More climbing." He pretended to protest but his original intention was to get the best view of Paris he could. They found the entrance on the left and began the climb. Even though he ran five miles most days, he had to stop halfway to catch his breath. "They should have an elevator."

Raphael giggled, not a bit short of breath. How does she do that? Is she more than just a museum guide? Does she train? When they reached the observation platform, they were alone. *A perfect place to take me out if that's her intent.* He balanced his weight over the balls of his feet, preparing himself for an attack, but none came.

The circular observation platform surrounded the entire base of the dome's exterior. A curved stone wall in the middle, separated the deck from the interior of the dome. Along the periphery, multiple Byzantine arched openings, supported by travertine columns, provided the panoramic view. Clouds were beginning to gather and the gentle breeze wafting across the plaza below was, at this higher elevation, a strong crosswind with intermittent heavy gusts. Jacob leaned out to gaze at the Paris skyline. He was overwhelmed. It was, without doubt, the magnificent panoramic view he wanted. All of Paris spread out before him. It made him forget about the burning in his legs. Another distraction.

Raphael stood next to him, pointing out the sights. She leaned closer, her right arm pressing against his, her skin cool and inviting. It seemed natural, lacking any indication of being contrived or sexual. At the same time, it wouldn't take much to push him over the platform's wall. He leaned back.

"Directly below us, you can see the Montmartre neighborhood. From up here it appears smaller than it looks when you wander through the narrow streets." She gazed ahead. "If you look straight out, you can see the Champs-Élysées with the Arch de Triomphe standing at its north end. To the left of that is the Eiffel Tower, a little over four kilometers away."

"What's that structure with the large gold dome?" He pointed to the building a little to the west.

"That's the Hotel de Invalides. It's the site of Napoleon's tomb. We can see it tomorrow if you'd like."

"I'd enjoy that," he said though sightseeing was the furthest thing from his mind He had a purpose in being up here.

"If you look carefully, you can see the Seine River in the distance. There's a Riverwalk that runs along the water. Dozens of floating restaurants and night clubs line the walkway. It's a romantic place to visit for dinner and drinks with a loved one." She blushed. She did that a lot along with the hand holding. "Everything to the left of the river is called the 'Left Bank' and everything to the right . . ."

"Is the Right Bank," he said, finishing her sentence.

"Yes." She jabbed him lightly with her elbow. "You're stealing my lines. If you keep it up, you won't need a guide." They laughed.

Jacob returned to the real business of why he wanted to climb the tower. It wasn't for the view. He lifted his special binoculars and scanned the crowd below as tourists wandered about. He needed a face. When he checked the terraced steps, he noticed the angry man he had bumped into at the Louvre. *Another coincidence? Maybe, but maybe not.* Sometimes, it simply took a while to uncover the connections. He forced himself to raise his level of awareness. The man was sitting and talking on a cell phone. He didn't look like a tail, but Jacob snapped several pictures of him anyway. He scanned the rest of the mall and took a few more photos of suspicious looking characters through his special binoculars.

He examined the windows of the buildings around the neighborhood. They were clear. He systematically scanned the rooftops of the closest buildings and then worked out from there. Jacob almost missed him. He was positioned several hundred yards away, on the roof of one of the tallest buildings behind the turquoise carousel. He zoomed in closer. His heart did a skip. It wasn't a man at all, but a woman, and she was adjusting the sights on a high-powered rifle. He had only a second to snap a few pictures before she aimed the rifle in his direction. He dropped to the deck and pulled Raphael down with him. At the same instant, a cracking sound shattered the quiet as small pieces of the travertine stone column broke off, showering them with debris.

He looked up. *Holy shit, that was close.* The bullet struck less than an inch from where his head had been seconds ago. He jumped up to recheck the shooter's position with the binoculars. She was gone. *Probably assumes she got me and left.* She might have if it hadn't been for the strong crosswind.

Raphael's eyes widened. "What was that all about?"

"I stumbled. I must be a little more tired than I thought. My legs gave out after climbing all those steps."

She giggled. "Or maybe it was the two bottles of wine we shared at lunch."

"Maybe. It was more wine than I'm used to drinking." He helped Raphael up and she brushed stone fragments off her skirt. She reached up and teased several strands of hair back down

147

over the scar over her left eye.

He stared at her. How did the shooter know he would be up in the dome? Did Raphael set it up? Did she give some kind of a signal? It would have been difficult. He'd been at her side ever since they met in front of the Louvre. *Except when I went into the camera store.* Did she call the shooter to say where they would be? She was the one who insisted that they take the time to tour the inside, which was to be expected from a guide, but maybe she was buying time for a sniper to get into position. It didn't make sense, though. It was his idea that they climb up the dome in the first place. *At least I think it was. Still . . .*

"Jacob?" asked Raphael. "Are you all right?"

"Uh, yeah. I hit my head when I fell. It left me a little stunned, but I'm fine now. We can head back down."

QUANTUM

TWENTY-FIVE

La Travesia Café
Near MontmartreParis, France

Jacob was right. He had been followed. At least now, he had a
face, maybe two.

When they left Sacré-Coeur, they headed down the steps
for the cover of the nearby trees lining the plaza. The clouds
brought a gentle rain and he led Raphael down several side streets
until they were able to take cover in a small corner café, one of
hundreds of such obscure little bistros along the side streets and
alleys of the region. It was the Café La Travesia. He selected a table
inside where he could keep an eye on the sidewalk and entrance.
He needed more time with Raphael, time to figure out how she
fit into the whole terrorist equation and what had just happened
on the church's observation platform. She seemed unaware, but
maybe she was just a good actress.

"I need a drink after all that," he said.

"More wine? Are you sure?" asked Raphael. "Alcohol
might not be such a good idea after a head injury."

"It's okay. Trust me, I'm a doctor."

She chuckled. "That sounds like a bad punchline from a
worse joke." They both laughed and made small talk, discussing
the sights at the Sacré-Coeur over another glass of wine and a
snack of escargot. A small candle sat in the middle of the table,
separating them, its light flickering in her eyes. Is was difficult to

not get lost in them.

Stay focused, Buddy Boy.

Jacob guided the conversation back to her, searching for any signs of deceit. There were none. Her eyes lingered on his, then turned away.

"So tell me, how does Raphael DuBoise, niece of Francois Mitterand wind up as a tour guide at the Louvre?" Jacob asked while keeping an eye on the front door.

"Actually, I'm not limited to the Louvre. I host tours for museums all over France, but mostly in Paris." She nibbled at her lip. So distracting. "Since I was a little girl, I've had an interest in French history. In fact, it was my major in college. Like my parents, I also enjoyed painting, but I'm afraid I wasn't very good, at least not good enough to make a living at it."

"So, you combined your two passions and became a museum tour guide," said Jacob.

"I guess that's pretty much it. My family has money, but I prefer to make it on my own."

"Do you enjoy what you do?" he asked.

"Oh, I love it most of the time. I seem to learn something new during each tour, but some clients can be a little too demanding. I think you Americans call them pains in the bottom."

"Something like that." Jacob chortled.

She must have realized what she had said. She reached across the table and grabbed his hand. "But not you Jacob, you're not a pain in the bottom. You've been a delight…other than your tendency to fall down and hit your head."

Jacob tried to look hurt, started to smile, then began laughing. She joined him and Jacob ordered another glass of wine for each of them. She swirled her glass and took a sip. "Earlier today you mentioned that you sculpt."

"Yes, I work mostly with various types of wood." He inhaled the wine's bouquet and studied how the liquid clung to the inside of his glass.

"Have you ever displayed your work?"

"Done a few shows around Cincinnati and one in New

York. I've sold several pieces, but like you said earlier, I'm not good enough to make a living with it."

"I'd love to see some of your pieces. Do you have any pictures?"

"I'm afraid you might be disappointed." He pulled out his cell phone and showed her photos of a half dozen of his favorite sculptures.

She looked at them and her eyes grew wide, zooming back and forth between them. "Your works are abstract conflicts of emotions. I can see the subtle lines of human faces in the wood grain of each piece. They're almost Dantesque, appearing to reflect a sense of violence and hopelessness, as though the images are gazing up from the depths of hell."

Jacob suppressed a grin. *That's were I sent them.*

"There's also a poetic tenderness in the flowing lines of your creations."

He didn't respond to the compliment.

Watch out, Buddy Boy. She's just buttering you up,
getting ready for the kill.

"You're a very complicated man, Dr. Jacob Savich." She stared into his eyes and put her hand over his. "You're also extremely talented. I should know. Art is my life and I've seen the best. I could arrange for you to have a show here in Paris if you'd like. My grandfather owns one of the most prestigious art galleries in France."

"Another Mitterrand?" Jacob asked.

Her mouth turned up at the sides. "Oh no, though I must admit, there are a number of them. He's my father's father, Marcelle DuBoise. He's my Pèpére."

"Pèpére?"

"My grandfather. At one time, I used to help him in the art gallery but not as much now since I've become a full-time guide."

Raphael looked at her watch. "Oh, my gosh. Speaking of my grandfather, I'm afraid I must be going. I have a date with him tonight and I'm late. He prepares supper for me every Friday. He's a dreadful cook, but I pretend to enjoy it anyway."

151

Jacob motioned for the waiter to bring their check. When he arrived at the table, Jacob pulled him aside and whispered, "Is there a back door? There happens to be a man outside whose been pestering this woman, and she'd like to avoid him."

"Shall I call the police, sir?"

"That won't be necessary, but if you show us to the back door, it would be greatly appreciated." He gave the man a fifty-Euro tip.

By the time they exited, dusk was settling in. He checked their surroundings. All looked clear and he hailed a cab. He turned to Raphael. "We're supposed to meet for another tour together tomorrow afternoon. I'll leave the schedule up to you."

"Since you have such an interest in sculpture, I think we should visit the Musée d'Orsay. The building was once an ornate train station. It was converted into an art museum that now houses some of the finest works of French Impressionism. It also contains an exquisite collection of priceless works by Rodin and Degas. I think you would enjoy it immensely. We can meet for lunch beforehand if you like."

"I'd enjoy that."

"Let's make it at noon at the Café du Marche on Rue Cler. Do you know where it is?"

"No, but I'll find it." He opened the car door. Should he shake her hand? Maybe kiss her cheek? He did neither. "Thank you for today, Raphael."

"And thank you for a perfectly lovely afternoon. Au revoir, Dr. Jacob Savich." She surprised him by kissing him gently on the cheek, turned, and got into the cab.

Jacob stood on the curb and watched as the car pulled away. He felt alone and a little bewildered.

> *Keep your game hat on and stay focused on the plan, Buddy Boy. Remember, you almost got shot in the head today and that woman of yours probably had something to do with it. Don't forget, you still might have to kill her.*

"Maybe, but she could have just as easily been a victim on

that tower," said Jacob.

Now that doesn't compute at all. She led you there, Buddy Boy. Can you come up with a single scenario to explain today, anything where you'd be the target of an assassination attempt without her somehow being involved?

Of course, the Entity was right. Nothing made any sense, and what was up with the hand holding and touching. Then there was that kiss? He thought of the line from The Godfather movie, "Keep your enemies close."

———————————•❖•———————————

Angry Eyes from the Louvre watched as Jacob left to walk back to his hotel. He had seen the kiss and made note of it. Remaining several blocks behind, he followed Jacob back to the Lancaster hotel. Then he called in his report.

"A kiss?" asked Faizel.

"On the cheek," said Angry Eyes.

"Still, it was a kiss."

"Yes, sir."

"I'll let you know where to be tomorrow."

TWENTY-SIX

Hotel Lancaster
Paris, France

As Jacob made his way back to his hotel, it gave him a chance to try to unravel the mystery of the enigmatic Raphael DuBoise: member of a world-wide terror network, or innocent civilian caught up in something well over her head? The over-riding questions were, if it's the former, what's the connection? How is she the key? Maybe tomorrow's meeting would help to resolve things. Meanwhile, he needed to talk to Mr. Hamilton.

He returned to his room and ordered a rare-steak dinner from room service. By the time he finished showering, it had arrived. After eating, he checked his watch. It was eight o'clock at night in Paris, two in the afternoon Eastern Standard Time in D.C. He picked up his secure cell phone and called Mr. Hamilton's office. The call bypassed his boss's secretary and went directly to a phone sitting on the man's desk.

"Hello, Dr. Savich. How's Paris?"

"Things here are fine considering someone took a shot at me today."

"Someone tried to kill you! Are you alright?"

"Yes. Fortunately, I saw the rifle before the sniper could fire, but it was close."

"I didn't think anyone even knew you were there yet, except Mr. DuBoise," said Mr. Hamilton.

"Obviously, they know me and where I am. I expected

some contact with the enemy but not quite so soon. After they found out we captured Rozhin, they must have figured that I might come to Paris to find Raphael."

"And did you meet him?"

"Yes, but Raphael's not a he. He's a she."

"A woman! That must have been a surprise."

"Yes, it was. I spent over seven hours with her today. That's whose photograph I sent to you earlier."

"Ah, what a pretty companion. This mission of yours appears to have its benefits."

Jacob ignored the comment. "Did you get any hits on the photo?"

"No, I ran it through the Homeland Security and FBI databases. She's not on any of their terrorist watch lists. That leaves us with: who is she and what were you able to find out about her?"

"Can't say for sure, sir. She certainly doesn't fit the profile of a terrorist, but we both know appearances can be deceiving. That's why I called you. I need to find out a few things regarding her family background."

"First let me open up my Homeland Security database." After a minute, he continued, "Okay I'm in. What's the last name?"

"Mitterrand," said Jacob.

"As in Francois Mitterrand, the former President of France?"

Jacob snickered. "Thought that might get your attention."

"He hasn't been in office since 1995 but the Mitterrand family is still an influential force in French politics and business. Do you have a specific family member for me?"

"Yes, how about a Philippe Mitterrand?" Jacob heard Mr. Hamilton type on his computer.

"Here it is, Philippe Mitterrand." He paused to read the information on the screen. "This is interesting. It could be significant. Philippe is president of Parisian Telecom. He was influential in consolidating all satellite communications within the European Union. It looks like he's been a pillar of Parisian society. His bio states that he's served on the board of directors of several of the city's most notable museums, and he's chairman of some charitable organizations. Not only that, he appears to be a devout Catholic — and a personal friend of the Archbishop of Paris."

Jacob leaned back in his chair. "Doesn't sound like he could be affiliated with any terrorist organizations. Is it possible that any of those charitable organizations he chairs are associated with a radical group, like the Muslim Brotherhood or CAIR?" asked Jacob.

"No, it looks like they're all related to Catholic charities and orphanages."

"Then what could he or Raphael possibly have to do with a large-scale terror attack on the United States?"

"I can't say unless it has something to do with disrupting European communications," said Mr. Hamilton.

"But I don't see what that would give the terrorists unless they're planning on blowing up the entire telecommunications system."

"That wouldn't accomplish anything for them. The Europeans have built in several layers of redundancy in the system. There are at least a dozen other communication centers scattered across Europe. As soon as one is down, the others automatically take over its functions."

"That brings us back to square one. How can Raphael be the key?" asked Jacob.

"I don't know, but I think you need to get a better handle on who this woman is. Perhaps she's somehow been recruited by the radical Islamists, maybe through a boyfriend. It wouldn't be the first time someone from a wealthy family was turned."

"Like when Patricia Hearst was kidnapped and turned by the domestic terror group, Symbionese Liberation Army years ago?"

"Exactly. She was the billionaire heiress who wound up robbing banks with her captors. So, Raphael's family ties don't preclude her from being a terror suspect. You'd better be careful around her, Dr. Savich." Mr. Hamilton finished reading the

report on Philippe Mitterrand. "There's nothing else of importance here. He's definitely not politically connected like his uncle
Francois. That's all I have."

Jacob reflected for a second. "How about a
Marcelle DuBoise?"

"Now that name definitely rings a bell. I recognize it
from CIA inter-departmental reports. You remember Mr. Martin
Darpoli, the man who orchestrated the assassination attempt on
President Wagner?"

"Darpoli? How could I forget him? He was the Scorpion
and the owner of Masterson Properties, a shell corporation
with ties to ISIS. His name came up when I interrogated Rozhin
Qaisar." Jacob leaned forward on the edge of his chair. "I knew
that son-of-a bitch was involved in this. Looks like a major piece
of the puzzle just fell into place."

"That's correct. After you thwarted his assassination
plans, the CIA and FBI joined forces in an effort to track down
his location. He fled to the Philadelphia International Airport
where he boarded a private jet. That plane belonged to Prince
Kabeer of Saudi Arabia, the Scorpion's financial backer. Several
months later, the Prince was arrested by the Saudi Ministry of
Intelligence and subsequently disappeared. He was probably
beheaded for treason and buried somewhere in the desert.
As it turns out, the prince had a priceless collection of French
Impressionist art. Almost all of it happened to disappear a month
before he was arrested by the Saudis." The phone went quiet for
a minute. "Now, here's the important part. Some of the art works
previously owned by Prince Kabeer, pieces by Monet, Seurat,
and Renoir, have reappeared on the market after having been
assumed to have been lost forever. They were sold through a fine
art gallery in Paris. Would you like to take a guess at the name of
the gallery owner?"

"Marcelle DuBoise! That's it. That's the connection between
Raphael and the terrorists. Marcelle is her grandfather. It looks
like the Scorpion has re-emerged and is selling the Prince's old
art collection to finance his activities."

"One might think so," said Winston. "The problem is he doesn't need the money from the paintings. He's already one of the wealthiest men in the world. It's believed he has access to over forty billion dollars of the Prince's money hidden in various numbered bank accounts scattered around the world. The FBI's been trying to track them down over the past few years, but no success thus far. He has contacts everywhere and when the bureau gets close, he simply wire-transfers the funds elsewhere."

"So, if he doesn't need the money, how do Raphael and the art gallery tie in?"

"I'm afraid that's your job to find out, Dr. Savich, but I wouldn't take too long. Something disastrous is in the works and I don't think we have much time to stop it."

Jacob raked his fingers through his hair. The newest information did not make him feel any better about his concerns regarding Raphael. "I have one piece of information that might help us. I was able to get a picture of the shooter who tried to kill me. I'm going to send it to you. Maybe we can get a hit through the NSA facial recognition programs."

"Forward it to me and I'll run it."

"I have another one of a suspicious man who bumped into me prior to the shooting today. He might be involved somehow. I'll send it also." He waited as the photographs were transmitted.

"Received them," said Winston.

"I have another request."

"What's that?"

"I'm going to need a little protection. Could you arrange for me to get a Sig Sauer 9mm? That's the gun I'm used to. I couldn't bring my own on the flight over here, and I'm a sitting duck without one."

"Consider it done. I'll have one available for you by morning. It'll be at one of our CIA safe houses in Paris." Mr. Hamilton gave him the address. "There's one other matter, Dr. Savich."

"Sir?"

"Try not to get yourself killed in the meantime."

158

TWENTY-SEVEN

DuBoise Gallery of Fine Art
Paris, France

"How was the coq au vin, my dear?" asked Marcelle. He was eightyish, a small man with a big smile and a full head of disheveled grey hair. His matching tangle of a beard was reminiscent of that of Claude Monet. In his eyes, a mischievous sparkle defied his age.

"It was wonderful as always, Pèpére," Raphael lied.

"Would you care for some more?" He lifted a chicken breast from the serving dish.

"Oh no, if I eat any more, I'm afraid I might burst." She laughed and patted her tummy. It growled. She was still hungry.

The two of them cleared the table and washed the dishes. After retiring to the living room, her grandfather poured them each a glass of brandy. "I enjoy our Friday evenings together, Raphael. I miss seeing you at the gallery."

"Well, I'll be there first thing tomorrow morning to help you with the books. How are things going?"

"Much better, especially since we started doing business with your new friend. Our commission on the works we've already sold is over seven million Euros, and he promises to provide us with more pieces in the future. He's saved the gallery.

Things were looking gloomy for a while, and I was afraid I'd have to close the doors, but now I've been able to pay off most of my overdue bills and the gallery is again on solid footing. It's all thanks to your friend."

Marcelle leaned forward, his old eyes twinkling in the dim light. "Speaking of which, how are things going between you and Mr. Sassani? Romantically, I mean."

"Pèpére! That's not a question to ask your granddaughter!" She took a sip of brandy. "If you must know, things are fine."

"Will he be the one?"

"The one what?" she answered innocently.

"You know what I mean. I'm getting older and I'd like to live long enough to see a few great-grandchildren."

She shook her head, revealing the scar over her eye. She pulled her hair back over it. "You're much too far ahead of me."

"Well, you aren't getting any younger, my dear. The opportunities are going to start drying up."

She raised her voice. "Pèpére!" He was right, of course. She stopped to gather her thoughts. "Our relationship isn't that serious, yet. He's very handsome and intelligent, but . . ." She bit at her lip.

"Something's missing?"

"Maybe…yes, something like that." She didn't want to admit it, but there was something definitely wrong with Faizel.

"Has he met Philippe? Maybe a conservative Catholic man like your uncle doesn't approve of a boyfriend with a Muslim background."

"Yes, they've met several times. In fact, Philippe was very impressed by his business expertise. They even had lunch together. Faizel has approached Philippe regarding some kind of business acquisition opportunity."

"Like what?"

"I'm not sure, but I think it has something to do with the merger of the European communication satellites with other countries. Other than that, everything's been quite secretive. It's a big enough deal that Uncle Philippe gave Faizel a personal tour of Parisian Telecom's corporate center."

He stroked his long beard. "It must be important if it captured Philippe's interest." Marcelle took his granddaughter's hand. "Listen Raphael, I want you to know that your happiness is the most important thing in the world to me. I'm sure I can speak for Philippe also. If you're uncertain about this Mr. Sassani, I don't want you to feel obliged to maintain a relationship with him. Yes, he has helped the gallery a great deal, but I'll find a way to make things work without him if I must."

Raphael leaned forward and gave him a kiss on the cheek. "Don't worry about me Pèpére. He's a sensitive and generous man. He treats me very well and he obviously cares about me." She was lying. There was a dark side to Faizel.

She finished her brandy and got up to leave.

"Until tomorrow then?" said Marcelle as he escorted her to the door.

"I'll be in the gallery at nine. Au revoir."

"Au revoir, my dear," He kissed her on the forehead and locked the door behind her.

TWENTY-EIGHT

Raphaels' Home
North Paris, France

Raphael caught a cab in front of the gallery. Twenty minutes later, she climbed the stairs to her second story flat, unlocked the door and stepped inside. It was only a one-bedroom apartment with a combined kitchen and living room. Uncle Philippe had offered to buy her a luxury condo on the Champs Élysées. He was wealthy enough. He could have easily purchased whatever she wanted, but she declined his offer, wanting to carve out a life on her own. After locking the door, she leaned against it, and looked around. It wasn't much, but it was hers. She felt safe and secure here.

Entering the bedroom, she kicked off her shoes and carefully placed them in the closet. She undressed, tossed her clothing into the hamper, and headed into the bathroom. While drawing a tub of hot water, she shed her bra and panties, letting them to fall carelessly to the floor. It had been a long day and she settled back into the bath, allowing the warm water to gently caress her body. It was so soothing she soon fell asleep.

Raphael awoke when she thought she heard a sound in the hallway. She stepped out of the tub and listened. "Hello?" There was no answer. *Just my imagination.* She had probably been dreaming. She stared at her image in the mirror, her body glistening from the water as it ran down across her skin. For a brief second, the image of Jacob Savich formed in her mind. She dismissed it. After drying herself, she wrapped the towel around her body, barely covering her breasts. While combing out her hair, she thought she saw some movement in the mirror. Before she could turn around, the intruder pounced upon her from behind like a cat attacking its prey. Her throat tightened and she wanted to scream but it was stifled by his hand as he pulled it tightly over her mouth. She clawed at the air as she struggled to fight him off. It was futile. He was too strong. When he pressed his dagger firmly against the skin of her delicate neck, she could feel his excitement pressing against the small of her back.

He loosened his grip. "You're hurting me." She whispered against the knife. "I want to see your face. If you're going to do this to me, I need to see your eyes!" There was no response from her attacker, but he allowed her to turn around. His face was almost beautiful, with intense dark-brown eyes that seemed to penetrate directly into her soul. They were always cold with an inexplicable hatred. Why, she didn't know. The man had every-thing, but the presence of the hatred was an undeniable fact. Something was wrong in his eyes, something not normal.

Raphael pulled away from the thoughts and resumed her role playing. She struggled slightly and tried to look frightened, but the facade melted away with a giggle. "Oh my, what are you going to do to me?"

Her attacker remained quiet while he lowered the dagger, re-sheathed it, and lifted Raphael into his arms, letting her towel fall to the floor on top of her panties. He carried her into the bedroom where he threw her onto the bed. That was the extent of their foreplay, just the usual domination game that he always insisted upon playing. He seemed to be unable to perform without it. *Maybe it's not role playing. Could he really cut my throat with his knife?* She shuddered at the possibility. There were those cold eyes.

He removed his shoes and socks, tucking the socks neatly in each shoe and methodically placed them under the bed. Then he carefully disrobed and meticulously draped his clothes over a chair. He admired his erection in the dresser mirror and smiled at the image before him. He was ready. Raphael felt her skin crawl. It was the same ritual every time. Any sense of spontaneity was abandoned as he crawled onto bed and mounted her. No cuddling, no caressing, and no kissing. There never was romance with Faizel. For him, sex seemed to be only about the physical act, more of a unilateral, technical performance.

Faizel pushed her against the mattress in a missionary position, pinning her arms down. He penetrated her and began pounding her against the bed. The mattress resisted and pushed back. What was he trying to prove, his manliness or his sexual prowess? She could never tell. Maybe he was trying to impress her, but the result was always the opposite. His breathing grew heavier until he extended his head back at his triumphant moment. She wanted to scream, but not out of pleasure. She never could climax with him. Her needs would have to wait until she was alone.

They both put on robes. Faizel opened a bottle of wine and poured two glasses. They retired to the couch where Raphael sat next to him, drawing up her legs to the side and resting her head on his shoulder. He massaged her neck. "Tell me, how well is Marcelle doing with the last several paintings I delivered?"

"He had two appointments today. One was a representative buyer for a private collector. He came for a repeat visit to examine the Renoir. There was no prior official record of the painting's existence and he initially doubted its authenticity, so he brought his own expert. After over an hour of inspection and testing, they were both satisfied that it was in fact an original Renoir. As soon as Marcelle confirms the ninety-five million euro transfer into the gallery's account, the purchase will be finalized."

"And the second?" asked Faizel.

"He's a buyer representing the Chicago Museum of Art. They're interested in the Monet, but he's trying to negotiate a lower price. However, grandfather is holding firm. He thinks they'll acquiesce. You should make a very handsome profit even after accounting for the commission."

"Perfect! Marcelle's done an excellent job. Tell him I expect to have a piece by Camille Pissarro available next month."

She first met Faizel several years earlier while she was working in her grandfather's Gallery of Fine Art. She was at the front desk when Faizel made an appointment to view a painting by Georges Seurat. It was a preliminary study for his famous "A Sunday Afternoon on the Island of La Grande Jette." After reviewing the authentication papers, he purchased the work for twenty-three million Euros. There was no hesitation on his part and the wire transfer of funds was completed within minutes. It was one of the fastest transactions she had ever handled. He mentioned that he wasn't a collector but only an investor in fine art.

She found him intriguing but didn't see him again until a year later when he returned with the same painting. He wanted Marcelle to sell it for him. Pèpére did so within a month, netting Faizel a seven-million-euro profit. Subsequently, Faizel returned at least bimonthly with a new French Impressionist painting. Marcelle never asked how he came to own the works and Faizel never offered an explanation. During one of his visits, Faizel asked Raphael out to dinner and the two had dated ever since. At first he had treated her well and was attentive. She thought she might be falling in love with him, but she was always plagued by lingering doubts. Faizel took, but never gave love.

He continued massaging her neck as he stared at the wall. "So, how was your day today? Did you have a good client this time? What was his name again?"

"Savich. His name is Jacob Savich." Her heart palpated as the warmth of a blush filled her cheeks. She turned her face away, hoping he wouldn't notice.

"Didn't you tell me he was a doctor of some type?" He continued to caress her neck.

"Yes, he's a plastic surgeon."

"So, what about his wife?"

"He was alone. I don't think he's married." Her face was burning hot. *Careful with what you say. Don't sound defensive.*

"What was he like?" Sassani continued to caress her neck,

each stroke getting firmer until she flinched. He seemed angry, but Faizel was usually in a sour mood.

She was taken aback by his questions. It seemed like an interrogation. He'd never expressed that much interest in her clients before. Was he jealous? Unusual. Other than anger, he'd never shown much emotion. She nibbled on her lip and told him everything she knew about Dr. Savich — almost everything.

"Is sounds as though you like him," he said, squeezing her neck now.

She pulled away. "You're hurting me, Faizel." He didn't respond. She continued, "He's okay, just the typical tourist."

"What are your plans for tomorrow?"

"In the morning, I'll be in the gallery helping Marcelle finalize the paperwork on the Renoir. Then I'm scheduled to meet Dr. Savich for lunch on the Rue Cler."

"The Café du Marche?"

"Yes, at noon. Afterwards, he wants to take a walking tour around the Eiffel Tower. Then we're going to proceed over to the Musée d'Orsay."

"It sounds as though you two have a busy afternoon scheduled." An awkward silence ensued, Faizel's hand again stroking the back of her neck, a little more gently.

"May I ask you a question?" asked Raphael.

"What's it about this time? I hope you're not going to ask about my family again. We've been through all that."

"No, it's not about your family." She turned to face away from him. "What color are my eyes?"

He huffed, clearly irritated. "What? Your eyes? What kind of a question is that?"

"It's a simple one. What color are my eyes? We've known each other for over a year now, so it should be easy to answer."

"Raphael, that's a stupid question, even for you. In fact, it's one of the most asinine ones you've ever asked, and I don't have time to get involved in your silly female games." She looked into his intense eyes, but instead of affection, all she could see was the distance between them.

Faizel abruptly looked at his watch. "I must leave, so I won't be spending the night. I have several important business meetings scheduled for the morning." He got up and removed his robe, letting it fall to the floor. He made no attempt to pick it up. After he dressed, she followed him to the door where he kissed her on the forehead, stepped back to look at her, and touched the scar by her left eye. "I think you need to do a better job of hiding this with your makeup."

He turned and studied himself in the hall mirror. He adjusted his silk tie, checked his teeth, raked his fingers through his thick black hair, and smiled at the image. Apparently satisfied, Faizel walked out the door without another word.

When the door closed, Raphael used her hand to brush her bangs down over the scar. She touched the place where he kissed her forehead. It was the same spot where her grandfather had kissed her a few hours earlier, but that kiss had been warm and tender. Faizel's kiss was cold and perfunctory, more of an obligation.

She needed to bathe again, to wash his scent off her. She scrubbed at her skin but this time the water wasn't warm and soothing. Rather, it was cold and intrusive. She put on pajamas and tore the sheets off the bed, letting them fall on the floor next to Faizel's robe. She climbed onto the bare mattress, pulled a cover up to her chin and cried. *I don't understand what happened between us. I've done everything he's ever asked me to do but it never seems to be enough.* He used to be so attentive and caring, always telling her how beautiful she was. He sent flowers almost every day. They dined together at nice restaurants and took long romantic walks along the Seine River. They held hands, laughed together, and kissed frequently. Now, he only stopped by on occasion for sex.

In all the time she'd known him, he had never taken her to his home. He never discussed his family. When she tried to ask about them, he'd cut her off. When she persisted, their relationship began to sour. He became more and more annoyed with her, gradually becoming distant and aloof. Then he started to repeatedly berate her and criticize her appearance.

What did I do? Was he married? She racked her brain, trying to piece together their history. We had been so happy, but the change came shortly after he met Uncle Philippe. Had he said something to anger Faizel? Couldn't be true. Philippe would never intentionally do anything to jeopardize her relationship.

Her tears resumed but were slowly washed away by thoughts of Dr. Jacob Savich until she fell asleep.

TWENTY-NINE

Lancaster Hotel
Paris, France

After his discussion with Winston Hamilton, Jacob opened the suite's minibar and mixed himself a glass of Sapphire and tonic. He kept reanalyzing the entire situation with Raphael as he sipped on his drink, his mind a broken record, the needle stuck in a groove replaying the events of the day over and over in his head. There were no obvious conclusions. He could make a solid case for her being a terrorist sympathizer, and an equally solid case against it. He sat back on the couch and turned on the TV to clear his mind. The only English station was running the movie *Lawless* with Tom Hardy, an uncomfortable reminder of his young life in corrupt Letcher County, Kentucky; a time when his family had been slaughtered. Halfway through the show, the drink began to take effect and his eyes grew heavy. He turned off the television, leaned his head back, and dozed off.

The dream was one of several variations of the same theme. His father and brother were working the fields on their family farm. Jacob could see the danger coming. He tried to run to warn them, but something always stopped him before he could get there. During this particular version of the dream, the ground had transformed into a muddy quagmire, pulling at his legs. His arms clawed at the empty air, desperately trying to grasp something to pull himself free. The harder he tried, the deeper he sank into the muck. He cried out, but the words got trapped in his throat. The inevitable result was always the same. He couldn't save them. Both his father and brother were cut down in a hail of gunfire. The assassins wore badges.

Jacob sat up in a sweat. It was two a.m. and his heart was pounding like a jackhammer.

There'll be no more sleep for you tonight,
Buddy Boy. You know what you have to do.

For some, the solution would be to get up and read a book. For others it might be surfing the internet. For Jacob, his normal form of relief after the dream was to go for a run. He put on a pair of sweatpants, a t-shirt, a hoodie jacket, and his running shoes. Out of instinct, he patted his side pocket, but it was empty. He preferred to carry a side arm when jogging, especially at night in a strange city, but that wasn't an option right now.

After dropping off his key with the front desk clerk, he crossed the hotel lobby and stepped through the door into the night. The breezy air was cool and refreshing. It helped to relax him and clear his head of the dream. Taking a right, he jogged a few blocks toward the Champs Élysées. It was hauntingly quiet with only a handful of stragglers making their way back to their hotels after a night of dining and bar hopping. The scene was in stark contrast to the frenzied swarm of shoppers and cars he had seen earlier in the day.

He crossed the avenue and looked to his right to see the Arc de Triomphe. Constructed by Napoleon, it was a monumental tribute to the man's military prowess. Even at this hour, it still illuminated the nocturnal sky. "City of lights," he whispered to the lonely night, then headed south down George Vth Avenue until he encountered a bridge lined with a wire mesh fence. It was covered with thousands of padlocks of various colors and sizes. He once read that they were attached by couples as a symbol of their undying love for each other. They then threw the keys into the Seine River so the locks could never be re-opened, insuring the perpetuity of their bond. He wondered how many of those relationships actually stood the test of time. His never had. The Entity never allowed it.

QUANTUM

He continued across the Seine. Glancing toward his right, he saw the illuminated Eiffel Tower with its lights still dancing across the water's surface. On the other side of the bridge, he caught sight of the same romantic River Walk that Raphael had pointed out earlier that afternoon. He headed down a flight of concrete steps on his left to gain access. The cobblestone walkway was wide enough for small truck traffic and was bordered by rows of mature Linden trees. Interspersed between them were antique streetlamps, given dignity by layers of patina. The breeze wandered through the leaves, shaking the small branches as the light glowed through the limbs, creating penumbra images of serpentine figures on the ground. He paralleled the water for about ten minutes, a tall stone retaining wall to his right and the Seine River slowly flowing by on his left. The night was peaceful and all he could hear was the slapping of his shoes on the pavement. He pushed himself to the point where the rhythm of his stride took over his consciousness and he became a machine, throwing one foot in front of the other. It was a time of increased clarity of thought. He passed flower shops and fruit stand kiosks which were closed for the night. The smell of jasmine and rosemary filled the air. He continued past a series of floating restaurants and night clubs, also recently closed. Multiple piles of construction material and barge-docking ring cleats were scattered along the walkway. *Watch your step*, Jacob warned himself. *Don't want to be sidelined with a broken ankle.*

He slowed a little to appreciate the upcoming Pont Alexandre III bridge. Named after a Russian Tsar, it was arguably the most ornate bridge in Europe. Even at three a.m., it was still illuminated by large flood lights, giving it a surreal appearance. In the center on either side were gold-gilded images of the Parisian coat of arms surrounded by copper statues of water nymphs lazily gazing down the river in either direction.

The illuminated walkway transitioned into darkness as it continued under the bridge. The light faded with each step, and the area took on the appearance of a foreboding tunnel, as though he were running directly into the ominous maw of some giant beast. *Maybe I should turn back.* The closer he approached, the more the stench of urine burned at his nose. *A hideaway for the homeless and the thugs who prey upon them. Perfect place for an ambush.* He slowed his pace, considering the possibility of turning back, but pressed on, forcing his senses to full alert, his eyes piercing the darkness, searching for any movement, his ears finely tuned to any out of place sound.

A loud crack rang out. A surge of adrenaline rushed through his body, preparing him for battle. He hit the ground and waited. Crack. There it was again. It wasn't a gunshot but more of a hard slap. It was followed by a whimper, the cry of a girl—and she was in trouble. He stood up, remaining in the darkness. To his right, a faint blue light was barely visible behind a steel mesh fence. A nightclub built into the bridge's buttress. Like the other bars along the river, it appeared to be closed for the night. The entrance, protected by the sliding steel gate was ajar. Careful to avoid making any noise, he slid through the opening. It took a few seconds for the room to come into focus.

The blue light emanated from a chandelier suspended over a large, curved bar to his left. To his right, a half-dozen bistro tables sat empty, chairs turned upside down on the tops. The whimpering came from shadows along the wall just to the side of the tables. He could discern several figures. He approached on his toes.

Directly in front of him, another slap echoed, followed by a cry. "I'm not a whore!"

"All French women are whores. Now spread your legs," a male voice said. It had a distinct middle eastern accent.

She was probably in her early twenties, her dark hair streaked with blond highlights. Her blouse had been ripped open and droplets of blood stained her bra, her left upper lip bruised and swollen. Three men surrounded her. One had her pinned against the wall with his left hand, pushing on her throat, while his right hand groped its way up under the poor girl's skirt. She tried to hold her knees together in defiance but was losing the battle. The second man, whom Jacob thought of as the

'Intimidator' stood in plain view of the girl. He was tall and lean with unearthly looking long arms. At the end of the right one he brandished a switchblade knife, threatening to use it on the girl's face if she resisted. The third man was a scrawny wide-eyed runt. He paced back and forth behind the other two, encouraging them with a twitchy carnivorous grin, ready to seize any scraps left over by his partners. *A jackal.*

> *Looks like it's time for some action, Buddy Boy.*
> *Let's take these dickless bastards out. We need*
> *to fuck them up.*

Jacob had seen these types before. There was always a leader, but he was never brave enough to act alone, so he needed a pack behind him to provide encouragement. The first thing to do was to take out the 'Groper' and then see what happens. Usually the others would scatter—sometimes not. *Sure could use that Sig about now. I'll just have to improvise.*

The three rapists were preoccupied with their victim and didn't hear Jacob approaching.

"I told you to spread your legs," the Groper yelled, his face inches from the girl's.

"No! I told you I'm not a prostitute!" the girl screamed back. She tried to break free.

As the Groper drew back his hand to hit her again, it was stopped in mid-swing.

"Don't you know that hurts, asshole?" said Jacob. He bent the rapist's arm back to the point of almost breaking it.

Everything after that happened within seconds. Groper tried a swing at Jacob's jaw. A mistake. Jacob blocked the punch, then struck like a rattlesnake. He slammed the folded knuckles of his right hand directly into Groper's Adam's apple. A sickening crunching sound accompanied a look of panic that exploded in the man's eyes. He fell to his knees, grasping his neck and desperately trying to suck in air through his damaged windpipe. *One down.* He was out of commission.

Jacob swung around to face Intimidator who stared at Jacob with rage in his eyes as he repositioned the knife in his right hand. The man stooped into a crouch, protecting his throat with his left hand so he wouldn't wind up like his partner. "Fucking American. You're going to die."

"Let's see what you've got, cupcake."

Intimidator made a sweeping roundhouse attempt at slashing Jacob across the abdomen, the move of an amateur. Jacob jumped back, easily avoiding the blade. He prayed the man was stupid enough to repeat the maneuver. He was. Instead of backing away when Intimidator swiped at him a second time, Jacob stepped into the attack giving him the advantage of leverage. He grabbed the attacker's right wrist, directly above the knife, and drove the heel of his left hand into the back of the man's elbow. Forward momentum of Intimidator's arm did the rest. A snapping sound pierced the room as Intimidator's arm fractured at the elbow, putting it at an impossible angle forward. Blood soaked his shirt where the bone had torn through the skin. Intimidator dropped his knife and fell to the ground, howling like a wounded dog. Jacob quickly picked up the knife and turned to face Jackal, but the coward was already long gone. He folded the knife and put it in his pocket.

Jacob searched Groper's pockets and found a refugee identification card. After pulling out thirty-four Euros from the guy's wallet, he threw it in the river. He frisked Intimidator and found forty-one Euros and the same kind of ID card. He kept everything.

He then turned his attention to the girl. "What's your name?"

"Ce...Celina. "Her eyes were glazed over and unfocused. She was in shock.

"Are you all right, Celina?"

She was shaking but seemed to understand English well enough. She slowly nodded her head yes. Jacob took off his hoodie jacket and placed it over her shoulders. Walking behind the bar, he moistened a towel, and gently wiped the blood from the corner of her mouth. "What happened here tonight?"

"It was after two ...th ...the club was empty ...my, my

boss told me to close up for the night. After he left, I was alone. I tried pulling the gate closed to lock it when those three men broke in and tried to rob us. We had no money. My boss already took all the cash with him. There was nothing here…s…so I guess they decided to ….

"I want you to have a seat in the back for a minute, Celina. Wait for me there. I have to take care of a few things."

Jacob stood over Groper and Intimidator, both still rolling on the ground in pain. "In case it hasn't occurred to you animals, you are guests here in France. When another country is gracious enough to open its doors to you and offer shelter, you should be grateful enough to abide by its laws and customs. In a civilized society, we don't treat women this way. They aren't our property. They aren't anyone's property, and if they say no, that means no. We're not savages here, and we don't live in the middle ages. If you want to live that way, go back to your hell-hole homeland where that kind of activity is acceptable." His voice was getting louder. The faces of Groper and Intimidator became the faces of the men who massacred his family. They needed to be destroyed. He was losing control.

Enough talking Buddy Boy. Just kill the bastards. Pull out that knife and cut off their dicks. Throw them in the water. Let 'em drown.

He was an instant away from doing just that, but he paused to compose himself. "You're lucky. I'm in a good mood tonight. Normally I'd slit your throats and dump you both into the river but tonight I'm going to give you a warning, which is more than you deserve. If I see either of you two around here again, I'll kill you both, no questions asked. In fact, if I see you anywhere in France, I'll do it. Now, get your sorry asses up and get the fuck out of my sight before I change my mind!"

They hesitated, so Jacob stomped on Intimidator's broken arm. He let out a painful howl. Jacob pulled him up by his only good arm and shoved him toward the gate. "I said get the fuck out of here! Take your friend to the hospital. I'm pretty sure I fractured his larynx and there's a good chance he won't survive until morning."

Jacob followed the two attackers through the gate and watched them limp out of sight. He returned to the girl. "Are you sure you're okay, Celina?"

"Ye…Yes." She wasn't convincing.

"How will you get home?"

"I live in an apartment nearby. It's only a ten-minute walk. I …I'll be fine." She still didn't sound very convincing. She looked back. "First, I must lock the gate. My boss will be furious if it's open when he returns tomorrow afternoon." She searched along the old stone wall at the side of the bridge abutment until she found what she was looking for, a loose stone. After pulling it out, she retrieved a key, locked the gate, and replaced the key back in its hiding place.

"Is that the extent of your security system: a hidden key, no alarm, no cameras? Isn't that a little risky?"

"N…Nobody's ever tried to break in before. There's nothing to steal except some cheap whiskey. Besides n…no one except my boss and I know the location of the hidden key."

"And, of course, me."

She stared into his eyes. "But I can tell that you, sir, are a good man."

Not everyone would agree. If you ever met the Entity, you wouldn't.

"I think I'll walk you home just in case one of those guys returns with a few friends." She didn't protest. When they arrived at the door to her building, Jacob gave her the money he had taken from her attackers. In addition, he pulled out several hundred Euros from his own wallet and handed it to her. "Take this. It's small compensation for all you've been through tonight." He also handed her the ID cards of her two attackers. "You might want to give these to the police and tell them about the two guys who tried to rob and rape you." He looked down the street for a second. "But you don't have to mention me. Say a stranger frightened them off. Stay home and call in sick tomorrow. Tell your boss that you'll no longer be able to stay here alone at closing time. If you want me to, I'll talk to him personally. I can be very convincing if I have to be." He held her hand. "There's too much evil in this world, Celina, and you're far too young and innocent to be dealing with it. Be careful. I'll come back in a few days to be sure everything's OK."

The young woman turned to enter her front door, but she suddenly turned around, and gave Jacob a hug. "Merci. You are a very good man, whoever you are. By the sad look in your eyes, I'm afraid you don't believe it." She then stood on her tiptoes and kissed him on the cheek. "Au revoir, my Lancelot." She disappeared behind the door. He'd never see Celina again. It was the second time he had been kissed that night. He resumed his run back to the hotel.

You know, you should've killed them, Buddy Boy.

I have a feeling they might come back to haunt you.

"Possibly, but the girl's seen enough violence for one night."

You gettin' soft on me, Buddy Boy?

"Maybe."

As Jacob resumed his run, his thoughts drifted back to Raphael DuBoise. It was hard to imagine how she could possibly be aligned with this type of vermin or be the key to a terror attack. The key? He continued to wonder until he returned to his room. He climbed into bed and slept peacefully. There would be no more nightmares.

THIRTY

Charles De Gaulle International Airport
Paris, France

Traffic was hectic as the car approached the airport. Faizel flipped on the limousine's intercom switch. "We're late. Head directly to Terminal One and drop me off near the baggage claim area." When they arrived, he exited the limo and turned to his driver. "You can park in the cell phone lot. I'll call you when I'm ready to leave."

"Yes sir, Mr. Sassani," said the driver, then slowly pulled away from the curb.

Faizel made his way through the automatic sliding glass doors and checked the bank of baggage carousels to his right. He didn't see the flight number listed, so he selected the Air China app on his cell phone and entered the number for flight 875 from Beijing to the Charles De Gaulle Airport. It was running forty-five minutes behind schedule. Good. He'd have at least an hour before they disembarked the plane and made their way to baggage claim. Could be longer. Plenty of time to get situated and make a few phone calls. He selected a bench where he had a commanding view of all arriving passengers as they came down the escalator.

Carla Coyne waited at the Marriott Champs Élysées when her special cell phone rang. "Yes." She reported that she had been watching the news on TV to see if there had been a report about the shooting at Sacré-Coeur. It wasn't mentioned.

"They will be at the Café du Marche tomorrow. It's on Rue Cler."

"I know the area. What time?"

"They should arrive around noon. Get there early to set up. I've made all the necessary arrangements. Do not underestimate Dr. Savich again. He's shrewd and resourceful. He'll spot you if you're not careful. The room is close to the target site so you won't need to try any more of your long-distance shots. Get rid of the silencer and utilize a full automatic shooting pattern to make it look like a random terrorist assault. I want the crowd to panic. The more collateral losses, the better, but make sure he's dead by the time you're finished. That's your priority."

"I understand."

"One more thing."

"Yes."

"There will be a woman with Savich. You are to eliminate her also. You missed your target yesterday so you're going to do the woman for free. You've come highly recommended. Don't make me regret my decision to utilize your talents. I only care about two words, success and failure. Thus far all I've received from you is failure. I'm not a man who tolerates that."

"I won't fail."

Sassani made his second call. "I want at least a dozen men tomorrow, six stationed on either end of Rue Cler. When Savich arrives, close in around him. Be careful. He's smart, so make sure you cover all possible escape options. Once our sniper opens fire, you do the same. I don't care how many others are killed. The more the better, but make sure he's dead. Once that's taken care of, eliminate our shooter."

When he heard the announcement that the flight from Beijing had arrived, he smiled and looked up. He withdrew a copy of the Journal of Computer Engineering. It contained the schedule for the upcoming International Conference on Computer Sciences. He patiently watched the escalator and twenty minutes later, he saw them. Dr. Chow was in front and Colonel Hushuan Meang was directly behind him. After stepping off the escalator, the Colonel searched the baggage claim carousel signs until he found the designation for their flight number. "This way," he ordered.

Chow looked to be frozen in place. Sassani gave him the signal by tapping the cover of the scientific journal with his index finger. Chow nodded and appeared to understand. He was to make contact via the web page again. Chow looked in Colonel Meang's direction. He hadn't noticed. Chow turned and ran to catch up.

Once they retrieved their bags and exited the airport, Sassani called his driver. "I'm ready."

"Yes sir, Mr. Sassani. I'll bring the car around immediately."

While waiting, he called another number. This one to China. "Dr. Chow and Colonel Meang have arrived. You are clear to proceed with the acquisition."

THIRTY-ONE

Chengdu, China

Five thousand miles away, Liu-Fawn was escorted from her Chengdu apartment. She recognized the two Chinese Army officers on either side of her as members of Meang's personal special intelligence unit. It was expected ever since the Colonel had confiscated her computer and phone. She took a deep breath of fresh air, happy to be outside after a month of strict house arrest. The sky was a cloudless blue. She feasted on what would be her last view of the outdoors. *Pity.* Chinese prison cells had no windows.

When they placed her in the back seat of their vehicle, she didn't try to resist. Any escape attempt would be futile. She knew what was happening. She had crossed the line one too many times. Her latest blog about the Chinese coronavirus must have struck a raw nerve at the Central Committee in Beijing. Her only regret would be the loss of Chow. This time the sentence could be years, maybe forever. She couldn't expect him to wait for her.

The ride was taking too long. They weren't headed toward the local Intelligence Ministry headquarters. They were headed out of the city and into the country.

"Where are you taking me?" she asked.

The two guards didn't answer.

"I said, 'Where are you taking me!'" she shouted.

The two soldiers continued to stare straight ahead.

"Are you going to drag me out in the woods and shoot

181

me? Is that your plan? Am I to be summarily executed with a bullet to the back of my head? Is that what things have finally come to in our country? Have we reverted back to the days of the Gang of Four and the Cultural Revolution?"

The two guards remained silent. She tried to kick out the passenger window. "You murdering cowards! Let me go!"

The guard in the passenger seat turned around. "You must remain quiet and not attract attention. You are being taken to see Dr. Chow."

Her jaw dropped and she collapsed back in her seat.

Chow and I are to be reunited in Paris? I don't understand. How is that possible? Chow hadn't mentioned this to me. Only Meang could do this, but why? Meang despises me.

In a flash, Liu-Fawn saw something barreling toward them from the side. A delivery truck rammed their car, knocking them into a ditch. The car rolled over and landed on it's side. She gasped for air as the sudden impact knocked the wind out of her lungs. Blood splattered across the shattered windshield. In a panic she checked herself for any injuries. No cuts or broken bones. The driver of her car was alive and moaning, bleeding profusely from his head. The other one who had been talking to her looked unconscious, his head twisted perpendicular to his neck. *Probably dead. What happened?*

Three men dressed in black uniforms and masks stormed out of the attacking truck and ran toward them. They aimed point blank at Colonel Meang's men and fired. They dragged Liu-Fawn from the car by her hair, handcuffed her, and threw her into the back of the delivery truck. The operation had been performed with military precision. It was over within thirty seconds.

What's happening? Who are these men? Apparently, they didn't want her dead, but whatever it was they wanted, it wasn't good.

She leaned her back against the inside panel of the truck until she was sitting up. "Where are you taking me?" she demanded.

The reply came in the form of a backhand across her mouth.

THIRTY-TWO

CIA Safe House
Paris, France

Jacob went to the hotel lobby and asked the doorman to call for a taxi. He wore his usual blue blazer over a yellow Polo shirt and khaki pants. Maybe he should stop in one of those fancy French tailors and pick up a new jacket. He was in Paris after all, the fashion center of the world. He vetoed the thought as quickly as it came. Fashion was not exactly his priority right now. Getting a gun was. A new, tailored sports jacket wasn't going to save his life.

When he got in the cab, he noticed the driver was the same one who had taken him to the embassy the day before. Coincidence? Maybe, maybe not. Ever since Sacré-Coeur, he had been suspicious of everyone.

"Bonjour, monsieur. We meet again," the man said.

"Bonjour."

"Will you be returning to the U.S. Embassy this morning?"

"Not today." He gave the driver an address several blocks away from the safe house. He didn't want to expose its exact location.

"Are you sure this is the correct place, monsieur? I don't get many requests for this area. It's well away from the typical tourist sites."

"It's correct. I wanted to explore some areas off the beaten path."

"Well monsieur, that's certainly where you're going to be, far away from the beaten path, as you say. I would advise you to keep your hand on your wallet and your eyes open for trouble."

Thirty minutes later they arrived at the destination. Jacob was relieved that this driver was not suicidal like to one who drove to Sacré-Coeur yesterday. He handed the cabby fifty Euros and, after making sure the car had pulled out of sight, he walked the remaining three blocks toward the safe house address. The sign over the storefront door read, "Magasin d'Antiquites," the French equivalent of an antique shop. When he entered, a bell chime announced his presence. He was greeted by the musty smell of most old buildings. To his left, a series of shelves contained hundreds of used books. Various paintings and musical instruments hung on the walls, apparently having been given up by previous owners in exchange for cash. On the right sat several glass display cases containing jewelry, guns, and small collectables. Along the rear stood a wooden counter on which sat an old brass cash register. Behind that, a black curtain looked to be concealing an office or storage area. All appeared to be as what one might expect in a typical antique shop—all except for the modern security cameras mounted in the corners of the ceiling. They slowly rotated back and forth scanning the entire room.

Jacob casually perused the items on display, making sure the cameras had a good view of his face. After several minutes, an elderly man pushed the black curtain aside and entered the room. Dressed in a long-sleeved, plaid shirt and baggy khaki pants, his long gray hair disheveled, and a pair of wire-rimmed glasses perched on the end of his small, beaked nose, he gave the appearance of an absent-minded librarian. Jacob was certain that he was anything but confused.

The man smiled disarmingly at Jacob and spoke English with a heavy French accent. "Bonjour monsieur, how may I help you this morning?" His right hand remained hidden under the countertop. Jacob imagined he had his hand wrapped around the grip of a gun.

"Bonjour," said Jacob. "I'm a student of French history and

I've been told that you might have some pieces of interest to me. Do you have any items related to the revolution? I'm particularly interested in muskets."

"I have a few of them, but you might want to consider purchasing an umbrella instead," said the clerk.

"Good idea. It's sunny right now, but perhaps it will rain later," replied Jacob.

It was a nonsensical exchange of questions and responses — senseless but critical. The clerk's right hand appeared from under the counter, without a gun. He walked over to the front door, locked it, and placed a closed sign in the window. "Follow me, Dr. Savich. Your package is upstairs." The French accent disappeared.

Jacob followed the man through the black curtain and into a storage area. The proprietor rolled a metal bookshelf to the side, exposing a steel door behind it. Above the door was another camera, identical to the ones Jacob had seen scanning the front room. The man entered his passcode into a wall-mounted keypad and Jacob heard the hum of an electronic lock sliding back. The door opened and Jacob entered a darkened hall where he encountered a floor-to-ceiling iron gate that looked much like the door to a jail cell. On the other side, a shotgun barrel was pointed through the bars, directly at his head.

"It's him," the store owner said before patting him down for a concealed weapon. Once satisfied, the proprietor closed and locked the steel door behind him. The gate in front opened. The guard with the shotgun lowered his weapon slightly, stepped aside and said, "This way." He pointed the tip of his gun in the direction of some steps. The man followed Jacob up a flight of stairs and down a darkened hallway. Jacob could sense the shotgun still pointed at the middle of his back.

"Security protocol," said the man.

"No problem." Jacob avoided any sudden movement that might be perceived as a threat. They walked past an office on the right where another person watched stacks of security monitors displaying images of the building's interior and periphery. They entered a brightly lit kitchen area on the left. It took a second for his eyes to adjust, and when they did, Jacob's mouth dropped. In front of him Winston Hamilton sat, relaxing in a chair, smoking a cigar and holding a book. A black fedora hat and Jacob's own 9 mm Sig Sauer sat on a table in front of him. Standing behind Winston, each holding a cup of coffee, were Tank, Dan, and Lisa.

Jacob forced shut his gaping mouth. "How did all of you get here?"

"My private jet," said Mr. Hamilton. "I made arrangements immediately after you called me last night."

"Thanks for the gun." Jacob picked up the Sig and checked the magazine. It was full. He slammed the clip back into the gun and tucked it into the belt holster along the small of his back. He then concealed it under his blazer. He stared at the group, running a hand through his hair. "Why are they here?"

"Well it's good to see you too, partner," said Tank with a laugh. "That's a hell of a welcome."

"How's the shoulder, Dan?"

His friend rubbed the area with his hand. "Good as new and ready for some action."

Jacob wanted to ask Dan about the medical problem. That would have to wait until they were alone. Instead he stared at the group. "I don't get it. This is supposed to be a solo operation."

Mr. Hamilton poured a cup of coffee and offered it to Jacob. "After that attempt on your life at Sacré- Coeur, I decided you might need a little backup. Mr. McClure from the embassy was able to make arrangements for the team to enter the country as registered members of the diplomatic corps. They each can claim immunity in case something goes wrong."

"Which will probably happen, knowing Jacob," said Dan patting his friend on the back.

Jacob turned to Lisa. "Aren't you supposed to be getting ready for something important in a month, like maybe your wedding? I thought you quit after the raid in West Virginia."

"I decided to put my retirement on hold for a little while. I couldn't pass up the opportunity to visit Paris and shop for a wedding dress. Besides, I can't have the best man getting killed. It might mess up the wedding plans a little."

"No problem. I can fill in if he gets shot," said Dan with a laugh.

Jacob noticed the crutches sitting in the corner. "Deets?"

"He's in the next room trying to hack into the French Police computers," answered Winston.

"Already in," Deets yelled from a room behind them.

"Shit," said Jacob. "Did you tell him to be careful? This is a low-profile mission. Officially, we're not even supposed to be in Paris, much less hacking into their systems."

Mr. Hamilton said, "Actually, I don't think this is going to remain low-profile much longer if that sniper attack at the Basilica is any indication." He took a sip of his coffee. "Where do you suggest we go from here, Dr. Savich?"

"We need to find the group's leader. He must be the one who ordered the hit on me yesterday. I'm almost certain it's the Scorpion but we still need to find out for sure. I going to try to draw him out into the open and I'll need Raphael DuBoise to do that. I'm scheduled to meet her this afternoon for lunch at a sidewalk café. Then we're supposed to walk to the Musée d'Orsay for a tour. I'm hoping that once I'm able to win her confidence, she'll give me a clue as to who the leader is."

Lisa's eyebrows shot up. "So, this Raphael DuBoise is a woman?"

"Yes, and don't say it. This is strictly business."

The Entity laughed in his ear.

Yea, Buddy Boy. Tell that to your dick.

Lisa shook her head. "And who selected the site for lunch?"

"She did."

"I thought so. Does anyone here besides me see a problem with this situation. A suspected terrorist schedules a lunch date with you at an outdoor café, one day after a sniper tries to kill you while that same woman is with you."

Jacob freshened his cup of coffee. "I'm comfortable with her."

"Then explain to me what happened at Sacré-Coeur yesterday? Were you comfortable with her while a shooter was trying to blow your head off? Tell me, Jacob, is she pretty, sexy even?"

"She's pretty enough. Why?" He knew his sister well enough to know what was coming next.

"Because, when a woman's involved, especially a beautiful one, you abandon all common sense. You're ruthlessly tough when it comes to male enemies, but women have a dangerous effect on you. You let your guard down and have this misdirected sense of nobility which requires you to protect them from harm. Have you stopped to consider the possibility that this Raphael of yours is setting you up for yet another assassination attempt?"

"Of course, I've thought about it, but I don't believe she's working with the terrorists."

"And you know this because?"

"Instinct."

"No offense, Jacob, but like I said before, when it comes to women, you're a patsy That makes your instincts about as reliable as weather forecasts. You remember what happened with Rozhin Qaiser? You hesitated because she was a woman—and she almost killed you! Dan's the only reason you're alive today. If Raphael isn't one of the terrorists, then why did Rozhin claim that she was the key?"

Jacob hated it when Lisa had valid points. "I haven't figured that out yet, but there must be an explanation that doesn't involve Raphael being a terrorist."

The room went quiet for a few seconds. It was apparent that everyone was in agreement with Lisa. Then she said, "You're not meeting anyone for lunch today unless we're there to back you up."

Tank and Dan said in unison, "She's right, Jacob."

"Thank you, but for now, I don't need to be protected from Raphael. I need her because she might be the only one who can lead me to the guy who's giving all the orders. I want her to trust me, and that won't happen if I'm surrounded by bodyguards. I can handle this on my own."

Mr. Hamilton put out his cigar and set his coffee cup aside. "If I may, Dr. Savich, your friends have presented some compelling arguments. Your opinion assumes that everyone else here is wrong and that you are correct. All instincts aside, that might not be valid. A mistake on your part could be a fatal one. If this Raphael is in fact the key and a terrorist sympathizer, you could be killed. Then the door is open wide for whatever attack is being planned. As they say about discretion . . ."

"All right, all right, I guess some level of caution is warranted. I still don't believe Raphael's setting me up, but you're correct, we should be prepared for all possibilities." He considered his options. "Let's take a look at a map of Rue Cler."

Mr. Hamilton called to Norman Deets who was still reviewing French police data bases, "Norman, can you print out an aerial map of the Rue Cler area of Paris?"

"I have it," said Deets. "Tank, could you give me a hand?" A minute later, Deets struggled into the kitchen on his crutches as Tank followed, carrying an armful of maps. He spread them out on the table. "From what I've read, it's a popular tourist site." Deets tapped his finger on a place on the map. "The French affectionately refer to it as a small step back in time to a Paris from a hundred years ago. A four-block section of the street is cordoned off on either end, preventing any vehicle traffic. Tourists and native Parisians stroll along the street, shopping without having to worry about dodging cars."

"At least we won't have to consider a potential ambush with a car bomb or a drive-by shooter," said Dan.

"Yes, but on the negative side, there are so many people on the street, it'll be impossible to monitor all of them with only the four of us," said Tank.

"Is there any way you can reschedule your meeting somewhere else, a place where we can control the situation and protect you better?" asked Lisa.

"Too late to reschedule now without raising suspicions. Besides, I have to draw the leader out and hope he makes a mistake. I can't do that if I spend all my time playing it safe."

"Well then, we'll just have to do the best we can." Lisa looked at the map. "Exactly where are you supposed to meet her?"

Jacob studied the map and pointed to the location of the café. "Right here at the corner of Rue Cler and the Champ de Mars. It's in the middle of the tourist area and there are multiple escape possibilities available. I'll try to get an indoor table close to a rear exit. If there is an attack, being inside will eliminate a number of their options. Here's what we're going to do."

After another half hour of outlining a plan he said, "We'd better get going. I want us to be in position early so we can do a little surveillance before Raphael arrives. We need to be careful so we don't spook her. Tank and I will enter from the north end of the street. Lisa and Dan will approach from the south. Look for anything suspicious. If you see something, notify the rest of the team, but I want everyone to hold their positions unless there's a definite threat. We don't need any heroics today. Protect yourselves while you're watching over me, and make sure nothing happens to Raphael. She is our prime objective."

"I will until she makes one wrong move," said Lisa. "Then she's mine."

"I'm serious. There's too much at stake here, so don't get trigger happy. We still need a lot more information from her before we're able to get a handle on the big picture." Everyone studied the map and identified potential sources of attack if one were to occur.

Jacob looked at Winston. "We should arrive in separate vehicles."

"Already arranged." Winston paused. "There's one other thing, Jacob."

"Yes?"

"I got a hit on that picture you sent me last night, the one of the sniper at Sacré-Coeur."

"And?"

"You were right. It was a woman. Her name is Carla Coyne, and she's an American."

QUANTUM

"Former military?" asked Dan

"Yes, she comes from a family with a long history of decorated heroes. From the initial reports, it looks like she was well on her way to following in the family's tradition. She had been accepted into the Army's Special Forces training program and had excelled in all areas of marksmanship and combat skills. Then suddenly, her career went sideways, and she left the service." He passed the photograph to the team members.

"She's beautiful," said Lisa with a frown. She turned to Winston. "What happened to her? Drugs?"

Winston read from the official report. "Doesn't say exactly but reading between the lines, it appears as though some of the men in her unit didn't appreciate the presence of a woman, especially since she was outperforming them. An officer took it upon himself to take her down a few pegs."

Lisa shook her head in disgust. "The bastard raped her, didn't he?"

"I'm afraid so, although that's not specifically confirmed in the official records. She leveled accusations of rape against the officer, but the base commander ruled that the charges were unfounded. She was reprimanded and sent to a military psychiatric hospital where she was found to be delusional and unfit for active duty. Her military career was derailed. A year later, she allegedly shot the rapist in the groin, essentially turning him into a eunuch for the rest of his life."

Jacob winced and Dan unconsciously covered his crotch.

"Probably did his wife a favor," said Lisa.

Winston continued, "After that, she disappeared and was court-martialed in absentia."

"Court martialed?" said Lisa. "They should have awarded her the Medal of Honor after what they put her through!"

"At least the son-of-a-bitch will never rape another woman," said Dan.

"She's been on the FBI's most wanted list ever since," said Winston. "That's how I was able to find her in the facial recognition program data base. Now, it appears as though she's re-emerged from the shadows as a hired assassin."

Winston turned to Jacob. "You must be careful with her, Dr. Savich. Don't allow yourself to feel any sympathy because of her history. She's extremely dangerous and very effective at what she does. If she makes another attempt on your life, it's unlikely she'll miss again."

"That's just great!" said Lisa. "Now we have two beautiful and dangerous women to worry about: Raphael DuBoise, a terrorist and Carla Coyne, a professional assassin."

"What about the other photograph I sent, the guy with a beard, sitting on the bench?" asked Jacob.

"He's a nobody," said Winston.

"That's a heck of a coincidence," said Lisa. "I think Raphael probably passed the bearded guy a note. I'm getting more and more nervous about this little lunch date of yours, Jacob."

No one responded.

THIRTY-THREE

Palais des Congrès
Paris, France

The Palais des Congrès conference center was the largest structure of its type in France. This week it hosted the International Conference on Computer Sciences. The meeting's director walked across the large stage and prepared to introduce the next speaker listed on the program.

Chow peeked from behind the curtain. The place was filled to capacity to the point that many were forced to stand against the back wall and along the sides, all vying for a better position to see the stage. Over four thousand people. *So many. Maybe this was a bad idea.* He considered feigning an illness. He could walk away. Someone else could read his presentation. *But no one else would understand.* Meang sat in the front row, his eyes glaring at the curtain as though he could see Chow trembling. Leaving would not be an option. He had already told Chow that for China, he was the propaganda equivalent of a dozen Olympic Gold Medal winners.

Chow checked his watch. It was exactly 11:07 a.m. The conference was running seven minutes behind schedule. He depressed the top button on the right side and the picture of Liu-Fawn appeared. He hadn't heard from her and was worried. He now found himself praying that she would be safe, without actually knowing what praying was about.

"The third paper to be discussed during this morning's session is titled, 'Quantum Applications in Future Computer Designs.' It will be presented by Dr. Chow Chi Wong from the People's Republic of China." The mention of his name over the auditorium's speakers sent a jolt of panic through Chow, his mouth so dry he could barely swallow. He pulled out a stick of Spearmint gum and chewed. A second glance at Liu-Fawn's picture brought the sense of calm he needed. He took a deep breath and walked across the stage to polite applause. He stepped upon a small riser, his head barely above the lectern as he gazed out over the tiers of velvet-clad seats containing conference participants from around the world. His eyes widened and his heart raced. He pulled the microphone down to his level and began, his voice shaky at first, but finding solid ground once he entered into the world of his scientific work. Confidence replaced nervousness. He was the world's expert on this topic. He would make them understand. Chow spoke in perfect English.

"Ladies and gentlemen, this is an exciting period in the development of computer technology. We are on the brink of an entirely new world that could have only been imagined just a decade ago. In the past, we were handcuffed by the standard binomial paradigms of digital technology. In 1965, Mr. Gordon Moore, the co-founder of Intel, noted that integrated circuit capacity appeared to double every two years as the size of processing units became smaller and smaller. This exponential improvement in processor capacity began to reach an asymptotic limit as the functional units approached the size of a single atom, the smallest building block in nature. It had been believed that this would serve as an impregnable barrier where Moore's Law, as it has been called, would fall apart. However, we may now be able to break through that wall by employing the quantum properties of the subatomic universe. At this level, mass almost disappears, creating almost infinite levels of energy and computing possibilities. This approach will eventually allow us to store all the information of human history in a unit as small as a single cluster of molecules."

Murmurs of excitement filled the auditorium. He waited until it was quiet.

"The potential of quantum technology is limitless. Trillions upon trillions upon trillions of calculations, which normally take massive supercomputers years to complete, could be done instantaneously in a space the size of a grain of sand. Data could be manipulated with unprecedented speed and efficiency.

"As exciting as this might be, the application of quantum theory to computer technology is still in the early theoretical stages. One major hurdle which we have all faced is that of qubit discordance and proper entanglement. However, using the calculations and procedures which I am about to discuss, this obstacle might be circumvented. First slide, please."

Chow directed a pointer toward the screen. "Using a two-dimensional array of Cesium atoms . . ."

The entire audienced hung on his every word. As Chow continued, the atmosphere became electric. Word spread as hundreds of reporters and spectators packed the hall in an attempt to see the speaker. As Chow proceeded to his summation, all those present realized they were witnessing a seminal event in the evolution of computer science. The theoretical implications were astronomical.

"Thank you for your attention today," Chow concluded. For several seconds the auditorium remained silent. Had he been wrong? Did they not understand the significance of this?

Then the audience erupted into a standing ovation. The warmth of pride flushed over him. He was finally recognized for what he had accomplished. He had been reborn. There was immediate speculation regarding an impending Nobel Prize nomination.

By the time of the noon reception break, Meang escorted Chow to a large reception area. Dozens of people waited in line to shake his hand. Chow had become a highly sought celebrity. Reporters from all countries were fighting to take his picture.

"Get used to this Chow," said Meang. "After today,

everyone will know who you are. In a few years, you'll be as famous as Stephen Hawking."

He was approached by a host of international corporations and major universities that wanted to recruit him. Hundreds of billions of dollars were potentially at stake. Colonel Meang had been acutely aware of the possibilities for some time. He remained always at Chow's side, prepared to discourage any enticements toward a non-profitable arrangement.

Chow was surrounded by his peers who peppered him with questions about the details of his research. Little did they know that what had been presented today was based upon his work from almost ten years ago. He had already far surpassed those discoveries. Conventional nano-technology had been pushed back into the history books. He had taken the quantum-based concepts from the theoretical to the actual. The scientist in Chow wanted to share his newest discoveries, but the Ministry of Intelligence would never allow that to happen. He thought of Liu-Fawn and what could happen to her if he said too much.

Chow scanned the eager faces of the crowd. He enjoyed the acceptance and praise of his colleagues, but at the same time, he was plagued by guilt. None of them were aware that because of his work, their own computer systems were already under the scrutiny of PLA unit 61398. The Ministry of Intelligence was privy to even the most confidential information on any data system in the world. The only thing standing between them and the Yaoguai was the list of activation codes that he alone controlled. They were stored in his wristwatch. Chow recognized the dangerous potential of Yaoguai if it ever fell into the wrong hands. It was the reason he had secretly installed his own failsafe measures.

Colonel Meang no longer looked like a member of the Chinese military. Today, he wore a charcoal-grey suit, white shirt, and red tie. He eagerly studied the group, recognizing a few of his intelligence counterparts from Israel's Mossad, Russia's KGB, and Britain's MI6. They were all members of a cordial fraternity of spies who wouldn't hesitate to kill each other if ordered to do so. He recognized Curt McClure from the U.S. Embassy. He was speaking to some of the others. *Probably trying to extract information. Once CIA, always CIA.*

Meang wasn't interested in them. He wanted to speak to representatives from the corporate world. That's where the real money would be. After testing the waters with several individuals from Apple, Hewlett Packard, and Google, he focused his attention on a man from IBM. He had devoted a great deal of his time speaking to Chow and was obviously trying to establish a rapport. Meang pulled the man aside. "Would you be interested in the possibility of having Dr. Chow on IBM's research and development staff?"

The man stepped back, annoyed. "I'm sorry. Who are you?"

The Colonel extended his hand. "I'm Colonel Hushuan Meang and I represent Dr. Chow in all matters. I repeat, are you interested in his working under the IBM umbrella? I know your company has been aggressively pursuing the development of a quantum-based computer system. From what I've read, your present prototype is still more theoretical than actual, and it takes up most of an entire building at your research facility in New York. This morning, Dr. Chow reported on his discoveries from over a decade ago. His addition to your staff would put you light years ahead of the competition."

Meang read the excitement in the man's eyes. He obviously recognized the potential of the gift being placed at his feet, a gift that could very well lead to a promotion to the position of vice-president of IBM in charge of research and development. The hook was set. All Meang had to do was reel him in.

The man looked skeptical. "Theoretically speaking, my company might be interested, but how would such an arrangement be possible? The People's Republic of China would never allow one of their greatest scientists to work for an American company."

Meang leaned closer to the man and whispered, "It could

be made to happen if Chow defected and sought political asylum in the United States."

"Defection!" the man replied too loudly.

Meang cringed and checked the room to see if anyone notice. *No damage done.* He raised his eyebrows at the IBM man.

Message received. He looked around before continuing in a whisper. "The international political ramifications would be shocking. Our own State Department would have to be involved and even if they agree, which is no guarantee, it's a process that could take months, if not years."

"Believe me," said Meang. "The United States government will jump at the chance to get a scientist of Chow's caliber. After the exposure of China's corona bioweapons and cyber-espionage programs, the U.S. will do whatever it takes to expedite the matter. Once he's in U.S. protective custody, it doesn't matter how long the official paperwork takes."

"But would Dr. Chow look favorably upon such a thing? Surely he'd never agree to leave his homeland."

"Dr. Chow is not a political animal and he has no family in China. He has never expressed an interest in communist dogma. He's simply a scientist who wants to pursue his research." Meang grinned. "More importantly, he will go wherever his girlfriend goes. She's a journalist who has been highly critical of China's record on human rights. As a result, she's come under intense scrutiny by the Ministry of Intelligence, and that generally translates into an arrest for treasonous behavior. She understands her situation and would be very receptive to the prospect of leaving China. In fact, if she were offered the chance to work as a political reporter at a prestigious newspaper in the West, I'm sure she'd grab at the opportunity."

Meang allowed the possibilities of his words to sink in. "Best of all, I have control of her."

The IBM executive flashed a smile. "Do you think the *Wall Street Journal* would be attractive enough? I can make that happen."

Meang nodded. *Like taking candy from a baby.* "I'm sure it

would be acceptable. If the two of us can reach an agreement before the Paris meetings conclude, I can guarantee that Dr. Chow will defect. He can be on IBM's payroll within the month."

"That brings us to the reality of numbers. You must have some personal financial incentives for arranging this."

"I do, in fact," said Meang. "I have a hundred million incentives."

The man gasped. "You're asking for a hundred million dollars in exchange for Dr. Chow? That's preposterous!"

"Not actually, especially when you consider the fact that your company will save billions in research dollars with him on your staff. IBM stands to make tens of billions in profit return on this investment. It's an offer that is more than fair. The amount is not subject to negotiation. I realize you must discuss this with your superiors, but you should let them know I'm prepared to present my offer to one of your company's competitors if necessary. I'll need to have your answer by this evening, or the offer will be withdrawn."

Meang turned and walked away to rejoin Chow who was still holding court with the other scientists. The Colonel knew full well that IBM couldn't afford to reject his offer. He was about to become a multi-millionaire.

———————◆———————

A soft chime echoed through the reception hall, signaling the beginning of the afternoon sessions. The group surrounding him dissipated as Chow was approached by the conference director. Colonel Meang remained at Chow's side as the director spoke. "Remarkable presentation, Dr. Chow. It appears as though you have been thrust into the world of a celebrity."

"Thank you." Chow wasn't sure what else he should say. The presence of Meang continuously at his side left him ultra-cautious.

The director continued. "Several of the more prominent presenters have been invited by the French President for a personal audience and a private tour of Paris tomorrow morning. It will include the usual tourist highlights plus some of the more exclusive areas of the city that are unavailable to the general public. I notice that you're not scheduled to speak tomorrow, so would you care to join us?"

Chow didn't know how Sassani knew about the invitation in advance, but he had emailed Chow that the offer would be extended after his presentation this morning. Chow looked at Colonel Meang much like a child would look to their parent for permission to buy some candy. The Colonel nodded his head in approval and said to the director, "Dr. Chow and I would be delighted to join your group tomorrow."

Chow also expressed his appreciation for the invitation, but a trickle of fear ran down his back. Something was about to happen. He had no idea what it might be, but he had no choice in the matter. His fate was in the hands of the Iranian, Sassani. He checked his watch and called up Liu-Fawn's image. *Hope you are safely out of China by now.*

QUANTUM

THIRTY-FOUR

Rue Cler Neighborhood
Paris, France

Carla Coyne arrived early that morning. She carried her duffel
bag up to the second-floor apartment where, as promised, the
key was hidden under the front mat. After unlocking the door,
she entered. It felt damp and smelled musty. Apparently, no one
had lived in here for some time, making it a perfect location. Two
living room windows were open, and the faded curtains were
blowing outward in the breeze. Walking over to the closest one,
she gazed down the street to her left. She decided upon the other
window which was closer to the corner and provided better visibility in both directions. She pulled a small kitchen table into a
position far enough away from the window that she couldn't be
seen from the street, but close enough that she could target the
sidewalk in front of the café.

Carla set her bag on the table and carefully removed its
contents. She assembled the rifle's bipod, connected the scope,
and centered the gun. Her instructions were to create enough
noise to panic the crowd. *Good idea.* The chaos would help conceal
her getaway.

She experimented with various shooting positions and
opted to sit in a chair behind the table. She brought the scope up
to her right eye and focused on the most likely positions for her
target. If he sat inside, a rifle shot would be impossible. Then,
she'd have to take him with a full-frontal assault on the ground.

That would be risky, but they promised he'd be forced to sit outside. She had to take them at their word, even if she didn't trust the contract issuer. There was something else going on here he wasn't telling her about. That could mean trouble.

After rechecking her equipment one more time, she inserted a thirty-round magazine and chambered a round. Satisfied that all was ready, she closed the windows and pulled the curtains shut. They would remain that way until it was time. Noon was still several hours away, so she walked over to the couch to wait for the call from her spotter.

The more she thought about the hit, the more unhappy she became. She was being paid to kill Savich. That was the accepted contract, but the woman being added, almost as an afterthought, introduced more risk into the equation. Last minute changes could affect her concentration. Besides, why should this woman be killed? They said the man was an international weapons smuggler, responsible for the deaths of thousands. She had no problem taking him out, but why the woman? Apparently, she was a nobody. It didn't make sense. *I don't kill people who don't deserve it, especially women.*

It wasn't the only problem with the assignment. The client had ordered her to spray the café with gunfire, creating the impression that it was a terror attack, but dozens of innocents would be killed in the process. *I'm a professional, not some mindless psychopath who shoots people at random.* The whole thing didn't feel right. A million-dollars had already been deposited into her account. *I should take the money and walk away from this deal.* She disappeared once before and could do it again.

Jacob arrived at the Rue Cler neighborhood an hour before he was to meet Raphael. It was close to where he had been jogging the night before, only several blocks away from the Seine River, and almost in the shadows of the Eiffel Tower. As planned, he entered the area from the north end and slowly strolled down the cobblestone street. Norman Deets had been right. It was a large marketplace, filled with both local Parisians and tourists in search of the romantic Paris that existed over a century ago. It was undoubtedly one of the city's hidden gems, brimming with sidewalk cafes, boulangeries, and specialty shops. Display tables spilled out of the stores and onto the street, showcasing fresh foods, clothing, and souvenirs. He caught the seductive aromas of fresh-cut flowers, chocolate, and pastries. It would be easy to become distracted.

Stay focused, Buddy Boy. You're in Paris to kill, not to sightsee.

Blending in with the tourists, he stopped occasionally to check an item. At one of the kiosks he purchased a small packet of souvenir photographs of Paris as he surveyed the street for potential ambush locations and possible response options. When he stepped into one of the fromageries, an older woman in a white cotton peasant dress greeted him. "Bonjour, monsieur." She walked over and asked in English, "May I help you?"

"Bonjour, madame," he said. "I'm just looking but thank you." He pretended to inspect the various cheeses on display in the front window. He needed to search the crowd out in the street for suspicious activity. There were many possibilities, but it was impossible to identify any one particular threat. Security in the area was almost non-existent. The French avoided packaging and instead shopped with small pull-behind carts. They were an excellent place to hide a weapon. Then there were the hundreds of tourists carrying backpacks. It would be easy to conceal a gun or bomb in any of them. After seeing no evidence of a tail, he turned to leave the cheese shop. "Au revoir, thank you."

"Au revoir, merci," the owner seemed to almost sing in response.

He repeated the same charade in several more shops until he reached the corner of Rue Cler and Rue du Champ de Mars. The sidewalk menu sign read, "Café du Marche." A waiter in a white apron approached and asked, "Will you be having lunch with us today, monsieur?"

The man was thin and had a twisted grin. He looked familiar. But that was probably true of many people you meet. Jacob didn't give it any more consideration. He was more concerned about Raphael and the many people wandering about on the street. An attack could come from anywhere.

"Yes. I need a table for two." He said to the waiter. "I prefer one indoors."

"I'm sorry, but there are none available, monsieur," said the waiter.

Jacob looked inside the restaurant. There were several vacant tables. "How about one of those?"

"I'm afraid they're already reserved. Lunch is a very popular time to dine on Rue Cler." The waiter escorted Jacob to the sidewalk. "We have several nice tables available out here. It's a beautiful day and perfect for people watching."

And a perfect spot for a me to be assassinated.

The waiter led him to a table by the curb. Jacob looked around and selected a bistro two-top further away from the street. It had a brick wall protecting his back. Nearby, to his right, was a narrow alley opening. Though he was exposed and out in the open, the location offered an excellent view of the street in all directions, and the alley provided a potential escape route if needed.

"I'll take this table by the wall." He took a seat before the waiter could protest. After ordering a glass of wine, he spoke into his wrist mike, "In position. All looks clear so far. Status report?"

"I'm a block away to your north and I have good visualization of the corner," said Tank. "I haven't seen anything suspicious but with this crowd, it's impossible to tell for sure."

"Roger that," said Dan. "I'm across the street, a block down to the south. I have eyes on you." Then he added, "Lisa's right behind me on the other side."

Jacob sat back and waited for Raphael while checking possible lines of fire. His instincts were telling him to be careful. He had to admit that Lisa was probably right. This meeting might have been a bad idea after all. It was Raphael's plan to eat here, and he was essentially placing his life in the hands of a woman he had known for only a day. He still had no idea who she truly was. *Maybe she's not just a harmless museum guide. Maybe she's simply a good actress who's pulled the wool over his eyes.* If so, he could be a sitting duck. If there's another assassination attempt, the team would never be able to get to him in time. *I'm on my own, and it's too late to back out now. It's game time.*

He started getting that familiar feeling that he was being watched, the same feeling he had right before the shooting at Sacré-Coeur. The crowd had doubled in size since he first set foot on Rue Cler an hour ago. There were hundreds of people within striking distance of his position, and he could identify over a dozen of them who looked like they might pose a problem. Across the street, people sat at café tables like his, drinking wine or espressos, chatting or reading. Jacob dismissed them as a harmless, local Parisians. He scanned the buildings across the street. If he were going to set up an ambush, that's where he'd position a shooter, but the windows of all the second-floor apartments were closed in an apparent attempt to keep out the early afternoon sun. *At least I don't have to worry about another sniper attack.* He returned his attention to the street and again spoke into his wrist mike. "Situation update."

"Negative here," replied Tank.

Dan's voice sounded muffled. "I have three possible bogies, but I can't tell for sure. They aren't doing anything suspicious, but that's the problem; they aren't doing anything at all. They should be wandering around the shops like the rest of the crowd. I'll keep a close eye on them."

"There are two more suspicious looking characters headed in your direction from the south," said Lisa. "I'm getting a bad feeling about this. Everybody close in more tightly and be ready."

Carla pulled the curtains aside slightly and searched the street below. A block to the north, she saw him. She double-checked the photograph. *Definitely Jacob Savich.* He was wandering in and out of small boutique stores, casually inspecting the merchandise, occasionally purchasing something. She knew what he was doing, looking for tails. *He's good – very good. Definitely a pro.* She could take him now, but he was still a little too far for a sure shot. Must be careful this time. No more mistakes like at Sacré-Coeur. In ten minutes, he'd be directly across the street. She could make that shot blindfolded.

She continued to wait for the right moment. Searching in the other direction to the south, she found another professional who was obviously covering his leader's back. Standard military black-ops procedure. Also, very good. She wouldn't have even noticed him if she hadn't already seen his photograph. He was the second contract target, the older one whom they called Dan Foster. Behind him and across the street, Carla noticed a beautiful blond woman wearing an earpiece and trying to hide the fact that she was speaking into a wrist mike. *Now who are you?* Another member of the Savich team? "You're not part of the contract, so you get to live so long as you don't get in my way."

Where was the big black guy? He must be there some-where. She scanned back in the other direction. There you are, Tank, contract number three. Two million dollars' worth of targets gathered together in the space of a hundred square yards. She could take all three of them today. It was tempting but would be extremely difficult. In fact, it would be almost impossible if she tried to kill them in addition to the woman who was supposed to join Savich. The chance of capture increased exponentially with each hit. No sense in being greedy.

What was she going to do about the woman? Following orders was what her brain said to do, but the prospect of shooting someone who could be an innocent bystander left a bad taste in her mouth. Checking the street one last time, she identified a half-dozen other suspicious looking characters. Who hired these guys? More bodyguards for Savich? She'd have to keep an eye on them also. The job was getting to be more complicated every minute. *Should have bailed when I could.*

She returned her attention to the primary target, Jacob Savich. She followed him until he was seated at a table almost directly across from her. She studied his eyes. They weren't the eyes of a weapons dealer. Something wasn't right. *Who the hell is this guy?*

He was checking the crowd and the buildings across the street, so she let the curtains slide slowly back into the closed position. She would wait a few minutes longer until the time was perfect. She checked her phone to be sure it was working and waited for the spotter's call.

Jacob continued to monitor the suspicious guys and kept an eye on the café across the street. Most of the customers had moved on. One man remained. He was wearing sunglasses and was deeply involved in reading a newspaper.

Something's going to happen soon. Not sure how, but he could feel it. He withdrew his Sig from its belt holster and chambered a round. After gently releasing the hammer, he hid it on top of the table under a napkin. What had made him successful as the team leader were his uncanny instincts, the ability to see things that most others missed. He was constantly considering the possibility of a problem, evaluating a situation from all angles, and formulating contingency plans for necessary countermoves. Like Winston Hamilton's game of chess, you had to look several steps ahead of your opponent if you were going to win. A wrong move in this game meant you were dead.

A man and woman strolled by and paused to study the menu poster near the café entrance. He tightened his fingers around the grip of the Sig. Anyone could be an assassin. The pair must have liked what they saw because the waiter escorted them to a table directly to the left of Jacob. Two children ran up and joined the couple. The kids were excited, running about, laughing, and doing what children do. He relaxed and allowed himself a minute to enjoy their innocence and spontaneity. No threat there, certainly not from a family. His eyes returned to the crowd. The suspicious men he had noticed earlier were still standing in the same spots, randomly scattered along the street. None of them had moved. In his mind he planned the sequence in which he would take them out if any decided to start shooting. Reaching under the napkin, he cocked the hammer on his Sig.

Jacob glanced in the direction of the café across the street. New customers had been seated and were ordering lunch. The reader with the sunglasses was still alone and sipping on his second cup of espresso, occasionally looking up over his paper to people watch and stroke his beard. He showed no interest in Jacob. The second-floor apartment windows were still closed. Everything looked secure, but his instincts nagged at him. *I'm missing something, but what?*

His thoughts were interrupted by Lisa's voice in his earpiece. "The package just passed me. She's headed in your direction from the south. She should be there in a few minutes."

Because of the crowd, he couldn't see her until she was only fifty feet away. Raphael wore a flowing white peasant dress, pink linen blouse, and low espadrille shoes. Her black hair blew slightly in the breeze. She had folded a light-weight jean jacket over her right arm, and she almost seemed to float above the street as she walked. He had forgotten how beautiful she was, and he was momentarily distracted as he stood to great her.

"Bonjour, Raphael."

"Bonjour to you, Dr. Jacob Savich," she said with a disarming smile. She looked at him with her flirtatious blue eyes and, like last night, stepped up on her toes to kiss him on the cheek. Mesmerizing. His world shifted, the emotional space separating them shrinking.

"Stay focused, Jacob!" Lisa hissed into his earpiece. "A kiss is exactly how Judas betrayed Jesus. She might be marking you for a shooter. And for God's sake, make sure she isn't hiding a gun under that damn jacket she has folded over her arm!"

Jacob took Raphael's jacket, and hung it over the back of a chair. No weapon. They each took a seat at the round bistro table, and Raphael ordered a glass of Sauvignon Blanc.

Across the street, the reader was showing a distinct interest in Raphael. *Probably nothing.* She was beautiful, and this was Paris, where the men weren't exactly shy about openly showing their interest in an attractive woman. In fact, every other man on the street was staring at her.

"*Think, Jacob!*" yelled the Entity.

"*You're missing something!*"

Suddenly he understood. It was so obvious. Why hadn't he seen it sooner? It had been over thirty minutes and the man with the newspaper was still reading the same page. He was either a very slow reader, or the paper was no more than a prop. Though the newspaper continued to obscure his face, Jacob finally recognized him. Angry Eyes! As soon as Jacob withdrew his Sig, time accelerated and slowed in unison.

When the waiter set Raphael's wine in front of her, one of the children sitting at the table next to them spilled her drink, startling the waiter and causing him to spin around. Jacob was momentarily distracted and immediately realized his mistake. When he looked back toward the reader, the man was talking on his cell phone. Jacob's internal radar went on full alert as he scanned the apartments across the street. One window was open! It had been closed only a few minutes ago, and now the curtains were blowing outward in the breeze. Then, as the sun peeked out from behind a cloud, a light reflection flashed inside the room. Telescope! All he could think about was the safety of the children next to him.

Everything happened within seconds. He checked the position of the family and quickly pulled Raphael to the ground away from them to divert any gunfire. A shot exploded from the window and the waiter who turned to help clean the child's spilled drink fell to the ground with a rosette of blood expanding over his chest. The family screamed and ran. At the same time, Jacob tipped his table over and used the top for cover. Aiming his

Sig, he fired a half clip through the open window, but the shooter was still able to get off several more rounds in his direction, but missing badly, most hitting the wall behind him.

The window went quiet, but now he and Raphael started receiving fire from the crowd. With no attempt to hide their weapons, several men began closing in. He looked to his left and checked on those around him. The children and their parents were unharmed and running down the street toward safety. One of the approaching shooters raised his rifle and was taking aim on the escaping family, but Jacob dropped him with two shots to the head before he could fire. He again checked on the children and they were safely away from harm. Jacob looked down at the dead face of his waiter. *The Jackal, one of the rapists.*

I told you to kill them last night, Buddy Boy.

The reader across the street briskly walked away. Jacob fired several shots at him but with the crowd blocking his lines of fire, he missed.

Panic spread as the terrorists closed in, firing indiscriminately in Jacob's direction. Parents screamed for their children. People tripped over each other and scrambled to get back on their feet. Many didn't make it. Bystanders fell to the ground with gunshot wounds. The cobblestones ran red with rivulets of blood. Two of the armed men were dropped by Lisa with precise 9 mm rounds to the back of their heads. Dan approached a third from behind and plunged his combat knife between the man's shoulder blades, directly into his heart. He was dead before he landed on the cobblestones. Tank spotted one heading out of a pastry shop, withdrawing an assault rifle from his shopping cart. Tank placed his left hand on the weapon and pulled it free. He wrapped his right arm around the man's neck. He struggled, but Tank was much too strong, reaching his arm further around the jihadist's neck until he could grab his jaw. "Allahu ak . . ." the man tried to yell, but before he could finish, Tank did a quick rotation with his hand. Through his earpiece, Jacob heard a loud snap. The man's neck was broken, and he was dead.

"Your north is secure," Tank said into his wrist mike.

"Hold on—Shit, I see two more running your way."

"We have more action coming from the south," said Lisa. "Where are all these guys coming from?"

"We can't control them all," said Tank, "and they don't seem to care who they're shooting. The body count here is rising faster than my blood pressure. You'd better run for it."

Using it for cover, Jacob and Raphael rolled the round tabletop along the sidewalk toward their right. Once they reached the mouth of the small alley, Jacob grabbed Raphael's arm and yelled, "Stay low and follow me!" He checked doors on either side of the alley, and all were locked.

"Cover the mouth of that alley," he commanded his team through his wrist mike. "Give me thirty seconds and then get the hell out of there!"

He and Raphael ran as fast as they could as they could. They heard a crescendo of sirens approaching Rue Cler from all directions.

Carla was already three blocks away, walking slowly to avoid attracting too much attention. *I missed again, damn it. I was on target, but that waiter stepped right into my first shot! I never miss at that short distance. Never.* Something affected her concentration. The woman. She had been instructed to kill her, but she didn't want to. The woman was obviously a victim. Why kill her? Did she really try to hit Savich? He couldn't be an international arms dealer. She could see it in his eyes. Arms dealers were interested in only one thing, themselves. Savich wasn't anything like that. He was tender and gentle with the woman. He looked with care toward the children seated next to him. Once the shooting began, his first concern was the safety of the family. He risked getting hit while protecting them. No arms dealer would do that. Then he shielded the woman seated with him. His own safety came last. He was a good man. *That fucking contractor lied to me.*

Carla's other concern was that Savich had initially returned fire, but then he was pinned down. She continued to receive fire from a multitude of other directions, but not from him, or his team. It had to come from the unknowns she had noticed earlier. She fumed. *Their job was to make sure Savich and the woman were dead. Then they were to eliminate me once their primary targets were neutralized.* She was set up! The bastard put out a hit on her! "That fuck!" She shouted to the sky. "Nobody does that and lives. I don't care who they are. It's time to stop taking orders and start fighting back."

THIRTY-FIVE

River Walk
Paris, France

Jacob and Raphael merged in with a wave of panicked people fleeing the shooting. They rushed through a maze of side streets until they reached an open area where the crowd dispersed in all directions, some jostling the two of them as they ran past. They stopped in front of a large park lined by batteries of old cannons. In the middle stood an ornate building with a large gold dome, the site of Napoleon's Tomb that Raphael had pointed out yesterday from atop Sacré-Coeur. That meant the Seine river must be close.

He started to move but Raphael pulled at his arm and stopped him in his tracks. "What happened back there, Jacob?"

"It was a terrorist attack," he lied.

"But they seemed to be mostly shooting at us. Why would they want to kill us? And what are you doing with that gun?"

He ignored the gun question. "No time to explain right now. We're still not safe." He needed to get back to familiar territory. "How close are we to the Champs Élysées? My hotel's only a few streets away from it. We can hide there."

"If we take a left at the next street, the Seine River is only a few minutes away. After we cross the bridge, it's only a short walk to the Avenue."

"Let's go," he said as he held her hand firmly. "Walk slowly like we're a couple of tourists lost in all the confusion." He stopped after only a block when he heard Lisa's voice over his earpiece. "Where are you?"

He raised his wrist mic to his mouth. "Still on the Left Bank, a block away from Napoleon's Tomb. I'm headed east toward the Seine River. How are Dan and Tank?"

"They're both fine. We're still trying to cover your six."

"I'm in the clear. Head back to the safe house."

"Where's the girl?" Lisa asked.

He turned away, his hand still firmly grasping Raphael's, and whispered. "With me."

"Don't let her get away. She set this thing up, Jacob. We need to get her to the safe house to interrogate her."

"She's not one of them."

"Are you blind? Of course she is Jacob! Open your eyes. She tried to have you killed, for the second time in two days!"

"I'm not so sure about that. They could have easily killed me while I was waiting for her. They had a spotter across the street. It would have been an easy shot, but they waited until she got there."

"Why would they do that?"

"I don't know. Maybe they wanted to eliminate her also. Whatever this whole thing is, maybe she's become a liability for some reason. Things aren't making a lot of sense to me right now and I still need to figure out what's going on. She's the only lead we have. Once I get her someplace safe, I'll let you know. In the meantime, have everyone return to the safe house."

When Jacob turned to face Raphael, her eyes were wide with tears threatening. "Who are you talking to?"

"Friends."

She yanked her hand from his and stepped back. "Friends don't talk on hidden radios. I want to know what's going on, Jacob! I heard part of what you said. Who thinks I'm a liability? And why would anyone want me dead?"

"I haven't figured that out yet but someone's definitely trying to kill both of us. Right now, I'm afraid we're on our own." He pointed ahead. "Look, there's the bridge." He recognized it as the one with the padlocks he had run across last night.

He stopped just as they were about to step onto the bridge. On the other side, two motorcycles waited, looking ready to head in their direction. One of the drivers pointed at them. Shit!

Jacob reached under his jacket for his pistol. He ejected his gun's clip and checked it. *Only three rounds left.* It wouldn't be enough for a gunfight with two assassins. The motorcycles accelerated toward them. "Come on. Those guys are coming for us."

He pulled on Raphael's arm and hurried her down the same concrete steps he had jogged down less than twenty-four hours ago. They ran along the River Walk, past the restaurants and nightclub barges, past the kiosks and small stores still under construction. Ahead was the Pont Alexandre Bridge, as spectacular in daytime as it was last night. He looked back. A few hundred yards behind them, the two motorcyclists were struggling to get down the concrete steps in pursuit.

"Run!" he yelled and pulled harder on Raphael's arm.

She stumbled for a second, hampered by her espadrille shoes. She looked back and screamed! "We can't outrun them. They're going to catch us."

The two sprinted as fast as they could but were running against a wave of tourists headed in the opposite direction. Dozens of construction vehicles were driving away in the direction of the motorcycles.

"Looks like the police ordered an evacuation after the shooting started," said Jacob, getting winded. Fortunately, the departing trucks slowed their pursuers even more. Suddenly, he felt the weight of Raphael pulling away from his hand and checked her. She'd turned her ankle in her heels and fell. He scooped her up in his arms and tried to run. They weren't going to make it. "I have an idea. There's a nightclub tucked under the Alexandre Bridge ahead."

"Yes, I've been there before. It's Le Showcase, but it's early and the club's probably closed. How's that going to help us?"

"You'll see."

Even in the daytime the area under the bridge was dark and foreboding. "They won't be able to see us in here and they might ride right past us." Jacob set Raphael down. She was limping and could barely walk. He checked the club's wrought iron gate. Locked. Feeling along the adjacent wall, he found a loose stone and pulled it out. The key he had seen Celina hide last night was still there. He grabbed it, unlocked the gate, and helped Raphael inside. "Hide behind the bar while I relock this."

Fifteen seconds later, the two motorcycles blew right past them. "We don't have much time," said Jacob. "It won't be long before they've figured out what happened and return for us. Is there a backway out of here?"

"Not that I know of. The club's built into the bridge so the gate must be only way."

They were trapped and it was just a matter of time before their pursuers returned, probably with reinforcements. He thought for a second. "Give me your bag."

"My handbag?"

"Yes. Quickly." He dumped the contents onto the top of the bar. He inspected her tube of lipstick, and a set of keys. Her wallet contained nothing but credit cards, a driver's license, and a few Euros in cash. Checking the cell phone, he found that the automatic tracking feature was inactive. He turned to face Raphael. "I'm going to have to pat you down. It'll be pretty thorough, and you might feel violated, but I have no other choice."

"What are you doing?" she asked with a confused look on her face as he proceeded to check her. No areas were off limits.

"Sorry about that. I needed to be sure you weren't wired."

"Wired? Why would I—"

"They're tracking us. That's how the guys on the motorcycles knew how to find us. I need to figure out how they're doing it."

"And?"

"Nothing, you're clean."

"What about you?" she asked.

"I couldn't possibly have a . . ." He stopped and patted the pockets on his blue blazer. Inside the left breast pocket, he found the object and showed it to Raphael. It looked like a large Euro coin with a coil of wire attached.

"What is it?" she asked.

"A tracking device. The man who bumped into me at Notre Dame yesterday must have planted it on me. That's how they've been able to follow us and right now someone's probably telling the two guys on the motorcycles to backtrack because we're still under the bridge."

Jacob tossed the device onto the bar and was about to smash it with the butt of his gun. He hesitated for a few seconds, as he looked through the gate.

"What?" asked Raphael.

"I have an idea. Stay here." He ran outside. The last of the construction vehicles was leaving the area. One was an open-bed pickup truck headed through the tunnel in the opposite direction of the assassins. He tossed the tracking device into the back. While out on the walkway he noticed a long coil of construction electric cord. He picked it up and returned to the safety of the darkness under the bridge. There wasn't much time. He tied one end of the cord to a metal boat cleat secured to the side of the bridge abutment. He looped the other end around the bars of the club's iron gate so that the cord traversed the river walk road in a diagonal fashion.

Jacob locked the gate and reached through the metal bars, tossing Raphael the key. "Remain hidden behind the bar in the back. You'll be safe there. If something goes wrong, they won't be able to get to you."

Jacob retreated deeper into the shadows of the bridge and held his gun ready. Less than a minute later, the two motorcyclists returned at full speed trying to again pick up the trail, now chasing a construction truck instead of Jacob and Raphael. As they entered the dark area under the bridge, Jacob pulled on the electric cord taut until it was high enough. It hit the first cyclist in the chest, knocking him off the bike. The force of the impact caused him to slide down the cord into the bridge abutment, breaking his neck. When the second cyclist saw what happened to his partner, he slid off his bike and skidded under the wire.

Before he could draw his gun and fire, Jacob shot him in the head. Quickly, he pulled both bodies farther into the dark recesses under the bridge.

He went back inside for Raphael. "We're safe but we must leave now."

"What about those two who are chasing us?"

"They got sidetracked."

He put his arm around Raphael's waist and helped her outside. She could walk but not run. Once outside, he pushed one of the motorcycles into the river. He picked up the second, helped Raphael onto the back, and they sped away.

"Where are we going?" she asked in his ear.

"Working on it."

THIRTY-SIX

Latin Quarter
Paris, France

Jacob drove for a half hour dodging in and out of side streets, increasing the distance between themselves and Rue Cler, repeatedly checking for a tail. Once satisfied they weren't being followed, he pulled to the side and took out his cell phone. He took a few steps and made a call to Winston Hamilton. " Lisa was right. It was another ambush."

"I know. The rest of the team arrived at the safe house ten minutes ago and gave me a report. Are you okay?"

"Yes, for now, but I'm not sure that Raphael and I are out of the woods yet. These guys always seem to be several steps ahead of us, but I may have fixed that. I found a tracking device in my jacket pocket."

"A tracker? How'd it get there?" asked Mr. Hamilton.

"It was planted on me yesterday after we visited the Louvre. Right now, I need a safe place where the two of us can get a chance to rest and figure this thing out. I was going to try my hotel but now I'm afraid they might have it staked out."

"Why not bring her to the safe house?"

Jacob turned away and whispered in his phone. "I don't want to risk jeopardizing its location until I can be certain of Raphael's status. I still have some unanswered questions. I need you to make arrangements for us to get a room at a small hotel on the Left Bank. Make sure it's off the main roads. Call me back when it's taken care of."

Need to ditch the motorcycle. It might have its own location GPS system. He abandoned the bike and left the keys in the ignition. "I figure it'll take less than fifteen minutes before someone steals it and takes off. That should keep the bad guys off our backs for a while."

He helped Raphael limp a few hundred yards until they found a small café. She grimaced but pushed forward through the pain. They were tattered and bruised from the attacks and neither had eaten for hours. Exhausted, they were running solely on adrenaline. They needed a place off the street to hide and rest until Mr. Hamilton called.

"We should eat. Are you hungry?" he asked.

"Are you kidding? I haven't even thought about food. Is it safe?"

"Nobody knows where we are now, so I think so. We must be careful though."

Jacob selected a table where he had a good view of the street. He sat in a chair opposite Raphael, his back to the wall. *Can I trust her?* Through his entire life he had prided himself on his ability to read others. It was a gift that had saved his life on more than one occasion. With Raphael, he drew a blank. She was a complete enigma. That made her extremely dangerous despite her having been a target on Rue Cler. He couldn't allow her to leave his side.

They shared a sandwich and ordered two more as a carryout for later. After they finished, Jacob's phone rang. Winston's only words were, "Hotel de Richelieu on Rue d'Arras."

"I'll call you back once I'm sure everything is clear."

He kept the hotel's location to himself until he was able to hail a cab. After helping Raphael struggle into the car, he gave the driver the hotel's name and address. It was only a half-kilometer away, down a small side street in the Latin Quarter. The place was inconspicuously sandwiched between larger buildings. The only identification was a bronze plaque by the front door emblazoned with its name. Inside, the hotel smelled of age but was clean, almost quaint. No frills or breakfast buffet here. Jacob handed the proprietor a hundred Euros. The man didn't ask for passports or any other forms of identification that might trigger a visit from Interpol or the group that was chasing them. The place was perfect enough for their needs. Most importantly, it was off the beaten path.

The room was larger than Jacob expected. After checking the windows and closets, he wedged a chair against the door. He placed his gun on the nightstand, then turned to Raphael. "We'll be safe here for a while, at least until I can figure out what to do next."

Raphael's eyes fixed on the only bed, her look of concern apparent. Jacob immediately smiled. "Don't worry. I'll sleep on the floor. Believe me, I've been in worse places." He sat on the edge of the bed. "Why don't you shower? I need to think a little bit."

While she was in the bathroom, Jacob removed the clip from his gun and left the empty weapon out in the open. It would be a test. He gathered Raphael's clothes and checked them for any surveillance devices he might have missed earlier. There were none. He removed the SIM card from her phone, then searched her purse for the second time to see if a device was hidden in the lining. He found nothing. Everything suggested that Raphael was as she claimed to be, an innocent museum tour guide with a prominent family history, somehow caught up in an international terror plot.

When she got out of the shower, she wrapped a towel around herself, cold and shivering. The hotel didn't offer complimentary robes, so Jacob pulled the comforter off the bed and gently placed it around her shoulders.

He took his turn in the shower, then gathered up their clothes and washed them, hoping that submersing them in water would destroy any hidden electronic tracking devices he might have missed.

After drying himself, he returned to the bedroom with the towel wrapped around his waist, relieved to see the Sig still sitting on the dresser where he had left it. Raphael had passed the test. He sat next to her on the bed, distracted by the warmth of her body. The scent of her perfume still lingered in her hair. He struggled to push the sensual image of her out of his mind, but he was losing the battle.

Stay focused, Buddy Boy. You still have no idea what's going on here. Her not shooting you proves nothing. She could still be the enemy.

Jacob had to admit that while he didn't believe Raphael was a terrorist sympathizer, he couldn't be absolutely sure yet. After all, Raphael had been called "the key" and she had been present during both attempts on his life. In addition, her grandfather had some connection with the Scorpion.

"Are you feeling any better?" he asked.

"Yes, the shower helped a lot. I needed it." She tucked a few strands of hair over her right ear. "I must look a mess."

"Don't worry. You look lovely." He hesitated before turning to face her, looking into her eyes. "Raphael, I know you've had a difficult day, but we need to discuss some important matters. It's urgent. As you've probably already guessed, I'm not simply an American physician on tour in France. Some dangerous things are beginning to unfold in Paris, and I'm here to figure out what they are."

"Do you mean like more terrorist attacks?"

"Maybe, but I believe it's something on a much larger scale."

"Are you with the CIA?"

"Not exactly. We're more like independent consultants."

Her eyes widened. "We? You mean it's not just you?"

"No, there's a team of us. My associates are the ones who saved our lives today on Rue Cler. Someone or some group tried to have us both killed."

"That's what you said earlier, but why me? I'm nobody."

"You're important for some reason, Raphael. The two of us must figure out why. My team members thought that you might be part of a terror network, but I don't share their beliefs."

Her face scrunched up. "Why would anyone believe that I

could be a terrorist?"

"We've been following some clues in our country and they eventually led us to Paris. The only recurring connection we've been able to uncover thus far is that whatever is about to happen, it somehow involves you."

"But I don't see how that's possible!" Tears threatened her eyes. A few escaped down her cheeks.

"In addition, they appear to be using you to get to me. They want me dead. I suspect they're afraid I might ruin their plans."

"What plans and who are they?" she asked.

He didn't answer. "First, I need to ask you a few questions. Did you know about that device in my sport coat pocket?" He studied her eyes carefully. If she tried to lie, he'd be able to tell.

"No, of course not. I've never even seen one of those things before." She was telling the truth.

"They were using it to track our location, and that's how they were able to stop us before we crossed the bridge today. But they needed more than just the tracking device to plan what happened at Rue Cler this afternoon. They couldn't have simply followed us there. The attack was too well coordinated, involved too many people, and required too much planning to be a spur of the moment thing."

"I often take my clients to that restaurant, so it wouldn't be surprising that someone might guess we would meet there."

"But this wasn't guesswork. Someone knew for a fact that we would be at that particular café at that specific time. There was a sniper already stationed directly across the street, waiting for both of us to arrive. It had to be organized by someone intimately familiar with your routine. Did you speak to anyone about your plans for today?"

She reflected for a minute and then, her face dropped. "There were two. Last night, I had dinner with Pèpére."

"That would be your grandfather, Marcelle DuBoise?"

"Yes, but he would never be involved in something like this. He's been a devout Catholic his entire life and could never be connected to any radical terrorist activities. Besides, he'd never do anything that would jeopardize my life."

"I agree with you. I don't think your grandfather is the problem. Who else knew?"

She blushed. "I saw a friend last night."

"A friend—as in boyfriend? Are you romantically involved?"

"Yes." She averted his eyes and looked to the floor. "He asked me what my schedule was like for today. He was persistent and very interested in what I was planning with you. He wanted specific details. I was afraid he might be jealous." She looked up at Jacob her pupils dilated with a shocked look on her face. "You don't think he could be one of them?"

"It's a possibility. What's his name?"

"Faizel Sassani, but he couldn't be involved in terrorist activity like this either. He's a respectable businessman from Iran. He imports rare artworks and contracts with my grandfather to sell the paintings through the DuBoise Fine Art Gallery."

"Tell me, was your Mr. Sassani aware that we would be at Sacré-Coeur yesterday?"

"He knew we were going to the Louvre, but I think that was it. I don't remember. Maybe he knew about Sacré-Coeur. I often take clients there. Why do you ask?"

"Because someone tried to shoot me while we were standing on the cathedral's observation platform. That's the reason why I pulled you down on the ground."

"Oh my God! You don't think Faizel could be responsible?"

"Do you have a photograph of him?"

She hesitated. "No, he would never allow his picture to be taken."

He asked Raphael to describe her boyfriend. After she did, he was almost positive that he knew the true identity of Mr. Faizel Sassani. If he was right, she was lucky to still be alive. Reaching for his secure cell phone, he called Winston Hamilton at the safe house.

He answered after the first ring. "Is there a problem with the hotel?"

"No, we're both safe here. I'm calling because I need some background information on a Mr. Faizel Sassani. I believe he could be an international businessman from Iran."

"Let me go down the hall to the communications room."

A minute later Jacob could hear Mr. Hamilton typing on a computer keyboard. "Nothing in the Homeland Security database. Let me try the NSA files."

There was more typing and finally he said, "I have something here. It's a Faizel Sassani and he is in fact a wealthy Iranian businessman, or I should say he was." He went on to explain the information in more detail. Jacob listened intently.

"Thank you, sir. That confirms my suspicions. There's one more thing. Could you have Deets send me a copy of the composite sketch of Martin Darpoli? I believe he can access it in the FBI files."

"I don't need Norman to hack the FBI computers for that. I've had one in my own files ever since the assassination attempt. It's on the way." Jacob received the picture less than a minute later. "Is there anything else, Dr. Savich?"

"That'll be it for now. A few more pieces of the puzzle are starting to fall into place, but I still don't have a handle on what the endgame is. I'll keep you posted."

Jacob terminated the call and turned to Raphael.

"What is it?" she asked.

"You were correct when you said Faizel Sassani was an Iranian businessman. He's recently completed some transactions around Paris." Jacob took her hand. "Have you ever been to his home?"

"No, I haven't," said Raphael. "I don't even know where he lives. We always meet at my apartment prior to going out. I always thought it was a little strange. For a while, I was afraid he might be married."

Jacob continued to study Raphael's eyes. She was telling the truth. "Well, he's not married but there is a major problem with him. Your Faizel Sassani doesn't exist — at least not anymore. He died some time ago. There's been no mention of him in any of our databases until two years ago when he applied for a business visa for France."

"How is that even possible?" asked Raphael.

"I believe the Iranian government must have helped your boyfriend establish a fake identity by assuming the name and background of the real Faizel Sassani. That man was probably murdered in preparation for the identity transfer. I suspect Sassani has many other false identities which he uses in emergencies in case he needs to disappear quickly."

Her brow furrowed. "That's horrible! Who is he then?"

"We'll get to that in a minute. When did you first meet him?"

"He came into my grandfather's art store a few years ago, when I was still working there. He said he was an investor in fine art and was looking for a painting by one of the French impressionists. I sold him a piece by Georges Seurat. After showing him the official documentation papers, he immediately had the twenty-three million Euros purchase price transferred to Pèpére's account."

"And that was unusual?"

"Oh yes. It generally takes months to complete such a transaction. Before a purchase of that magnitude is finalized, the buyer typically insists on authenticity confirmation by one of his own experts, but Faizel said that he was in a hurry and he trusted me."

"Is that when you started your relationship together?"

"No, I didn't see him again until about a year ago when he returned the Seurat painting for resale. He made a very large profit, and at the time, I believed he simply had a keen appreciation for the art valuation market. That's when he first asked me out to dinner. We've been dating ever since." Her face reddened and she dug her toes into the carpet. She seemed embarrassed and scooted closer to Jacob's side, her arm almost touching his. "He has returned to the gallery on many occasions to sell more museum-caliber paintings. I'd say at least one every two months." She stopped and looked at Jacob. "But if he didn't exist until a couple of years ago, how did he come by so many pieces of collectable art? Each one must be worth in excess of fifty million Euros."

"It's a little complicated. We believe that years ago, he was adopted by a Saudi prince who had been one of the wealthiest men in the world. He had a fondness for the French Impressionists and had acquired an art collection which would have been the envy of even the world's most prestigious museums. The Prince also had a fondness for power and was involved in an attempt to overthrow the Saudi monarchy. His plans were uncovered by work that my team had done. As a result, we believe that he wound up somewhere under six feet of sand in the middle of the desert, all compliments of the Saudi Intelligence Ministry. Your Mr. Sassani escaped and was apparently able to transfer most of the art collection from his father's estate into hidden vaults. He's a multibillionaire in his own right."

Raphael shook her head, exposing the scar on her face. Another tear ran down her cheek. "So, who is this man?"

"I'm going to show you a composite sketch of someone. It was taken from descriptions given by a number of witnesses who knew him in the United States." He handed her his cell phone and she studied the screen.

"Does this look like your Mr. Sassani?"

Jacob had his answer as soon as she looked at the picture. Her hands shook and she started to sob. The phone fell to the floor. Again, she asked, "Who is he?"

"In the world of the international terrorists, he's referred to as the Scorpion."

"Scorpion?"

"Correct, and he's a very dangerous man." Jacob didn't mention that the man had murdered his last girlfriend whom he had been using to gain information about President Wagner's inauguration schedule. There would be nothing to gain from telling her what the Scorpion usually did to women after he was finished using them. "In the United States he was known as Mr. Martin Darpoli. It's one of many aliases he has used. We believe he has close ties to ISIS."

"ISIS!" The dam ruptured and Raphael sobbed uncontrollably as she buried her face in Jacob's shoulder. "I knew something wasn't right about him. How could I have been so stupid as to trust this man?" She bent over at the waist and buried her face in her hands.

"You weren't stupid, Raphael. He's very clever and has a knack for using woman to get what he needs."

She straightened up, her face full of questions. "But what can he get from me? I have no important connections other than the museums. Is he planning on blowing up the Louvre?"

"I can't say exactly, but it wouldn't surprise me. For the radical Islamists, the type of art displayed in the Louvre is a symbol of western decadence. Many of the paintings glorify Christianity and the jihadists consider them to be an affront to Allah. However, my instincts tell me that Sassani is looking for an attack on a much larger scale."

"But I . . .I still don't understand. If he's not looking for access to the Louvre . . ., why me?"

He had no answers — yet.

Raphael placed her hand over his and gently squeezed. She looked up and stared into his eyes. "Thank you, Jacob. You and your friends saved my life today. I guess I have become a liability, but I don't know why. I don't know anything. Now it looks like a man whom I thought I might have loved is behind it all." She leaned closer to him. "You're a good man Jacob Savich."

She slowly melted against him and kissed him on the cheek. Jacob felt her breath on his neck and sensed the warmth radiating from her body. He turned his face toward her and kissed her in return, on the lips. She didn't resist, opening her mouth, her tongue coaxing his, the kiss becoming more passionate. Jacob kissed her like it would be the last kiss of his life. Maybe it would be if he didn't solve this mystery soon. He inhaled her sighs and breathed in the scent of her hair.

Raphael stood and slowly made her way to the lights, turning off all except for a small table lamp on the dresser behind her. Jacob followed her with his eyes, consuming every move she made as she walked across the room. She stood in front of him and let the bedspread fall to the floor, leaving a silhouette of soft light glowing around the delicious curves of her naked body. Her eyes stared into his, hot and sultry.

He immersed himself in the lithe sensuality of her. She was stunning, exquisitely soft, looking like Monet's *Woman with a Parasol,* a figure of ethereal beauty untainted by the harsh depravities of life.

Raphael gazed down into his eyes and coaxed her hair down, trying to hide the small scar over her left eye. Jacob stood, gently took her hand away, and pushed the hair back. He caressed her face in his hands, lost himself in her soft blue eyes, and kissed the scar. "You should never be self-conscious about that, Raphael. You're undoubtedly the most beautiful woman I've ever known."

Raphael reached toward him and placed her finger on his mouth, tracing the outline of his lips. "Sweet words from a very beautiful mouth, Jacob Savich." He opened his mouth slightly, kissed her finger, then proceeding to the others, gently sucking on each of them as he did.

"I want you," she whispered, running her nails down across his broad chest, continuing lower toward his abdomen, firm and rippled. He wrapped his hands around her, his fingers tracing along the center of her back and across her round bottom. He pulled her closer until they collapsed together on the bed, locked in a deep passionate kiss. Jacob kissed her neck and caressed her breasts, kneading them slowly. He put his finger in her mouth to moisten it and returned to her breasts, touching her nipples, soft as a whisper, then gently pinching each. She moaned softly as he replaced his hand with his mouth and nibbled. Her breathing grew heavier as his kisses made their way down her body and toward her thighs. He lingered between them with his mouth, his tongue exploring the depths of her secret essence. She felt all the energy of her body flow to that one spot as her hips matched the rhythm of his oral thrusts.

"My God," she yelled. "That's it!" Her chest heaved rhythmically with each deep breath until she spasmed in ecstasy as she came the first time.

When he returned to her mouth several minutes later, she slowly coaxed the towel from around his waist and tossed it onto the floor. They feverously explored each other. She wrapped her fingers around his shaft, hard and throbbing, on the verge of release, but stopped him with a flick of her finger. The slight pain was exquisite, making him want her even more. "Not yet," she whispered in his ear, then resumed stroking him slowly and deliberately, staring deep into his eyes until she saw his soul, bringing him back to the verge, but not letting him finish. Her slightest touch was a symphony of excitement. He was ready. So was she. "Take me, Jacob," she whispered and gently bit his earlobe.

Jacob rolled on top and grabbed her by the hips, lifting her off the sheets, entering her, plunging as deep as he could. Raphael arched her back, leaning her head off the side of the mattress, trying to take in as much of him as possible, more than was possible. The heat of their bodies melted their hips together until their love making exploded into an uncontrolled feral intensity. They were like two wild animals, joined in unbridled passion, becoming lost and found at the same time. Thoughts of the past and the future were irrelevant as they ravenously devoured each other's separateness until they merged together as one. Their passion transcended time and reality as the problems of the outside world dissolved into insignificance. There were no assassins, no Scorpion, no Jacob, and no Raphael, only their singularity in a parallel universe where nothing else existed but rapture. He pulled her closer, kissing her hard and deep, wanting every part of himself to be inside her. They remained that way, wildly immersed in the throes of passion, until the dam exploded open. They came as one.

After recovering, they rolled over onto their backs and stared at the ceiling. Jacob was speechless. *What the fuck were you thinking, Jacob? Sure, it was great, the best, but this was a bad idea — a very bad idea.* He needed to stop this before it went any further.

It wasn't the voice of the Entity he was hearing. It was his own demand for common sense.

Raphael rested her head on his chest, hearing his strong heartbeat. "I've never met anyone like you, Jacob. You've been my protector, my warrior." She bit him on the neck and raked her nails across his chest.

Not good Jacob. Stop this, and right now. He didn't pull away. She kissed his chest slowly working her way down across his belly. She lingered between his legs and took him into her mouth, a cornucopia of unimaginable delights.

Screw it. You're overanalyzing, Jacob.

He again took her into his arms and kissed her hard on the mouth. Still locked in the kiss, she rolled over and pinned him against the bed. "I'm in charge this time." A smile turned the corners of her mouth. Such a nice mouth. She raised up and sat astride him, slowly lowering herself down on him until he was deep inside her. His instincts were to take over, but she controlled the rhythm as they took the second time more slowly, gradually submerging themselves in the moment. Neither one of them was in a hurry. They savored every minute, experimenting with each other, finding sources of unimagined pleasure, until they rolled off the bed onto the floor. Unfazed, she continued to slowly raise and lower herself on his shaft, prolonging the inevitable. Both held out as long as they could, not wanting it to end, but the passion overcame them like a powerful tsunami. They climaxed again in perfect sync. Still inside her, Jacob gently kissed her lips.

When finished, Raphael whispered, "It may sound cliché, but I've never experienced anything like this before."

"Neither have I." He was being honest. He had been with many women in his life, but it had never been like this, not with this level of intensity. Prior relationships never lasted. He had issues. He didn't need a psychiatrist to explain them. It was the Entity. Any successful relationship required a foundation of honesty, and it was impossible for Jacob to be completely honest regarding his dark life. How do you tell a potential partner that you need to kill people? It's a hard pill to swallow, even if the killing was done for what he considered to be righteous reasons. Too many factors had worked against Jacob having a normal life in the past. The only way to have one now would be to leave the team behind, just as Lisa was planning to do. Could he do that? This situation with Raphael seemed somehow different, so perfect. Normally, the Entity would vehemently protest any strong feelings like this toward a woman. However, it had been uncharacteristically silent tonight.

Sometimes you find a special person, a woman who can purge the demons from your soul and unlock feelings you never thought possible. Could Raphael be that person? Feelings like these could become distracting and dangerous. Jacob's life had just become more complicated.

THIRTY-SEVEN

Notre Dame Square
Paris, France

It had been a fitful night and Chow had barely slept. He hadn't heard anything from Liu-Fawn yet. He could only hope she was somewhere safe. Mr. Sassani had reassured him that she would be fine, but Chow wasn't convinced. What other choice did he have but to follow the plan that had been outlined for him? He wasn't told what would happen or where, but he knew something would occur today, and he suspected it might be dangerous. Any mishaps could result in his death, and probably, that of Liu-Fawn also. For the second time in a week he found himself praying. He didn't actually understand how to do it or to whom he should be praying. He had never done it before. It just seemed to be a good idea and it made him feel better.

A loud knock rattled the door to his room. He trembled. Meang had that effect. When he opened it, the Colonel stood in the hall wearing a grey tweed blazer over white, button-down shirt and grey slacks. A strange sight, seeing Meang in anything but his military uniform. A telltale bulge under the left side of Meang's jacket revealed that he was armed. Chow chomped down on a fresh stick of spearmint gum. Was it going to happen today? Did Meang plan to shoot him?

"Chow, it's getting late," said Meang, but without his typical sneer. He was smiling, something Chow had never witnessed before. "If you don't hurry, we'll miss the tour bus."

"I'm ready," Chow said as he started to shut the door. He stopped. *I almost forgot.* He made a one-hundred-eighty degree turn and rushed back into his room.

"Now what?" said Meang.

"I forgot my watch." He scrambled to search the room. It was sitting on the bathroom sink.

"You and your obsession with time. If we don't hurry, it's not going to make any difference. They'll leave without us."

"Got it!" Chow retrieved the timepiece and strapped it onto his left wrist. He decided to hide it until he had a better idea about what was going on. Liu-Fawn was still unaccounted for and the watch and its codes were his only bargaining chip. He checked the time. It was 8:23 a.m. in Paris which made it 3:23 p.m. in China.

He pushed the top button on the right side and caught a quick glimpse of Liu-Fawn's picture on the screen. *Where are you now? Are you safe?* "Hope I'm doing the smart thing for both of us," he whispered to the image.

"Chow! Now!" ordered Meang.

He chewed faster on his gum.

When Chow exited, Meang patted him on the shoulder. "We don't want to be late. After today's tour, we will embark on an exciting journey, a new future for both of us — and Liu-Fawn."

What does that mean? They didn't sound like the words of a man planning to shoot anyone today. He and Meang rushed through the hotel lobby. They made it to the bus in plenty of time. Chow counted twenty-three others plus a tour guide, who began talking as soon as the bus pulled down the Champs Élysées. Chow looked at the faces of the people shopping along the exclusive avenue. So many Chinese. Except for the high-end stores, it was almost like being at home. Even many of the advertising signs were in his native language. He commented on it to Colonel Meang who was still smiling. "It's a testimony to the success of the economic policies instituted by our Ministry of Finance. China has the fastest growing middle-class population in the world." He leaned closer and grinned. "But our economy still pales to that of America's. That's the place to be, Chow."

What? Meang's words seemed like a hypocritical betrayal of the entire foundation of communist ideals. While millions of his countrymen at home were starving, thousands of Chinese nationals in Paris acted like wealthy capitalists, shopping at expensive designer stores, and buying frivolous adornments they didn't need. Liu-Fawn was right. The entire system has been corrupted by greed. China wasn't any different from western capitalist countries. It was simply a matter of who held the power.

After special private tours of the Arc de Triomphe and the Eiffel Tower, the group was to have been treated to a traditional French lunch of wine and cheese at a quaint sidewalk café on Rue Cler. However, the entire area had been cordoned off by the French police after a terrorist attack yesterday. The lunch stop was relocated to a small café overlooking the large open courtyard in front of the Notre Dame Cathedral. Everywhere the group went, they were followed by an international entourage of reporters and photographers. For Chow, who had never set foot outside the confines of his home city of Chengdu in China, it was a surreal experience.

When they finished lunch, the guide escorted the group of scientists outside to see the Cathedrale de Notre-Dame. Despite the cathedral being covered in soot and surrounded by police barricades, the crowds in the plaza were huge. The guide huddled the group together. "It's a tragedy. The cathedral was a source of great pride for the citizens of Paris. The central spire was completely destroyed by the fire but most of the original structure remains intact. Fortunately, the twin bell towers are unaffected. The major relics and works of art inside have been preserved. We can't go in, but I can show you the exterior architecture." The guide bragged about the eleventh century engineering skills required to construct the flying buttresses that supported the immense building. "The famous rose windows . . ."

Chimeras and gargoyles glared down from the towers, warding off evil spirits. Gauging by the devastation caused by the fire, it appeared as though they had failed. Chow didn't hear most of what was said during the tour. Thoughts of Liu-Fawn and how she was doing distracted him. What was supposed to happen today? Would the two of them truly be reunited in a safe place as promised by Mr. Sassani? Who he could trust? Why was Meang so happy today? He was never happy.

He had to hide the watch. Couldn't take the chance that it, or the codes would fall into Meang's hands. *Not here.* Too many tourists and construction workers. He checked the plaza clock. *Not much time left.* The tour would be over within the hour.

The crowd in the plaza had doubled since his group had arrived, leaving barely enough room to walk. The guide had difficulty keeping them together as she tried to negotiate her way toward the next tour site, a concrete abutment on the opposite side of the plaza. The sign read, "Crypte Archèologique." While trying to keep up, Chow almost tripped over the legs of a man sitting on a bench, reading a book. He glared up at Chow with angry, black eyes. Chow was taken aback by the hateful scowl after having received so much fond attention by the French up until now. The look was reminiscent of Meang—before today. Chow hurried. He caught up with Meang and the rest of the group as they were walking down a flight of concrete steps. "Where were you?" Meang asked.

"Got held back by the crowd."

"Make sure you stay at my side. I don't want you getting lost."

The tour guide stopped in front of a set of glass entrance doors. A sign read "Closed for Repairs." She turned to face the group. "This is the entrance to a subterranean city which was excavated by our archeologists several decades ago. Unfortunately, the water used to put out the cathedral fire ran down and resulted in a partial cave-in. It's been closed to the public, but we are in luck. The mayor was so disappointed that you weren't able to see the cathedral, he authorized a special private tour of the Crypte. Some areas are still off limits, but I promise you'll find it to be well worth your time this afternoon. The site offers us a haunting glimpse into the past, when Paris was little more than a small

Roman village established shortly after the death of Christ. At that time, the city was twenty feet below its present elevation. That's why this entire complex and much of historic Paris is now honeycombed by interconnecting subterranean tunnels. It's a little unstable down there, so I must caution that at all times you should wear the hard hats that we will distribute. Stay on the walkways and please watch your step. It's slippery."

She unlocked the doors and led them farther down several more flights of stone steps toward a civilization long ago forgotten. Midway through the tour, the guide said, "On your right is the entrance to an ancient Roman bath. The baths served as a social gathering places throughout the empire. It's too unstable to see right now and will be closed for several more months. We'll have to pass by it. Be careful. Watch your step."

A length of yellow construction tape prevented entrance to the bath. Narrow stone steps led down into the darkness. Meang was distracted by what appeared to be a message on his cell phone. The Colonel's face turned red and his smile had been replaced by his usual scowl. Something had upset him. Chow took the opportunity to slip away from the group unnoticed. He ducked under the tape barrier and snuck down the steps to the bath area until he reached a flat area at the bottom. The area was covered with layers of two-thousand-year-old dust and debris. It was damp but dry, and the walls were smothered by a thick layer of black mold. He continued farther until the light almost completely disappeared. Feeling along the stone walls, he found the perfect spot. Chow removed his precious watch and pushed the side button for one final glimpse of Liu-Fawn, then hid it within a crack in the stone wall. He laid a rock at the base to mark the spot, then sighed in relief. "Yaoguai is secure." He couldn't allow anyone access to all the activation codes that unlocked the power of Yaoguai until he could be sure of what was going on with Meang and Sassani. He headed back up the stairs and rejoined the group on the plaza level outside.

Meang was yelling into his cell phone and pacing about, his voice so loud those nearby were staring at him.

"What do you mean you don't have her? What happened!" he screamed in Chinese. After a minute, during which the person on the other end appeared to be explaining something, Colonel Meang spit into the phone. "Then find out who took her! Shut down the border! Close the damn airports! You'd better get her back or you're going to spend the rest of your life planting rice in a concentration camp!"

He terminated the call and glared at Chow. "Where have you been?"

"I lost my hard hat and it rolled down some steps. It was difficult to find."

Meang jammed his finger in Chow's chest. "I told you to remain at my—"

He never finished the sentence. A fountain of red spewed from where his mouth had been seconds ago. Meang's body collapsed onto the pavement. Panic struck the crowd and they stampeded in all directions. Chow's face and shirt were covered in droplets of Meang's blood as he stood in a catatonic-like state. He hadn't expected anything like this. Multiple shots rang out and bodies began falling all around him, transforming the Notre Dame plaza into a giant Jackson Pollack painting with huge blotches of dark red covering the ground.

Chow's ears rang from all the gunfire. The muffled screams of victims surrounded him like a scene in a silent horror film. During the frenzy, several men grabbed his arms. *What's happening?* His heart exploded in his chest. He tried to fight back but they were too strong, forcibly dragging him toward a dark sedan. Once thrown inside, a black hood was forced over his head as the car sped away.

THIRTY-EIGHT

Latin Quarter
Paris, France

Light from the window hit Jacob's eyes. They fluttered open and he saw Raphael staring down at him, her face bathed in the glow of the late morning sun. She looked even more radiant now than she had yesterday, so soft and vulnerable. Something had changed. *She's special, maybe even someone who can reconnect me toward a normal life.*

"Last night was wonderful, Jacob Savich."

"I would have to agree, Raphael DuBoise."

He kissed her gently on the lips. There was no denying it. He had feelings for her, something he had never experienced before. He waited for the voice of the Entity. It remained quiet.

They showered together and enjoyed sex one more time, the warm soapy water offering new options. "Your ankle seems better," he said.

She flashed a coyish smile and touched his face. "I think last night must have healed it. You're a very gifted physician, Jacob."

In spite of my Entity.

After drying off, she said, "I'm starving, and those leftover sandwiches from yesterday aren't looking very appetizing right now."

"We could use a little fresh air," said Jacob, feeling a wry smile he couldn't contain spread across his lips. Last night had taken a lot of energy. "There's a small café around the corner.

We can order lunch there. No one knows where we are, and I'm certain they can't track us anymore. Otherwise they would have already tried to storm our hotel room." He reloaded his Sig and tucked it into the holster at the small of his back. They exited the hotel through the lobby door and headed around the corner, keeping their heads down.

The café was small and quaint. Jacob found a rear exit by the kitchen. "This'll work," he said, pulling a chair for Raphael at a table near the back. He sat facing the front door. After setting his Sig Sauer on his lap, Jacob placed their order. They shared an egg soufflé with a side of fresh fruit, followed by several cups of espresso. Jacob was getting a better understanding of what was happening but still had no idea where things were ultimately headed.

They were safe for now, but they couldn't remain hidden forever. Sassani would continue to search for them, and he seemed to have unlimited resources. Jacob needed to get a better handle on the situation before he and Raphael were killed and before Sassani could launch his attack. Halfway through lunch, they heard sirens, a lot of them. They weren't far, maybe less than a mile away, coming from the direction of the Notre Dame Cathedral.

Raphael grabbed his hand. "Could that be another terror attack?"

"Maybe. We should probably head back to the hotel." He paid the bill and took Raphael's hand. They zig-zagged through the neighborhood, checking for tails, before they returned to the secure confines of their room. As soon as they entered, his cell phone rang.

"Jacob, it's Curt McClure from the embassy."

Jacob sat on the edge of the bed. "Do you have something for me?"

"Maybe. Have you been watching the news?"

"I've been kind of busy trying to stay alive. Why?"

"Turn on your TV to CNN. They have an English Channel in Paris."

Jacob reached over to the nightstand and found the remote in a drawer. He flipped on the TV, leaned forward, and watched the screen. A reporter was standing in the plaza that surrounded the Notre Dame cathedral, bodies scattered on the ground behind her. "Another terror attack has rocked the city of Paris this afternoon, the second in only two days. Gunmen opened fire on a large crowd of unsuspecting tourists. Dozens have been killed or wounded." The cameraman zoomed in on a bloodied park bench, the bullet-ridden body of a nun on the ground in front of it, her white habit stained red. Jacob's breathing shallowed as he leaned forward studying the screen. A book, splattered with bloody droplets sat upon the bench. He recognized the name *Les Miserables* on the cover. *Angry Eyes, you bastard!* It was the same book the man dropped after running into Jacob outside the Louvre. *Sassani was behind the attack.*

Jacob flipped off the TV and paced the room, listening to Curt's voice on his cell phone. "I think I've figured out what's going on in Paris and why you're here," he said. "I have some important information we need to discuss in person. How soon can you meet me at the embassy?"

"I'll be there in a half-hour. I need to make a few arrangements first."

Jacob pulled out his secure cell phone and contacted Winston Hamilton. Sir, we've had a major breakthrough. I'm going to need a few things.

Thirty minutes later, Dan and Tank, each holding a handgun, picked up Raphael and Jacob at their hotel.

THIRTY-NINE

No Go Zone
Paris, France

All was quiet for the first fifteen minutes of the ride. Chow could tell the car had turned down a multitude of different side streets. He had no idea who had taken him or where he was going. He only knew he was flanked by at least one man on either side of him. No one spoke.

He choked. "Would it be possible to remove the hood now? I can't breathe."

There was a brief discussion amongst the men. It wasn't English or French, and they sounded angry. He sensed that someone in the front passenger seat approved his request because the man on his left removed the hood. He immediately regretted losing it. The car reeked with the stench of body odor. He gagged and almost vomited. The men laughed — sinister and too loud.

They must work for Sassani, but they are not the kind of men I would expect. Mr. Sassani was a sophisticated gentleman. These men acted more like kidnappers than rescuers.

It took a few more seconds for his eyes to adjust to the light, but his vision was still blurred. His glasses were spotted with Meang's blood and body tissue. He cleaned them with the edge of his shirt. There were four men in the car with him: a driver and passenger in the front, and one on either side of him in the back. All wore heavy, black beards. The one in the front passenger seat turned to face him after the hood was removed.

He had dark black circles under his eyes.

Realization dawned. It was the same man he had almost tripped over near the Crypte, the one reading the book, the one with the angry looking eyes.

"Are you taking me to see Mr. Sassani?"

Angry Eyes seemed to understand his question and translated it for the other three. They all laughed — too loud again as they repeated the translation over and over. There was no reply to his question. What was so funny? His hands trembled.

Finally, Angry Eyes answered, "You will see Mr. Sassani soon."

"And what about Liu-Fawn? Will she also be there?" asked Chow.

Again, the translation and the subsequent laughing.

"The Chinese woman? Yes, she will be there."

There was no more conversation. *Same level of oppression, just different oppressors.*

The car sped through intersecting canyons of side streets and alleys. It no longer looked like Paris. Litter rolled in the streets and clogged the gutters. Abandoned cars sat everywhere. Gangs hung on street corners while men armed with automatic rifles patrolled the rooftops. Down some of the streets, old furniture, mattresses, and coils of barbed wire barricaded any exit. Graffiti defaced the sides of many buildings. The word ISIS painted in large red letters ran down the walls like fresh blood from a wound. Some buildings were scarred by bullets or scorched by fires. Battles had been waged here. It was almost as though their car had left France and was somehow transported into the center of a war-torn city in the Middle East.

After turning down a few more narrow streets, the car came to an abrupt stop in front of a three-story brick building.

"Is this where I am to meet Mr. Sassani?" asked Chow.

No reply. Not good. The four men spoke to each other rapidly in loud voices. They always seemed to be arguing with each other.

"You don't understand. I was to be taken to see Mr. Faizel

Sassani. I want to see him now!" Still no reply, only the unintelligible orders being issued by Angry Eyes.

The man jerked the car door open and pulled Chow out by his shirt, causing him to stumble and scrape his knees on the sidewalk. Blood soaked through his pants.

What have you done, Chow? Where is Liu-Fawn? Hopefully not here.

He was shoved through the front door of the building and dragged up three flights of stairs. Men armed with assault rifles met him on the top floor. One of them had unearthly long arms, the right one in a cast. He looked like he had recently been in a fight — one which he had lost. They opened a door and pushed Chow inside.

The rancid smell of rotting food and urine hit him in the face like a sledgehammer, causing him to gag again. A stained couch and an old wooden kitchen table with three chairs were the only furnishings in the small flat. The only light struggled its way through the cobwebbed panes of two grimy windows. In the center of the room sat Liu-Fawn, gagged, and tied to one of the wooden chairs. Tears streamed down her cheeks, her eyes wide with fear and panic, her upper lip swollen, and her clothes torn.

He ran to Liu-Fawn's side and touched her bruised cheek. She winced. Rage exploded inside Chow's chest. He turned and charged toward Angry Eyes, his face inches away. "What's the meaning of this? I want to see Mr. Sassani immediately!"

His demand was answered with the butt of a rifle to his left kidney. The pain seared through his body like a bolt of lightning. He doubled over, barely able to breath, each attempt causing more excruciating spasms of pain. The two guards pulled him to one of the chairs and restrained him with ropes. A dirty rag was shoved into his mouth, so tight he was convinced he would suffocate. Angry eyes yelled, "Quiet Chow! You're lucky to still be alive. The only thing I will promise you is a quick and painless death as long as you cooperate. If you do not, things will not go well for you and your pretty friend. Now shut up! Mr. Sassani will be here when it's time."

FORTY

No Go Zone
Paris, France

A well-dressed Faizel Sassani gave the cab driver the address. "I'm afraid I can't take you there, monsieur. No driver in Paris would. It's too dangerous."

He offered the cabbie a one hundred Euro tip. "Maybe this will help change your mind."

"I still can't take you there. That money's no good to me if I'm not alive to spend it." After the passenger doubled the offer, the driver said, "What I will agree to do is to take you within several blocks of the address, but that's the best I can do." A rosary hung from his rearview mirror. He kissed its crucifix before accepting the fare.

A half-hour later, the cab driver let Sassani out eight blocks from his destination. "This is as far as I can go, monsieur. Its closer than I should have come. Are you sure you want to head into this neighborhood alone? It's a rough place and gangs regularly prowl the area looking to rob tourists like yourself."

"This is the place."

"Suit yourself. Faites attention à vous, keep your eyes open. A man dressed in an expensive Italian suit is a tempting target and you're sure to be accosted. There will be no help for you if it happens. Even the French Police Nationale won't patrol this neighborhood. They call it a 'No-Go' zone."

"I understand, but I'll be fine. Merci beaucoup." He paid

the fare and left the generous tip as promised. He exited the cab, and it accelerated away. Sassani walked to his right for a block, and then headed east, down a narrow street. The sidewalks were an obstacle course of cracks and potholes. More dangerous were the gangs patrolling the neighborhood.

The cab driver was correct. It didn't take more than ten minutes before he was accosted by a small group of teens, demanding money. He stared them in the eyes. "As-salamu alaykum."

The teens hesitated, not expecting a formal Muslim greeting from a tourist. The gang's leader gazed up to the surrounding rooftops. Armed guards aimed rifles down at him and his friends. The shock of realization hit him. The man they intended to rob was the Scorpion. The teen took several steps back, bowed his head, and quickly apologized. "We are sorry. We meant no disrespect. We assumed you were just another lost western tourist. May Allah be with you and protect you on your journeys." The teens turned and hurried away, looking for other targets.

The Scorpion continued to follow a maze of garbage-littered streets until he reached his destination. Two guards at the front door stepped aside to let him enter the building. "The prisoners are on the third floor," the one with the cast said.

As he climbed the three flights of stairs, he avoided the stained hand railing. He opened the apartment door, entered, and brushed dust off the front of his suit. Glancing around the room, he scowled. "This place is unfit even for goats." His eyes fixed upon Dr. Chow and Liu-Fawn, bloodied, gagged, and tied to chairs. "Remove those restraints immediately!" he demanded. "After all, we don't want our two guests to think we're savages."

The guards did as they were told. Once free, Chow and Liu-Fawn removed their gags and rubbed their wrists to get the circulation flowing. Chow still had some dried blood smears on his glasses. The Scorpion removed them, cleaned the lenses, and replaced them. Chow seemed confused.

"Are you thirsty?" asked the Scorpion. He turned to

the guards. "Get a couple of bottles of water for our guests." Liu-Fawn looked at Chow for assurance. He nodded and they accepted the bottles cautiously.

"I must apologize for the actions of my men. At times they become…what's the phrase—over exuberant in their work. I'll have them get you something to eat as soon as we've had a chance to talk." The Scorpion paused to wipe away some dirt from one of his fingers. "I had intended to place you and Liu-Fawn in nicer accommodations until we could finish our business arrangement, but I'm afraid interference by outside forces has precluded that option. I've been forced to adjust my plans and accelerate my schedule."

Chow set down his empty water bottle and looked up. "Business arrangement? What arrangement, Mr. Sassani? You promised to get Liu-Fawn and me to safety in another country. You said it was for the sake of science and my research. You never mentioned a business arrangement."

The Scorpion slowly shook his head. "Now, Dr. Chow, you're a very intelligent man. Did you actually believe that I would go through all of the expense of kidnapping you and smuggling your girlfriend out of China simply out of the goodness of my heart?"

"But I thought—"

The Scorpion held up his finger to silence Chow. "Here's what we need to do, Dr. Chow. I'm prepared to fulfill my promise to you and your girlfriend. The two of you can live out the rest of your lives together in peace and freedom. All I ask in return is that you provide me with some information."

"Information?"

"Your list of activation codes."

"How do you know about the codes?"

"How I know makes no difference. The important thing, as far as you are concerned, Dr. Chow, is that I want them."

"But I don't have them anymore."

Sassani leaned forward. "Then we might have a problem, because you and your girlfriend are not leaving here until I get the codes. I can be very persuasive when I want something, so it's in your best interest to turn them over to me immediately."

"But I told you, I don't have them, Mr. Sassani!"

"Where are they?"

"I hid them so the likes of you could never gain access to them."

Sassani slowly shook his head. "That was an unwise comment, Dr. Chow. I was hoping we could do this in a civilized manner, without any discomfort for you and your little friend over there. I was willing to live up to my end of the agreement, but what do I get in return? Disrespect. You need to understand your position here. You have no leverage. I'll do whatever I must to get what I want. Now where are the codes?"

Liu-Fawn screamed, "Don't tell him anything Chow! Don't you see? He's not going to relocate us to another country. He's going to kill us as soon as he gets what he wants! He's just another oppressor, a monster, like Colonel Meang!"

The Scorpion lowered his eyes and looked to the floor. "I don't believe anyone was talking to you Liu-Fawn, and I definitely wasn't asking for your opinion." He looked to the guards. "Has anyone heard me ask for the lady's opinion?"

They shook their heads.

The Scorpion stood and walked over to her, removed his suit coat, and carefully draped it over one of the wooden chairs. The two guards restrained her as the Scorpion turned to Chow. "As I said before, I was hoping we could handle this situation as civilized gentlemen, but you're leaving me little choice here. All I ask for is a little cooperation on your part, but all I'm getting from you two is resistance and insults. If you provide me with the information I want, I promise to provide a life of luxury for you and your little lady friend here." He gently caressed Liu-Fawn's left cheek. "She's such a beautiful creature. It would be a shame if anything happened to her. Don't you agree, Dr. Chow?"

Chow lowered his head. "Please don't hurt her, Mr. Sassani."

"Don't you want a better life for her, Chow?"

Liu-Fawn pulled away and spit in the Scorpion's face. "Don't believe his lies, Chow!"

The Scorpion said nothing. He extended his right hand and one of the guards placed a clean towel in it. He wiped the spittle away and tightly wrapped the towel around his hand. Without warning, he delivered a vicious punch to the same cheek he had so gently caressed moments ago. Liu-Fawn's head snapped to the side, the punch almost knocking her unconscious, her left eye already beginning to swell shut.

"Stop!" cried out Chow.

The Scorpion faced him and smiled. "Pardon, what did you say?"

"Please stop."

"Have you had a change of mind?"

Chow didn't answer. The Scorpion withdrew a long knife from a belt scabbard along the small of his back. He walked over and held it a few inches from Chow's eyes. "Do you know what this is Chow?"

He looked down at the floor and slowly shook his head.

"No? Well you soon will because you and your girlfriend are about to become intimately familiar with it. This knife is called a Pesh-Kabz dagger. It's an Afghan tradition to give one to a young man as a symbol of his entry into manhood. My grandfather gave me this one only days before he and the rest of my family were slaughtered by the Americans. 'It was an unfortunate accident, the result of unanticipated collateral damage from an off-target bomb,' they claimed. I don't accept that feeble excuse. I am entitled to revenge for what they did, and I will have it!" His words were slow and measured. "You're going to help me, Chow. Don't make the mistake of trying to deny me what I deserve. I've become very proficient at using this dagger. I used it to kill over thirty American soldiers in Kandahar by the time I was fourteen. I won't hesitate to use it on your little girlfriend."

He slowly rotated the dagger in his hand, causing the dim light to reflect off the blade and into Chow's squinting eyes. "Now, must I show you how efficient I have become at using this? Must I start whittling away on your little lady-friend's face? I can make this last a very long time if I must,"

"Don't do it, Chow. He's just going to kill us anyway," whimpered a barely intelligible Liu-Fawn.

"No, please stop!" Chow cried out. "I'll tell you whatever you want to know! Don't hurt her anymore. Please."

"Good. That's all I wanted to hear. That wasn't so difficult, now was it? I'm glad we've been able to reach an understanding." The Scorpion grabbed one of the wooden chairs and pulled it over to face Chow. He dusted it off with the towel and sat down, his face close to Chow's—too close. Chow pulled back.

The Scorpion waited for a few seconds, his eyes boring into Chow's soul. "Now what do you have for me doctor?"

"How can I be sure you won't kill us as soon as you have what you want?"

"Because, I'm still going to need your help after I get the codes. That's your life insurance, Chow. But if you lie to me, that insurance policy is going to lapse. Then, I'll turn Liu-Fawn over to my men to do with as they wish. She will suffer a humiliating and painful death which you will be forced to watch. Do you understand?'

"Yes," said Chow. "The codes have been downloaded into my wristwatch. It's hidden in the walls of the Crypte Archèologique." He described the exact location in the cordoned off Roman bath. "The place is marked with a rock on the ground. When you try to access the codes, you must push the buttons along the side in a precise sequence to open the watch. Failure to follow my instructions exactly will cause the watch to self-destruct and the codes will be erased."

Chow paused, ashamed that he had given up the information. "What now?"

"My men are going to retrieve your watch tonight, as soon as we can gain access to the Crypte. For your sake, it'd better be exactly where you described. Then, you and I are going to take a small trip across the city. Liu-Fawn will remain here until we finish our business together. She's my insurance policy. If all goes well, you'll be released, unharmed, and transported to safety."

The Scorpion walked over to Liu-Fawn and made a sudden slash across her left cheek with his dagger. She screamed out in pain as blood ran down her face.

Chow pulled at his restraints. "Why? I gave you everything you wanted!"

"That's for her spitting on me and to let you know what's in store for her if you've lied to me, Dr. Chow." He whispered to the two guards, smiled, and turned. "I'll see you in a couple of days." He then disappeared out the door.

FORTY-ONE

United States Embassy Building
Paris, France

It was dark by the time Dan's car dropped Jacob off at the American Embassy. Tank kept an eye out for followers while they pulled away and headed to the safe house where Raphael would be protected. Curt McClure met Jacob in the lobby, but rather than leading him to his Cultural Attaché office on the second floor, he led Jacob down a flight of stairs to the lower level. They entered a small room with no windows. Jacob felt the pressure in his ears when the heavy sound-proof door closed behind them.

"The room's completely sealed off from the outside world," said Curt. "It even has its own ventilation system. The walls are lined with copper mesh to prevent any electronic eavesdropping." He flipped a switch next to the door and a black box in the corner hummed to life.

"White Noise Generator?"

"Yes, it jams any extrinsic devices we might have missed and keeps outsiders from eavesdropping on the embassy's more confidential discussions. It's similar to the one used inside the situation room at the White House. This particular room is swept for bugs twice a day. Our enemies are everywhere, and I can't say with one hundred percent certainty that the embassy's security systems haven't been compromised. Even our friends would like to know what we're up to, so we can't be too careful, especially when we need to conduct exceptionally sensitive conversations."

"And I guess we're about to have such a conversation?" asked Jacob.

"Yes, have a seat."

They each took a chair on opposite sides of a conference table, a bottle of Evian water in front of them. Jacob took a large drink from his bottle, draining half of it. He rested his elbows on the table and folded his hands. "So, what do you have for me, Curt?"

"The news media are labeling that massacre at Notre Dame another terrorist attack." Curt leaned forward in his chair and lowered his voice. "It was much more than that. The killings were used to disguise something even more sinister. Do you know of a man by the name of Dr. Chow Chi Wong?"

"No, should I?"

"He's from the People's Republic of China and he's one of the world's most notable computer research scientists. He's being touted as a future Nobel Prize winner. The man is to computer science what Einstein is to relativity."

"And?"

"During this afternoon's shootings, he was kidnapped from the Parvis de Notre Dame. His bodyguard, a Colonel Meang from the Chinese Ministry of Intelligence, was assassinated in the process."

Jacob furrowed his brow. "What would terrorists stand to gain by kidnapping a Chinese scientist? Ransom?"

"We don't think so," said Curt.

Jacob took another mouthful of water. "So, what's all this have to do with me being in Paris."

"I know you're involved in something big, and it's my belief that it's tied to Dr. Chow in some way. You've been extremely active in Paris and a lot of people here are trying very hard to look the other way to cover up your activities. I'm convinced you're somehow involved in the Rue Cler shootings and I suspect that's only the tip of the iceberg. Whatever you're up to it's off the books and probably extremely illegal. Only a select group of individuals can accomplish that level of cooperation from the French. That tells me you're politically connected, probably to the highest levels of our government. You must be working on something of critical importance to the U.S. and Europe." Curt leaned back and twirled his pen the same way he had during their first meeting. Annoying, but the Entity said nothing. After a few seconds, Curt leaned forward. "I want to be a part of it."

Jacob almost choked. "What?" He set the water bottle on the table and stared into McClure's eyes.

"I want to join you."

Jacob ran his hand through his hair and looked at the ceiling. *McClure must know something.* Maybe it was another big piece to the puzzle. He had to feel the man out some more before agreeing to team up with him. "Why would you be interested in getting involved in my mission here? You seem to already have a pretty cushy job as a Cultural Attaché."

"To tell you the truth, I'm bored. Don't get me wrong. Paris is a great assignment, one which many of my peers would jump at the chance to get. It's true, there's a lot happening here with all the recent terror attacks and yellow vest protests, but I need to get back into the trenches where this war is being waged: on the streets, in the alleys, and in the gutters. I can't do that if I'm stuck sitting behind a desk or attending endless diplomatic dinners."

"I generally work alone, Curt. The fewer people involved in my activities, the safer it is for me, and for them." The last thing he needed was to partner up with someone he'd only met a few days ago. McClure was smiling. *He must be holding some big cards and he isn't going to turn them over until I agree.* Jacob needed whatever information the guy had.

McClure stopped twirling his pen and pushed the issue. "I can be a valuable asset, Jacob. I have over twenty years of experience on the front lines, and I'm well-connected to many influential people in Paris; ones who could pave the way for whatever you have to do. I have access to information that can help you. We should pool our resources if we're going to stop this thing you're working on, whatever it is."

Jacob stared down at the table for a minute before answering. "Let's just say that theoretically, I'd be willing to consider your help. What do you have to offer, and what's it have to do with this Chow fellow?"

"Fair enough." Curt smiled. Genuine or fake? Jacob inwardly shook his head, not knowing for certain if he could trust this guy. He made his decision. He would take a chance on McClure.

Curt continued, "This afternoon I spoke to some of the people in our information technology department at Langley. They informed me that Dr. Chow has been working on a process which will revolutionize the way in which we think of computers. Old systems rely on the process of binomial theory."

Jacob nodded. "Basically, a series of on and off switches arranged in sequence to code data in bytes."

"Correct. Apparently, that limits the future capabilities of computer technology. Every major tech company in the world has spent billions of dollars to break through that barrier but they haven't succeeded. It appears that Chow has. He's developed a photon-based system based upon the principles of quantum physics. The concept of bytes has been replaced by something called qubits. I don't understand how they work but they provide infinitely greater processing and storage capacity. Langley claims that Chow's system might have the ability to solve trillions upon trillions upon trillions of problems simultaneously, well beyond the abilities of our most advanced systems. It can do so in an instant, and it accomplishes this with a computer inconceivably smaller than anything we've ever seen before."

Jacob slowly shook his head. "Hard to believe, but if true, the military and economic implications would be staggering. Whoever possesses this technology stands to make hundreds of billions in profits, but I still don't see what this would have to do with any terrorist group. What they would gain by kidnapping Chow. They don't care about financial gain as much as the destruction of Western Civilization and the world-wide imposition of Sharia Law."

"True, but it takes a great deal of cash to finance a large terrorist organization." Curt's voice almost dropped to a whisper. "Here's the heart of the problem. More important than financial considerations is the impact such a computer can have on national security systems. Because of the quantum computer's ability to instantly analyze complex data, all cryptography becomes useless. Even the most sophisticated cyber-security systems could be easily penetrated in milliseconds. In fact, every significant information system in the world might have already been compromised. It's possible the Chinese have access to some of our top-level secret discussions. That includes those of every other major power in the world. They may already know about military contingency plans designed by our Joint Chiefs, and God only knows what else. We know for a fact that they've been pirating technological information from our business leaders, including plans for our most sophisticated weapons systems. The Chinese haven't taken military advantage of the situation because they can't afford for the United States to collapse. They own too much of our national debt and their economy is too dependent on ours. However, terrorist organizations don't share the same concerns. They would love to have all Chow's power at their fingertips."

Jacob stood and paced the room, his arms folded across his chest. "That's a dangerous capability in the hands of an enemy," he said. "The problem is that the recent attacks in Paris haven't been the work of any worldwide terrorist organization like ISIS or Al Quaida. I know for a fact that the shootings at Rue Cler and the Notre Dame Plaza were orchestrated by just one man." He couldn't figure out what Chow could possibly have to do with Raphael. "The quantum computer factor could be a piece of the puzzle, but I don't believe it's the primary reason for his kidnapping."

So, who's this guy pulling all the strings?"

"He has a multitude of different aliases. In Paris he's known as Mr. Faizel Sassani."

McClure's eyes went blank. "Never heard of him. If he's such a major player in the world of terrorism, his name would have come across my desk. You mentioned other alias identities."

"In the world of terrorism, He's known as the Scorpion."

Curt's jaw dropped and he leaned forward on the edge of his chair. "Holy shit! The guy who tried to assassinate President Wagner? This Sassani guy is the Scorpion? The State department and Homeland Security have been looking for that guy for years.

"He's been able to slip into and out of so many different identities, it's been impossible to track him down. That's about to change soon. Now we know he's in Paris and he has to remain nearby until he can get whatever he needs from Dr. Chow."

Curt picked up his pen but set it back down on the table. "We won't be able to figure what that is unless we get our hands on this Chow fellow."

Jacob stopped pacing. "Before the Scorpion kills him or smuggles him out of France."

"The problem is, we have no idea where he's being kept."

Jacob squinted his eyes and held up his index finger. "But we're getting close. See if you can find anything in your database on Sassani."

McClure sat at one of the room's secure computer consoles while Jacob waited. After ten minutes of searching, Curt said, "Here it is. Faizel Sassani. He's an Iranian businessman who entered France a couple of years ago, but there's no picture included in his file. Somehow, he's been able to avoid photographic documentation in spite of living here on a temporary visa. That's almost impossible to do."

"He's one of the wealthiest men in the world and pretty much able to buy whatever he wants. That includes anonymity," said Jacob.

McClure continued with his search by opening an Iranian database. "Now I have a photograph." He showed Jacob.

"I already checked with Langley and the man in this picture is dead, probably murdered. The Scorpion took over Sassani's identity a few years ago. The important question is, does he have any business interests in Paris?"

"Let's see." After a few minutes of typing, Curt looked up. "Nothing."

"What about transactions under the name Martin Darpoli?"

"Another Scorpion alias?" Curt entered the name into the data base. "Not much on him either, except that he visited Paris for a few weeks several years ago."

"Damn, I was hoping—wait a minute. What about the Masterson Properties Corporation? It used to be the Scorpion's shell company."

Curt returned to the computer and typed. "Bingo! Here we are! The company owns a condo on the Champs Élysées."

"That must be it! Now that we know where he is, we can get him before he can go any further with his plans. I want you to arrange for the French police to conduct a raid on his Champs Élysées condo ASAP. We must hurry on this. Once he realizes we're on to him, he's going to bolt. Then things are going to start happening quickly."

"What if he's already gone?"

"Then we'll have to find Chow on our own," said Jacob. "Is there anything else on Masterson Properties?"

"They own a hotel in St. Tropez and an apartment building in Paris."

"What's the area like?"

"Low end."

Jacob leaned forward on the edge of his chair. "Masterson Properties was involved in the luxury hotel business. There's no reason he would purchase an apartment building in a depressed neighborhood unless—"

"He needed a secure place somewhere in Paris as a base of operations," Curt finished the sentence.

"Exactly! That must be where he's keeping Chow. Let me guess, it's in the middle of one of those No-Go zones you mentioned a couple of days ago."

"Right smack dab in the middle of the worst. The French police haven't set foot in there in years. Too dangerous.

It'll be impossible to get Chow out of there alive without a full military assault."

"I need to make a few phone calls. We're going to need some surveillance. For right now, your job is to get the French on that damn condo."

FORTY-TWO

Champs Élysées.
Paris, France

The Scorpion paced the floor like a caged animal. He hadn't heard from Raphael and was concerned that she might have betrayed him. In fact, after the failed assassination attempt on Rue Cler, he was almost certain she had.

It wouldn't take much for her to realize that she had been targeted along with Savich. She didn't know where he lived, but Savich was smart, certainly clever enough to avoid two attempts on his life. He might even be shrewd enough to figure out the location of his home.

He glanced at the briefcase and luggage sitting by the front door. "It's time to move on," he said to the room. He checked the bags. Everything was there: the fake identities, the clothes, the passports, the credit cards, and the cash.

Before leaving, he made some last-minute arrangements. *Raphael betrayed me. Nobody does that and lives, especially a woman.* He should have killed her long before this. She must pay for what she has done. Maybe he could throw Dr. Savich off balance in the process.

He opened his laptop and sent a message to his shooter, instructing her to call him immediately. Within a minute his cell phone rang.

"What do you need?" she asked.

"You've failed to hit your primary target for the second

time! The Chinese colonel was little consolation."

"What's so important about him?" she asked. "You told me he was an international arms dealer, selling weapons to terrorists. You said that he was responsible for the deaths of thousands of innocent people. I don't believe that this man is an arms dealer at all. I think you lied to me."

The Scorpion ground out a cigarette into a silver tray. "You're not being paid to think. You're being paid to kill the people I tell you to kill. When I want your opinion, I'll ask you." His voice got low and steely. "Now here's what you're going to do. You have only one more chance to redeem yourself. If you succeed, I'll forgive your past two failures and let you live."

He told her the plan and where she was to go later that evening. "Don't disappoint me again. or you'll never have to opportunity to return to your little pastry shop in Limone."

He heard a gasp on the other end of the line. "That's right. I know who you are, Carla Coyne. Did you really think I'd hire someone without knowing their identity? Don't think about running. I have contacts everywhere and I'll find you. By the way, you should be aware. I also know where your mother lives in Texas." He paused to let that little fact sink on. "Now take care of things the right way this time! Kill Raphael and her damn grandfather!"

He hung up the phone, grabbed his bags, and walked out the door onto the Champs Élysées. By the time he was two blocks away, he saw the police cars racing up the avenue toward his former home.

Carla screamed into the dead phone line. "You fucking asshole! You'll let me live? You threaten me? You threaten my mother? Nobody gets away with that, not even the U.S. military! You're a fucking dead man!" She made her own call.

FORTY-THREE

CIA Safe House
Paris, France

The commercial Bell helicopter sat on the pad, rotors turning, and waiting for its only passenger of the day. The plane was owned by Vista Tours, Inc. They provided private corporate transportation across France and helicopter tours around Paris. The sole owner and operator was a retired U.S. Air Force major from Oklahoma. On the side, he also served as a contract employee for the U.S. government. He checked his watch. Today's passenger was over ten minutes late, but the pilot didn't care. He wasn't being paid by the hour. His compensation was based upon the job and the level of risk involved. This one was somewhat hazardous and that meant a sizable paycheck.

When the passenger finally arrived, he loaded his gear and jumped into the passenger seat. He gave the pilot the coordinates for their destination, and they were entered into the helicopter's GPS system. After the two men put on their headsets, the pilot said, "I know the area well. We'll be heading to the south first. I need to follow a typical sightseeing route to the site. We don't want to raise any suspicions by setting a direct course for the target. Buckle up. Our ETA is about fifteen minutes."

"Roger," the passenger said. There would normally be no further conversation between the two men during the flight. There rarely was when the CIA was involved. No communication was necessary. The pilot's sole job was to fly the plane to wherever the passenger wanted to go and then forget whatever happened. That's how he liked it. No fuss, no muss, just a fat tax-free cash payment when it was over. During the flight, the passenger assembled a device. It looked like a tiny bird.

"What the hell is that?" asked the pilot, breaking the normal silence protocol.

The passenger held up the device and inspected it closely. "Its official name is Videoroam but I call it The Hummingbird. It's the smallest video-capable drone made. It was developed for military reconnaissance. It's fast, highly maneuverable, and virtually undetectable by the enemy." He placed the control module on his lap and checked the video feed. He tested the controls. All was ready. He stared forward in silence until they neared their target site.

Pointing to the west, the passenger asked, "Can you hover over there for a while?"

The pilot slowly shook his head. "Too dangerous. This isn't a stealth aircraft, and the locals who live there will definitely hear us. They won't care who we are. I guarantee they'll start shooting, and they have weapons much more powerful than automatic rifles to fire at us. We need an alternate plan. What's the range of your device?"

"About two miles, but I'd prefer to halve that number to be safe."

"Roger that. I can keep us well within those parameters." He nodded to his right. "Do you see that white building on top of the hill?"

"Sure, it's the Sacré-Coeur Basilica on Montmartre, the highest point in Paris."

"It's also a popular tourist site. I can safely hover there for a while. If anyone's curious, they'll assume that it's part of a sightseeing tour. However, you should keep what you do down to twenty minutes, max. Any more than that and we'll start to attract too much attention from the Paris Aviation Control Center."

"That should work. My battery pack is good for at least

twenty minutes. It's two minutes to the target, ten minutes of work and two minutes to return. That'll give me a six-minute buffer in case anything goes wrong." The passenger launched his drone and guided it toward the No-Go zone. Looking through the camera's lens, he guided his "Hummingbird" to the apartment building and began taking a dozen photographs from above and along all sides.

"Got everything I need." He guided the drone back to the copter. "We can head back."

"We need more time," said Tank. "I have to admit, it's pretty good intel, but I'm not sure how well it's actually going to help us."

"The French Police missed him at the condo, so this is our only option," said Jacob.

The team was in the safe house, reviewing the aerial images provided by the drone. Maps and over a dozen photographs were scattered over the kitchen table. Jacob said, "These images are as good as any on site surveillance, Tank. In many ways, they're better."

"Sure," said Tank. "We know where they have shooters stationed on the rooftops, and we can see the three guards protecting the front door of the apartment. But that's not nearly enough information to launch a rescue attempt. Photographs are no substitute for boots on the ground. Too many missed variables."

"The front guards are in addition to the two in the alley protecting the back," said Dan.

"That's worse," said Tank. "We still don't know how many snipers might be sitting inside the adjacent buildings, ready to shoot through an open window. Remember what happened on Rue Cler?"

Winston Hamilton lit up a cigar and leaned over the photos. "Rescuing Dr. Chow will admittedly be a Herculean task, but maybe Deets and I can help. We can use the same type of infrared satellite we accessed in West Virginia during the training compound raid. It'll allow us to see inside the target building and those nearby. I'll have to make a call to Parker Davis at the White House to make the necessary arrangements, but it won't be a problem."

"That's all fine and good," said Tank, "but there's still no way we'll be able to get to the apartment. That building's in the middle of a No-Go zone. It's essentially a war zone for outsiders. We'd have to slug our way through a half-mile of streets and alleys in enemy territory just to get close to the building. If we do happen to make it, there must be hundreds of armed jihadists surrounding the place. They'll be ready to defend that building with their lives. We can't even be certain Chow's actually in there. If we do get lucky enough to find him, there's zero chance of our getting him out alive. Once they know we're coming, they'll probably just shoot the poor bastard."

"They won't kill him. He's too valuable." Jacob sipped at a cold cup of coffee and made a face.

Tank crossed his huge arms across his chest. His biceps stretched his black tee to its limits. "We don't know that for certain. Look, I'm just trying to be realistic here. There's probably going to be a lot of shooting, so we'll never be able to maintain the element of surprise. The noise alone is going to bring out an army of militants. Not only that, we'd still have to do all of this within a maximum fifteen-minute window. It's not possible."

The team members remained quiet. It was hard to argue against Tank's logic. "You know me. I'm ready to mix it up as much as anyone. I'm not afraid of a good fight, but I still think we need more time to plan this thing."

Dan stepped forward and scanned through the photos. The tremor in his right hand had become more noticeable since West Virginia. "I'm afraid time is a luxury we don't have, Tank. Like Jacob said, the Scorpion knows we're on to him. He's already abandoned his condo, so, whatever he has in mind, he's going to do it soon. We have to make this happen, and we need to do it ASAP."

Tank was right. As things stood now, this was a suicide mission. It was essential, but it was also impossible unless something changed. They needed an idea, a plan on how to rescue Chow and get everyone out alive. Right now, they didn't have one.

The team discussed their dilemma for the next hour but were unable to come up with a solution. Jacob poured another cup of stale coffee, grimaced and spit it out. He threw the cup in the sink. "We're fucked." He placed his hands on the table and again leaned over to study the drone's images and topographical maps, hoping for inspiration. He picked up one of the maps and brushed some of Mr. Hamilton's cigar ashes off the surface. Beneath it was an old, illustrated copy of *Les Miserables*. Jacob lifted the book off the table. "Who's reading this?"

"I am," said Mr. Hamilton and took a long draw on his cigar. "I found it in the antique store downstairs. It's one of the few English texts they had. I hadn't read it since college, and I needed something to do while you all were running around Paris having fun."

"I had to write an essay on it in college," Lisa said. "It's the story of the tribulations of Jean Valjean, right?"

"Yes. For twenty years, he was relentlessly pursued by Inspector Javert for stealing a loaf of bread to feed his starving family," said Winston. He looked at Jacob. "Why are you asking about the book?"

"Probably a coincidence. The man who was a spotter for the sniper at Sacré-Coeur was reading it. The same man was holding the book when he bumped into me outside the Louvre. He's the one who planted a bug in my sport coat. 'Angry eyes,' I called him. I hope it's not a bad omen, that same book being here."

He opened it carefully. Time had turned the edges of the pages a mottled yellow and there was the unmistakable musty smell of age as he leafed through it. Something was itching in the back of Jacob's mind, but he didn't know exactly what it was. He couldn't quite put his finger on it, but something was there, trying to talk to him. What was it trying to tell him? He hesitated and began turning back several pages. It was there in one of the illustrations. The seed of a plan was sown and beginning to germinate. He carefully studied the maps and drone images again, rapidly switching back and forth between them. His heart rhythm picked up. He turned to Raphael. "Do you know much about this area?"

"Somewhat. We studied it in one of my 'History of Paris' classes in college, but that was over fifteen years ago."

He explained the details of his plan to everyone. "Could this work? I mean, is it even possible?" asked Jacob.

Raphael nibbled at her lower lip. After a minute, she smiled. "It'll be tricky, but yes, I think it could work. You're going to want my help, though. We'll need some bolt cutters and a can of fluorescent spray-paint."

Mr. Hamilton put out his cigar in an ashtray and studied the drone images. "It's a brilliant move. Considering the time restraints, it'll be challenging, but I believe it's doable. If this thing is going to happen, there are some other matters I'll need to discuss with Parker Davis. We're going to need more help than just the satellite coverage. President Wagner will have to talk to the president of France to smooth out some ruffled feathers in advance. The man's been taking heat from the French press ever since Rue Cler and the shootings at Notre Dame."

Jacob showed the map to Dan. "Three doors down from the apartment is a building with a steeply-pitched mansard roof. After he explained Dan's part to the team, Dan said, "That's terrific. How am I supposed to get there? I sure can't walk in by myself and a helicopter insertion will be out of the question. It's not that I'm afraid to do it but those guys'll hear me before I'm a thousand yards out. I wouldn't be surprised if they have stinger missiles."

"Can you pull this off?" asked Jacob. "That gunshot wound to your shoulder was less than a couple weeks ago."

Dan rotated his arm around the shoulder. "It was only a flesh wound. I was shot up much worse than this in Afghanistan and still manned my sniper position for over forty-eight hours." He touched the shoulder. "This thing is only a minor inconvenience." He put on his old army hat, the one with the bullet hole in the top. "Besides, I'll have my good luck charm with me."

But what about that neurological problem you're trying to hide?

Mr. Hamilton patted Dan on his good shoulder. "It looks like you're going to be doing a little traveling tonight, Dan. I'll make the necessary calls."

Jacob called Curt McClure on his secure cell phone and told him what was about to go down.

"Thanks for the invite," said McClure. "By the way, someone's been calling the embassy, trying to get ahold of you. She left a number."

"She?"

"Yeah."

Jacob wrote it down on a scratch pad.

"Okay, get here as soon as you can. We need to get started right away," said Jacob.

"I'll be there in fifteen minutes," said McClure. He made it in ten.

FORTY-FOUR

Beneath Paris, France

The light faded as the moon disappeared behind a thick layer of clouds. Jacob couldn't have asked for better conditions. *Dark and no traffic.* He checked the park in all directions. "All clear, go ahead."

Tank divided the chain with bolt cutters. "I'm surprised they don't have a guard posted here."

"Who, besides us, would be crazy enough to try to break into this place?" said Lisa.

The heavy rusted gate screeched in protest as Tank coaxed it open. The sound pierced the silence of the night, forcing the team to stop for a minute in case the noise had attracted any attention. No lights flipped on in nearby buildings and the silence returned. Raphael led the way down several flights of rough-hewn stone steps. Once they reached the bottom, she said, "You can turn on your flashlights now. No one can see us from above. Watch your step. It's very slippery in spots."

Lisa held her nose. "This is awful!"

"It's better than it used to be. In the eighteenth century it was referred to as 'The intestine of the Leviathan,' and for obvious reasons. Thirty years ago, the sanitary sewers were isolated from the street rainwater by using separate pipes. The Parisian government installed elevated metal walkways so at least we don't have to wade through the sludge. The system is over two thousand kilometers long and it's almost like a centuries-old underground expressway running beneath the streets of Paris."

"Expressway for rats," said Lisa as one ran across her foot. She pulled her leg back.

Raphael continued, "It was made famous in the book *Les Miserables*. It's how Jean Valjean was able to escape from the grasp of Inspector Javert."

"So, it can take us fairly close to where we want to go?" asked Tank.

"That's what I'm counting on," said Jacob. "The drone photographs showed a series of manhole covers less than fifty yards from the apartment building's entrance. That's where we'll exit. Dan will cover us once we come back up to the surface."

"Isn't this going to start transitioning into smaller and smaller pipes?" asked Lisa. "I'm not exactly looking forward to crawling through miles of sewerage."

"Don't worry, it won't be a problem," said Raphael. "When they originally built this section in the fourteenth century, they constructed these high-arched tunnels out of brick and mortar. They didn't have precast concrete pipes and they had to make the sewers large enough for workers to walk through. The high ceilings will allow us easy access throughout much of the older city. Considering when it was first built, it's remarkably complex. It's considered to be such an amazing engineering feat that there are guided tours available."

"I can't believe tourists actually pay money to do this!" said Lisa, still holding her nose.

"Yes, but that's in a newer section of the sewer which is only a few hundred years old. Those walls have been power washed and a ventilation system was installed, so it's less offensive than it is here. We broke in through an accessory service entrance several miles away from where the tourists enter."

After twenty minutes of walking, Raphael checked her map. "Here we are. This is the first junction. Hand me that can of spray paint." She drew an arrow on the wall indicating the direction back to the entrance. "Getting there isn't so difficult but getting back can be almost impossible. This system is a complex labyrinth of branching tunnels. If you miss a turn and get lost, the result could be disastrous. You might never find your way out. People have been known to disappear and die down here."

Jacob checked his watch. "How much longer?"

"Less than an hour," said Raphael.

"Good, Dan should be in position by then."

Thirty minutes after crossing the border into southeast Germany, Dan's car arrived at the Ramstein U.S. Air Base. The guard at the side entrance gate inspected his credentials and noted the time. It was 2:30 a.m., but the visit wasn't entered into the official log. There was to be no record of his having been there. An MH-X Stealth Black Hawk helicopter was already waiting for him on the tarmac, rotors turning. In a crouched position, he approached the copter, loaded his gear, and jumped aboard. He asked the pilot, "Do you have the coordinates?"

"They're already entered into the computer, sir. Once you fasten up, we'll take off." They were airborne ten seconds later. Though he had been in a similar helicopter several years ago, Dan was still impressed by the almost complete lack of noise.

"How long?" asked Dan.

"A little over an hour. We're already entering French air space. We can't be seen on their radar, but I'll stay at treetop level to be safe."

The pilot glanced over at Dan. "Have you ever flown in one of these before?"

"Flew in some of the earlier models when I was in the Special Forces."

"And maybe once in Washington a few years ago?"

"Maybe." Dan continued to look straight ahead into the night.

"I thought I recognized you. You're Dan Foster! A buddy of mine was flying the helicopter on the day you took out one of the terrorists trying to assassinate President Wagner. Shot him while hanging out the copter door and flying at over two hundred miles an hour. All the while you were receiving heavy automatic fire in return. It was an impossible shot, but you made it; dropped the bastard with two shots right in the head. You helped save the President. They should have given you a medal."

"Maybe, but officially I wasn't there." Dan hesitated. "I'm not here either. Neither of us are."

"Roger that, sir."

It took fifty-seven minutes. Light from the instrument panel reflected off his visor as the pilot studied the darkness in front of them. "Paris is directly ahead."

Once they reached the drop area, Dan pointed out the building. The pilot balked. "Are you sure about this, sir? I've dropped a lot of people into some pretty hairy spots, but this has to be one of the worst. There's an awfully steep pitch on that roof. It'll be a miracle if you don't lose your footing and slide off. It looks like a four-story drop straight to the ground."

"That's why we selected it. Nobody in their right mind would consider stationing a shooter here, so it isn't likely to be guarded."

"Roger that sir. I'll keep us as steady as I can until you're there."

"Hooah," said Dan.

"Hooah," replied the pilot. "Make sure you get some bad guys for me tonight. I lost a brother in Syria."

"That, I can promise you, captain," said Dan. He put on his leather rappelling gloves, shouldered his weapon, checked his sidearm, and secured a coil of nylon repelling rope to his utility belt. After giving a thumbs-up sign, he reached out for the fast rope. "Hold on," he told the pilot and reached over the seat and grabbed his hat. "Almost forgot my lucky charm. It's kept me safe more times than I can count."

"Roger that, sir. Mine's a photo of my family. Keep it in my pocket on every mission."

Dan secured the hat firmly atop his head. He reached out and tried to grab ahold of the "fast rope." It fell out of his hand. "Dammit!"

The pilot looked over his shoulder. "Everything okay back there, sir?"

"I'm fine. Just been a while since I last made a drop at night." He held firm onto the rope and disappeared into the darkness through the copter's side door. He hadn't made a rapid drop since he had been in the Special Forces over a decade ago and he was a little rusty. When he landed, he lost his balance. *Oh shit.* He slid most of the way down the steep slate roof before finally stopping his fall by grabbing the edge of a chimney. He gave a small prayer of thanks and looked up to see the super-silent helicopter already gone. He hadn't even heard it leave.

Dan tied one end of his nylon rope around the narrowest of the building's three chimneys and attached the other end to a carabiner on his waist harness. His hands fumbled. *Damn.* Parkinson's Disease, the doctor called it. He didn't have time for any fucking disease. He was a special forces sniper, one of the best in the world and his job was to protect others on his missions. No way was this going to affect him. He shook off the tremor and searched the roof for a position that would provide adequate cover and optimize potential lines of fire in all directions. He found one and settled in. The target building sat across the narrow street, around thirty yards away. Only two guards protected the front door instead of the three noted on the drone images. Two more were stationed on adjoining rooftops. Fortunately, none of the guards had noticed his helicopter drop. The streets were empty; no surprise considering it was just after three in the morning. He affixed a night vision scope to his flash-sound suppressed sniper rifle. and whispered into his throat mike, "In position." He crouched down behind the chimney. There was nothing left to do now but wait for the team.

"This should be it," said Raphael as she looked up the silo-like column above her. Several small circles of light peeked through holes in the cover.

"Are you sure?" asked Jacob.

"As sure as I can be, considering we're ten meters underground and I haven't seen the surface in a couple hours."

"I need some confirmation before we exit. If we're not in the right spot, they'll cut us down in seconds." Jacob spoke into his wrist radio. "Dan, do you read?" There was no response, only static. He repeated the call, again with no reply. "We're too deep to get reception. I'm going up to the surface."

Jacob climbed the steel rungs of the sewer well, slipping twice on wet ones before reaching the top. He rotated the cover clockwise to unlock it and carefully pushed it aside slightly so as to avoid making too much noise. The cover scraped against the concrete. He froze, hoping he hadn't been heard. All remained quiet. He inhaled, filling his lungs with the cool fresh air, then whispered into his radio. "Dan, do you read?"

Only static, then Dan replied, "Here. What's your 20?"

"Not sure. I'm going to need your help on that. Check the manhole covers and see if one looks out of position a few inches. That should be us."

Dan studied the street through his night vision scope. "Got it! Now wiggle the cover a little to be sure."

Jacob did.

"Confirmed. You're about fifty yards from the entrance to the building. I see only two guards between you and the door."

"Roger that. Wait for further instructions." Jacob climbed back down the ladder.

"OK, here's the plan. Lisa, you escort Raphael back out to the entrance and proceed with phase two. Take care of her."

Lisa smiled. "I'll protect her with my life if I have to."

The comment sent a foreboding chill down Jacob's spine. Lisa and Raphael were the two most important people in his life. He understood the possible risks they might be facing. "You both should be fine but be prepared for surprises. I'll send Dan as backup as soon as we're finished here. Don't start until he gets there."

Lisa turned to leave when Jacob stopped her. "And Lisa, just follow the plan. No improvising. I'm still not one hundred percent sure that we can trust this person. It could be a trap. If you suspect an ambush, abort." He touched her arm. "Remember them."

"Always." She turned to follow Raphael back to the entrance.

Jacob watched as the two disappeared down the dark tunnel.

"What's with that?" Curt asked Tank.

"What's with what?"

"The 'remember them' comment."

Tank sighed. "It's something Lisa and Jacob say before every mission. They're remembering how their family was butchered when they were just kids."

The three men completed a last-minute weapons check. Each had several grenades and smoke bombs in case they got into trouble. They attached silencers to their handguns and applied camo paint to their faces. After slinging assault rifles over their shoulders, they climbed the rungs up to the surface. Before exiting, Jacob asked in his throat mike, "Still clear?"

"There are several small problems you should be aware of," said Dan.

Jacob looked down at the other two on the rungs below him. They were his responsibility. He didn't need any surprises. Sweat beaded up on his brow. "Define small problems."

"First of all, there's a streetlamp sitting almost directly over your position. I should have mentioned it earlier. You'll be seen as soon as you exit the sewer."

"Can you shoot it out?"

"Sure, but as soon as I do, the guards are gonna get suspicious and start shooting at anything that moves. You guys will have to come out one at a time, and you'll be sitting ducks."

"Terrific." Adrenalin was pulsing through his body.

He hated waiting when it was time for action. "And the second problem?"

"We now have three guards at the building's entrance. One just came around the corner a minute ago."

"Where'd he come from?"

"Not sure. He might have been checking on the apartment's rear door or he might have come from one of the adjacent buildings."

"Deets, are you getting this?" asked Jacob.

"Roger. I have Dan on satellite but can't see you."

"That's because we haven't surfaced yet. How's it look inside the building?"

"One guard in the back. As best I can tell, there are four individuals inside on the top floor. Three of them haven't moved. My guess is that one of them might be Chow and the other two are probably guards. Looks like they're sleeping. The remaining one's pacing about the hall outside and appears to be standing watch."

"Could there be any others on the lower floors?"

"Hard to be sure. With the satellite, I'm looking almost straight down. There could be more sitting below the top floor, camouflaged by the heat signatures of the ones above. Let me try a digital filter." After a few seconds, he added, "Actually, it looks like there could be several overlapping images. That means there might be more than we thought."

"So, we don't know for sure exactly how many we're dealing with," said Jacob. Sweat was now dripping down his cheeks. He could hear Tank and Curt below him, changing their hand positions on the rungs, getting restless. "That's terrific! How about the surrounding buildings?"

"There are two roof guards, one stationed on either side of the target building. There are about two dozen people in each of the apartment buildings on either side. They're all horizontal and appear to be asleep."

"Keep tabs on them. They could be radicals, or they might be innocents. For now, we have to assume that everyone's a threat. We don't need any more surprises like we had in West Virginia."

"Roger that. I'll keep a close eye on them."

"Dan, do you have visualization of the two roof guards?" asked Jacob.

"Got 'em. Should I take them out?"

"Do it."

Within five seconds, both men were down with barely a sound.

"Are we clear?" asked Jacob.

"Hold on—the three guys in the front are all clustered together, lighting cigarettes. There's no way I can get all of them without at least one getting off a shot. If that happens, we'll lose the element of surprise, and then we're gonna be knee deep in shit."

"We need to separate them. Go ahead and shoot out that streetlight after all."

"Roger that. It might work." Dan set his sights on the light and fired, pfft. A bright light flashed as the lamp exploded, then darkness as a storm of broken glass fell onto the pavement. Immediately one of the guards turned toward the noise, threw down his cigarette, and raised his automatic rifle. He stepped into the middle of the street, cautiously heading toward the broken lamp.

Jacob heard the glass crunching under the guard's shoes as he approached. He was getting too close. If they got into a gunfight now, it'd be all over before they even got started. They'd lose any hopes of rescuing Chow.

The guard stopped almost on top of the sewer lid. Jacob raised his Sig and silently prayed. "Come on Dan."

Dan watched the second guard follow about ten feet behind the first, providing cover for his partner. The third remained near the apartment entrance, checking the street in both directions for trouble. There was a suppressed "pfft" sound and suddenly the back of the third guard's head exploded against the building's front door. Dan quickly centered his sights on the middle one and dropped him a second later with a shot through the neck, severing his spine. The man closest to the sewer began to turn around when he heard his partner hit the ground. Another "pfft" and he was dead before he had a chance to realize what had happened.

"You're all clear to the door," said Dan.

Jacob pushed the lid completely aside and crawled onto the street, Tank and Curt right behind him, providing cover. Staying low, the three ran for the shadows of the nearest building and made their way along a wall to the front door of the apartment.

Jacob said to Curt, "There's an alley on the right side. Take it to get around to the back door and eliminate the rear guard. If you see anyone else, shoot. No innocent civilian is going to be out on the street this late."

"Roger that." Curt took off for the rear. Jacob noticed he was still limping slightly.

"*Terrific,*" said the Entity. "*You're gonna have a problem with this one.*"

Tank and Jacob quietly coaxed the front door open. All was clear.

"Careful, this seems a little too easy," whispered Tank. "Could be a trap."

"Doesn't feel like it. They're probably not expecting a rescue attempt." Jacob headed down a hallway and disappeared into the first door on the left. A second later, Tank heard the characteristic "pfft, pfft" of a silencer followed by the sound of two bodies hitting the floor. Jacob returned to the hall giving a thumbs-up signal. He cleared the remaining apartments on the first floor. They were empty.

They headed up the stairs to the second floor and followed the same procedure. When Jacob opened the last apartment door on the right, he found a woman and small child sleeping. She woke up startled, but before she could scream out a warning to the guards, Jacob shook his head no and pointed his gun directly at her child.

Shoot, Buddy Boy! Do it now!

Jacob ignored the Entity. He'd never pull the trigger on

an innocent kid, but the mother didn't know that. She remained quiet. Jacob tied and gagged them both.

As he and Tank were halfway up the stairs leading to the third floor, the woman started kicking the walls. They froze on the seventh step.

Hearing the racket below, one of the guards peeked over the railing. Before he could raise his rifle, Tank dropped him with double tap shots to the forehead. The dead man fell over the railing and landed in front of Tank. He and Jacob jumped over the body and ran up the remaining steps two at a time. They stormed the room. Jacob dove low. There was only one guard. He had a cast on his right arm, and Jacob recognized him as Intimidator, one of the rapists from several nights ago. He killed the man before he could get off a shot.

Should'a done that a couple nights ago, Buddy Boy.

As Tank cleared the rest of the floor, Jacob turned his attention to the two people gagged and tied to chairs in the middle of the room. They were awake, wide-eyed, and looked frightened. Jacob whispered into his throat mike. "We have two hostages. I repeat, two hostages, and one of them is a woman! From the looks of her, she's had a rough go of it. They tortured her. We're going to need a medical evacuation when we finish."

"Done," said Winston.

Tank returned. "Rest of the floor's clear."

Jacob turned to the man and woman. "We're Americans and we're here to rescue you. I'm going to cut your restraints but you both must remain silent. Do you understand?"

Chow and Liu-Fawn nodded their heads.

Jacob removed their gags while Tank cut their arms and legs free. "Can you walk?"

"Yes," said Chow. "But I'm afraid Liu-Fawn is going to need some assistance.

"Okay, but we have to hurry." Jacob led Chow towards the stairs while Tank threw the woman over his shoulder and headed down the steps, keeping his automatic rifle pointed forward. They made it to the front door when Deets yelled into his radio. "We have a problem!"

Multiple shots rang out from behind the building and Curt came running around the corner limping more than he had earlier, throwing his injured leg out to the side and then swinging it forward with his hip. "We've got company."

"How many?" Jacob yelled back.

"More than we can handle, and they're really pissed off."

The sewer opening was only fifty yards away but with the two hostages and Curt's bad leg it might well have been five hundred.

"We'll never make it," yelled Tank.

Dan yelled into his throat mike, "Run! I'll slow 'em down for you!" He fired at the first of the men pursuing his teammates. They were getting close, but he dropped them all with head shots. The problem was the noise from their guns was drawing even more people from the surrounding apartment buildings. It was a group of at least thirty men and some of them started to fire on Dan's position. Bullets ricocheted off the chimney next to him, showering him with pieces of concrete and brick. One of them ran forward, dropped to a knee, and aimed an RPG launcher in his direction. Dan immediately fired on the man, but the shot was rushed. *Damn tremor, missed his head.* The result was better. The errant shot hit the man in the right shoulder as he was about to launch the rocket. He spun around in a pirouette motion and when the grenade was fired, it headed toward the middle of his fellow attackers. The closest man was hit directly in the chest, immediately disintegrating him and killing at least a dozen of his comrades in the process.

The attacking horde retreated, buying the team precious seconds to escape. Dan slammed a fresh magazine into his rifle and continued to spray the enemy with cover fire, driving them back farther. Once he was sure the team and the two hostages

QUANTUM

had made it safely back to the sewer opening, he rappelled down the side of the building. He lost his good-luck hat in the process. *Damn. No time to look for it.* He ran to join his teammates, as they laid down suppressive fire for him. Dan fell ten feet away from the sewer opening after taking a round in his left leg.

Jacob yelled, "Dan's been hit! Tank, get Chow and Liu-Fawn down the ladder. Curt, cover me." Jacob rushed forward, grabbed Dan by the back of his tactical vest, and started dragging his friend back to the safety of the sewer. By now the crowd had recovered from the RPG blast and they were again resuming the chase. Jacob and Dan received heavy fire from all directions as bullets exploded off the pavement. A wet, thud sound changed everything. Suddenly, Dan felt heavier. Jacob looked back to see his friend bleeding from a large hole in his right chest. *Shit, shit, shit.* Jacob dragged Dan closer to the opening.

"I'm...I'm not going to make it. S...save yourself," said Dan. He coughed up blood—too much.

"Never. We're either going home together or not at all. Tank, get Dan down the ladder while I cover us. If I'm not down there in thirty seconds, leave without me. You need to get Chow and his friend to safety."

The scream erupted from the bottom of Jacob's gut, clawing away at the fraying fibers of his sanity. He wanted to kill anyone—everyone.

Kill em, Buddy Boy. Kill em all!

He unloaded three full clips into the crowd, dropping dozens but they kept attacking. Jacob didn't care. He was going to die and take as many with him as he could. "Die you fuckers." He tossed away a spent clip and reached for another. *Shit!* He was out. His brain refocused. The mission was to get Chow to safety. *Get your paybacks later.*

They kept coming, screaming, attacking toward him, a swarm of killer hornets. There was no time to close the lid. He pulled a couple of smoke bombs from his tactical vest and hurled them in the direction of the hoard, blocking their vision. Heaving

three grenades into the resulting cloud did the job. Multiple
screams of pain pierced the murky darkness. Jacob locked the
sewer lid and joined his team at the bottom.

He checked with Tank who looked up and shook his head.
Jacob dropped to one knee. Dan's sightless eyes stared up at him.
He placed his hand on Dan's head and brushed his palm over his
eyes, closing them from the world. "I'll always remember what
you did for us, my friend." He paused for a second to say a prayer
and gather his composure. The sounds of the crowd trying to
unlock the sewer lid brought him back to the present. There were
others to think about. "Anyone else hit?"

Curt checked the rescued hostages. "They're okay."

"Tank?" Jacob asked.

"Solid here."

"There's blood on your shirt."

"No problem. The bullet hasn't been made that can bring
me down. I gotta stay alive to take care of those sons of bitches
who killed our friend."

"Then let's head out. We don't have much time until
those crazy bastards get the lid open and decide it's safe to come
after us."

Tank threw Liu-Fawn over his shoulder and grimaced.
Jacob did the same with Dan's body. "I've got you my friend."

Curt covered their six while Jacob led the way with his
flashlight. The group slowly struggled to return to the accessory
entrance descending farther back into the darkness of the sewer,
like falling into a black hole. The stench no longer mattered. The
burning in his lungs didn't matter. Nothing did but protecting
Chow and stopping the Scorpion. Every few hundred yards, Curt
fired a half-dozen rounds behind them in case anyone followed.

About twenty minutes in Jacob said, "There's Raphael's
first guide arrow straight ahead. We should be in the clear now.
Five more to go." They followed the arrow and repeated the
process, careful not to miss any of them. An hour later, they
made it back to where they had started and emerged from the
sewer system into the coolness of the dark night.

QUANTUM

Chow fell to the ground next to Liu-Fawn and cradled her head in his lap, stroking her bloodied hair away from her face. Jacob laid Dan's body in the grass and folded his jacket under his friend's head. He hailed Winston Hamilton on his radio. "Dan's gone."

The phone was silent for a few seconds before Winston said, "Sorry, Jacob. I know you and Dan were close. He was a good man."

"He died doing what he did best, protecting others from harm." Jacob inhaled the cool night air. "The packages are secure. The woman will need a hospital."

"Help's on the way. I had Dan's helicopter pilot hover nearby just in case we needed him. I'll send your coordinates. He should be there within five minutes to take her and Dan's body to the military hospital at Ramstein."

"Roger that. I'll set up an infrared marker. I don't think the enemy has any idea where we are, but just to be sure, we'll establish a defensive perimeter until the copter gets here. Then we'll bring Chow to the safe house."

"How is phase two coming?" asked Winston.

"Don't know. Lisa hasn't reported in. I haven't had a chance to tell her we lost Dan. She should have aborted the mission by now." He tried to hail Lisa on her secure radio. No response.

FORTY-FIVE

DuBoise Fine Art Gallery
Paris, France

After exiting the sewer system, Lisa and Raphael headed for the Marcelle DuBoise Fine Art Gallery three miles away. Jacob suspected that after he discovered Raphael's treachery, the Scorpion would want to exact some revenge for her betrayal. Her grandfather would be an easy target and the two women were headed over to pick him up and transport him to safety.

"Are you certain this will be okay?" asked Raphael.

"Winston assured us that everything will be fine. Dan should be here within the hour to provide backup. We can proceed as soon as I hear from him. Until then, I'll keep an eye on the front of your grandfather's building."

Lisa parked their car a block away from the gallery and waited to hear from Dan. He never arrived.

Lisa checked her watch. "He's at least an hour late." She tapped on the steering wheel with impatience and monitored the surrounding streets. Finally, she turned to Raphael. "Something's wrong. We need to get your grandfather now."

"But Jacob said we should wait for your backup," said Raphael.

"I don't think Dan's coming. Can't wait any longer. Sassani's men are going to be here soon. I can feel it." She drove their car up to the gallery's front door and got out to check their surroundings. When satisfied all was clear, she escorted Raphael to the door while keeping an eye on the street. Raphael rang the buzzer and stepped back so Marcelle could see her clearly on the gallery's security camera. After what seemed like an eternity, he released the electronic lock and the door opened. The two women rushed in and ran up the stairs to his second-floor apartment. Raphel's grandfather greeted her in a long sleep shirt, his hair and beard even more disheveled than usual.

Raphael hugged him. "Pèpère, you're okay!"

"Of course, I'm okay, except for you waking me up. It's five in the morning, child. What are you doing here at this hour? And who is this woman with you? She looks like military."

"I'm afraid you're in grave danger, Pèpére, and it's all because of me. It has to do with my former friend, Sassani."

Marcelle laughed and waved his hand around the room. "My apartment is one of the most protected sites in Paris. I have the best security systems available and the paintings are stored in a heavy vault upstairs. No one can get to them."

"It's not the paintings I'm worried about. It's you, Pèpére. Sassani has the manpower and weapons to break through your front door in seconds if he wants, but he's not interested in robbing you. He wants to kill you to get even with me."

His bushy grey eyebrows pinched together. "But why? You've never done anything to hurt anyone."

"He thinks I betrayed him—which I did. He's a very evil man and he's already murdered thousands of people, so he won't hesitate to shoot you. We must leave now! This woman and her team are going to protect us. Hurry, there's no time to waste!" She told him what he was to do.

Raphael grabbed Marcelle by the arm and helped him down the steps to the front door, with Lisa in the lead, her automatic rifle ready for action. Lisa exited first and looked into the shadows of an alley across the street. It was there. The pinpoint flash of a red laser lit up the wall of the DuBoise Building. She breathed out a sigh of relief. *It's game on now. You'd better not be targeting us Carla.* She waited in a crouched position behind her car. The shooter didn't fire.

"So far so good," she said to herself and prayed that Jacob had been right about this. She turned to wave the other two towards her. When they reached Lisa, they dropped down next to her. Only then did the first volley of automatic rifle fire begin. Bullets flew over their heads, peppering the wall behind them. Up to this point all was proceeding as planned.

It happened in the blink of an eye. A black sedan screeched to a stop right next to Lisa's car. *What the hell is this?* Two men jumped out, firing assault rifles. Lisa hit one of the assailants, center chest with a three-round burst. He died instantly. The second gunman raced around her car, firing his weapon as he ran. Lisa fell to the ground. Raphael and her grandfather landed face down on the sidewalk next to Lisa. More gunshots rang out, but they were from the shooter hidden in shadows across the street. Carla Coyne stopped the second gunman with a single shot to the forehead. He fell back against the hood of his vehicle and slid to the ground. Dead.

Seeing his comrades already down, the driver of the car sped away. He grabbed his cell phone and called Sassani. "Praise Allah, we got the grandfather. There were two women there. They surprised us. It was Raphael and another woman. I've never seen her before. She was armed, but we were able to kill them all. Two of our men sacrificed themselves in the process. May Allah smile upon their souls."

"What about our shooter? She was supposed to be there."

"I didn't see her."

Sassani gritted his teeth. "We'll deal with her later. Good work. You can return home now. You and your family will be well rewarded for your dedication."

FORTY-SIX

CIA Safe House
Paris, France

Shortly after dawn, the time returned with Chow to the safe house. They were drained after Dan's death. None of them had slept in over thirty-six hours, and they were running on fumes, but there was no time to rest. Jacob needed to question Chow as soon as they had a chance to sit down. Winston made a fresh pot of coffee and poured a cup for everyone, including Raphael. She and her grandfather's deaths had been staged to help protect them from future reprisals from the Scorpion and his organization. Lisa was on her way to the airport to board a plane headed home so she could prepare for her wedding. Winston handed a cup to Jacob. "I'm sorry about what happened to Dan. He was one of the bravest warriors I've ever known."

"He was that and more. He was a good man and a loyal friend who gave up his life to protect the rest of us."

"I'm going to make sure he receives the honor he deserves."

"Thank you, Mr. Hamilton. It'll mean a lot to me and the team. I'm going to make sure he didn't die in vain. Someone is going to pay, but to make that happen we need to focus on the task at hand, and that is to stop the Scorpion!"

"We have Chow," said Winston, "but now what? We still have no idea what the Scorpion's planning and I'm afraid we're running out of time."

Chow entered the room, his face drawn and his eyes downcast. "How is Liu-Fawn?"

Winston said, "She's stable and should be ready for discharge from the hospital in a week. She sustained a concussion and a cracked cheek bone, but I've been told surgery won't be necessary. Her facial lacerations required sutures, and I think she might need some plastic surgery in the future to minimize scarring." Winston glanced at Jacob who nodded in agreement. "Other than that, and IV fluids to treat dehydration, she'll be fine."

"That's good news," said Chow, his eyes perking up. "Where is she?"

"In Germany at one of our best military medical facilities in Europe. She's getting the finest treatment available and is completely protected from any more harm." Winston took a sip of his coffee and set the cup on the table. "How are you Dr. Chow?"

"I'm fine as long as Liu-Fawn is safe." His eyes glazed over, looking distant. "Mr. Sassani is a very rich and powerful man. He has the ability to get to almost anyone."

"There's an entire United States military base surrounding her," said Tank. "Even he can't get to her there. You have absolutely nothing to worry about. That, I can promise."

"Tank is right, Dr. Chow" said Curt. "As far as Sassani and his organization are concerned, you and Liu-Fawn are already dead. We've arranged for the French press to report that you and a female friend were kidnapped by terrorists outside the Notre Dame Cathedral several days ago. The official story is that you were both killed during a rescue attempt. Even the Chinese government will believe you're dead. It gives you the perfect opportunity to establish a new life somewhere else."

Winston gestured toward a chair. "Have a seat, Dr. Chow. There are several serious matters which we must discuss. I know you must be tired, but I'm afraid the situation is urgent, and time is of the essence. We know you have developed a quantum-based computer system and your work is probably decades ahead of any research being done elsewhere in the world."

QUANTUM

Chow opened his mouth to speak and closed it without saying a word. He fidgeted with the wrapper on a pack of spearmint gum and popped a stick in his mouth.

"I understand your reluctance to speak to us, Dr. Chow. You really don't know who we are and don't know whether or not you can trust us. I'm sure your government has told you over the years how evil the United States is. We aren't perfect but what you've been told is a lie, mere political propaganda. Otherwise our men wouldn't have risked their lives to save you. I assure you that you can place your faith in us."

Chow nodded slowly. "I believe that. One of your men even died to save us, something for which Liu-Fawn and I will be forever grateful. The answer to your question is yes, I have developed such devices. They are called Yaoguai. They are much smaller and infinitely more powerful than any computer system you could have ever imagined."

Winston leaned forward in his chair. "You used the word 'devices.' You have more than one?"

"Billions of them, and they have been incorporated into every electronic device China has exported over the past three years. Almost every electronic product in the world, from coffee makers to flash drives to cell phones, contains at least one component part made in China, and they all contain Yaoguai. Even this building which I assume is a highly secure CIA facility must contain at least one. That means your systems have been compromised. Every one of the surveillance cameras and security monitors I saw on my way in probably contains a Yaoguai device. Each individual unit has the ability to recruit any computer within its range and convert it to a slave device. Once they are integrated into the system, it makes the Chinese Ministry of Intelligence privy to any and all information stored in them. It's the primary reason our PLA Unit 61398 has been successful in stealing so many aspects of American and European industry. Even the most secure systems haven't been immune. It has allowed China to bypass years of research and development simply by looking over the shoulders of western corporations and

289

duplicating their discoveries. At the same time, my devices are so inconspicuous, the most seasoned cybersecurity companies are unable to detect them."

"So, your devices constitute a world-wide integrated network?" asked Winston.

"Yes."

Jacob ran his hand through his hair. There had to be a lot more than hacking and industrial espionage involved in whatever the Scorpion had planned. Hacking had become commonplace over the past several decades and almost every computer system in the world was now vulnerable to intrusion. "What else have you been able to do?"

"The initial device was improved to the point where it can now perform the equivalent of ten to the thirty-seventh power calculations in an instant," said Chow. "That's well over a trillion, trillion, trillion. It's more than stars in the universe. As a result, all encryption systems around the world have been rendered useless. Nothing is beyond the Ministry's grasp. The Chinese government has been able to sit in on every strategic meeting of each major power in the world. They know the strengths and weaknesses of every military, including the planned deployment of the most confidential military assets in case of war."

Curt flipped a chair around backwards and straddled it, leaning his arms on the back. "Then why haven't the Chinese tried to manipulate our financial institutions? It sounds as though they could easily do so."

"They have manipulated various stock markets to some extent. Wang Liuang, my former boss at the LCT Corporation, has been one of the beneficiaries of such illegal financial maneuvers. It's made him a multibillionaire. However, my government wouldn't want to do much more than obtain some marginal financial advantages. They don't want to totally destabilize the American economy unless there would be an all-out war. China's economy is too intertwined with that of America's."

"Maybe the Scorpion wants Chow's devices to hack into financial institutions and transfer monies into his own accounts," said Curt.

Chow looked up in a start. "The Scorpion? Who's that? I've never heard that name before."

Winston lit up a cigar, drew in a mouthful, and exhaled to the ceiling. "It's how Mr. Sassani is known in the world of terrorists," he said. "His true identity remains unknown."

Jacob turned to Curt. "I don't think financial gain is the Scorpion's goal. It's not his modus operandi. Access to top secret information and stirring up financial instability doesn't give him the kind of devastating weapon he seeks. No, we're missing something." He added more sugar to his coffee as he considered the situation. "What about our nuclear program? Could he gain access to that?"

Winston tapped a long cigar ash into a tray. "I know where you're going with this, Dr. Savich, and I don't think it's a concern. I have intimate knowledge as to how our nuclear deployment programs work. From what Dr. Chow has told us, his device would allow the Scorpion to look at the list of potential targets, but he couldn't actually initiate a nuclear weapons launch. There are too many built-in failsafe measures which bypass computer control and are strictly directed by human decision making. A team of two separate individuals, each with a launch key retrieved from a secure safe, confirm a complex code of over a hundred fifty characters. Within several minutes of presidential authorization, the target coordinates are entered manually, and the launch initiated. There is no changing the course."

"Exactly. That brings us back to intelligence gathering or acquisition of wealth through financial transfers," said Jacob. He gave a slight shake to his head. "I don't see him interested in either. He already has access to over forty billion dollars in cash and gold equivalents. He has another twenty billion available in hidden art assets. No, there's more to this puzzle than what we've considered thus far. The Scorpion's sole focus has been the destruction of the West and more specifically the United States. He doesn't care how many people he kills in the process. The more the better as far as he's concerned. This man tried to destroy the entire U.S. government and murder tens of thousands of innocent citizens by attempting to detonate a dirty bomb in Washington a few years ago."

Chow removed his gum and covered it in the foil wrapper. His hands trembled. "He told me that he wanted revenge for something the Americans did to his family. It had to do with some off-target bomb. I had no idea how insane with revenge he actually was. There . . ." he stammered, "there is another aspect to this situation, one much more dangerous than we've discussed. I was hoping it would never surface, but now I understand why the Scorpion, as you call him, wanted me. It's the Yaoguai-II Program."

"Yaoguai is one of the primary reasons I came to Paris, said Jacob. "Now there's a Yaoguai-II for us to deal with?"

Chow nodded and looked up, his pupils dilated. Jacob saw fear in them. "Yaoguai was originally designed to spearhead China's cyber espionage program using my quantum technology," Chow continued. "While Yaoguai-II is an extension of the original program, it's become something entirely different. It can be used as a weapon to shut down any system it controls so it can essentially neutralize any nation's nuclear capability, an extremely dangerous capability if it falls into the wrong hands. The threat of any retaliatory nuclear attack could be eliminated. China's Ministry of Intelligence has always known that they could never catch up with the extensive nuclear programs of the United States and Russia. They didn't have the power of adequate nuclear deterrence and never would, so they wanted me to develop a program whereby their nuclear disadvantage could be neutralized. That's when I developed Yaoguai-II. I told my superiors that it wouldn't be ready for deployment for at least another few years. That was a lie on my part. It's ready now but seeing the potential for abuse, I didn't tell them the truth. I didn't want Yaoguai-II implemented until I had fully understood how they planned to use it."

Winston sat in his chair, directly across from Chow. "Let me make sure I understand. Are you telling us that with the

Yaoguai-II program, someone can abort any attempt to launch a nuclear device? A human decision must be made, and two specific persons must ultimately press the button, but the actual launch sequence is controlled by a series of computers. If Yaoguai-II has the ability to shut those down, it makes any nuclear arsenal worthless. It changes the entire balance of power in the world."

"That's correct," said Chow.

"But the Scorpion has no access to a nuclear weapon," said Jacob. "The interruption of a launch sequence would be meaningless as far as he's concerned."

Winston frowned and the blood drained from his face. "If Yaoguai-II can stop a nuclear launch by shutting down its control systems, am I correct in assuming that it can also neutralize any computer program anywhere in the world?"

"Yes," said Chow. "No system is safe."

Winston removed his glasses and cleaned them with the corner of a paper napkin. Now his own hands trembled. "If Yaoguai has already infiltrated over ninety-five percent of the world's computer systems, then Yaoguai-II could achieve a level of destruction comparable to a world-wide nuclear Armageddon."

"Precisely," said Chow. "That's the potential of Yaoguai-II that I had hoped no one else but I would realize. The entire civilized world has become dependent upon computers to run almost every aspect of our lives. Yaoguai-II has the ability to give a self-destruct command to every one of the systems it has infected. That means, when the appropriate instructions are given, all power grids around the world can be shut down. Communication abilities will be eliminated. Cell phones and land lines will become useless. Internet access would disappear. Contact between branches of the military and between nations would be severed. Water treatment plants would cease to function leading to a lack of clean water and world-wide spread of disease. Electric supply grids to hospitals, financial institutions, businesses, traffic control, and everything else which keeps civilization running will be permanently interrupted. All air traffic control will stop. Planes will start falling out of the sky like rain, crashing into cities. The world's financial systems will collapse. The list of potential targets is endless. Containment procedures for biological warfare programs would malfunction, exposing the globe to more severe pandemics than we've ever seen, even worse than the Wuhan virus. It can send civilization back hundreds, if not thousands of years. Worst of all, every nuclear reactor on the planet would go into melt-down mode, disseminating vast clouds of nuclear contamination across every continent. The destructive potential is limitless. Deaths could be in the billions. Once started, it's almost impossible to stop. The world as we know it would come to an end, and I'm afraid that the Scorpion now has the power of Yaoguai-II under his control."

The group was speechless. Everyone froze in place as the enormity of Chow's words sunk in. Jacob was the first to ask the obvious question, "But why would any nation want a weapon like that? It would result in destruction of their own country. It makes no sense."

"I suspect Dr. Chow has already factored in the dilemma of potential self-destruction, haven't you?" replied Winston.

"Yes. I built two protective measures into the system. First of all, Yaoguai II was designed to be very specific. Each infected information system has been assigned its own activation code. Yaoguai-II has the ability to individually track and identify the location of every computer it controls. Only those systems whose codes have been specifically activated can be destroyed. In that way, a particular country or part of the world can be protected if desired. Those codes are arranged by geographic location and target priority levels. From what you've told me so far, I don't believe the Scorpion is interested in sparing anyone. He was never interested in Yaoguai's specificity."

"And the second protective measure?" asked Winston.

Chow offered a slight smile. "I have designed an antidote program which has the ability to neutralize Yaoguai-II if any of the activation sequences are initiated. Therefore, if a code is triggered, the recipient system can be immunized from self-destruction." His smile vanished. "However, there are some limitations to its use. It must be utilized within minutes of activation, and at the same location. If too much time passes, the process becomes irreversible."

"If Yaoguai now controls over ninety-five percent of the world's systems, wouldn't your antidote program entail tracking hundreds of billions of computers and activation codes at one time?" asked Raphael.

"Yaoguai can do that in a nanosecond," replied Chow. "Its only limitation is that the rest of the world is controlled by digital systems which are painfully slow by comparison. That creates a relative bottleneck in the transmission of codes."

"And the Scorpion needs you for the activation codes?" asked Jacob.

"No, I'm afraid he already has them. They were stored in my watch which I hid in the Crypte Archèologique on the afternoon I was kidnapped. I was forced to tell him about the watch's location, or he was going to torture Liu-Fawn." Chow looked down at the floor.

"Completely understandable," replied Jacob. He turned to Curt. "Can you check on that?"

Curt opened his cell phone and made a call. A minute later he replied to the receiver. "Thanks, I owe you." He turned to Jacob. "The French police were called early this morning. There was a break-in at the Crypte last night. Two security guards were killed in the process."

"So, we must assume that the Scorpion already has what he wants," said Jacob.

Winston furrowed his brow and leaned in closer, his face inches from Chow's. "That begs the question, Dr. Chow. Why are you still alive if the Scorpion has the codes?"

Chow met his stare. "For Yaoguai to be used as an effective weapon of mass destruction, simultaneous world-wide dissemination of the activation codes is mandatory to avoid the digital bottleneck of regular internet transmission. Using the traditional internet would be too slow. Yaoguai-II would fail because individual countries would have time to institute automated protective measures. That means he must gain access to a rapid global information delivery system. I suspect he believes that he needs my help in doing that." He turned to look at Jacob. "Unfortunately, he's wrong. He has everything he needs if he has my watch."

"Rapid dissemination!" Jacob exclaimed. "Now I know why they called Raphael the key. I know where Sassani is headed. We must hurry!"

FORTY-SEVEN

Parisian Telecom Headquarters
Outskirts of Paris, France

The smell of burning oil filled the interior of the van as it sped past the historic regions of Paris and up into the surrounding hills. Old buildings gave way to thick green vegetation as the city of Paris fell distant in the rearview mirror. The transmission towers of Parisian Telecommunications loomed ahead. Curt pushed the Citroen van to its limits, mercilessly grinding through the gears. "The campus is less than a mile ahead."

From the back seat, Raphael asked, "What if we can't stop him in time? What if Sassani successfully transmits the activation sequence?"

"Technologically," said Chow, "it'll be extremely difficult for him to accomplish without a computer engineer there to help him. But if he is successful, there's still the antidote program. The problem is that I've never had the chance to fully test it."

"Terrific," said Jacob. "That means we'd better get there before the Scorpion does. You'd better step on it, Curt."

It was early evening by the time their van sped down the entrance drive toward the front gate. The parking lot was almost empty except for Philippe's car, still in his personal parking place near the front. When they reached the gate, the security guard was nowhere to be seen. A single bullet hole blemished the center of the guardhouse window.

Tank jumped out of the car and checked inside. He looked

at the others and shook his head. "The Scorpion's already been here. The guard's dead."

"Oh my God, Philippe!" cried Raphael. "We must find Philippe before the Scorpion does!"

The van screeched to a halt in front of the main building. The team ran up to the entrance, withdrew their side arms, and pushed on the door. It should have been locked. It wasn't. When they entered, there was an alarming lack of activity. The place was dead quiet. Curt cautiously walked over to the reception desk where the evening security chief would have normally been watching a bank of monitors. His body was on the floor with two bullet holes in his forehead, a large pool of clotting dark blood surrounding his body. "It looks like we're too late."

Jacob scanned the lobby. "No, we're not. Look around. The lights are still on and the security monitors are working. The power grid hasn't been interrupted yet. That means the Scorpion hasn't initiated the activation sequences."

He looked at Raphael. "Where's Philippe's office?"

"Follow me." Raphael ran to a bank of elevators near the rear of the lobby. When the doors opened, they found another dead body. Raphael screamed. It was Philippe's secretary. She had been shot in the chest. Tank pulled the body out of the way and the group took the elevator to the top floor. They ran down a hallway toward Philippe's office and stopped ten feet away.

"The door's partially ajar," whispered Jacob. He signaled for Tank to go high right while he would cover low left. "Curt, stay in the hall with Raphael and Dr. Chow. No matter what happens, keep them alive!" He checked his Sig to be sure a round was chambered and used the tip of the gun to coax the door fully open. He and Tank exploded into the room. It was empty.

"Looks like a fucking bomb went off in here," said Tank. Lamps were knocked over. Drawers were pulled out and papers strewn all over the floor. Behind the desk they found the bloodied body of Philippe Mitterand. His face had been beaten and he had bullet holes over both knees. His right hand was missing. It had been severed at the wrist.

QUANTUM

"From the looks of it, he put up a pretty good fight," Tank said trying to stay out of earshot of Raphael.

Chow entered the office and stared at Philippe's body. "The Scorpion tried to torture information out of him. He needed to know how to interface Yaoguai with the satellite transmission systems." He shook his head. "What kind of a monster does something like this?"

"The kind who would kill billions and destroy all civilization just for the sake of personal revenge," said Jacob.

Raphael rushed into room. Jacob stopped her. "You don't want to see this." He tried to shield her eyes from the sight, but he was too late. She saw her uncle's mutilated body and fell to her knees, sobbing. "Philippe. Oh my God, Philippe, what has he done to you?" Jacob put his arm around her and pulled her away. She buried her face in his chest. "This is all my fault! He used me to get to Philippe!" Jacob held her tightly in his arms and gently stroked her hair, his heart torn in half at the sight of her anguish.

Curt knelt over the body and felt the skin. "He hasn't been dead long. His body's still warm and the blood on the carpet hasn't clotted yet. We're only a few minutes behind Sassani, five minutes max."

"That means there might still be enough time to stop him," said Jacob.

Raphael abruptly stopped crying. She wiped her tears away with the back of her hand. "I know where he's headed. We must hurry."

Jacob held her by the shoulders and looked into her eyes. She wouldn't be any good to them if she was in shock. "Are you sure you're up to this?"

"There'll be time enough for grieving later, after we get this bastard. Now follow me!"

The group ran right behind her as she rushed back toward the elevators. They exited on the basement level and followed a trail of blood along the walkway to the operations building. The first door was locked, but Tank was able to kick it open. They entered a small antechamber and stopped in front of a second door. A guard lay dead against it with two shots through his chest. Recessed into the wall, near the right side of the door, was a one-square-foot stainless steel box with a black glass top. On its cover laid the severed right hand of Philippe Mitterand, a red laser light repeatedly scanning his lifeless palm print. Each time it did, a mechanical female voice repeated, "Identification confirmed, Mr. Mitterand. Please enter your access code—Identification confirmed, Mr. Mitterand. Please enter your access code."

Below it, a bloodied computer keypad protruded from the same wall.

Jacob turned to Raphael. "What's the code?"

"I don't know! He showed me the room, but he never told me his passcode."

"Shit!" He turned to Tank. "Can you kick it down?"

Tank tried several times. It was hopeless.

Jacob again turned back to Raphael. "What's Philippe's birthday?"

"May 17, 1956."

Jacob tried the date. It failed. He asked, "Your birthday."

She gave it to him. Again, the door failed to open.

The computerized voice returned, "You have only one more code entry option, Mr. Mitterand. If that fails, the doors will be secured for twenty-four hours."

"He's in there and we know it," said Jacob. "He's erasing all of civilization and destroying billions of lives, but I can't get in there in time to stop him!" Jacob pounded on the door with his fist. He again looked at Raphael. "Think! You must know the code. They said you were the key."

She looked to the ground, nibbled at her lower lip, and slowly shook her head. "I don't have it."

Meanwhile Chow was studying the bloody smudges on the computer keypad. "None of the blood smears cover the numbers so the code must be all letters. That eliminates any significant dates. The darkest stained letter is "R" which suggests that it's the first letter to be pushed in the sequence." After a second, he continued. "I think I might understand the password.

It's not the woman, but her name. That's the key. Raphael's name is the password."

Jacob stared at him. "We'd better be right. We only have one more try before we're shut out. I'm certain the Scorpion is almost finished with what he came here to do." Jacob stood in front of the keypad and carefully entered r, a, p, h, a, e, l.

Before he could press the enter key, Chow yelled, "Wait."

Jacob stared at him, an impatient look in his eyes. "What?"

"I almost missed it. There's a blood smear on the Caps Lock key. You must use all uppercase characters."

"I hope you're right about this, Dr. Chow."

"I'm positive."

Jacob typed, R, A, P, H, A, E, L.

They all held their breath and waited. A soft hum was followed by a loud click. The electronic lock system disengaged, and the door opened. Jacob turned to Curt and said, "Remain in the hall with Raphael and Dr. Chow! Don't try to enter until I tell you!"

When Jacob and Tank stormed the room, they almost tripped over the body of a computer technician lying a few feet inside the door. A second body was sitting at a desk, a bullet hole in his forehead. To the left stood the Scorpion, his face and shirt peppered with the bloody droplets of his victims. He glared at the intruders with the bulging eyes of a madman. The only remaining communications technician sat at his computer console, typing instructions as the Scorpion held a semi-automatic against the back of the frightened man's head. In front of the tech was Chow's watch, a micro-USB cable connecting it to the computer terminal. When the man looked up from the screen, he said, "It's ready." The Scorpion responded by depressing the transmit button and putting a bullet into the tech's head. He tried to fire another round into the dead man's computer to destroy it, but nothing happened. He racked the slide of the gun and immediately turned the gun towards Jacob and Tank. He pulled the trigger, but again, nothing—just a click. He had used up the last of his ammunition killing Philippe and the guards. He flashed a satanic smile. "You're too late! It's done! You have failed Jacob Savich. America and its allies are destroyed."

"That's where you're wrong," said Jacob. "You're the one who's failed." He yelled out to the hallway. "You'd better bring him in now, Curt! The activation sequences have been transmitted!"

The Scorpion's jaw dropped as Chow rushed into the room, still very much alive. Chow immediately began working at the computer terminal, his fingers typing frantically.

Jacob said to Curt, "Protect Chow with your life." He then faced the Scorpion. "You're wrong, Sassani or whatever the hell your name is. It's not over. You and I have some unfinished business."

The Scorpion threw his empty gun at Jacob. He missed, pulled his Pesh-Kabz dagger from its scabbard, and held it up for Jacob to see. "It's an old family heirloom given to me by my grandfather when I became a man. He's the same grandfather that your country murdered with a bomb. You destroyed my entire family and village!" He stared at his dagger, "I'm an expert with this knife and now I'm going to use it to make you pay."

"So, that's why you're so pissed off at the world. It's all about revenge, but you've made a huge mistake. You've been fucking with the wrong country, and you're definitely fucking with the wrong guy. Your lust for vengeance has been your own undoing." Jacob turned and set his gun on one of the computer tables. He said to Tank, "He's mine. Just make sure nothing interferes with Chow."

He stared at the Scorpion. "Ironic, you held that dagger on the day you became a man, and tonight you're going to be holding it on the day you die." Jacob removed his combat knife from its ankle sheath and held it up. "I have a knife too, but mine's bigger." The two men slowly approached each other, circling around cautiously, as Chow rapidly worked at the computer console, trying to abort the activation commands.

Jacob assumed a defensive posture, centering his balance evenly over the balls of both feet. He pulled his elbows in to protect his sides and tucked his head down slightly to protect his throat. He slowly closed the distance between himself and his opponent. The two men tested each other, thrusting with their knives, looking for an opening. Jacob gave one and in response, the Scorpion slashed at Jacob's neck. The attack was easily dodged, and Jacob caught the Scorpion in the face with a left-hand counterpunch, breaking his nose. He was knocked back and blood trickled down his face. His eyes widened, filled with rage. He again made a sweeping slash with his dagger. It was an angry, undisciplined maneuver that Jacob easily avoided. Jacob intentionally gave him another chance and the Scorpion took the bait, again lunging forward in a slashing motion. Jacob countered by blocking the attempt and drawing his blade across the Scorpion's face. A deep gash opened from the man's left ear to the corner of his mouth. He howled like an unearthly primordial creature and grabbed at the wound. His paralyzed faced bled through his fingers. He completely lost control and charged forward, wildly swinging his knife back and forth. Jacob blocked the dagger with his own blade, pivoted around his left foot, and pulled his knife across the Scorpion's right wrist, severing his radial artery and nerve, leaving the hand paralyzed. Blood pumped out of the cut and his knife fell to the floor. The Scorpion stood motionless, short of breath, blood running down his face and onto his chest. His right arm hung useless at his side. For all practical purposes, the fight was over, but the raging flames of hatred still burned in his eyes. In that fire Jacob saw himself, consumed by his own relentless need for revenge.

I am him, and he is me. Jacob returned his knife to its ankle sheath.

> *Whoa. What're you doing, Buddy Boy? We're not finished here. We need to end this thing once and for all. Do it tonight or we're going to have to face this asshole again down the road.*

"I'm finished. It's over."

"You're right," yelled Sassani. "It's over. The transmission is sent and there's nothing you can do to stop it. I have my revenge.

I've taken everything from you. I've destroyed your country."

"You've failed, Sassani. You're a fool, blinded by revenge. You failed when you tried to assassinate our president a few years ago, and you've failed again today. You haven't destroyed anything. I imagine you might have caused a few isolated power outages, but Dr. Chow had a fail-safe system built into his programs. He designed an antidote to Yaoguai just in case some sick fuck like you got hold of it. Right now, it's in the process of negating all of your activation commands."

"You're lying!"

"Look around you. The lights are still on! The monitors are on! We still have power!"

The Scorpion scanned the room in disbelief and snarled at Jacob. "This isn't over Savich! We have armies of thousands all over the world and we'll hunt down every last one of you. It'll never be over until you're all dead." He picked up his dagger with his left hand, and charged toward Chow, screaming and slashing haphazardly in all directions.

A shot echoed through the room. The Scorpion took a step back, dropped his dagger, and pressed his left hand against his neck. Bright red blood pumped out between his fingers. He turned to his right with a look of horror in his eyes. It wasn't Jacob who had shot him, and it wasn't Tank. Raphael stood only ten feet away, the pistol still aimed at him. She was alive—and she was smiling. "Now, it's over." She dropped the gun.

The Scorpion tried to yell but nothing came out of his mouth, only the gurgling sounds of bloody froth escaping from the hole in his neck. He looked up at the ceiling for a second, then fell to the ground, his pupils dilating, and his soulless eyes slowly fading into oblivion. The Scorpion was no more.

Jacob turned to Chow. "Did you stop it in time?"

"I'm not sure. The only thing we can do now is to wait and see if the world comes to an end."

FORTY-EIGHT

La Madeleine Catholic Church
Paris, France

The world did not come to an end. Chow's antidote worked. Soon after Yaoguai was neutralized, Winston Hamilton arranged to have Chow flown to Ramstein Air Force Base in Germany where he remained at Liu-Fawn's side until she recovered.

Raphael and Jacob sat close together in a large black limousine, on their way to the La Madeleine Catholic Church for the funeral mass of her Uncle Philippe.

"I'm sorry I have to leave you next week, Raphael, but I must return home for my sister's wedding and my best friend's funeral. Are you sure you can't come with me?"

"I would love to, Jacob, but I have too much to do here, clearing up the estate of my Uncle Philippe. I also have to sort out everything with the inventory of paintings at the art gallery. Pèpére wants to retire and he's beginning the process of transferring ownership to me." She ran a hand down his chest. "Will you be coming back to Paris soon?"

"As soon as I can. At some point we need to discuss our future."

They rode in silence for a few minutes, wondering what life might bring them. He kissed her on the cheek and gently took her hand. "How are you doing?"

"It's difficult, but I'll get through it."

"You must be very angry with them."

"With whom?" asked Raphael.

"With the ones who caused all of this anguish, the ones who killed your Uncle Philippe."

"But the Scorpion is dead, Jacob. We both saw to that. He's the one who was the ultimate source of this nightmare."

"Yes, but there were others, men who helped the Scorpion. They're still out there waiting to prey upon the innocent. Don't you feel the need for vengeance?"

"I guess there will always be a part of me that demands it, but the desire for vengeance can be all-consuming, and ultimately self-destructive. It's almost like drinking a poison in the hopes that it will kill someone else. I need to push the feelings of hate aside before I can ever hope to free up my life to pursue more important things." She gazed into his eyes and squeezed his hand. "You've been my rock. I don't know if I could have gotten through this past week without you. You're a strong and decent man, Jacob Savich. I love you for that. Though I've only known you for a short while, it's almost as though our souls are somehow joined together. I feel closer to you than I have to any other man in my life."

Jacob fidgeted, uncomfortable with the attention on him.

"I can tell you've had your own issues, Jacob, but we both must set our anger and our desire for revenge aside. It's a thirst that can never be quenched. There could never be enough bullets in all of France to stop the pain, so we must let it go for both of our sakes."

He nodded slightly without answering and continued to hold Raphael's hand as they exited the limousine and entered the cathedral. Tank followed just to Jacob's left, scanning the crowd, a thick bulge under his coat. Once inside, they took a pew in the front and listened to a eulogy delivered by the Archbishop of Paris. A veil of red draped over Raphael's blue eyes as tears slowly trickled down her cheeks. Her trembling hand dabbed at them with a tissue. Jacob hated seeing her in this much pain.

QUANTUM

Philippe was a well-respected man throughout Europe, and he was missed by many. Hundreds of the most influential people of Paris were in attendance. As was his habit, Jacob checked the large crowd looking for potential danger. He studied every nook and cranny of the huge church. There were still many more Scorpion disciples out there, and they wouldn't hesitate to kill Raphael in retaliation for the Scorpion's death. He scanned and rescanned the crowd, looking for any inappropriate activity, maybe a suspicious face.

His eyes came to rest upon a man sitting in one of the side pews next to a column in the back. He seemed out of place. His demeanor defied the solemnity of the funeral service. His eyes weren't full of sorrow or respect, but rather they reflected the fire of an unrelenting hatred of those here, a hatred Jacob had seen before. He had shaved his dark beard but Jacob recognized him. *Angry Eyes.*

The Archbishop concluded his remarks. "Philippe is leaving a world filled with chaos and evil. He's headed for a better place, leaving the darkness of this life and entering into the light of the Lord. Let us pray for him."

The words caused Jacob to ponder. *Meanwhile we're left in the darkness of this world to confront the forces of evil. Maybe that's one of the main purposes of religion, to provide the promise of peace and light when we're surrounded by so much wickedness. I could use some of that light myself.*

As they left the church, Jacob lifted his eyes to the clear blue sky. He bathed in the life-giving warmth of the sun as he felt Raphael's cool hand take hold of his. She spoke graciously to those around her, people she didn't even know, people who were expressing their condolences. She remained remarkably poised in spite of her grief. Jacob admired her strength in the face of so much personal suffering.

He would do anything for this woman, readily giving up his own life to protect her. Jacob had to admit to himself that for the first time in his life, he felt love, and for the first time in years, there were no protestations from the Entity. In fact, he hadn't heard a word from it since she killed the Scorpion. It felt as though an obtrusive weight had been lifted from his soul. He was now free to pursue evil, not under the dictates of the Entity, not guided by revenge, but because it was a righteous thing to do.

He stepped away from Raphael and the well-wishers and scanned the crowd still mingling around the church. He spotted Angry Eyes standing under a tree along the perimeter talking into his cell phone. Jacob reflected back on the words his father had spoken to him as a young boy, after he and Lisa had been attacked by bullies at school. "If someone tries to hurt you, strike back with massive retaliation, so much so that the bully and his friends would never consider threatening you again. But when you do it, don't lash out blindly. Do it with purpose and have a plan." Today, Jacob had a plan.

When he looked back into the face of Angry Eyes, he saw the face of the Scorpion, the face of a man destroyed by hatred. He also saw himself, driven by anger and the need to avenge the deaths of his own family. Jacob recalled the words he had spoken to the Scorpion at Parisian Telecom, "Your lust for vengeance has been your undoing." *Perhaps that hatred has been destroying me also.* What was it Raphael said? "We must cast the anger and need for vengeance aside if we are ever to be free to pursue happiness." Certainly, they were wise words, maybe ones he would begin living by. He would make an effort to reject the anger—maybe someday—but not today.

He whispered into his wrist mike, "Rooftops?"

"We had three rooftop shooters arrive during the service. One was armed with an RPG launcher. All have been neutralized."

"Good work, Carla," said Jacob. "What about the plaza area around us?"

"Tank reports that there are two characters lingering along the periphery. They're showing an unhealthy interest in you and Raphael. From the looks of the bulges under their jackets, they're definitely packing. Should we take them?"

"Not yet, not unless they make a move. What about Angry Eyes? Do you have him?"

QUANTUM

"He's in my sights as we speak," said Carla. "I think he's trying to make contact with one of the roof snipers on his cell phone. No one's answering and he's looking a little nervous. Shall I shoot?"

"No, I don't want to disrupt the funeral. Raphael's been through enough already. He's not going to try anything on his own. Too much of a coward. I suspect he and his two buddies will be hanging around for a little while until they find out what happened to their shooters. Wait until we leave, and the crowd begins to disperse. Then he's yours." Was he missing anything? "The cemetery?"

"Curt's been there for several hours and he's already disposed of two bags of garbage, so you and Raphael should both be safe. Tank and I will be there shortly after we clean up things here. We've got your back covered," said Carla.

Jacob rushed to catch up to Raphael as she was entering the limo. When he closed the door, he briefly glanced back at Angry Eyes. "There will always be more Angry Eyes to confront in this world, but after today there will be fewer," he muttered.

"What was that, Jacob?" asked Raphael.

"It's nothing—nothing at all for you to worry about." He patted her hand. She rested her head on his shoulder as the car pulled away.

This is for you, Dan

Several minutes later three bullets pierced the center chest of Angry Eyes. Within seconds, his two associates fell to the ground, each with a bullet wound to the head. It was a new start.

EPILOGUE

Winston Hamilton's private jet landed at Philadelphia's Northeast Executive Airport. A limousine was waiting for him on the tarmac as he disembarked the plane. Winston had no luggage. He would be in the city for less than three hours and would return to his home in Georgetown. The limo took him to the Downtown Marriott Hotel where President Jack Wagner was scheduled to deliver an address to the National Association of Hospital Administrators. He would be discussing his proposed measures to address the financial impact of future pandemics on our nation's health care systems.

When the car pulled up to the front entrance of the hotel, Winston exited and pulled his black suede fedora low over his forehead. He was immediately met by a member of President Wagner's Secret Service detail and led down a rear hallway to a service elevator that took him to the Presidential Suite on the top floor. President Wagner had requested a personal briefing and felt it would be best to do so away from the prying eyes of the D.C. news media. Winston took a seat on the couch as the president's personal assistant asked, "May I get you something to drink?"

"A cup of coffee would be nice, thank you. I prefer it black, without sugar."

He set his fedora on a side table and waited. An hour later President Wagner entered, followed by his entourage of Secret Service agents and assistants. Wagner excused all of them except Parker Davis, the head of White House security.

He turned to Winston who had stood to greet him, "Parker

reports that your team has done an excellent job, Mr. Hamilton. Once again, our country is deeply indebted to all of you."

They shook hands. "Thank you, Mr. President. I'm afraid things got a little messy over in Paris."

The President gestured for them to sit. "Considering the organization you were up against, it was unavoidable. Fortunately, except for a few select individuals, most of Paris has been unaware of your activities. I've had to hold a number of confidential conversations with their president. Publicly, he's been able to credit their special security forces with the elimination of several major terror cells in Paris. He's successfully placated their news media and most of his political opponents."

Winston said, "I've read that the entire European community is reconsidering their present immigration policies until a more thorough review process can be implemented. For its part, France has begun the process of eliminating the No-Go zones that have been the source of so much of the terrorist activity in its cities. They've also shut down several of the militant mosques where radical mullahs have been recruiting members for the ranks of ISIS."

"The globalists are protesting but the French have finally seen the light," said Wagner. "They've decided to back up their rhetoric with aggressive action. The French courts have begun the process of stripping citizenship from confirmed terrorist sympathizers. They're taking a zero-tolerance approach to terrorism by implementing a program based upon the one I initiated in the U.S. last year. It places more emphasis on immigration control, improved screening procedures, and assimilation."

"That's definitely a step in the right direction, Mr. President."

Wagner leaned back in his chair and folded his arms. "Tell me about this Scorpion fellow."

"He's no longer a problem, Mr. President. We still don't know exactly who he was, but we do know that the motivation behind his attacks wasn't the result of any religious zeal. From what we've been able to ascertain, his actions were based solely upon a desire to exact revenge for the bombing of his family and village, probably in the mountainous Hindu Kush area of Afghanistan. I think they were probably the victims of collateral damage during a MOAB bomb release."

"One of the many tragedies of war."

"Yes, but that is no excuse for what the Scorpion has done, Mr. President."

"But he's no longer a threat?" asked Wagner.

"He no longer exists."

"Good. It did give us quite a scare when we started seeing some of our power grids shut down for several minutes. Fortunately, your people were able to abort the attack."

"It was a close call, Mr. President and the Scorpion almost succeeded. If the team had stopped him a minute later, the results would have been devastating."

Wagner pick up the coffee pot and turned to Winston. "Refill?"

"Thank you, Mr. President."

After filling Winston's cup, he said, "That brings me to the subject of the Yaoguai Program. What's the status of that thing?"

"Dr. Chow, the designer of the program, has reassured me that Yaoguai has been destroyed, but there's no way I can verify that. He's somewhat evasive when we discuss the issue. I'm concerned that Yaoguai could still become a viable weapons system. That's why I've taken measures to keep Dr. Chow happy. I've given him a new identity and have provided generous funding for his future research. We've also made arrangements for his girlfriend to pursue her journalism career. If she's happy, I know Dr. Chow will be happy."

"Oh yes, Liu-Fawn. I've heard about her brave exploits in China. She was a champion of individual rights, but she made many enemies in Peking. I understand she's now writing political pieces on her home country — under an anonymous name of course."

"Of course, Mr. President," said Winston. "For obvious reasons, I won't reveal their new identities or where they are now living."

"Plausible deniability," said President Wagner.

"Exactly, Mr. President. You need to be able to isolate yourself from this process. With all due respect, you'll not be president forever, sir. Unfortunately, political winds change, and we don't know who'll be running the country ten years from now. Unlike you, Mr. President, there are some politicians who place their own interests and those of their party ahead of the country. For now, I think it's best if a mind like Dr. Chow's remains hidden."

"So, where do we go from here?" asked Wagner.

"Well sir, although the Scorpion is dead, we still have the rest of radical Islam causing problems. They're an ongoing threat and continue to be a financial powerhouse. Dealing with them will require total elimination of their cash flow."

"It's like playing global Wack-a-Mole," said the President. "Every time we eliminate one terrorist organization, another pops up somewhere else, using a different name, but with the same agenda, always regrouping and rearming, always looking for targets."

"We will be ready to do whatever we need to protect our citizens," said Winston. "The solution to the jihadist movement is twofold. First of all, every time we find a cell, we must immediately isolate it, squeeze as much information as we can from its members, and then destroy it. Secondly, we must get ahead of this curve. Instead of being reactive, we must become more pro-active."

"Like your team did in Paris? You went after the Scorpion."

"Yes, we have to find their leaders and eliminate them. When they're replaced, we eliminate the replacements. Anyone who preaches the violent overthrow of our country must be neutralized. In addition, we must eliminate any and all aid to countries which provide logistical or financial support for the radicals. In other words, reward our friends and punish the friends of our enemies. It's going to take years, if not decades. Unfortunately, there will be an ongoing need for the team until such time when we can change the culture of radical Islam."

"How can we ever hope to accomplish that?" said the President. "Trying to win their hearts and minds has never worked before."

"I'm afraid it never will, Mr. President."

President Wagner looked at his watch. "I'm afraid I must leave you, Winston. I'm late for my speech."

"I know you're busy, sir but I have a special request. It concerns a man who once saved your life, though you never met him. Like you, he was a special forces veteran."

The car dropped Jacob off in front of the reception building. The driver asked, "Will you need an umbrella, sir?"

Jacob looked at the cloudy skies. "It looks like the worst of the storm has passed." He entered the front doors of the Arlington National Cemetery visitor's center. He walked past the life-like statue of a bugler in full military dress, playing taps. After browsing the displays, he exited the far side of the center and took a left onto Eisenhauer Drive. The hills around him were a wave of perfectly spaced white headstones. The nation's fallen heroes had been laid to rest in sites arranged with military precision. It was a sobering experience, the peaceful quiet disrupted only by the sounds of birds singing their morning chorus. A few rays of sunlight struggled to peak through the lingering clouds as he strolled past the graves of Audie Murphy, General John Pershing, and Five-Star General Omar Bradley until he found what he was looking for. It was a headstone adorned with special gold lettering and a gold star, a recognition reserved for Medal of Honor recipients. It read, "Daniel Foster, Staff Sergeant, United States Army, Medal of Honor."

Jacob stood in silence and prayed for a minute. He whispered, "You deserve this as much as anyone I know." The rain returned, camouflaging the tears running down his cheeks. He placed his hand atop the headstone, the same way he used to place his hand on Dan's shoulder. "You're in good company. Rest well, my good friend. I will remember you always."

He returned to his car and was taken to Reagan International Airport to catch his flight to Paris.

The crisp morning air flowed in from the ocean. Fifty feet to his left, waves threw themselves onto the rocky beach. The smell of fall filled the air as scrub oak trees relinquished their leaves to autumn, creating drifts of yellow along the path. He was relatively new at this, so Chow maintained a slow pace, just as the American had instructed him. "Take it easy at first and gradually increase your distance and speed every week. In time, you'll find that the shortness of breath and the burning pain in your legs will dissipate as you begin to enter the zone."

"What zone is that?" Chow had asked.

"You'll know it when you're there. It's a place where sadness lessens and there's more clarity of thought. Your mind will become free to focus on what's most important. I know this from personal experience."

The American, who Chow only knew as Jacob, was right. He was beginning to feel more at ease as he ran, but thoughts of what had happened to himself and Liu-Fawn continued to haunt him. He had almost lost the most precious thing in his life. Then there was the Yaoguai issue which still plagued Chow's conscience daily. He pushed his pace faster as he headed south along the promenade, the Atlantic Ocean still on his left and the city of Plymouth, Massachusetts to his right. The town was small enough to be relatively obscure, but large enough that he and Liu-Fawn wouldn't be noticed.

It was the perfect place for them to hide. Thanks to the Americans, they had no concerns about reprisals from their homeland. They were given a new home, new identities, and new looks. Liu-Fawn wrote freelance articles for the *Wall Street Journal*, untethered from the worries of being sent to prison for what she reported. He taught post-graduate physics at a local university. In the basement of their home, Mr. Hamilton had provided a cutting-edge research lab where Chow continued his work on quantum applications for information systems. Of necessity, he was again forced to live a life of anonymity and obscurity, but it was something he now readily embraced as long as Liu-Fawn was at his side.

After finishing his run, Chow stopped at the Plymouth Bay Café for a cup of coffee. It was his daily reward for completing the morning exercise program. He sipped on it as he finished his route by walking the final mile to his home. It gave him time to think about what he should do with Yaoguai. Chow still had the cloud of responsibility for the device hanging over his head. It was his personal creation, his baby, the culmination of decades of his hard work. No one else in the entire world had been able to accomplish what he had done, but his creation had been twisted into an instrument of evil. It almost caused the end of civilization.

By the time he climbed the front porch steps to his new house, he had come to the unavoidable conclusion regarding his problem. Yaoguai must be destroyed.

He walked inside and hugged Liu-Fawn. She was in the middle of writing a series of articles exposing the political corruption surrounding the Liuang Computer Technology Corporation. Chow gazed into her eyes. The fire and determination were still there but there was also a sadness brought about by the events of the past several months. The facial scars inflicted by the Scorpion's knife were fading but the emotional scars would probably never heal.

She and Chow briefly discussed dinner plans. Afterward, he walked down the steps toward his laboratory. He looked at the watch, always there on his left wrist. He didn't bother to check the time. That no longer seemed to be so important to him. He opened the micro port by pushing the series of buttons on the side and interfaced the watch with his laptop.

Good morning, Dr. Chow. How may I assist you?
Chow typed a specific code on the keypad and hit the

"enter" key.

Partial termination program authorization code received. What is it you wish to eliminate?

Chow's entered several specific vector codes stored in his watch.

List of target sites to be eliminated:
- **All hardware and software systems involved in your research at your former laboratory in China.**
- **All Yaoguai manufacturing systems at Liuang Computer Technologies.**
- **Elimination of all Ministry of Intelligence cyberespionage programs in the PLA Unit 61398.**

Please confirm by pressing the enter key.

Chow did as instructed.

Orders executed per your instructions, Dr. Chow. Will there be anything else?

Chow exhaled a sigh of relief. He had removed a great threat to the world's stability. *The next part is going to be more difficult.* He entered a sequence of twenty-one random characters.

Are you sure you would like to proceed with full termination, Dr. Chow? This is an irreversible command.

He typed,

Affirmative

He planned to destroy the entire global Yaoguai network. All infiltrated computers around the world would be scrubbed free of Yaoguai's influence. It could no longer be used as a weapon of mass destruction. The next step was simply a matter of typing the word "initiate" and pushing the "enter" key. It was the final fail-safe measure he had attached to Yaoguai.

He typed **initiate** and hesitated as his finger hovered over the "enter" key. This was much more difficult than he had anticipated, almost the same as destroying one's own child. He unwrapped a piece of spearmint gum, placed it in his mouth, and chewed rapidly as his finger paused over the "enter" key.

Still, he hesitated. *Perhaps I can save it.* Yaoguai wasn't inherently evil. It was only made so by those who try to use it for their own purposes. It might still benefit mankind. He could reconfigure its programming so that only he could control it. That way, the power of Yaoguai couldn't be abused. There were still problems posed by the threat of nuclear programs in Iran and North Korea. The conflict between Pakistan and India was always a potential trigger. What would happen if some crazy radical got control of a warhead? With the new Yaoguai, only he would have the power to disarm them and defuse those situations, to prevent world-wide nuclear Armageddon. He could activate Yaoguai whenever he felt it was needed to protect the world from itself. *I could never be corrupted by Yaoguai's power.*

His finger trembled and continued to hover over the "enter" key.

QUANTUM

www.ingramcontent.com/pod-product-compliance
Lightning Source LLC
Jackson TN
JSHW022346200125
77244JS00004B/133